TROUBLED SLEEP

LES CHEMINS DE LA LIBERTÉ

(*The Roads to Freedom*)

I

L'ÂGE DE RAISON (*The Age of Reason,* 1947)

II

LE SURSIS (*The Reprieve,* 1947)

III

LA MORT DANS L'ÂME (*Troubled Sleep,* 1951)

IV

LA DERNIÈRE CHANCE (*in preparation*)

TROUBLED SLEEP

by Jean-Paul Sartre

TRANSLATED FROM THE FRENCH BY

GERARD HOPKINS

VINTAGE BOOKS

A Division of Random House, New York

VINTAGE BOOKS EDITION, January 1973

Copyright 1950 by Alfred A. Knopf, Inc.

Library of Congress Cataloging in Publication Data

Sartre, Jean Paul, 1905–
Troubled sleep.

Translation of La mort dans l'âme.
Original ed. issued as v. 3 of the author's The roads
to freedom.
I. Title.
[PZ3.S2494Tr6]   [PQ2637.A82]   843'.9'14   72–3997
ISBN 0–394–71840–2 (pbk.)

Manufactured in the United States of America

PART ONE

❀❀❀❀❀❀❀❀❀❀❀❀❀❀❀❀❀❀❀❀❀

New York, Saturday, June 15, 1940, 9 a.m.

Aɴ ᴏᴄᴛᴏᴘᴜs? He pulled out his knife and opened his eyes; it was a dream. No, it wasn't. The octopus was a reality, it was draining him with its suckers: it was the heat. He was sweating. He had gone to sleep about one o'clock; at two the heat had waked him. He had plunged into a cold bath and had then got back into bed without drying himself. Almost at once the furnace had resumed its roaring under his skin, and he had begun to sweat again. At dawn he had fallen asleep, he had dreamed that the house was on fire. The sun must be pretty high by this time, and not for a moment did Gomez stop sweating; he had been sweating uninterruptedly for forty-eight hours. "Christ!" he muttered, passing a damp hand over his streaming chest. This *was more* than mere heat; it was a sickness of the atmosphere: the very air was in a fever, the air was sweating, one sweat with a carapace of sweat. He must get up; he must put on his shirt and start sweating in that. He said: "*Hombre!* I haven't a dry shirt left!" His last, the blue one, was soaked, because he had had to change twice a day. None left: he would have to wear this sopping, stinking rag until his things came back from the laundry. Cautiously he got to his feet, but he was unable to prevent the flood. Drops crept down his flanks like lice, tickling him. His crumpled shirt lay across the back of the armchair, a mass of creases. He felt it: nothing ever gets really dry in this bitch of a country. His heart was thumping; his mouth was parched, as though he had got drunk last night.

He put on his trousers, went across to the window, and pulled aside the curtains. From the street the light glared up at him, dazzling white as a catastrophe; thirteen more hours of daylight. With anguish and fury he gazed down at the roadway. Everywhere the *same* catastrophe: over there, on the good, black earth, under a pall of smoke, blood and screams; here, between the low, red-brick houses, sunlight, merely sunlight, and sweat. But the catastrophe was the *same*. Two Negroes were strolling by, laughing; a woman was just going into a drugstore. "Oh, God!" he muttered. "Oh, God!" He looked at the screaming confusion of discordant colors. Even if I had the time, even if I were in the mood, how could I *paint* in light like this! "Oh, God!" he exclaimed, "oh, God!"

There was a ring at the bell: Gomez went to open the door. It was Ritchie.

"It's worse than murder!" said Ritchie as he came in.

Gomez gave a start. "What?"

"This heat—it's worse than murder! Hello!" he went on accusingly, "you're not dressed yet? Ramon's expecting us at ten."

Gomez shrugged. "Didn't get to sleep till late."

Ritchie grinned at him, and Gomez added hastily:

"Too hot. I can't sleep."

"Always like that at first," said Ritchie breezily. "You'll get used to it." He gave Gomez an appraising look. "See here, you taking salt pills?"

"Of course, but they don't do any good."

Ritchie shook his head, and there was a touch of severity in his friendliness. Salt pills *ought* to prevent sweating. If they didn't work on Gomez, that must be because Gomez was *different* from everybody else.

"Wait a minute!" Ritchie frowned: "You should be acclimatized by this time: Spain's plenty hot."

Gomez's mind went back to the dry, tragic mornings in Madrid, to the noble light of the sun above the Calle de Alcalá when it was still speaking of hope. He shook his head.

"It's not the same kind of heat."

"Less humid, eh?" asked Ritchie with a kind of pride.

"Yes, and more human."

Ritchie was holding a newspaper; Gomez stretched out a hand to take it, but his courage failed him. His hand fell back.

"This is my big day," said Ritchie cheerfully; "Delaware holiday. I come from there, you know."

He opened the paper at page thirteen. Gomez saw a photograph of La Guardia shaking hands with a fat man; both of them were smiling broadly.

"The guy on the left is the Governor of Delaware," Ritchie explained. "La Guardia received him yesterday at City Hall. An important occasion."

Gomez wanted to snatch the paper from him and look at the front page. But he thought: "What the hell do I care?" and went into the bathroom. He started running cold water into the tub and shaved hurriedly. Just as he was getting into his bath, Ritchie called to him:

"How are you getting along?"

"Just about washed up. Not a clean shirt to my name, and just eighteen dollars left. And Manuel's due back on Monday and I shall have to give him back his apartment."

But his mind was on the newspaper. Ritchie was reading it while he waited; Gomez could hear him turn the pages. He dried himself carefully; but it was no use: the towel was wringing wet. He put on his damp shirt with a shiver and went back into the bedroom.

"The Giants did pretty well."

Gomez looked at Ritchie with no idea what he was talking about.

"Baseball—yesterday—the Giants won."

"Oh yes, baseball. ... ."

He bent down to tie his shoes. He tried to read the front-page headlines upside down. Finally he asked:

"What about Paris?"

"Didn't you hear the radio?"

"Haven't got a radio."

"Finished, washed up," said Ritchie without any show of excitement. "They got in last night."

Gomez went over to the window, pressed his forehead to the blazing pane, and looked at the street, at the meaningless sun, at the whole meaningless day. There would be nothing now any more but meaningless days. He turned away and dropped onto the bed.

"Hurry up," said Ritchie. "Ramon doesn't like to be kept waiting."

Gomez got up. Already his shirt was wringing wet. He began to knot his tie in front of the mirror.

"Think he'll agree?"

"In principle, yes. Sixty dollars a week, and you write up the art shows. But he wants to see you."

"He'll see me all right," said Gomez. "He'll see me."

Then he swung round. "I've got to have an advance. Do you think he'll give it to me?"

Ritchie shrugged. After a brief pause he said:

"I've told him you were in Spain, and he doesn't exactly think you've got Franco written on your heart; but I didn't say anything about—about what you'd been doing there. Better not tell him you were a general; nobody knows what he really thinks about things."

A general! Gomez looked at his shabby trousers, at the dark sweat stains already showing on his shirt. He said bitterly:

"Don't worry, I'm not likely to boast. I know what it costs a man here to have fought in Spain: for six months now I haven't had a job."

Ritchie showed signs of annoyance. "We Americans don't like war," he said dryly.

Gomez stuffed his jacket under his arm. "Let's get going."

Ritchie slowly folded his paper and stood up. On their way downstairs he asked:

"Your wife and boy in Paris?"

"I sincerely hope not," said Gomez briskly. "I hope Sarah was smart enough to slip away to Montpellier." He added: "I haven't had any news of them since the 1st of June."

"If you get this job, you'll be able to bring them here," said Ritchie.

"Yes," said Gomez. "Yes, yes. We'll see!"

The street, the dazzle of windows, the sun blazing down on the flat, roofless warehouses of blackened brick. In front of every door was a flight of white stone steps; over toward the East River there was a heat haze; the city looked shrunken. No shade anywhere: in no street in the world did one feel so terribly exposed. White-hot needles pierced his eyes; he raised his hand to screen them. His shirt was sticking to his body. He shivered.

"It's murder!"

"Yesterday a poor old man fell down just ahead of me," Ritchie said. "Sun-stroke—br-r! I don't like to see corpses."

"You'll see plenty if you go to Europe," Gomez thought.

"It's forty blocks," Ritchie went on. "We'd better take the bus."

They stopped in front of a bus stop. A young woman was waiting. She surveyed them with an expert and sullen eye, then turned away.

"Nice-looking gal," said Ritchie with schoolboy eagerness.

"Obviously a bitch!" Gomez commented resentfully.

He had felt dirty and sweaty beneath her stare. She was not sweating. Nor was Ritchie: he looked pink and cool in his fine white shirt; there was but the merest gloss on his snub nose. Handsome Gomez! Handsome General Gomez! The general had gazed into blue eyes, green eyes, black eyes half-hidden under fluttering lashes; while this bitch here had seen nothing but a little south European, earning fifty dollars a week, sweating in a ready-made suit. "She took me for a wop." All the same, he stared at her long, shapely legs and was conscious of a little uneasy stirring of the flesh. "Four months since I had a woman." In the old days desire had been like dry, hot sunlight in his belly, but now the handsome General Gomez knew only the squalid, furtive cravings of the voyeur, the Peeping Tom!

"Cigarette?" suggested Ritchie.

"No, my throat's on fire. I'd rather have a drink."

"We haven't time."

Ritchie, looking slightly embarrassed, gave him a friendly pat on the shoulder. "Try to smile," he urged.

"What?"

"Try to smile. If Ramon sees you looking as glum as that he'll be afraid of you. I don't ask you to be obsequious," Ritchie added hurriedly as he noticed Gomez's movement of irritation. "Try to smile quite impersonally when you go in, and forget you're smiling; it doesn't matter what you're thinking."

"Oh, I'll smile," said Gomez.

Ritchie looked at him anxiously. "Worrying about your kid?" he asked.

"No."

Ritchie made a painful effort to apply his mind to the situation. "About Paris, then?"

"Paris can go to hell, for all I care," said Gomez with violence.

"It's better they should have taken it without a fight, isn't it?"

"The French could have defended it," Gomez replied without a trace of emotion in his voice.

"Hell! A city like that, in the heart of a flat plain."

"They could have defended it. Madrid held out for two and a half years."

"Oh, Madrid," Ritchie repeated with a vague gesture. "But why defend Paris? It would have been crazy. They would have destroyed the Louvre, the Opéra, Notre-Dame. The less destruction, the better. As things are going now," he wound up with satisfaction, "the war will be over soon."

"Why, of course!" said Gomez ironically. "At this rate we'll be having a Nazi peace inside three months."

"Peace," Ritchie declared, "is neither democratic nor Nazi; it's just peace. You know I don't like these Nazis, but they're only men, after all. Once they've conquered Europe, their troubles will begin, and they'll have to pipe down. If they've got any sense, they'll just let each country run itself inside a European federation. Something like our United States." He spoke slowly and with deliberation. "If that stops you from having a war every twenty years, that will be all to the good."

Gomez looked at him with a feeling of irritation. There was, he thought, an immense kindliness in Ritchie's gray eyes. The man had a happy temperament, he loved humanity in general, children, birds, abstract painting; he imagined any conflict in the world could be settled with ten cents' worth of common sense. He had small sympathy for immigrants from the Latin countries; he got on much better with Germans. "What does the capture of Paris mean to him?" Gomez mused as he turned away to look at the multicolored display on a news-stand. He realized suddenly that there was something ruthless about Ritchie.

"You Europeans," Ritchie was saying, "set such a store

by symbols. All of us knew a week ago that France was finished. So what of it? Naturally, you take it to heart because you've had a home there, you've got memories, I can see all that. But why should you really care about the capture of Paris, so long as the city is unharmed? As soon as the war is over, we'll go back there."

Gomez felt himself borne up on the wings of a tremendous and angry joy.

"Why should I care about *that?*" he asked, his voice quavering. "I'm glad! When Franco entered Barcelona the French shook their heads, they said it was a pity, but not one of them raised a finger. Well, now it's their turn, and I hope it chokes 'em! I'm glad!" he shouted above the din of the bus, which was drawing up to the curb. "I'm glad!"

They got in behind the young woman, and Gomez managed to get a good look at her legs. They stood in the aisle at the back. A fat man, wearing gold-rimmed spectacles, drew hastily back, and Gomez thought: "I must stink." A man in the back row of seats had opened his paper. Gomez, looking over his shoulder, read: "Toscanini acclaimed in Rio, where he is conducting for the first time in fifty-four years." And lower: "New York Premiere: Ray Milland and Loretta Young in *The Doctor Takes a Wife.*" Elsewhere in the bus other newspapers unfolded their wings: "La Guardia receives Governor of Delaware"; "Loretta Young"; "huge fire in Illinois"; "Ray Milland"; My husband has Loved me Since the day I started using Pitts' Deodorant"; "ask for Chrisargyl, the Honeymoon Laxative"; a photograph of a man in pajamas smiling at his young wife; La Guardia smiling at the Governor of Delaware; " 'No cake for the miners,' declares Buddy Smith."

All these people were busy reading. The large black and white pages spoke to them of themselves, of their worries, their pleasures; they knew who Buddy Smith was and Gomez did not; they kept the giant headlines that read "Paris Captured" or "Montmartre in Flames" turned to the floor, to the driver's back. They read on, and the papers they held screamed out their news to deaf ears. Gomez felt old and tired. Paris was far away. He alone among a hundred and fifty million people was concerned about it; his was no more than a small personal preoccupation, scarcely more important than the thirst burning his throat.

"Let me have a look at your paper," he said to Ritchie.

The Germans Occupy Paris. Pressure toward the South. Havre Captured. Assault on the Maginot Line.

The headlines screamed, but the three Negroes talking behind him went on laughing, not hearing a thing.

French Army Intact. Spain Takes Tangier.

The man with the gold-rimmed spectacles was feeling about methodically in his briefcase, from which he finally fished out a Yale key, which he studied with satisfaction. Gomez felt ashamed; he wanted to put away the paper, as though it were indiscreetly telling his own most intimate secrets. The vast uproar of unhappy voices that set his hands trembling, these appeals for help, these death rattles, all these things seemed crudely incongruous, like his own foreign sweat, like his own unpleasant smell. *Hitler's Good Faith Doubted; President Roosevelt does Not Believe; . . . The United States Will Do Everything in Its Power for the Allies;* His Majesty's Government will do everything in its power for the Czechs; the French will do everything in their power for the Spanish Republicans. Bandages, medicaments, cases of canned milk. A mere drop in the bucket! *Students Demonstrate in Madrid, Demand Return of Gibraltar to the Spaniards.* Catching sight of that word "Madrid," he could read no further. "It serves them right, the sons of bitches! Sons of bitches! I only hope they'll set all Paris on fire and reduce it to ashes." *Tours* (from our special correspondent Archambaud): *Battle raging; French say enemy pressure lessening; Nazi losses heavy.*

Of course the pressure is lessening, and it will go on lessening until the last day of the war, until the last French newspaper stops publication. Heavy losses! Mere words, hope's final little bluster that deceives nobody. Heavy Fascist losses around Tarragona; pressure lessening; Barcelona will hold out . . . and then, twenty-four hours later, headlong flight.

Berlin (from our special correspondent Brook Peters): *France has lost the whole of her industry; Montmedy captured; the Maginot Line stormed; the enemy in flight;* pæans of triumph, sounding brass, sunlight; they are singing in Berlin, in Madrid, in their uniforms; in Barcelona, in Madrid, in *their* uniforms; in Barcelona, Madrid, Valencia, Warsaw, Paris; tomorrow, London. At Tours gentlemen in black jackets are scurrying down hotel corridors. It serves them right! It serves them right—let 'em take the whole damn thing, France, England, and the rest. Let 'em land in New York—it serves them right!

The gentleman in the gold-rimmed spectacles was looking at him. Gomez felt ashamed, as though he had spoken his thoughts out loud. The Negroes were smiling, the young woman was smiling, the driver was smiling. *Not to grin is a sin.*

"Here's where we get off," Ritchie said, smiling.

On the posters, on the magazine covers, all America was smiling. Gomez thought of Ramon and began to smile.

"Ten o'clock," said Ritchie; "we shan't be more than five minutes late."

Ten o'clock; three o'clock in France. Livid, hopeless, an afternoon lay hidden behind this colonial morning.

Three o'clock in France.

"A fine mess!" said the man.

He sat there as though turned to stone. Sarah saw the

sweat trickling down the back of his neck. Her ears were filled with the din of automobile horns.

"No more gas!"

He opened the door, jumped out on the road, and stood there in front of the car, gazing at it affectionately.

"Hell!" he muttered between clenched teeth. "God damn it to hell!" He laid the flat of his hand on the scorching hood. Through the window Sarah could see him standing against the glitter of the sky, amid all this vast uproar. The cars that had been following them all morning stretched forward into the distance in a cloud of dust. Behind them, horns, whistles, sirens, a warbling of metallic birds, a hymn of hate.

"Why are they so angry?" asked Pablo.

"Because we're blocking their way."

She would have liked to jump out of the car, but despair kept her riveted to the seat. The man looked up.

"Come on, get out!" he said irritably. "Can't you hear? Help me push."

They got out.

"Go round to the back," said the man to Sarah, "and push, push hard!"

"I'd like to push too," said Pablo.

Sarah leaned against the car and pushed with all her might, her eyes shut, in a nightmare. The sweat was soaking through her blouse. The sun jabbed at her eyes through their closed lids. She opened them: in front of her the man was pushing, his left hand flat against the door, his right steering the wheel. Pablo had flung himself against the back bumper and was clinging to it, shrieking wildly.

"Be careful not to get dragged forward," Sarah warned.

The car rolled apathetically to the side of the road.

"Stop! Stop!" shouted the man. "God in heaven, that's far enough!"

The horns had stopped blowing; the stream of cars began to flow forward once more. They brushed past the broken-down car. Faces flashed by, pressed against the windows. Sarah felt herself blushing beneath all those staring eyes and took refuge behind the car. A tall, skinny driver, at the wheel of a Chevrolet, leaned out:

"Sons of bitches!"

Trucks, heavy and light, private cars, taxis with masked meters, carriages. With each vehicle that passed by, Sarah felt her heart sink a little lower and Gien, her destination, seemed a little farther distant. Next came a procession of horse-drawn wagons, and Gien creaked away into a still more hopeless remoteness. Finally, the road became a black congestion of pedestrians. Sarah withdrew to the edge of the ditch; the crowd terrified her, as it trudged by slowly, painfully. To all of them wretchedness imparted a family likeness; any one who joined them would soon look as they did. I don't want to, I don't want to become like them. They did not look at her; they avoided the car without even glancing at it; they seemed no longer to have eyes. A great hulking fellow, wearing a straw hat and carrying a suitcase in either hand, brushed the car and bumped against the fender. He made a half turn, then resumed his tottering progress. His face was dead white. One of the suitcases was covered with multicolored labels: Seville, Cairo, Sarajevo, Stresa.

"He's dead with fatigue," Sarah exclaimed. "He'll fall down any moment."

He did not fall. Her eyes followed the stiff straw hat with its red and green ribbon, bobbing along gaily above the sea of hats.

"Take your suitcase and go on without me."

Sarah shuddered but said nothing; she looked at the crowd with terrified disgust.

"You heard what I said?"

She turned to him. "Can't we wait until a car comes along and beg a gallon of gas? There are bound to be some more cars when these people have gone by."

The man gave her a sinister smile.

"I advise you to try."

"Well, why not? Why not try?"

He spat contemptuously and for a moment said nothing.

"Didn't you see those cars?" he asked at last. "They were pushing along, jammed nose to arse. How could they stop?"

"Suppose I manage to find some gas?"

"You won't. Do you think anyone is going to lose his place in line for you?" He looked her up and down, with a mocking laugh. "If you were a good-looking babe of twenty, I'm not saying there wouldn't be a chance."

Sarah pretended she had not heard him. She pressed her point:

"But suppose I did manage to get some?"

He shook his head with stubborn obstinacy. "Nothing doing. I won't go any farther, not if you raise five gallons, not if you raise twenty-five. I've caught on." He folded his arms.

"Just stop and think for yourself," he said with surly earnestness. "You jam on your brakes every minute; you skid; you let in your clutch, then you throw it out again every few yards; you change gear a hundred times an hour. That's what wrecks a car!"

There were brown stains on the windshield. He took out his handkerchief and began rubbing at them with anxious care.

"I oughtn't to have let you talk me into coming."

"You only need a little more gas," Sarah told him.

He shook his head without answering; she would have wished to claw at his face. But she controlled her temper and, keeping her voice calm, asked:

"What are you going to do then?"

"Stay and wait."

"Wait for what?"

He did not answer. She seized his wrist and gripped it

as hard as she could: "You know what will happen if you stay here? The Germans will deport all men of military age."

"Well, well, you don't say! And I suppose they'll cut off the kid's hands and rape you, if they can bear to. All that is a lot of hooey; I bet they're not half as bad as people say."

Sarah's throat was dry and her lips trembled. In a perfectly colorless voice she said:

"All right. Where are we?"

"Twenty-four kilometers from Gien."

"Twenty-four kilometers! Just the same, I won't let this brute see me crying."

She got in the car, pulled out her suitcase, got out again, took Pablo by the hand.

"Come along, Pablo."

"Where to?"

"To Gien."

"Is it far?"

"Quite a long way, but I'll carry you when you get tired." Then, defiantly, she added: "We'll surely find some kind people who will help us."

The man stepped in front of them, barring the way. Frowning, he scratched his head uneasily.

"What do you want?" Sarah asked grimly.

He did not know what he wanted. He looked first at Sarah, then at Pablo; he seemed to be hunting for an answer.

"I see! You're going off like that, are you?" he said without conviction. "You're going off without so much as a word of thanks?"

"Thank you," Sarah said hurriedly, "thank you."

The man had found what he was looking for—anger. He was working himself up into a fury, and his face turned crimson.

"How about my two hundred francs? Where are they?"

"I don't owe you anything," said Sarah.

"Didn't you promise me two hundred francs? This very morning? At Melun? In my garage?"

"Yes, on condition you took us to Gien. But you're abandoning me and the child halfway."

"I'm not abandoning you; it's this old bus." He shook his head, the veins were standing out on his temples. His eyes were glittering and he looked thoroughly pleased with himself. Sarah was not in the least frightened.

"I want my two hundred francs."

She fumbled in her bag.

"Here are a hundred. I don't owe them to you, and you're certainly richer than I am. I'm giving them to you just for the sake of peace and quiet."

He took the money and put it in his pocket; then he held out his hand again. His face was very red, with his mouth open and a brooding look in his eyes.

"You still owe me a hundred francs."

"Not one sou more will you get from me. Let me pass."

He made no move, caught in the trap of his own ill temper. He did not really want the hundred francs. He did not know what he wanted; perhaps he just wanted the boy to give him a kiss before parting. These confused feelings he translated into his own language. He took a step toward her, and she guessed that he was going to take her suitcase.

"Don't you touch me!"

"My hundred francs, or I take the suitcase."

They stood staring at each other. It was quite obvious that he did not want to take the suitcase; and Sarah was so tired that she would gladly have given it to him. But since the scene had reached this stage, it had to be played out. They hesitated, as though they had forgotten their parts; then Sarah said:

"Just you try to take it! Just you try!"

He seized the case by the handle and began to pull. He

could have twisted it free with a single jerk, but he did no more than pull, keeping his face averted. Sarah pulled as well. Pablo started to cry. The crowd of pedestrians had already receded into the distance; the procession of cars had begun again. Sarah knew she was making a fool of herself. She tugged violently at the handle; tugging more violently still, he managed to wrench the suitcase free. He stared in astonishment, first at Sarah, then at the suitcase. Perhaps he had not really wanted to take it from her, but it was done now; he was holding it in his hand.

"Give me back that suitcase," Sarah cried.

He made no reply; he looked foolish, obstinate. Anger flared up in Sarah and set her running toward the cars.

"Thief!" she shouted. "Help!"

A long, black Buick was passing at the moment.

"Come on," said the man, "don't make a fuss!"

He took her by the shoulder, but she wrenched herself away. Ease and precision of speech and movement came back to her. She jumped onto the running-board of the Buick and clung to the handle of the door.

"Thief! Help! Thief!"

A hand shot out of the car and pushed her off.

"Get off or you'll get yourself killed."

She felt she was going mad; it was rather pleasant.

"Stop!" she shouted. "Thief! Help!"

"Get off there! How can I stop? The car behind would bump into me."

Sarah's anger ebbed suddenly. She jumped to the ground and stumbled. The garage man caught her and set her on her feet. Pablo was crying and yelling. The game was up; Sarah wanted to die. She fumbled in her bag and brought out a hundred francs.

"Here you are! You'll be ashamed of yourself later on."

The man took the bill without raising his eyes and let go of the suitcase.

"And now please let us pass."

He stood aside. Pablo was still crying.

"Don't cry, Pablo," she said, but there was no tenderness in her voice. "There, there, it's all over now; we're going."

They walked away, leaving the man grumbling behind them:

"Who'd have paid for the gas, I'd like to know?"

The long-bodied, dark-colored ants filled the whole width of the road. Sarah tried at first to walk between them, but the bellowing of horns drove her stumbling into the ditch.

"Keep behind me."

She twisted her foot and stopped.

"Sit down."

They sat in the grass. The insects crawled past, enormous, slow, mysterious. The man turned his back on them; he was still clutching his useless hundred francs. The cars creaked like so many lobsters, scraped like so many crickets. Human beings had become insects. She felt frightened.

"He's a bad man!" said Pablo. "A bad, bad man!"

"No one is bad!" Sarah told him passionately.

"What for did he take the suitcase, then?"

"You mustn't say *what for*, Pablo. Say: *why* did he take the case?"

"Why did he take the suitcase?"

"He was frightened," she said.

"What are we waiting for?" asked Pablo.

"We're waiting for the cars to go by, so we can walk in the road."

Twenty-four kilometers. Eight would be about the limit of the boy's strength. Impulsively she climbed to the top of the bank and waved her hand. The cars passed her and she felt she was being *seen* by hidden eyes, by the strange eyes of flies, of ants.

"What are you doing, Mamma?"

"Nothing," said Sarah, bitterly. "Just being silly."

She returned to the ditch, took Pablo by the hand, and together they gazed at the road in silence. At the road and at the shelled tortoises moving over its surface. Gien, twenty-four kilometers away. After Gien, Nevers, Limoges, Bordeaux, Hendaye. At Hendaye, consulates, formalities, humiliating periods of waiting in official anterooms. It would be a stroke of luck if they found a train for Lisbon. At Lisbon it would be a miracle if they found a boat for New York. And in New York? Gomez hadn't a sou; perhaps he was living with some woman; if that were so, her cup of misery and shame would be filled to the very brim. He would open her telegram. "Christ!" he would say, and turn to the fleshy blonde sitting with a cigarette between her coarse lips. "My wife's turned up again," he would say, "that's the finishing stroke." He'd be on the dock. All the other people would be waving handkerchiefs, but not Gomez! He would be scowling at the gangplank. "If I had only myself to consider," she thought, "you would never hear another word from me. But I've got to go on living in order to bring up the child you wished on me!"

The cars had vanished, the road was empty. Across the road lay yellow fields and hills. A man passed by on a bicycle; pale and sweating, he was pedaling away for dear life.

He gave Sarah a wild look, and, without stopping, "Paris is burning!" he called to her. "Incendiary bombs!"

"What?"

But he had already caught up with the crowd of cars, she saw him hitch on to the back of a Renault. Paris burning. Why go on living? Why protect the young life at her side? So that he might wander from country to country with bitterness and terror in his heart? So that for fifty years he might endure the curse that lay upon his race? So that at the age of twenty he might be machine-gunned on some stretch of road and fall, holding his guts in with his hands? From your father you inherit pride, sensuality, and a wicked nature; from me, your Jewish blood. She snatched at his hand.

"Come along! It's time we were moving."

A vast crowd was sweeping over road and fields, close-packed, mulish, implacable—a human flood. Not a sound but the scraping of boots and shoes over hard earth. Sarah experienced a moment of panic; she wanted to run some-where, anywhere, into the open countryside; but she pulled herself together, took a firm grip on Pablo, and dragged him along, letting herself be swept forward. Stench. The hot, stale stench of human beings, the sweet acrid stench of destitution, the unnatural stench of think-ing animals. Between two red necks topped by derby hats she could see the last of the cars, her final hope, vanishing into the distance. Pablo began to laugh, and Sarah gave a start.

"Ssh!" she said shamefacedly. "This is no time to laugh." But he kept on, noiselessly.

"What are you laughing at?"

"It's like a funeral," he explained.

She felt the presence of faces, of eyes, to right and left of her, but she dared not look at them. They plodded on, clinging to their plodding as she clung to life; walls of dust rose in the air and broke upon them; they kept on plod-ding. Sarah, very upright, her head high, kept her eyes focused far ahead, staring between the two necks in front, and she kept saying to herself: "I won't become like them!" But, in a very short time, the collective plodding became part of her very being, mounted from her thighs to her belly, beat within her like a huge, laboring heart. The heart of *all* those about her.

"The Nazis would kill us if they caught us, wouldn't they?" Pablo asked suddenly.

"Hush!" said Sarah. "I don't know."

"They'd kill everybody, wouldn't they?"

"Oh, do stop talking; I tell you I don't know."

"Well then, we should run."

She tightened her grip on his hand.

"Don't run. Stay where you are. They won't kill us."

There was a sound of rasped breathing on her left. She had been hearing it for the last five minutes without giving it any serious thought. It seemed to have worked its way into her, to have settled in her lungs, to be *her* breathing. She turned her head and saw an old woman with gray, sweat-matted locks, an ancient crone of the cities, with bloodless cheeks and heavy pouches under her eyes; she was panting. She had probably lived for sixty years in some Montrouge slum or some back shop in the Clichy quarter; and now here she was, turned loose upon the roads. She was clutching an elongated bundle to her side; at every step she staggered, lurching forward first with one foot, then with the other; her head moved in sympathy with her legs. "Who on earth suggested she should come away, at her age? Haven't people enough unhappiness as it is, without deliberately going out of their way to find more?" Kindliness surged in her breasts like milk. "I'll help her, I'll take her bundle, her weariness, her misery." Gently, she asked:

"Are you all alone, madame?"

The old woman did not so much as turn her head.

"Are you alone, madame?" Sarah asked more loudly.

The old woman looked at her with expressionless eyes.

"Let me carry your bundle," said Sarah. She waited a moment, eying the bundle covetously. "Do give it me," she added earnestly. "I'll carry it as long as my little boy is able to walk."

"I'm not giving my bundle to nobody," said the old woman.

"But you're completely exhausted; you'll never get to where you're going."

The old drab shot a glance of hatred at Sarah and sidled away. "I'm not giving my bundle to nobody," she replied.

Sarah sighed and said no more. Her unused kindliness distended within her like a gas. They don't want to be loved. Several heads turned toward her. She flushed. They don't want to be loved, they're not used to it.

"Have we still far to go, Mamma?"

"Almost as far as it was just now," replied Sarah, her nerves on edge.

"Carry me, Mamma."

Sarah shrugged her shoulders. "He's pretending," she mused. "He's jealous because I offered to carry the old woman's bundle."

"Try to keep on walking for a bit."

"I can't, Mamma. Carry me!"

Angrily she snatched her hand away. He will exhaust all my strength and I shan't be able to help anybody. She would end by carrying the child as the old woman was carrying her bundle; she would become one of them.

"Carry me," he said, stamping his foot. "Carry me!"

"You aren't tired yet, Pablo," she murmured with severity. "You only just got out of the car."

The boy resumed his jog-trot progress. Sarah walked on, staring straight before her, forcing herself not to think of him. At the end of a few moments she glanced down out of the corner of her eye and saw that he was crying. He was crying very quietly, making no sound, as though keeping his tears to himself; now and then he raised his small fists to rub the tears from his cheeks. She felt ashamed, she thought: "I am being too hard. I am kind to everybody else out of pride, and hard to him because he belongs to me." She was inclined to give herself to everybody, she forgot her own troubles, forgot she was a Jewess, one of the persecuted, she found a way of escape into a huge movement of impersonal charity, and for that reason she hated Pablo because he was flesh of her flesh, and the mirror of her race. She laid her large hand on the boy's head. "It's not your fault," she thought, "if you've got your father's jaw and your mother's race." The old woman's whistling inhalations were in her own lungs. "I have no right to be generous." She changed her suit-case to her left hand and bent down.

"Put your arms round my neck," she said good-hu-moredly, "and make yourself as light as you can. Upsa-daisy!"

He was heavy. He laughed blissfully, and the sun dried his tears. She had become just like the others, a beast of burden in the general herd. With each breath she took, it was as though tongues of fire were licking her lungs; a sharp, half-imaginary pain gnawed at her shoulder; a weariness that was neither generous nor willingly in-curred set her heart thumping—the weariness of a mother and of a Jewess, *her* weariness, *her* destiny. Hope died in her: she would never get to Gien. Not she nor any of them. None of those around her had any hope left, neither the old woman, nor the two necks with derby hats, nor the couple pushing a tandem bicycle with flat tires. We are just caught up in the crowd, and the crowd is walk-ing and we walk; we are no more than the feet of this interminable vermin. Why walk when hope is dead? Why live?

When the screaming started she was scarcely surprised; she stood still while the others scattered, scrambled up the bank, flung themselves flat in the ditches. She dropped her suitcase and stood in the middle of the road, alone, proud, and erect. She heard the roaring in the sky, she saw her shadow already lengthening from her feet, she clutched Pablo to her breast; there was a deafening din in her ears: for a moment she was as though dead. Then the noise lessened; she had a glimpse of tadpoles in the watery spaces of the sky; the others were climbing out of the ditches; she must start once more to live, she must start once more to walk.

"He was pretty swell, you know," said Ritchie; "he bought us lunch, and he's given you a hundred dollars' advance."

"True," said Gomez.

They were on the ground floor of the Museum of Modern Art, in the gallery devoted to loan exhibitions. Gomez turned his back on Ritchie and the pictures; he leaned his forehead against the window and looked out at the asphalt and at the meager grass of the tiny garden.

"Perhaps now I shall be able to think of something else than my stomach," he said without turning round.

"You ought to be pretty pleased with life," said Ritchie expansively.

The words contained a discreet hint: you've found a job, everything's for the best in the best of all possible new worlds; it's up to you to show proper enthusiasm. Gomez glanced gloomily at Ritchie over his shoulder. Pleased? It's you who feel pleased, because I'm not going to be a burden to you any longer.

He felt thoroughly ungrateful.

"Pleased?" he said. "That remains to be seen."

A touch of hardness showed on Ritchie's face. "Well, aren't you pleased?"

"That remains to be seen," said Gomez again, with a mirthless chuckle.

He pressed his face again to the glass and looked out at the grass in a mingled mood of longing and disgust. Until this morning, thank God, colors had left him cold; he had buried the memory of the days when he wandered the streets of Paris spellbound, mad with pride at the thought of the destiny awaiting him, saying to himself a hundred times a day: "I'm a painter." But Ramon had given him money. He had drunk Chilean white wine, for

the first time in three years he had talked about Picasso.
Ramon had said: "After Picasso, I don't see there's much
a painter can do," and Gomez had smiled; he had said:
"But I see," and a dry flame had started once again to
flicker in his heart. When they came out of the restaurant,
it was as though someone had operated on him for cata-
ract: at the same moment every color had blazed into life
to do him honor, as in '29, with its dance-halls—the
Redoute, the Carnaval, the Fantasia; people and things
had shown a rush of blood to the surface. A violet dress
had glowed to purple, the red entrance to a drugstore
had turned to crimson, colors had drummed in every
object with a mad pulsation. The world had thrilled and
vibrated till it seemed that it must burst; it was as though
everything were on the point of exploding, of falling down
in an apoplectic fit. The air had sounded a shrill cacoph-
ony of brilliance, had whirled and dazzled like a merry-
go-round. Gomez shrugged his shoulders: Here were
colors pouring on his head just when he had ceased to
believe in his destiny. I know perfectly well what ought
to be done about it, but somebody else will do it. He had
clung to Ritchie's arm, walking quickly, with a fixed stare,
but the colors had thrust at him from every side, bursting
in his eyes like tiny flasks of blood and gall. Ritchie had
pushed him into the museum, and here he now was, with
there, on the other side of the glass pane, this green,
nature's green, crude, unrendered, an organic secretion,
like honey or curdled milk; there that green was, to be
taken, to be *handled.* I shall take it, I shall work it to a
pitch of incandescence. . . . But what business is it of
mine? I'm no longer a painter. He heaved a sigh: an art
critic is not paid to spend his time worrying about wild
grass; his business is to think about what other men have
thought. At his back were other men's colors displayed
on canvas: concentrations, essences, thoughts. *They* had
had the good fortune to be achieved; somebody had in-

flated them, breathed into them, pushed them to the very limits of their nature, and they had accomplished their destiny, there was nothing more for them save to be preserved in museums. Other men's colors: that was now his lot.

"Oh, well," he said, "I'd better start earning my hundred dollars."

He turned round. Fifty pictures by Mondrian were set against the white walls of this clinic: sterilized painting in an air-conditioned gallery; no danger here, where everything was proof against microbes and the human passions. He went up to a picture and stared hard at it. Ritchie was watching Gomez's face and smiling in anticipation.

"It doesn't say a thing to me," Gomez muttered.

Ritchie stopped smiling, but the expression on his face was one of understanding.

"Sure," he said tactfully. "You can't expect it to come back all at once, you must get back into your stride."

"My stride?" Gomez echoed the words ill-temperedly. "Not *that*."

Ritchie turned and looked at the picture. On a gray ground was a black vertical line crossed by two horizontals; at the left-hand extremity of the upper horizontal was a blue disk.

"I thought you liked Mondrian."

"I thought so too," said Gomez.

They stopped in front of another picture; Gomez stared at it and tried to *remember*.

"Have you really got to write about these?" Ritchie asked nervously.

"I haven't got to, no. But Ramon would like me to devote my first article to Mondrian. I suppose he thinks it would strike the high-brow note."

"Watch yourself," said Ritchie. "Don't start off by being too destructive."

"Why not?" asked Gomez, beginning to bristle.

Ritchie's smile spread a gentle irony. "Obviously you don't know the American public. The one thing it can't stomach is to be startled. Start in by making a name for yourself: say simple, sensible things, and say them with charm. And, if you absolutely must attack someone, at least don't pick Mondrian: he's our God."

"Naturally," said Gomez; "Mondrian doesn't pose any questions at all."

Ritchie shook his head and made a clucking sound with his tongue several times in sign of disapprobation.

"He poses a whole lot," he said.

"Yes, but not embarrassing questions."

"Oh," said Ritchie, "you mean questions about sex or the meaning of life or poverty? I was forgetting you studied in Germany. *Gründlichkeit*, eh?" he said, slapping the other on the back. "Don't you think that is a bit dated?"

Gomez made no reply.

"As I see it," said Ritchie, "it is no part of the painter's business to ask embarrassing questions. Suppose somebody came along and asked me whether I wanted to go to bed with my mother: I would fling him out on his ear, unless he was carrying out a piece of scientific research. I don't see why painters should have the right to ask me questions in public about my complexes. Like everybody else," he added in a conciliatory tone, "I have my troubles. But when I think they're getting me down, I don't slip off to a museum; I call up a psychoanalyst. People should stick to their jobs: a psychoanalyst gives me confidence because he started off by being psychoanalyzed himself. So long as painters don't do that, they're talking at cross-purposes, and I shall not ask them to make me look at myself."

"What will you ask of them?" Gomez put in, more for the sake of saying something than because he wanted to know. He was looking at the picture with surly hostility. He was thinking: "Transparent as water."

"I ask them for innocence," said Ritchie. "This picture—"

"Well, what about it?"

"It's just seraphic!" said Ritchie ecstatically. "We Americans like painting to appeal to happy people or to people who are trying to be happy."

"I'm not happy," said Gomez, "and I would be a bastard if I tried to be, what with all my friends either in prison or shot."

Ritchie clucked his tongue again. "Look," he said, "I know all about your personal troubles. Fascism, the defeat of the Allies, Spain, your wife, your kid—sure! But it's a good thing to rise above all that occasionally."

"Not for one single, solitary moment!" Gomez protested. "Not for a single moment!"

Ritchie flushed slightly.

"What did you used to paint, then?" he asked in a hurt tone. "Strikes? Massacres? Capitalists in stovepipe hats? Soldiers firing on the people?"

Gomez smiled. "You know, I've never much believed in revolutionary art. And at present I don't believe in it at all."

"Well then, we agree, eh?" said Ritchie.

"Perhaps. The trouble is I wonder if I haven't lost my faith in art of any kind."

"And in revolution?" Ritchie asked.

Gomez said nothing. Ritchie smiled again.

"You know, you European intellectuals are really very funny. Where action is concerned, you suffer from an inferiority complex."

Gomez swung round suddenly and gripped Ritchie's arm. "Come on, let's get out of here. I've seen all I want to. I know Mondrian by heart. I can turn out an article on him any time. Let's go upstairs."

"Where to?"

"To the second floor. I want to see the others."

"What others?"

They walked through three galleries devoted to the loan exhibition. Gomez, pushing Ritchie ahead of him, did not stop to look at anything.

"What others?" Ritchie repeated testily.

"All the others. Klee, Rouault, Picasso—the ones who ask awkward questions."

At the foot of the stairs Gomez stopped. He looked at Ritchie with a puzzled expression and said almost timidly:

"These are the first pictures I've looked at since '36."

"Since '36!" Ritchie repeated, taken aback.

"That was the year I went to Spain. At that time I was trying my hand at copperplate engravings. I hadn't time to finish the one I was working on, I left it on my table."

"Since '36! But what about Madrid? What about the Prado?"

"The pictures had all been packed up, hidden away, dispersed."

Ritchie shook his head. "You had a bad time of it!"

"Not a bit of it." Gomez burst into a guffaw of laughter.

There was a hint of disapproval in Ritchie's astonishment. "Take me, now," he said; "I never touched a brush in my life, but I just *have* to go to all the exhibitions; it's a necessity of my nature. How can a painter go four years without looking at any pictures?"

"Wait," Gomez warned, "wait a minute. In a few seconds I shall know whether I am still a painter."

They climbed the stairs and entered one of the galleries. On the left-hand wall there was a Rouault, red and blue. Gomez came to a halt in front of the picture.

"That's one of the Magi," said Ritchie.

Gomez said nothing.

"I don't care so much for Rouault," said Ritchie, "but I can see you like him."

"Oh, shut up!"

Gomez examined the picture a moment longer, then looked down. "Come along."

"If you're fond of Rouault," said Ritchie, "there's something of his at the end of the room that I find much more beautiful."

"Let's not bother," said Gomez. "I've gone blind."

Ritchie looked at him and opened his mouth, but said nothing. Gomez shrugged his shoulders.

"No one who ever fired a rifle at his fellow men can look at these pictures properly."

They went downstairs again; Ritchie held himself stiffly and looked very formal. "He thinks there's something odd about me," Gomez reflected. Ritchie undoubtedly was an angel; the obstinacy of an angel could be read in his limpid eye; his great-grandparents, who had been angels too, had hanged witches in Massachusetts. "I am dripping with sweat, I am poor and my thoughts are dubious because they are European thoughts; the nice-looking angels of America will end by hanging me too." Over there, across the Atlantic, were the concentration camps; over here was the gallows. Gomez had a wide range of choice.

They had reached the counter near the entrance. Gomez glanced absent-mindedly through an album of reproductions. Art is optimistic.

"We do make magnificent photographs," said Ritchie. "Look at these colors: it's the original picture itself."

A dead soldier, a shrieking woman: the recorded images of a heart at peace. Art is optimistic; suffering is justified as soon as it becomes the raw material of beauty. I *am not* at peace, I *don't want* to find justification for the suffering I have seen. Paris. . . . He turned sharply toward Ritchie.

"If painting is not *everything*, then it is merely a bad joke."

"What's that?"

Gomez slammed the album shut. "No man can paint Evil."

Ritchie's expression froze into distrust; the look he turned on Gomez was that of a country cousin. Suddenly he gave a full-throated laugh and dug his companion in the ribs.

"I understand, old fellow. Four years of war! What you need is to be re-educated."

"Why bother?" said Gomez. "I'm just about ripe to be a critic."

They relapsed into silence; then Ritchie, speaking very quickly, said: "Did you know there is a movie theater in the basement?"

"I have never set foot in the place before."

"They show film classics and documentaries."

"Do you want to have a look?"

"I must stay around here," Ritchie said. "I have a date at five o'clock a few blocks away."

They crossed to a panel of varnished wood and read the program.

"*The Covered Wagon.* I've seen it three times," Ritchie said. "But *Diamond Mining in the Transvaal* might be interesting. You coming?" he added without eagerness.

"I don't care for diamonds," said Gomez.

Ritchie appeared to be relieved. He grinned broadly, confidingly, and, clapping his friend on the back, "See you again," he said in English, as though he were recovering his native language along with his freedom.

"This is where I ought to say thank you," Gomez thought. But finding no fitting words, he shook hands in silence.

Outside, the octopus; a thousand suckers closed in upon him; he was dripping with moisture, his shirt was soaked through in a moment. A white-hot blade passed before his eyes. No matter! No matter! He was happy to have escaped from the museum: the heat might be cataclysmic, but it was genuine. The fierce Indian sky, too, was genuine, thrust upward by the tall peaks of skyscrapers until it was higher than all the skies of Europe. The brick houses between which he was walking were genuine and so ugly that no one would have dreamed of painting them. A soaring block in the distance looked like one of Claude Lorrain's ships—a faint brush-stroke on canvas; but it was genuine and Claude Lorrain's ships were not: pictures are so many dreams. Gomez thought of the village in the Sierra Madre where they once fought a battle from dawn to dusk: the red on the road was genuine. "I shall never paint again," he thought with a bitter pleasure. *Here*, on this side of the mirror, *here* and nowhere else, with himself crushed by the heat descending upon *this* blazing pavement, Truth had reared high walls around him, stood blocking every vista of the horizon; there was nothing in the whole world but this heat, these stones, nothing at all save dreams. He turned into Seventh Avenue. The human tide flowed over him, its waves crested with a fine spray of bright, dead eyes; the sidewalk throbbed, incandescent colors bespattered him, steam rose from the crowd as from a damp sheet laid out in the sun; eyes and grins everywhere, *not to grin is a sin*, eyes vague or definite, flickering or slow-moving, all dead. He did his best to go on pretending that these were real men, but no, impossible! Everything was falling to bits within his hands, his momentary feeling of happiness ebbed dismally; these eyes were like the eyes of portraits. Do these people realize that Paris has fallen? Do they even give it a thought? They were all walking with the same hurried concentration, splashing him with the white spume of their eyeballs. They are not real at all, he thought, they are ghosts. Well then, where are the real people? he wondered, and, answering himself, mused: Certainly not here. And I am no more real and genuine than any of them. A make-believe Gomez took the bus, read the paper, smiled at Ramon, talked of Picasso, looked at the Mondrians. I was striding through Paris, the rue Royale is deserted, the place de la Concorde is deserted, a German flag is flying over the Chamber of Deputies, an SS regiment is parading under the Arc de Triomphe, the sky is dotted with airplanes. The brick walls crumbled, the crowd returned to the bowels of the earth, and Gomez walked lonely through the streets of Paris. Through Paris, through the truth, the *only* Truth, through blood, and hatred, and defeat, and death.

"God-damned French swine!" he muttered, clenching his fists. "They couldn't take it, they scattered like rabbits, I knew they would, I knew they were doomed." Turning right into Fifty-sixth Street, he stopped in front of a French bar and restaurant called A la Petite Coquette. He looked at the red and green façade, hesitated a moment, then pushed through the door; he wanted to see what kind of face New York's Frenchmen were pulling today.

Inside, it was dark and almost cool; the blinds were lowered, the lights lit.

It was pleasurable to Gomez to find himself in artificial light. At the far end of the establishment, the restaurant lay swathed in shadow and silence. A big fellow with a crew haircut sat at the bar, staring through his eyeglasses; now and then his head dropped forward, but he recovered immediately, with a great show of dignity. Gomez sat down on a stool at the bar. He knew the bartender slightly.

"Double Scotch," he said in French. "Have you got today's paper?"

The bartender produced a *New York Times* out of a drawer and handed it to him. The bartender was a blond young man, with melancholy and precise manners. But for his Burgundian accent, he might have passed for a native of Lille. Gomez made a pretense of glancing through the

Times; then suddenly he looked up. The bartender was gazing wearily at him.

"The news is pretty bad, eh?" Gomez said.

The bartender shook his head.

"Paris is captured," Gomez said.

The bartender, grunting in melancholy fashion, filled a small glass with whisky, which he emptied into a larger one; then he repeated the operation and slid the large glass toward Gomez. The American with the eyeglasses looked glassily at them for an instant, then inclined his head as though bowing reverentially.

"Soda?"

"Yes." Gomez continued unabashed: "I'm afraid France is done for."

The bartender sighed but said nothing, and with a sharp stab of joy, Gomez thought the other was too disconsolate to be able to speak. He stuck to his point with a feeling akin to tenderness.

"Don't you think so?"

The bartender sprayed soda water into Gomez's glass. Gomez's eyes never abandoned the other's moonlike and weepy face. How delicious to choose his moment and in a different voice to say: "What did you do for Spain? Well, it's your turn to roast in hell!"

The bartender raised his eyes and a finger; suddenly he began to talk in a deep-pitched, slow, and very calm voice, slightly nasal, marked heavily by a Burgundian accent.

"Late or soon," he said, "you have to pay."

Gomez chuckled. "Yes, you have to pay."

With one finger the bartender stabbed at the air above Gomez's head; he looked like a comet foretelling the end of the universe. He did not look at all unhappy.

"France," he said, "will learn what it costs to abandon her natural allies."

"What on earth does the man mean?" Gomez wondered.

He had meant to stare the other out of countenance with a look of insolent, rancorous triumph; now that very triumph glittered in the bartender's eye.

Gomez chose his words carefully; he was feeling his way. "When Czechoslovakia—"

The bartender shrugged his shoulders and interrupted. "Czechoslovakia!" he said with contempt.

"Well, what about it?" Gomez said. "It was your fault that Czechoslovakia fell!"

The bartender smiled. "In the reign of Louis the Well-Beloved, monsieur, France had already committed every sin it is possible to commit."

"I see!" said Gomez. "You're a Canadian?"

"I am from Montreal," said the bartender.

"You should have told me."

Gomez laid the *Times* down on the counter. After a brief pause he asked: "Don't any Frenchmen ever come here?"

The bartender pointed at a spot behind Gomez's back. Gomez turned. Seated at a table covered with a white cloth, an old man was dreaming over a newspaper. A *genuine* Frenchman, with a worn, gnarled, ravaged face, with hard, bright eyes and a gray mustache. Compared with the florid American cheeks of the man with glasses, the Frenchman's cheeks looked as though hewn out of some inferior material. A *genuine* Frenchman, with genuine despair in his heart.

"Oh," said Gomez, "I hadn't noticed him."

"That gentleman is from Roanne," the bartender explained. "He comes in here regularly."

Gomez gulped down his whisky and got off his stool. "What did you do for Spain?" With unconcern, the old man watched Gomez approaching him. Gomez took his stand squarely in front of the table and stared greedily at the old face before him.

"Are you a Frenchman?"

"Yes," said the old man.

"Have a drink with me," said Gomez.

"Thank you, no. Today scarcely calls for drinks."

Gomez, his heart thumping in an access of cruelty, asked: "Because of this?" and pointed to the newspaper headline.

"Because of that."

"But that is why I want to buy you a drink," said Gomez. "I lived in France for ten years, my wife and son are still there. Whisky?"

"Very well, but no soda."

"One Scotch without soda, one Scotch with," Gomez ordered.

They relapsed into silence. The American with the eyeglasses swung round on his stool and looked silently upon them.

Suddenly the old man asked: "You are not Italian, are you?"

Gomez smiled. "No," he said, "no, I am not an Italian."

"The Italians are all bastards," said the old man.

"What about the French?" Gomez inquired suavely. "Have you relatives in France?"

"Not in Paris. I have nephews in Moulins." He surveyed Gomez with attention. "I can see you have not been here long."

"And you?" asked Gomez.

"I settled here in '97. That is a good while ago. I don't like these people," he added.

"Then why do you stay here?"

The old man shrugged. "I'm making money."

"You're in business?"

"Hairdressing. I have a shop two blocks away. I used to go to France for two months one year out of three. I was expecting to go again this year. Now, with all this—"

"Yes, with all this," said Gomez.

"I have had forty customers in my place since morning.

Some days I get as many as forty. They all want shaves, haircuts, shampoos, electric massages. Wouldn't you think they might mention my country? Well, think again! They sit reading their newspapers without a word, and I read the headlines while I shave them. Some of them have been coming to me for twenty years, but they have nothing to say. They were lucky I didn't cut or maul them, my hand was trembling so. In the end I shut up shop and came here."

"What do they care?" Gomez said.

"If they do care, they cannot find the words that save. The name Paris must mean something to them, and yet they will say nothing about it, just because it does mean something to them. That's the way it goes!"

Gomez remembered the crowd on Seventh Avenue. "Do you imagine those people in the streets are thinking about Paris?" he said.

"In a way, yes, but not like you and me. Americans do not enjoy the process of thinking. When they do concentrate, it is in order to escape all thought."

The bartender brought the glasses. The old man took his and raised it. "Well," he said, "your health."

"Here's to you!" said Gomez.

The old man smiled sadly. "It is hard to know what to drink to, isn't it?" Then, with sudden determination, "I drink to France," he said. "To France, no matter what!"

Gomez had no desire to drink to France. "To the day when the United States gets into the war," he said.

The old man barked. "What a hope!"

Gomez emptied his glass and turned to the bartender. "The same."

He was thirsty for another drink. A moment ago, he had felt he was alone in his concern for France; the fall of Paris had been his own private affair: it constituted at once a misfortune for Spain and a righteous punishment for the French people. But Gomez also sensed that France was vividly present here in this bar and that the tide of France, no matter in how vague or abstract a form, pulsed through six million minds. It was beyond measure; yet here he was, all ties with Paris broken, a newly arrived immigrant, preyed upon, like the rest of them, by a collective obsession.

"I don't know if you follow me," said the old man, "but I have been living here over forty years, and this is the first time I have felt I was a foreigner. I know Americans," he went on, "and, God knows, have no illusions. But I did think somebody here in America would stretch out a hand to me or say a word to me." His lips twitched. "My customers have been coming to me for twenty years," he said again.

"A true Frenchman," Gomez thought, "one of those who once dubbed us *Frente crapular*." Still, the old man was not consolatory. "He is too old," Gomez concluded.

The old man, staring wide-eyed and without conviction, declared: "Perhaps they are leaning backwards to be fair and neutral."

"Could be," said Gomez.

"Indeed, yes," said the old man. "Could be, indeed! Anything could be in this country." In the same tone he went on: "I owned a house at Roanne. I hoped to go back and live there when I retired. Now I feel I will be fated to die here. That sort of thing changes a man's point of view."

"*Certainly,*" Gomez thought, "*certainly,* you are fated to die here." He turned his head; he wanted to escape. But he pulled himself together, flushed suddenly, fixed his look on the old man's eyes, and asked in a wheezy voice: "Were you for intervention in Spain?"

"Intervention? What do you mean?" the old man asked, bewildered. He looked at Gomez with interest. "Are you a Spaniard?"

"Yes."

"You fellows had a pretty rough deal."

"The French didn't help us much," Gomez said in a toneless voice.

"True. Well, what are the Americans doing? Nation or citizen, it's the same thing: every man for himself."

"Yes," said Gomez, "every man for himself." That old man did not lift a finger to defend Barcelona; Barcelona fell; Paris has fallen, and both that old man and I live in exile, both alike.

The bartender rustled up two glasses. They reached for them without for a moment ceasing to look at each other.

"Here's to Spain!" said the old man.

Gomez hesitated, then said between clenched teeth: "Here's to the liberation of France."

Silence fell between them. It was pitiable: two old broken marionets in a New York bar, drinking to France, to Spain. What a farce!

The old man carefully folded his paper and got up. "I must go back to the shop. That last drink was on me."

"No," said Gomez. "No, no. Bartender, they're all on me."

"Many thanks, then."

The old man reached the door. Gomez noticed that he walked with a limp. "Poor old devil," he thought.

"Same again," he said to the bartender.

The American got off his stool and staggered toward him. "I'm plastered," he said.

"Ah?" said Gomez.

"Hadn't you noticed it?"

"As a matter of fact, I hadn't."

"And d'you know why I'm plastered?" he asked.

"I don't give a damn," said Gomez.

The American belched noisily and collapsed on the chair the old man had just vacated. "'Cause the Huns have taken Paris." A gloomy look came into his face, and he added: "It's the worst news since 1927."

"What happened in 1927?"

The man laid a finger on his lips. "Ssh," he said. "Personal." He laid his head on the table and seemed to have fallen asleep. The bartender left the counter and came across to Gomez.

"Keep an eye on him for a coupla minutes," he said. "This is his reglar time. I'd better go find his taxi."

"Who is he?" asked Gomez.

"Works on Wall Street."

"Did he really get drunk because Paris is captured?"

"If that's what he says, I guess it's true. Only last week it was because of what was happening in the Argentine, and the week before because of the Salt Lake City disaster. Gets drunk every Saturday, but never without some reason."

"He's too sensitive," said Gomez.

The bartender hurried out. Gomez rested his head in his hands and stared at the wall; he had a clear vision of the engraving he had left on his table. It had needed a dark mass on the left to give it balance. A bush, perhaps. Yes, a bush. He saw in memory the engraving, the table, the big window, and he began to cry.

Sunday, June 16

"THERE! There! Just over the trees."

Mathieu was asleep and the war was lost. Even in the depths of his sleep it was lost. The voice woke him with a start: he lay on his back, eyes shut, arms pressed close to his body, and he had lost the war. His mind was rather hazy about where he was, but he knew that he had lost the war.

"To the right!" said Charlot excitedly, "Over the trees, I tell you! Haven't you got eyes in yer head?"

Mathieu could hear Nippert's slow drawl. "Ah, what's the hurry?" said Nippert. "What's the hurry?"

Where are we? Lying in the grass. Eight city slickers in the country, eight civilians in uniform, rolled up in pairs in army blankets, lying on a spread of canvas in the middle of a vegetable garden. We've lost the war; they gave it to us to do something with it and we've lost it. It had slipped through their fingers and got itself lost somewhere up north with a great crash.

"Ah, what's the hurry? What's the hurry?"

Mathieu opened his eyes and stared at the sky. It looked pearl gray, cloudless, bottomless, merely negative presence. Another morning was slowly gathering like a drop of light, which would fall on the earth and drench it with gold. The Germans are in Paris and we have lost the war. Another morning, another beginning. The world's first morning, like every other morning: everything waiting to be done, all the future in the sky. He freed one hand from the blankets and scratched his ear: the future didn't concern him, that was for others to bother about. In Paris the Germans were looking at the sky, reading in it the signs of victory and of many morrows. I've got no future. The silky texture of the morning stroked his face; but against his right hip he felt the warmth of Nippert's body; against his left thigh the warmth of Charlot's. Years and years still to be lived: years to be killed. He had got to kill every detail, all the successive minutes, of this triumphant day now starting, light morning breeze in the poplars, midday sun on the cornfields, the smell of warm earth at evening. When night comes, the Germans will take us prisoner. The sound of booming grew louder; he saw the airplane in the rising sun.

"It's a wop," said Charlot.

Sleepy voices tossed insults into the sky. They had grown used to the lazy patrolling of German airplanes, to a war that had become cynical, wordy and inoffensive; it was *their* war. The Italians didn't play the game: they dropped bombs.

"A wop, eh?" said Lubéron. "You're telling me! You can hear how regular that engine's running. It's a Messerschmitt, take my word—Model 37."

Tension relaxed beneath the blankets; the faces, turned skywards, smiled at the German airplane. Mathieu heard a few muffled explosions, and four small round clouds formed in the sky.

"The bastards!" said Charlot. "Shooting up the Germans *now.*"

"Enough to bring a basketful of eggs down on *us*," said Longin irritably.

And Schwartz added contemptuously: "Won't them fellows never learn?"

There came the sound of two more explosions, and a couple of dark fluffy clouds appeared over the poplars.

"The bastards!" said Charlot again. "The bastards!"

Pinette had raised himself on one elbow. His bright little face, so typically Parisian, looked pink and clean. He fixed his companions with a disdainful expression. "Just doing their job," he said dryly.

Schwartz gave a shrug. "What's the point, now?"

The ack-ack had gone silent; the two little clouds were shredding out; nothing could be heard but the regular and triumphant throb of an engine high up.

"Can't see him any longer," said Nippert.

"I can—there he is, just where I'm pointing."

A white vegetable thrust from the ground in the direction of the airplane. Charlot crouched naked under his blankets.

"Keep still," said Sergeant Pierné nervously; "you'll give us away."

"Oh, yeah? In this light they'll take us for cabbages."

All the same, he withdrew his arm as the airplane passed overhead. His pals grinned as they followed the bright little speck of sunshine across the sky; it was a morning's distraction, the first event of the day.

"He's getting up an appetite," said Lubéron.

There were eight of them there who had lost the war, five orderly-room clerks, two observers, and a meteorologist, all lying side by side among the leeks and carrots. They had lost the war much as a man loses an hour—without noticing it. Eight of them: Schwartz the plumber, Nippert the bank clerk, Longin the tax-collector, Lubéron the insurance agent, Charlot Wroclaw, sunshades and umbrellas, Pinette, the ticket-puncher, and two teachers, Mathieu and Pierné. They had spent nine boring months, first in the pine woods, later among the vineyards; then, one fine day, a voice from Bordeaux had announced the news of their defeat, and they had realized that they had backed the wrong horse.

A clumsy hand brushed Mathieu's cheek. He turned to Charlot. "What is it, angel-face?"

Charlot was lying on his side; Mathieu could see his healthy pink cheeks and open mouth.

"What I want to know," said Charlot in a low voice, "is shall we be moving today?" A worried look passed around and around over his cheerful countenance, as though it did not know where to perch.

"Today? I don't know."

They had left Morsbronn on the 12th; there had come this disorderly retreat, and then, suddenly, this halt.

"What the hell are we doing here? Can you tell me that?"

"Waiting for the God-damned infantry, so they say."

"If the God-damned infantry can't get out, that's no reason why we should let ourselves get nabbed with 'em." He added apologetically: "You see, I'm a Jew. And I've got a Polish name."

"I know," said Mathieu gloomily.

"Shut up," said Schwartz. "Listen!"

A continuous muffled rumbling reached their ears. The day before, and the day before that, it had gone on from dawn to dusk. No one knew who was firing, or on what.

"Must be close to six o'clock," said Pinette. "Yesterday they started at five forty-five."

Mathieu raised his wrist above his eyes and turned it round in order to consult his watch. "Five past six."

"Five past six," said Schwartz. "It'd surprise me if we left today." He yawned. "Oh, well," he said, "another day on the veldt."

Sergeant Pierné yawned too. "Oh well," he said, "better shake a leg."

"Yes," said Schwartz. "Yes. Better shake a leg."

No one moved. A cat streaked past them, zigzagging. It suddenly stopped and crouched as though ready to pounce; then, its purpose forgotten, it stretched itself out lazily. Mathieu, propped on his elbow, was watching it. All at once he saw two bandy legs wrapped in khaki puttees and he raised his head. Lieutenant Ulmann, with arms folded, stood before them and was contemplating them, eyebrows raised. Mathieu noticed that he had not shaved.

"What the devil d'you think you're doing there? Have you gone mad? Answer me, what d'you think you're doing?"

Mathieu waited a few moments and then, seeing that no one replied, said, without moving: "We thought it'd be nicer to sleep in the open, sir."

"You did! With the sky full of enemy planes! That happy thought of yours may cost us dear; it may set them bombarding the division."

"The Germans know perfectly well we're here; all our moves were made in broad daylight," Mathieu remarked patiently.

The lieutenant seemed not to have heard him. "I issued strict orders that you were not to leave the barn," he said. "And what the hell do you mean by lying down in the presence of a superior officer?"

There was a lazy stirring at ground level, and the eight men sat up on their blankets, blinking sleepily. Charlot, who was stripped to the skin, covered his nakedness with a handkerchief. The air was fresh. Mathieu shivered and felt round for his blouse to throw over his shoulders.

"So you're there too, Pierné! Aren't you ashamed of yourself, a noncom? You're supposed to set a good example."

Pierné compressed his lips and said nothing.

"Never seen such a thing in my life!" said the lieutenant. "Perhaps you'll explain why you left the barn?" He spoke without self-assurance, in a violent but weary tone. There were dark shadows under his eyes, and his fresh complexion looked blotchy.

"We were too hot in there, sir. We couldn't sleep."

"Too hot? What do you want? An air-conditioned bedroom? I'll see that you spend tonight in the schoolhouse, with the others. Don't you realize there's a war on?"

Longin gestured with his hand. "War's over, sir," he said with an odd little smile.

"Over, hell! You ought to be ashamed to talk about it's being over when less than twenty miles from here there are fellows getting killed for trying to cover our retreat."

"Poor bastards," said Longin. "Just set down there to be popped off while the armistice is being signed!"

The lieutenant flushed angrily. "You're still soldiers, anyway, and until you've been demobilized and sent home, you'll go on being soldiers and you'll obey your officers."

"Even in a prison camp?" asked Schwartz.

The lieutenant said nothing, but looked at the soldiers with mingled timidity and contempt. They returned his gaze without embarrassment or impatience; it seemed doubtful whether they even felt the novel thrill of unexpectedly seeing themselves as objects of fear. After a brief pause the lieutenant gave a shrug and turned on his heel.

"I should consider it a favor if you would get up at once," he said over his shoulder.

He moved away, holding himself very upright and walking trippingly, like a dancer. "His last dance," thought Mathieu. "In a few hours there'll be German shepherds herding us eastwards, higgledy-piggledy, officers and men alike." Schwartz yawned and his eyes watered; Longin lit a cigarette; Charlot was tearing up handfuls of grass. They were all afraid to get up.

"You see?" said Lubéron. "He said he'd make us sleep in the schoolhouse. That means no move."

"That was just for something to say," Charlot remarked. "He doesn't know any more than us."

Suddenly Sergeant Pierné burst out with "Who does know? Who does know?"

No one replied. A moment later Pinette jumped to his feet. "Anyone coming along for a wash?" he inquired.

"O.K." said Charlot with a yawn.

He got up. Mathieu and Sergeant Pierné got up too.

"Tha Cadum Kid!" exclaimed Longin.

In his pink, hairless nakedness, with his fresh complexion and his prominent little belly gleaming in the golden light of dawn, Charlot looked exactly like France's number-one baby. Schwartz, as usual, padded along behind him.

"You're all gooseflesh," he said, tickling him. "You're all gooseflesh, baby-face."

Charlot put on his regular act of squealing and wriggling, but this morning there was something half-hearted about the performance. Pinette turned to Longin, who was smoking with a mulish look on his face.

"You not coming?"

"What for?"

"To wash."

"Why the hell should I want to wash?" said Longin. "To please the Heinies? They can take me as they find me."

"Who said anything about being took?"

"Come on, come on!" said Longin. "Come along!"

"We may make a get-away!" said Pinette.

"You believe in Santa Claus?"

"Even if they do take us, that's no reason for staying dirty."

"You don't catch me washing for them."

"Balls to that!" said Pinette.

Longin chuckled but said nothing. He lay there snuggled in the blankets, with a look of superiority. Lubéron, too, hadn't moved; he was making believe to be asleep. Mathieu took his knapsack and walked over to the trough. There were two metal pipes from which water flowed into a stone basin; it was cold and stark like a naked body. All night long Mathieu had heard its hopeful, childish, interrogative murmuring. He plunged his head into the trough. The babyish song became a silent, glittering freshness in his ears and nostrils, a bouquet of wet roses and water plants in his heart: bathing in the Loire, rushes, a small green island, childhood. When he stood up again, Pinette was furiously soaping his neck. Mathieu smiled at him; he was very fond of Pinette.

"What crap Longin does talk!" said Pinette. "If the Heinies do turn up, we got to be clean." He stuck a finger in his ear and twiddled it vigorously.

"If you like cleanliness so much," shouted Longin from where he was lying, "you'd better wash your feet too."

Pinette looked at him pityingly. "Nobody sees your feet."

Mathieu started to shave. The blade was an old one and made his skin smart. "When I'm a prisoner I shall let my beard grow." The sun was getting higher. Its long beams struck obliquely through the grass; under the trees the grass was young and tender, a hollow of sleep in the morning's flank. Heaven and earth were full of signs— signs of hope. Among the poplar leaves a multitude of birds, obedient to some invisible signal, struck up a full-throated chorus, a small metallic storm of extraordinary violence; then, mysteriously, they fell silent. As if, uncertain where to alight, a feeling of insecurity seemed to be prowling amid the grassy expanses, amid the patches of vegetables as chubby as Charlot's cheeks. Carefully Mathieu dried his razor and put it back in his knapsack. His heart was in league with the dawn, the dew, the shadows. Deep within him was a feeling as of a feast day. He had got up early and shaved as though for a feast day. A party in a garden, a first communion or a wedding feast, with gay dresses flickering in arbors, a table spread on the lawn, the warm droning of sugar-drunk wasps. Lubéron got up and went to piss against the hedge. Longin went into the barn, carrying his blan-kets under his arm. A moment later he came out again, wandered idly across to the trough, and, with a mocking, idle expression on his face, wet a finger in the water. Mathieu had only to look at his wan face to realize that there would be no feast day, either now or ever again.

The old farmer had come out of his house. He stood smoking his pipe and looking at them.

"Morning, pop," Charlot cried.

"Morning!" said the farmer, shaking his head. "Morn-ing!" He came forward a few steps and halted close to them. "Not gone, then?"

"As you see," said Pinette dryly.

The old fellow chuckled; he looked in no very good humor. "I told you; there's no chance of your ever going."

"Maybe so."

He spat between his feet and wiped his mustache. "What about the Boches? Won't they be coming today?"

They broke into laughter.

"Maybe yes, maybe no," said Lubéron. "Like yourself we're just waiting for them; we're dolling up to receive them."

The old man gave them a funny look. "It's not the same for you," he said. "You'll be coming back." He sucked at his pipe and added: "Me, I'm an Alsatian."

"We know, pop, you've told us often enough," said Schwartz. "Change the record."

The old man shook his head. "Funny sort of war," he said. "It's the civilians who get killed, and the soldiers who get off free."

"Nonsense! You know as well as we do that they won't kill you."

"I'm from Alsace, I tell you."

"Me too," said Schwartz, "I'm Alsatian."

"Maybe," said the old man, "but when I left Alsace, it belonged to them."

"They won't do you any harm," said Schwartz. "They're human like the rest of us."

"Like the rest of you, eh?" said the old man with a sudden spurt of indignation. "Would you go chopping the hands of kids off?"

Schwartz burst out laughing. "He's filling us up with propaganda from the other war," he said with a wink at Mathieu.

He took his towel, dried his great muscular arms and turned to the old man. "They're not all crazy, you know. They'll give you cigarettes, yes, and chocolate—propaganda, that's what they call it, and you needn't be afraid of taking it either, it won't commit you to anything." Still laughing, he went on: "As things go today, pop, you're better off being born in Strasbourg than in Paris."

"I don't want to become a German at my age," said the farmer. "Shit! I'd rather they just shot me."

Schwartz slapped his thigh. "Did you hear that? Shit!" he said, imitating the old man's voice. "I'd rather be a live German than a dead Frenchman, say I."

Mathieu jerked up his head and looked at him; Pinette and Charlot were looking at him too. Schwartz stopped laughing, turned red, and wriggled his shoulders. Mathieu turned away his eyes; he had no wish to sit in judgment, and besides, he liked this great strapping, good-tempered, hard-working lout; not for anything in the world would he have added to his embarrassment. No one spoke. The old man shook his head and glanced round the circle with a resentful expression.

"Ah," he said, "we shouldn't have lost this here war! We needn't have lost it."

They were silent; Pinette coughed, went over to the trough, and began playing with the faucet, looking rather foolish. The old man knocked out his pipe on the gravel, ground his heel into the earth to bury the ash, then turned round and went slowly back into his house. There was a long silence; Schwartz stood very stiffly, his hands on his hips. After a moment he seemed to wake up. He forced a smile. "I was only kidding."

No answer; the other fellows were all looking at him. Then, quite suddenly, though nothing had visibly changed, something gave way; it was as though the taut spring of some mechanism had been eased, a sort of motionless dispersal of energy. The sullen little group that had formed around him broke up. Longin began to pick his teeth with his knife, Lubéron cleared his throat, and Charlot, with a look of innocence, started to hum. They could never harbor a grievance long except in matters of leave or rations. Mathieu caught a brief whiff of wormwood and mint; after the birds, now the grass and flowers were coming awake; they were scattering their scents just as the birds had scattered their cries. "I'd forgotten the smells," thought Mathieu. Fresh, gay odors, green and sharp and acid; they would grow sweeter, more and more lush and feminine as the blue of the sky deepened and the German caterpillar trucks drew nearer. Schwartz sniffed noisily and looked at the bench that they had pulled up last night against the wall of the house.

"Oh, well," he said.

He walked over to it and sat down, his shoulders hunched, his hands hanging between his knees; but he kept his head up and stared in front of him with a hard look in his eyes. Mathieu hesitated a moment, then went to sit down beside him. A few moments later Charlot detached himself from the group and planted himself in front of them. Schwartz raised his head and looked up at him, unsmiling.

"I'd better start washing my things," he said.

There was a silence. Schwartz was still looking at Charlot.

"*I* didn't lose this war. . . ."

Charlot seemed embarrassed; he began to laugh. But Schwartz followed up his thought.

"If everyone had behaved like me, we might have won it. I did nothing anyone can blame." He scratched his cheek, with a surprised look in his eyes. "It's damn funny!" he said.

"It's damn funny," thought Mathieu. "Yes, it's damn funny." He gazed into nothingness and thought: "I'm a Frenchman," and he found that damn funny, for the first time in his life. "*It's damn funny*. We have never really seen France; we have only been in it. France was the air we breathed, the lure of the earth, elbow room, seeing the kind of things we see, feeling so certain that the world was created for man; it was always so natural to be French, it was the simplest, most economical way in the world to feel oneself universal. No explanations were required; it was for the others, the Germans, the English, the Belgians, to explain by what misfortune or fault none of them was quite human. And now France is lying on her back, and we can take a good look at her, we can see her like a large broken-down piece of machinery, and we think: That is it—it was an accident of geography, an accident of history. We are still French, but it no longer seems natural. It needed no more than an accident to make us realize that we were merely accidental. Schwartz thinks that he is accidental, he no longer understands himself, he finds himself embarrassing. He thinks: 'How can a man be French?' He thinks: 'With a little luck I might have been born a German.' And then his face takes on a hard look and he sits listening to the onward surge of his adoptive

country; he is waiting for the glittering armies that will
celebrate his change of heart; he sits waiting for the moment when he may trade our defeat for their victory, when
it will seem *natural* to him to be victorious and German."

Schwartz got up with a yawn. "I'm going to wash some
clothes," he said.

Charlot swung round and joined Longin, who was talking with Pinette. Mathieu was left alone on the bench.

It was Lubéron's turn to yawn noisily. "Christ! What a
boring life!" he declared.

Charlot and Longin yawned. Lubéron watched them
yawning and yawned again himself. "What we need," he
said, "is a whorehouse."

"You mean you could hump it at six o'clock in the morning?" Charlot asked indignantly.

"Me? No matter what time, night or day."

"Not me. I'd as soon take a kick in the arse as frig a
wench at this time of day."

Lubéron cackled. "If you were a married man, you little
turd, you'd have learned to do the job whether you felt
like it or not. The great thing about frigging a woman is
that you needn't bother to think about anything."

They stopped talking. The poplars rustled, an antique
sun trembled among the leaves; from far away came the
companionable rumble of artillery, so daily familiar and
reassuring that it had seemed like one of the sounds of
nature. Something detached itself from a point above their
heads, and a wasp struck at their group in a long, quivering
dive.

"Listen!" said Lubéron.

"What is it?"

There was a sort of emptiness around them, a strange
tranquillity. The birds sang, a cock crowed in the farmyard; far away, someone was hammering rhythmically on
metal. Despite these sounds there was an overwhelming
sense of silence: the guns had stopped.

"Oh boy!" said Charlot.

"Mmm."

They strained their ears, staring at one another.

"That's how it'll begin," Pierné said without any particular show of interest. "At a given moment, over the whole front, there will be silence."

"Over what front? There isn't a front."

"I mean everywhere."

Schwartz came toward them shyly. "You know, I think there must first be some sort of bugle call," he said.

"Balls!" said Nippert. "Communications have all broken down; it might take twenty-four hours before we heard the armistice was signed."

"Perhaps the war ended at midnight," Charlot suggested with a hopeful grin. "The cease-fire is always given at midnight."

"Or at noon."

"Nonsense, you dope, at midnight: zero hour, get it?"

"Stop talking," said Pierné.

They were silent. Pierné sat listening intently, his face nervously twitching; Charlot's mouth was hanging open; across the rustling silence they listened to Peace—a peace without glory, without bells, without drums or trumpets, peace that was like death.

"Shit!" said Lubéron.

The rumble had begun again; it sounded less muffled, nearer, more threatening. Longin clasped his long hands, making the finger-joints crack. Bitterly he growled: "God in heaven, what are they waiting for? Don't they think we've fought enough? Haven't we lost enough men? Must France be utterly bitched up before they decide to stop the slaughter?"

They felt nerveless and flabby, spinelessly indignant; their faces wore that leaden look which comes from indigestion. The echo of drums on the far horizon sufficed to make them feel that the great tidal wave of war was sweeping down on them once more. Pinette swung round and faced Longin. There was the darkness of storm clouds in his eyes, his hand gripped the edge of the trough.

"*What* slaughter? Tell me that. *What* slaughter? Where are the dead and wounded? If you've seen any, you're lucky. All *I've* seen is a lot of fart and crap artists like you careening along the roads in a royal blue funk."

"What's biting *you*, angel-face?" Longin asked with a fiercely spiteful concern. "Not feeling good?" He looked at the others with the glance of a confederate. "Our friend Pinette has always been a nice guy, we used to like him because he was as good at swinging the lead as the rest of us, he never volunteered if there was any dirty work to be done. It's too bad he's turned hero just as the war is over."

There was a glitter in Pinette's eyes. "Who says I'm a hero, you bastard!"

"I do! You want to play the little soldier."

"Well, that's better than shitting your breeches, like you."

"Am I shitting my breeches just because I say the French Army took a hell of a beating?"

"A lot you know about the French Army." Pinette was so angry that his words tumbled headlong over one another as he spoke them. "I suppose Weygand has been talking things over with you."

Longin's smile was lazy and insolent. "No need to talk things over with Weygand: half the effectives are in flight, the other half are surrounded. What more do you want?"

Pinette swept the words away with a peremptory gesture. "We shall regroup on the Loire and establish contact with the northern armies at Saumur."

"You really think that, you fathead?"

"That's what the captain told me. Ask Fontainat."

"Well, the northern armies had better get a move on, that's all I can say, with the Boches already at their backsides. As to our turning up at the rendezvous, well, I'm not taking any bets."

Pinette, black as thunder, was breathing heavily and shuffling his feet. He looked at Longin, shaking himself violently as though to free his back from some load, and when he spoke, it was with the fury of a man at bay. "Even if we retreat as far as Marseille, even if we have to march right across France, there's always North Africa."

Longin folded his arms with a contemptuous smile. "What's wrong with Saint-Pierre-et-Miquelon, you dumbbell?"

"You think you're smart, don't you?" Pinette advanced toward him. "You think you're damned smart, don't you?"

Charlot jumped in between them. "Come on, fellows," he said, "what do you want to scrap for? Everyone knows a fight won't settle anything, and anyhow, there won't be any fighting any more. No more war, never again!" he declared with burning conviction. He was staring hard at both of them, and trembling with passion, passion to make peace among them all—between Pinette and Longin, the Germans and the French.

"It ought to be possible," he went on in a voice almost of supplication, "it ought to be possible to come to an understanding with them. After all, they don't want to crush us."

Pinette diverted his fury toward him. "If the war is lost, it's bastards like you who are responsible."

Longin gave an ugly laugh. "Just another dope who can't see straight, that's all."

There was an interval of silence; then, slowly, all of them turned toward Mathieu. He had been expecting this: after every argument they looked to him to settle it because he was a man of education.

"What do you think?" Pinette asked.

Mathieu lowered his head and said nothing.

"Are you deaf? I'm asking what you think."

"I think nothing," said Mathieu.

Longin crossed the path and came to a halt in front of him.

"You don't say so? I thought school teachers thought all the time."

"Well, you see: not all the time."

"You're not a God-damned fool: you know perfectly well that further resistance is impossible."

"How should I know that?"

Pinette in his turn joined them. They stood, one on either side of Mathieu, like his good and evil genius.

"*You* aren't a heel," said Pinette. "You can't want the French to lay down their arms without fighting it out to a finish!"

Mathieu shrugged his shoulders. "If I was the one fighting, I might have an opinion. But it's the other fellows who are getting wiped out, it's on the Loire that they're fighting; I can't decide for them."

"So you see," said Longin, with a bantering glance at Pinette, "it's not for us to decide whether the other fellows get it in the neck."

Mathieu looked at them uneasily. "That's not what I said."

"What d'you mean, that's not what you said? You just said it."

"If there was a chance," Mathieu said, "the slightest chance—"

"Well?"

Mathieu shook his head. "How can we possibly know?"

"What d'you mean?" Pinette asked.

"He means," Charlot interpreted, "that we can only wait and see, instead of getting all worked up about it."

"No!" Mathieu exclaimed. "No!" He jumped up, clenching his fists. "I've done nothing but wait ever since I was a child!"

They stared at him with no idea what he was talking about. With an effort he mastered himself.

"How can it possibly matter what we decide or what we don't decide?" he said. "Who is asking us for our opinion? Do you realize the jam we're in?"

They recoiled from him, frightened.

"Oh, sure we do," said Pinette, "sure we do, we know."

"You said it," Longin remarked. "A poor God-damned soldier has no opinions." His cold, slobbering smile gave Mathieu the creeps.

"And prisoners even less," he answered dryly.

Everything is asking us for our opinion. *Everything!* We are encircled by questions: the whole thing's a farce. Questions are asked of us as though we were men, as though somebody wanted to make us believe we still are men. But no. No. No. What a farce, this shadow of a question put by the shadow of a war to a handful of make-believe men!

"What's the use of having an opinion? *You're* not going to decide."

He stopped talking. He thought suddenly: life has got to go on. Day after day we have got to gather in the rotten fruit of defeat, to work out in a world that has gone to pieces that total choice I have just refused to make. But, good God! *I* didn't choose this war, nor this defeat; by what phony trick must I assume responsibility for them?

He was conscious within himself of the panic fury of the trapped beast, and, looking up, saw the same fury in the eyes of his comrades. Let them clamor to the skies: "We have nothing to do with this mess! We are guiltless!" His passion ebbed; oh, yes, to be sure, innocence was in the morning sunlight, you could touch it on the blades of grass, an almost tangible presence. But it was a lying presence: what was true was the indefinable fault that they had all committed, *our* fault. A phantom war, a phan-

tom defeat, a phantom guilt. He looked in turn at Pinette
and Longin, and his clenched hands relaxed; he did not
know whether he wanted to help them or to beg them to
help him. They, too, looked at him and then, averting their
eyes, slunk away. Pinette was staring down at his feet;
Longin was smiling at some private pleasantry, but his
smile was stiff and embarrassed. Schwartz was standing
with Nippert a little apart, talking together in the Alsace
dialect; already they looked like conspirators. Pierné was
spasmodically opening and closing his right hand. Mathieu
thought: "So this is what we have come to!"

Marseille, 2 p.m.

IT WAS true, of course, that he *thoroughly* disapproved of melancholy, but when the mood was on one, it was the very devil to shake it off. "I must have an unhappy temperament," he thought. There were many reasons why he should rejoice; in particular, he ought to congratulate himself on his narrow escape from peritonitis, on being quite well again. Instead of which, he was thinking: "I have outlived my day," and the knowledge was bitter to him. When one is melancholy, reasons for rejoicing become melancholy too, so that one rejoices in a melancholy way. "Besides," he thought, "I am dead." For all practical purposes he had died at Sedan in May 1940: all the years of life remaining to him were only boredom. He sighed again, following with his eyes a large green fly moving across the ceiling; then he concluded: "I am a second-rater." This idea was profoundly disagreeable to him. Until now Boris had made it a rule never to question himself introspectively, and it had always worked very well; besides, so long as his main problem had been merely that of getting himself decently and neatly killed, the fact that he was a second-rater had not very much mattered; on the contrary, he had less to regret. But now all this was changed: destiny had decided that he was to live, and he was being forced to realize that he had no vocation, no talents, no money—none of the qualities, in short, which are necessary for living, with the single exception of good health. "How bored I am going to be!" he thought, with a sense of frustration. The fly made off, buzzing loudly. Boris put his hand under his shirt and stroked the scar that seamed his stomach in the neighborhood of his groin; it gave him pleasure to feel the little gully in his flesh. He stared at the ceiling, stroked his scar, and remained plunged in gloom. Francillon came into the ward, strolled with unhurried steps between the empty beds in Boris's direction, and came to a sudden halt, simulating surprise.

"I've been looking for you out in the yard," he said.

Boris said nothing.

Francillon folded his arms indignantly. "Two o'clock in the afternoon and you're still in bed!"

"I'm pissed off," said Boris.

"You feel blue?"

"No, not blue: just pissed off."

"Well, snap out of it," said Francillon. "It'll all end some time."

Francillon sat down by Boris's bed and began to roll a cigarette. He had large, prominent eyes and a beaked nose; he was a frightful-looking creature. Boris was very fond of him: sometimes the mere sight of him made Boris burst into uncontrollable laughter.

"Won't be long now," said Francillon cryptically.

"How long?"

"Four more and you go."

Boris counted on his fingers. "That means the 18th."

Francillon grunted confirmation, licked the gum on his cigarette paper, lit the cigarette, and leaning forward confidentially: "No one here?"

All the beds were empty: the boys were out in the yard or off in the town.

"Look for yourself," said Boris. "Unless, of course, there are spies under the beds."

Francillon leaned still closer. "On the night of the 18th," he explained, "Blin will be on duty. The old crate will be on the runway ready to take off. All aboard by midnight, we take off at two, we reach London by seven. What do you say?"

Boris made no reply. He fingered his scar and thought, "Lucky guys, they're in clover!" a thought that made him feel gloomier than ever. "He's going to ask me what I've decided."

"Well, what about it?"

"I think you're lucky devils," said Boris.

"What d'you mean, lucky? All you have to do is come along with us. Don't say you've not been invited."

"No," Boris admitted, "I won't say that."

"All right, then. What have you decided?"

"Nothing doing," Boris said morosely.

"Surely you aren't going to stay on in France?"

"I don't know."

"The war isn't over yet," said Francillon, an obstinate look on his face. "Anyone who says it's over is a coward and a liar. You've got to be where the fighting is; you've no right to hang on in France."

"You're telling me," said Boris bitterly.

"Well, then?"

"Well, then, I'm waiting for my girl to turn up, I told you that before. When I've seen her, I'll decide."

"You can't let a girl stand in your way: this is a man's job."

"Well, that's the way it goes," Boris said dryly.

Francillon looked cowed and said nothing. I wonder if he thinks I've got cold feet. Boris gazed into Francillon's eyes trying to read his mind; but a trustful smile reassured him.

"Seven o'clock you get there?" Boris asked.

"Seven o'clock."

"The English coast must look grand at daybreak. There are big white cliffs at Dover."

"Ah!" said Francillon.

"I've never been up in a plane," said Boris. He brought his hand out from under his shirt.

"Scratching your scar?"

"No."

"I keep on scratching mine; it itches. Seeing where mine is placed, it's hard for me to scratch it in company," said Francillon.

There was a pause, then Francillon went on: "When's she coming, your girl?"

"I don't know. She was meant to come here from Paris."

"Well, she'd better get a move on," Francillon warned. "We fellows can't wait."

Boris sighed and turned over on his stomach. In a detached tone Francillon went on: "I haven't breathed a word to mine, though I see her every day. I'll drop her a line the evening we take off; by the time she gets it, we'll be in London."

Boris nodded without replying.

"You surprise me!" Francillon exclaimed. "Honestly, Serguine, you surprise me!"

"You wouldn't understand," said Boris.

Francillon was silent; he stretched out his hand and picked up a book. They'll be flying over the cliffs of Dover by dawn. It didn't bear thinking about: Boris was no believer in Santa Claus, he knew that Lola would say no.

"*War and Peace*," Francillon said. "What is that?"

"A novel about war."

"War I?"

"No. Another war. But they're all alike."

"Yes," Francillon agreed, laughing, "they're all alike." He had opened the book at random and was frowning over its pages with a pained look.

Boris fell back in bed. He thought: "I can't do that *to her*, I can't go off for the second time without asking her how she feels about it. If I stay on here because of her," he thought, "it will be a proof of love. But, good Lord!" he thought, "what an odd proof of my love." On the other hand, had any man the right to stay behind for a woman's sake? Francillon and Gabel, of course, would say no; but they were too young, they didn't know what love was. "What I want someone to tell me," thought Boris, "is not what love is like; I've paid to learn that. I want to know what love is worth. Has one the right to stay behind just to make some woman happy? Put like that, I should be inclined to say no. But has any man the right to go away if that hurts somebody?" Boris recalled something Mathieu had once said: "I'm not such a coward that I should be scared to hurt somebody if it was necessary." All right, only Mathieu's actions were always at variance with his words; he never had the courage to make anyone miserable. Boris caught his breath; a sudden doubt assailed him. What if all this was only a mad impulse? "Suppose my anxiety to get away is dictated by pure egotism, because I dread getting shit on in civilian life? Maybe I'm out for no more than adventure. Maybe it's easier to get yourself killed than to go on living. On the other hand, suppose I'm staying on because I want to be comfortable, because I'm frightened, and to have a woman handy." He turned over. Francillon was bent over the book, his concentration full of mistrust, as though he was determined to unmask the author's lies. "If only I could say: 'I'll come,' if the words can get out of my mouth, I say them." He cleared his throat, opened his mouth, and waited. But the words did not come. "I can't hurt her like that." It came to Boris that he didn't want to go without first consulting Lola. "She's bound to say no, and that'll be that." But suppose she didn't arrive in time, he thought. This possibility had not yet occurred to him. "Suppose she doesn't get here by the

18th? Shall I have to make up my mind independently?
What if I stay and she turns up on the 20th and says: 'I'd
have let you go.' A fine fool I'd look then. Worse, what if
I go and she arrives on the 19th and kills herself. Oh hell!"
His mind was a whirl of conflicting thoughts; he closed his
eyes and dozed off.

"Serguine," Berger cried from the door, "there's a girl
outside asking for you."

Boris started up and Francillon raised his head.

"It's your girl."

Boris dangled his legs over the side of the bed and
massaged his scalp.

"Too good to be true," he yawned. "No, it's the day my
sister comes."

Francillon, in a daze, repeated: "It's the day your sister
comes? You mean the babe that was with you the last
time?"

"Yes."

"She's not bad," Francillon said without any enthusiasm.

Boris rolled on his puttees and put on his blouse. He
saluted Francillon with two fingers, crossed the ward, and
went downstairs, whistling softly through his teeth. Halfway down the stairs he stopped and began to laugh. "It's
screamingly funny!" he thought. "It's funny to think how
gloomy I feel!" He wouldn't get much fun out of seeing
Ivich. "She's no damned use to a fellow when he feels
low," he mused; "she would only make me feel worse."

Ivich was waiting for him in the yard of the hospital. A
few soldiers, walking about the yard, eyed her casually,
but she took no notice of them. While Boris was still some
way off, she smiled.

"Good afternoon, little brother," she called.

Catching sight of Boris, the soldiers broke into speech
and laughter; he was very popular. Boris waved to them,
but felt vaguely disappointed that no one said: "This is
your lucky day!" or "I wouldn't mind finding that babe in

my bed!" Truth to tell, Ivich had aged a good deal and after her miscarriage had lost most of her appeal. Of course Boris was still proud of her but in a different way.

"Good afternoon, you little horror," he said, his fingers grazing her neck.

These days there was always about her an odor of fever and eau de Cologne. He studied her dispassionately.

"You look poorly," he said to her.

"I know. I'm a hag."

"You've given up using lipstick."

"Yes," she said, a harsh note in her voice.

They said no more. Ivich was wearing an oxblood-red blouse with a high collar, very Russian, which accentuated her pallor. It was a pity she did not expose her shoulders and neck a little; she had beautifully rounded shoulders. But she had taken to high-necked gowns and excessively long skirts, almost as though she were ashamed of her body.

"Are we going to stay here?" she asked.

"We can go out if you like. I'm allowed to."

"The car is waiting," said Ivich.

"*He's* not with you, is he?" Boris asked, frightened.

"Who?"

"Your father-in-law."

"Why on earth should he be?"

They crossed the courtyard and passed through the main gate. At sight of M. Sturel's immense green Buick, Boris felt a certain annoyance.

"Next time, tell him to wait at the corner," he said.

They got into the car, so absurdly large a car that they felt lost.

"We could play hide-and-seek in it," Boris muttered.

The chauffeur looked over his shoulder and smiled at Boris—a thickset fellow with obsequious manners and a gray mustache.

"Where to, madame?"

"Where would you like to go?" Boris asked.

Ivich thought for a moment. "Somewhere where there are lots of people."

"How about the Canebière?"

"No, not the Canebière. But I don't mind, if you really want to."

"Take us down to the docks, on the corner of the Canebière," Boris said.

"Very good, Monsieur Serguine."

A lazy swine, thought Boris. The car started, Boris sat back looking out of the window; he did not want to speak because the chauffeur could hear everything.

"What about Lola?" Ivich asked.

Boris turned toward her: she looked completely un- ruffled; he raised one finger to his lips, but she repeated the question, loud and clear, as though the chauffeur were about as important as a discarded onion peel:

"Have you heard from Lola?"

He shrugged his shoulders without replying.

"Have you?"

"No," he said.

Throughout the time that Boris was in hospital at Tours, Lola had placed herself within easy reach of him. Early in June he had been evacuated to Marseille, she made a brief visit to Paris, to draw all her money from the bank just in case the worst might happen, before re- joining him. Since then "things had happened," and now Boris knew nothing of her.

A jolt threw him against Ivich; they took up so little room in the back of the Buick that he was reminded of the time when they first landed in Paris: they played at being two orphans lost in the capital and they often sat close to- gether, as now, on a settee at the Dôme or the Coupole. Boris raised his head to tell Ivich what he was thinking, but at sight of her dejected expression, he merely said: "Have you seen the papers? Paris is captured."

"Yes, I know," Ivich said indifferently.

"What about your husband?"

"I've heard nothing, either." She leaned toward him and in a low, hurried whisper said: "I hope he's dead."

Boris, glancing quickly at the chauffeur, noted that he was watching them in the rearview mirror. He nudged Ivich and she relapsed into silence; but an ugly smile, which she made no effort to conceal, lay across her lips. The car drew up at the foot of the Canebière. Ivich, alighting, ordered the chauffeur cavalierly: "You will call for me at the Café Riche at five."

"Au revoir, Monsieur Serguine," the chauffeur said in a syrupy voice. "Five o'clock, Café Riche."

"So long!" Boris said, vexed. He thought: I shall go back by street-car. He took Ivich by the arm and they set off up the Canebière. Several officers passed. Boris did not salute them, and they seemed to take no notice of his failure to do so. Boris felt annoyed by the way in which the women turned to stare at him.

"Given up saluting officers?" Ivich inquired.

"What's the point?"

"The women are taking a lot of notice of you," she went on.

Boris said nothing; a brunette smiled at him as she passed. Ivich turned sharply.

"He *is* a handsome dog, isn't he," Ivich called after the brunette's retreating back.

"Ivich!" Boris begged. "For heaven's sake, don't draw attention to us!"

This was his latest ordeal. One morning somebody had remarked that he was handsome, and ever since, everybody repeated it. Francillon and Gabel nicknamed him "Love Mug." Naturally, Boris took no notice, but it was annoying all the same because good looks are not a sign of virility. He would far rather all these bitches would concentrate their attention on showing off their legs and all

these men ogle Ivich—but not too much: just enough to
make her feel that she was attractive.

Almost every table outside the Café Riche was occupied; they sat down amid a crowd of lush dark-haired
trollops, of officers, of soldiers in smart uniforms, of
middle-aged men with pudgy hands—a whole world of
harmless, conventional, hidebound folk much the better
off for being killed, as painlessly as possible of course.
Ivich was tugging at her short hair.

"Don't you feel well?" Boris asked.

She merely shrugged. Boris stretched his legs and
realized how utterly bored he was.

"What will you have?" he asked.

"Is their coffee drinkable?"

"So-so."

"I'm dying for a cup of good coffee. The stuff they make
up north is perfectly foul."

"Two coffees," Boris ordered. Turning to Ivich, he
asked: "How are you getting along with your in-laws?"

All feeling seemed to die out of Ivich's face. "Not too
badly," she said. "I have grown to be just like them." She
went on with a little laugh: "My mother-in-law told me I
looked like her!"

"What did you do with yourself all day?"

"Well, yesterday I got up at ten, I dawdled as long as
possible over dressing; that took until half past eleven;
then I read the papers—"

"You don't know how to read the papers," Boris said
sternly.

"No, I don't. At lunch they started discussing the war.
Mamma Sturel shed a few tears as she thought of her be-
loved son; when she cries, her lips turn upward and I always think she is about to laugh. Then we settled down
to our knitting and she bared her woman's heart. Georges
was a delicate child, you will be glad to hear; he had an

attack of enteritis at the age of eight. Mamma Sturel
would find it terribly difficult to choose between losing
her husband and her son; but better her husband, she is
more the mother than the wife. Then she discussed her
ailments—womb, bladder, bowels, and the rest. Apparently
her physical condition is not what it should be."

An amusing *mot* occurred so swiftly to Boris that he
strongly suspected he must have read it somewhere. And
yet probably not. *"Les femmes entre elles parlent de leur
intérieur ou de leurs intérieurs;* Women among themselves
speak of their intimate circles, be they social or gynecologi-
cal." Expressed thus, it sounded a whit pedantic, like some
maxim of La Rochefoucauld's. Under another form: *"Une
femme, faut que ça parle de son intérieur ou de ses
intérieurs;* Try to stop a woman speaking of what's in her
home or home in her." Or *"Quand une bonne femme ne
parle pas de son intérieur, c'est qu'elle est en train de
parler de ses intérieurs;* When a female isn't discussing
her outward feelings, she discusses the outward pressure
on her innards." That, on the whole, was the version he
liked best. He wondered whether he should quote it for
Ivich's benefit. But Ivich seemed to have lost her sense of
humor nowadays. Instead he said simply: "And so—?"

"And so I went up to my room till dinner."

"What did you do?"

"Nothing. After dinner we all listened to the news on
the radio, then we discussed what we had heard. Apparently everything is all right, we must keep cool. France
has weathered worse crises. Then I went back to my room
and made myself some tea on the electric plate. I keep it
hidden because it usually blows out a fuse. I sat back in
my armchair until they all went to sleep."

"And then?"

"Then I breathed more freely."

"You should join a lending library," said Boris.

"When I read, the letters dance about in front of my eyes," Ivich said. "I am forever thinking of Georges. I can't but hope we shall hear he's been killed."

Between Boris and his brother-in-law there was no love lost and he had never understood why in September 1938 Ivich had run away from home to fling herself into the arms of that lanky nonentity. But he had to admit that as soon as the fellow realized she was pregnant, Georges had really behaved admirably: of his own accord he had insisted on marrying her; though by that time it was too late: Ivich already hated him for getting her with child. She said that to look at herself sickened her; she buried herself in the country and refused to see even her brother. She would certainly have committed suicide if she had not feared to die.

"What filthy muck!"

Boris gave a start. "What?"

"This," she said, pointing to the coffee.

Boris took a sip. "Certainly it is not very good," he admitted. He thought for a moment, then he said: "I expect it'll get worse and worse."

"The Land of the Conquered!" said Ivich.

Boris glanced nervously around him, but nobody was paying any attention; people were discussing the war calmly and rather sadly, as though they had just come back from a funeral. A waiter passed by carrying an empty tray. Ivich glowered at him, her eyes ink-black.

"Lousy, swinish!" She shuddered.

The waiter gazed at her in surprise. He wore a gray mustache; he might have been Ivich's father.

"This coffee, I mean," said Ivich. "Lousy, swinish! Take it away."

The waiter eyed her with curiosity; she was much too young to intimidate him. When he realized what the trouble was about, he sneered: "You want Mocha coffee? Have you by any chance heard there's a war on?"

"Maybe I haven't," Ivich countered sharply, "but my brother has; he's just been wounded. He probably knows a lot more about it than you do."

Boris, flushing with embarrassment, looked away. Ivich had become a pretty tough customer; she now gave back as good as she got; but nostalgically he recalled the old days when, shaken by anger, she used merely to toss her head so that her hair fell over her face and growl. It had caused a good deal less trouble.

"I wouldn't choose the day the Boches have taken Paris to complain about a cup of coffee," the waiter grumbled, thoroughly vexed. He walked off. Ivich stamped her foot.

"They never stop talking about the war, and they never stop getting beaten either. Anybody would think they're proud of it. I only hope they lose their war, once and for all, and let's stop bellyaching about it!"

Boris stifled a yawn; nowadays he found Ivich's outbursts dull. When she had been young, he had enjoyed seeing her tugging at her hair, stamping her foot, and squinnying up her eyes; the sight was enough to amuse him for the rest of the day. But today her eyes were dismal; it was as though she were remembering something. At such times she looked like their mother. "She's married," he thought with shocked awareness, "a married woman with her parents-in-law, a husband at the front, and a family car." He looked at her, puzzled, then away because he felt that she was about to become hateful.

"I'm off!" He started up; his mind was made up. "I'm going away with them. I can't stay in France."

Ivich talked on.

"What's that?" he asked.

"Our parents."

"What about them?"

"I say they should have stayed in Russia. You're not listening to me."

"If they had stayed, they'd have been tossed into jail."

"Anyhow, they shouldn't have had us naturalized. Otherwise we could go home now."

"Home is France," Boris said.

"No, home is Russia."

"Home is France. We were naturalized, we are French!"

"Exactly," said Ivich, "that's why they shouldn't have done it."

"But we have."

"What do I care? If it shouldn't have been done, we are as free as ever we were."

"If you were in Russia," said Boris, "you'd get the shock of your young life!"

"What do I care? Russia is a great country, and I would feel proud to live there. Here I spend my life feeling ashamed of myself."

She paused hesitantly. Boris looked at her blandly, unwilling to argue with her. "Surely she will stop soon," he thought hopefully. "I don't see that there's much more she can say." But Ivich, inventive as ever, lowered one hand in an odd downcast gesture as though she were plunging into water.

"I loathe the French," she said.

A man who was reading his paper near by looked up at them dreamily. Boris returned his gaze. Almost at once the gentleman rose as a young woman moved toward him; he bowed, she sat down with much handshaking and many smiles. Boris turned to Ivich, reassured. But there was no holding her now.

"I loathe them, I loathe them," she insisted.

"You loathe them because they make bad coffee!"

"I loathe them for everything."

Boris had hoped that the storm would abate of itself; but now he saw he was wrong; he must face the music.

"I'm fond of the French," he said. "Now they've lost the war, everybody jumps on them; but I've seen them fighting, and I know they did all they could."

"There," said Ivich, "you see!"

"What d'you mean, I see?"

"Why do you say *they* did everything they could? If you felt like a Frenchman, you'd have said *we*."

It was from a sense of modesty that Boris had not said "we." He shook his head and frowned.

"I don't feel either French or Russian," he said. "But when I was up there with the boys, I felt glad to be with them."

"They're rabbits," she said.

Boris pretended to have misunderstood her. "They certainly are tough rabbits."

"I don't mean that. They run like rabbits—like this!" She set her right hand scuttling across the table.

"You're like all women," said Boris. "The only thing you think about is military valor!"

"It's not that at all. But since they chose to have this war, they ought to have fought it to a finish."

Boris raised his hand in a weary gesture. "Since they chose to have this war, they ought to have fought it to a finish." He knew all about that. It was what he had said only yesterday evening to Gabel and Francillon. But—he let his hand drop: when other people don't think as you do, it is difficult and tiring to prove them wrong. But when they share your point of view and you've got to explain that they're mistaken, it's hopeless.

"Leave me alone," he said.

"Rabbits!" Ivich repeated, with a little grin of anger.

"The fellows I was with weren't rabbits," said Boris. "They were gallant and tough as leather."

"You've told me they were afraid of dying."

"Well, aren't *you* afraid of dying?"

"I'm a woman."

"Certainly they were afraid of dying, and they were men," said Boris. "That is what real courage means. They knew the risks they were running."

Ivich looked at him suspiciously. "You're not going to tell me *you* were afraid?"

"I wasn't afraid of dying, because I believed I was there for that very purpose." He looked at his nails, and added, in an impersonal tone: "But that didn't prevent me from being scared stiff—which was a bit of a bore."

Ivich gave a start. "Scared stiff? Why?"

"I don't really know. Perhaps because of the infernal noise."

As a matter of fact, his fear had lasted for only ten minutes, or maybe twenty, at the very beginning of the attack. But he did not in the least mind Ivich thinking him a coward: it would give her a healthy jolt. There was bewilderment in the way she was looking at him; she was flabbergasted that anyone who could be a Russian could be frightened, and not only a Russian, but a Serguine and her own brother. Presently, ashamed, he hastened to add.

"Anyhow, I wasn't frightened all the time."

She smiled at him, relieved. Gloomily he thought: "We no longer see eye to eye about anything." There was a short silence; Boris swallowed a mouthful of coffee and very nearly spat it out again: it was as though he had poured gloom down his throat. But he reflected that he was about to go away, and felt a little comforted.

"What are you going to do now?" asked Ivich.

"I suppose they'll demobilize me," Boris said. "You know, most of us are quite fit now; they're keeping us here because they don't know what to do with us."

"And later on?"

"I—shall try to get a job as a teacher."

"You haven't got a degree."

"No. But I might teach in a private school."

"Would you enjoy teaching small boys?"

"My God, no!" he said emphatically. He flushed and added humbly: "I'm not cut out for that."

"What are you cut out for, brother of mine?"

"I wonder."

A gleam came into Ivich's eyes. "Would you like me to tell you what we were cut out for? To be rich!"

"Not that," he said irritably. He looked at her for a moment and, holding his cup between his fingers, repeated: "Not that!"

"What for, then?"

"I was trained and primed to be killed," he said, "and then I was cheated out of my death. I'm completely at sea, I've got no gifts and no preferences for anything."

He heaved a sigh and relapsed into silence, ashamed at having talked about himself. *What I can't face is leading a mean, obscure existence. Fundamentally, I suppose that is what she meant just now.*

Ivich guessed what he was thinking.

"Hasn't Lola got any money?" she asked.

Boris gave a start and banged the table with his fist. She had the power to read his mind and to translate his thoughts in the most insufferable way.

"I don't want Lola's money!"

"Why? She used to give you money before the war."

"Well, she's not going to give me any more."

"Then we'd better both of us commit suicide," Ivich said passionately.

Boris sighed. *Now she's off again,* he thought wearily. *If only she'd be her age.* Ivich was smiling at him.

"Let's take a room down by the old harbor and turn on the gas."

Boris negatived the proposal with a simple movement of his right forefinger. Ivich did not press her point; she looked down and began tugging at her hair. Boris saw that there was something she wanted to ask him. At the end of a moment, avoiding his eye, "I've been thinking—" she began.

"The devil you have!"

"I've been thinking you might let me join up with you.

The three of us could live together on Lola's money."

Boris all but choked. "So that's what you've been thinking!" he said.

"Boris," Ivich said with sudden passion, "I just can't go on living with those people."

"Do they treat you badly?"

"On the contrary, they keep me wrapped up in cotton wool: I am their son's wife, and all that. But I loathe them, I loathe Georges, I loathe the servants . . ."

"And you loathe Lola," remarked Boris.

"Lola's different."

"She's only different because she happens to be far away and because you haven't set eyes on her for two years."

"Lola's a singer, she drinks, and she's lovely to look at. . . . Oh, Boris!" she cried, "they're so *ugly!* If you leave me with them, I shall kill myself. No, I shall not kill myself, which is much worse. If you only realized how old and evil I feel sometimes!"

"There we go, with all stops out," Boris mused. He took a sip of coffee to help him to swallow. One can't make *two* people miserable, he thought. Ivich had stopped tugging at her hair. A little color returned to her broad, pallid face; she was scrutinizing him with an expression in which determination fought with anxiety; there was something in her face now that reminded him of the old Ivich. Perhaps she might regain her youthful appearance, who could tell? Perhaps she might once more be pretty. He said: "All right, provided you do the cooking, you little she-devil!"

She seized his hand and pressed it as hard as she could.

"Do you really want it? Oh, Boris! Do you really want it?"

I shall be teaching at Guéret. No, not Guéret, that's a high school. At Castelnaudary, in a private school. I shall marry Lola; a school teacher can't live with a concubine. Tomorrow I shall start working up my courses. He ran his fingers through his hair, clutched a lock and tugged, as though to make sure that it was firmly affixed to his scalp. I shall go bald, he decided; no doubt of it: my hair will fall out before I die.

"Of course I want it," Boris said.

He watched an airplane catch the morning light as it turned, and to himself he said: the cliffs, the lovely white cliffs, the cliffs of Dover.

Padoux, 3 p.m.

MATHIEU was sitting on the grass; he watched black smoke eddying above the wall. Now and then a flame would leap up in the smoke, turn it blood-red, and then burst. Each time that happened, sparks leaped skywards like fleas.

"They're going to set the place on fire," said Charlot.

Butterflies of soot fluttered all about them. Pinette caught one and crushed it pensively between his fingers.

"Here is all that's left of a military map," he said, displaying his blackened thumb, "drawn to scale, too: one mile to a half inch."

Longin pushed open the trellised gate and came into the garden; his eyes were streaming.

"Longin's crying!" said Charlot.

Longin wiped his eyes. "The swine! They were almost the death of me!"

He flung himself down on the grass. He was holding a book with a tattered cover. "They made me work the bellows while they piled all their shithouse paper on the fire. The smoke blew in my face."

"Job finished?"

"Finished, my arse! They threw us out because they

were starting on top-secret stuff. Top-secret my arse! Why, I typed those orders myself."

"What a filthy stink!" Charlot exclaimed.

"Just the smell of burning."

"No; I mean if they're burning divisional orders, there's something very stinking going on."

"Exactly. A filthy stink, a smell of burning, just as I said."

They laughed. Mathieu pointed to the book and asked: "Where did you find that?"

"Oh, over there," Longin said vaguely.

"Where, over there? In the schoolhouse?"

"Yes." He clutched the book to him mistrustfully.

"Are there any more?" Mathieu asked.

"There were, but the guys from the Q.M. have been helping themselves."

"What is it?"

"A history book."

"What history?"

"I haven't looked to see."

Longin gave a quick glance at the cover and announced sullenly: "*History of the Two Restorations.*"

"Who by?" asked Charlot.

"Vau-la-belle," read out Longin.

"Who's Vaulabelle?"

"How should I know?"

"Will you lend it to me?" Mathieu asked.

"When I've read it."

Charlot crawled through the grass and took the book from him. "Hey, boys! It's volume three."

Longin snatched it back. "What the hell does that matter? I only wanted something to occupy my mind." He opened the volume at random and pretended to read, the better to stake his claim on the book. That formality accomplished, he looked up.

"Our captain has been burning up his wife's letters,"

he said. He raised his eyebrows and goggled at them like a village idiot, giving with eyes and lips an advance pantomime of the astonishment he knew his words would produce. Pinette, emerging from a sulky daydream, looked at him with interest.

"You're not kidding us?"

"Of course not. He burned all her photos as well, I saw them go up in flames. She comes from near Bordeaux, you know."

"No kidding!"

"I'm telling you!"

"What did he say?"

"He said nothing. He just watched 'em burn."

"And the others?"

"The others said nothing either. Lieutenant Ullman pulled a lot of letters out of his wallet and tossed them in the fire."

"That's funny," Mathieu muttered.

Pinette swung round on him. "Wouldn't you burn your babe's photos?"

"I haven't got a babe."

"If you had a babe, you would—"

"What about you?" Mathieu asked. "Have you burned your wife's photos?"

"I will when the Heinies turn up."

They were silent. Longin was now reading in earnest. Mathieu glanced at him enviously, then got up. Charlot tapped Pinette on the shoulder.

"What you say to having your revenge?"

"All right."

"What's the game?" Mathieu asked.

"Trumps."

"Can three play?"

"No."

Pinette and Charlot sat down astride the bench. Sergeant Pierné, who was writing on his knees, moved along a little to make room for them.

"Writing your memoirs?"

"No," said Pierné, "I'm studying physics."

They began to play. Nippert was sleeping on his back, his arms flung out. The sound of his breathing was like water going down a drainpipe; his mouth gaped. Schwartz sat apart, daydreaming. No one spoke a word; France was dead. Mathieu yawned. He watched the secret documents going up in smoke; he looked at the rich black earth between the growing vegetables, and his mind was a void: he was dead; the afternoon bleached and dead, it was a tomb.

Lubéron came into the garden. He was eating, and blinking his wide albino eyes. His ears moved in concert with his jaws.

"What are you eating?" asked Charlot.

"A piece of bread."

"Where did you get it?"

Lubéron pointed vaguely beyond the wall without replying and went on munching. Charlot suddenly stopped talking and looked at him as though scared. Sergeant Pierné, his pencil raised, his head thrown back, was also looking at him. Lubéron went on eating, without any hurry. Mathieu noticed his air of importance and realized that he had news to tell. He caught the infection of the general nervousness and took a step backward. Lubéron quietly finished his meal, then wiped his hands on his trousers. "It wasn't bread," thought Mathieu.

Schwartz sauntered up, and they waited silently.

"So that's that!" said Lubéron.

"What? What?" Pierné urged roughly. "What's what?"

"That."

"The—"

"Yes."

A dazzle of steel, then silence. The blue, flabby flesh of
the afternoon had been swept by eternity as by the sweep
of a scythe. Not a sound, not a breath of air; time had become frozen; the war had withdrawn. No more than a
moment ago they had all been part of the war, though
temporarily sheltered; they had all still believed in mir-
acles, in France the immortal, in American aid, in mobile
defense, in Russia's coming into the war. Now the war was
behind them, a thing finished, accomplished, lost. Mathieu's last dregs of hope turned to the mere memory of
hope.

Longin was the first to pull himself together. He
stretched out his long hands as though to touch the news
with extreme caution. Timidly he asked: "Then—it's
signed?"

"This morning."

For nine months Pierné had been longing for peace—
peace at any price. Now he stood there pale and sweating;
the shock made him lose his temper.

"How do you know?" he burst out.

"Guiccioli just told me."

"How does he know?"

"Radio. The news came through just now."

Lubéron had assumed the patient, impersonal voice of
a radio announcer; he enjoyed playing the part of in-
exorable fate.

"But the gunning?"

"Orders for cease-fire at midnight."

Charlot's face was flushed, but his eyes shone. "You're
not kidding us?"

Pierné rose to his feet. "Any details?" he asked.

"No," said Lubéron.

Charlot cleared his throat. "How about us?"

"What do you mean, us?"

"When are we going home?"

"I just told you, there are no details."

There was a silence. Pinette kicked a stone into the carrots.

"The armistice!" he exclaimed angrily. "The armistice!"

Pierné nodded his head. His left eyelid began fluttering in his ashen face like a window shutter on a gusty day.

"The conditions will be harsh," he observed with a pleased chuckle.

They all began to laugh.

"You said it!" Longin remarked. "You said it!"

Schwartz joined in the laughter. Charlot turned and looked at him in surprise. Schwartz stopped laughing and blushed furiously. Charlot kept on staring at him: it was as though he were seeing him for the first time.

"So now you're a Heinie," he said quietly.

Schwartz made a vague, violent gesture, turned on his heel, and left the garden.

Mathieu felt overcome with weariness. He dropped on to the bench. "How hot it is!" he said.

"We're being looked at." A crowd growing more and more dense was watching them swallow this bitter pill of history. The crowd grew older and backed away from them, muttering: "There stand the vanquished of 1940, the army of defeat. By their fault, we are in fetters." There they stood, unchanged beneath the changing scrutiny of the crowd, judged, summed up, explained, accused, excused, condemned, imprisoned within this ineffaceable day, buried beneath the drone of insects and the rumble of guns, in the hot smell of growing things, in the air quivering above beds of carrots; there they stood, guilty forever in the eyes of their sons, of their grandsons, and of their great-grandsons, they, the conquered of 1940 to all eternity.

Mathieu yawned. Millions of men were watching him yawn. "He's yawning! Did you ever see anything like that? One of the vanquished of 1940 has the effrontery to yawn!" Mathieu bit back that yawn, one of yawns innumerable over the face of earth. He thought: "We're not alone in this."

He looked at his comrades, and his mortal eyes met the timeless, petrified eyes of history. For the first time greatness had fallen upon their shoulders: they *were* the fabulous soldiers of a lost war. Statues! I have spent my life reading, yawning, tinkling the bell of my own little problems, I decided not to choose, only to find that I had already chosen, that I chose this war, this defeat, that today has been waiting for me since the beginning of time. Everything must be done over again, and yet there's nothing that can be done. The two thoughts interpenetrated and canceled each other out; only the unruffled surface of Nothingness remained.

Charlot made a quick little movement of head and shoulders; he began to laugh, and the flow of time was resumed. Charlot was laughing, laughing in the teeth of history, making of his laughter a defense against petrifaction. There was malice in his glance. "Do we look like saps?" he cried. "Do we look like God-damned saps?"

They turned toward him, stunned; then Lubéron joined in his laughter. Wrinkling his nose as though in sudden pain, he snorted down his nostrils. "You said it, pal! God-damned saps, that's what the Heinies made of us!"

Charlot, with a sort of drunken gaiety, exclaimed: "They caught us with our pants down, they turned up our delicate arses and now for the spanking!"

Longin laughed too. "The soldiers of 1940 or the champion sprinters in history!" he said.

"The best cross-country runners in the world!"

"The speed-kings of the Olympic Games!"

"I should worry!" Lubéron put in. "A nice sort of welcome we shall get when we turn up at home! A grateful people will vote us its heartfelt thanks!"

Longin squealed with delight. "A deputation to meet

us at the station, with the local glee club and the athletic clubs."

"And I'm a Jew!" Charlot laughed till the tears poured down his face. "What a field day for the anti-Semites down our way!"

Mathieu caught the infection of this hateful merriment. He had just experienced an appalling moment, he had been flung, shaking with fever, between icy sheets; then his statuesque eternity cracked, flew apart into a thousand fragments of laughter. These men were laughing, they were making the great refusal, and in the name of all the guttersnipes of the world they were spurning the obligations of greatness. "Oh hell, why worry so long as you enjoy good health and have plenty to eat and to drink? I despise one half of the world, and I shit on the other. Their austere lucidity had driven these men to lay aside the consolations of greatness. They were denying even their right to suffer, they were refusing to strut as *tragic,* even as *historic* figures. They could not so much as bring themselves to admit that we are just a lot of cheap down-at-heel actors, we aren't worth a tear, a bundle of *predestined* failures. They could not even comfort themselves with the thought that life is a gamble. All they could do was laugh, banging their heads against the wall of Absurdity and the wall of Fate and bouncing from one to the other like so many rubber balls. Their laughter was an instrument of self-punishment, of self-purification, of vengeance. At one and the same time they were less than human and more than human; they had stopped short of despair and they had transcended it. They were men. For a fleeting moment their open mouths displayed to high heaven the black horror of their sores. Nippert was still snoring, his mouth gaping was itself an outrage. Then their laughter drooped under its own weight, drew out to a great length, then shook to a standstill: the ceremony was over, the armistice consecrated. Officially they were living in the era *after*. Time flowed smoothly on, a sun-warmed brew of weak tea. Life beckoned and they must live it.

"So that's that!" said Charlot.

"Yes, that's that," said Mathieu.

Furtively Lubéron withdrew his hand from his pocket, raised it to his mouth, and began to chew. Under his rabbity eyes his jaw moved spasmodically. "That's that," he said. "That's that."

Pierné's attitude was fussy and triumphant. "Didn't I tell you?"

"What did you tell us?"

"Don't try to be dumber than you look! What did I say after Finland, Delarue? And after Narvik, remember? You treated me like a bird of ill omen, and because you're smarter than I am, you kept tying me up into knots."

His cheeks were flushed. Behind his spectacles his eyes glittered with spitefulness and triumph. "We ought never have started on this war; I always said so. If it weren't for this war we wouldn't be where we are now."

"Things might be even worse," Pinette declared.

"Impossible: nothing can be worse than war."

Pierné rubbed his hands unctuously, his face shone with the light of innocence. He kept rubbing his hands together, cleansing them of war. He had taken no part in it; it had formed no part of his life. For ten months he had sulked, refusing to see, to speak, to feel. The very alacrity with which he had executed orders proclaimed him a crank and voiced a protest. He had lived in a constant state of absent-mindedness, strung to a pitch of tension, his thoughts elsewhere. And now he had his reward. His hands were clean, and what he had foretold had come about. It was the *others* who had been defeated—Pinette, Lubéron, Delarue, and the rest—not he.

Pinette's lips began to tremble. "I suppose you think

everything's all right?" he asked in a broken voice. "You're satisfied?"

"Satisfied?"

"You've got your defeat!"

"*My* defeat? It's yours just as much as mine."

"You wanted it; it's yours. We never wanted it; you can have it."

Pierné's smile expressed surprise at being misunderstood. "Who says I wanted it?" he asked patiently.

"You did, just a moment ago."

"I said I'd foreseen it. To foresee a thing isn't the same as to want it."

Pinette looked at him but said nothing. His face was a mask of obstinacy, he pouted and his lips looked for all the world like an animal's snout. His bewildered eyes rolled in their sockets.

Pierné pursued his advantage. "Why should I want it, can you tell me that? You'll be saying next that I'm a fifth-columnist."

"You're a pacifist," Pinette replied with an effort.

"Well, what of it?"

"It amounts to the same thing."

Pierné raised his shoulders and spread his hands in a gesture of hopelessness. Charlot ran to Pinette and put his arm round his neck. "Stop arguing," he said good-naturedly. "What's the point? We've lost, and it's nobody's fault, no one has anything to be ashamed of. It was bad luck, that's all."

Longin smiled knowingly. "Bad luck?"

"Yes," Charlot went on, eager to conciliate. "Let's be fair. It was bad luck, damned bad luck. But what of it? Everyone has his turn. Last time *we* won; this time *they* win, next time we win again."

"There won't be a next time," Longin observed. He raised his finger and, with a paradoxical air, added: "We've

fought the war to end all wars, and that's God's truth!
Winners or losers, it all comes to the same in the end: we
fellows of 1940 have managed what our fathers failed to
manage. From now on there'll be no nations, and there'll
be no wars. Today we've been beaten to our knees; tomorrow, the English. The Boches are masters of the world
now, they'll restore order everywhere, and then full speed
ahead for the United States of Europe."

"United States my arse," Pinette growled. "We'll be
Hitler's slaves!"

"Hitler? Who in hell is Hitler?" Longin asked rhetori-
cally. "Sure, there had to be someone like Hitler. How do
you expect nations to get together if they're left free to do
as they like? Nations are like individuals, each out for
himself. Who's going to talk about your Hitler a hundred
years from now? Hitler will be as dead as a doornail, and
so will the Nazis."

"You God-damned fool!" cried Pinette. "Who in hell
is going to live a hundred years?"

Longin seemed scandalized. "That's no way to think,
angel-face. We've got to learn to look beyond our noses;
we've got to think about the Europe of the future."

"Will the Europe of the future feed my guts?"

Longin raised his hand in a gesture of pacification; it
hung poised in the sunlight. "Bah!" he said. "Bah! The
grafters and wise guys will always get on!" The episcopal
hand, descending, played with Charlot's curly hair. "Don't
you agree?"

"There's only one thing I agree about," Charlot said:
"if this armistice has to be signed, the sooner the better.
That way fewer guys will be killed and the Heinies won't
go hog-wild on us."

Mathieu stared at him in amazement. So they were all
slinking away, all of them! Schwartz was changing skin,
Nippert was taking refuge in sleep, Pinette was finding relief in anger, Pierné in innocence; Lubéron, grounded in

the here and now, was focusing his attention on food, stuffing every hole and cranny of his carcass; Longin was embarked upon the seas of futurity. Hurriedly every one of them had assumed that attitude which would allow him to go on living.

Mathieu sat up with a jerk and in a loud voice said: "You make me puke!"

They showed no surprise; they simply looked up at him with shoddy little smiles; he was more surprised than they. His own words still echoed in his ears, and he wondered how he had come to utter them. For a moment he hesitated between confusion and anger, then he settled for anger. Turning his back on them, he pushed open the wicket and crossed the road. It was blinding and empty; Mathieu plunged into the brambles, which caught and clung to his puttees. He ran down the copse-crowned slope until he reached the stream. "Hell, shit!" he said aloud. He stared at the water and, without knowing why, repeated: "Hell, shit!" A bare hundred yards from him a soldier, stripped to the waist and streaked with sunlight, was washing his shirt. There he is, whistling and kneading his lump of soggy dough. He has lost the war and he doesn't know it. Mathieu sat down; he felt ashamed. What right have I to take this high line? They've just heard that the bottom has been knocked out of everything; now they're shifting for themselves as best they can; they're not used to such crises. I am, and much good it does me. To come down to brass tacks, I'm as much an escapist as any of them. What is anger but a way of escape?

He heard a faint crackle in the undergrowth, and Pinette came and sat down on the bank. He smiled at Mathieu, Mathieu smiled back, but for a long moment neither spoke.

At last Pinette said: "Look at that poor guy down there. He doesn't know what the hell about anything."

The soldier, bending above the water, was washing his

shirt with a thoroughness that had suddenly become un-
necessary. An anachronistic airplane thrummed above
them. With an expression of apprehension that made them
both laugh, the soldier looked up through the foliage at
the sky. The whole scene had the picturesque quality of
an old historical play performed in modern dress.

"Shall we tell him?"

"He'll hear soon enough," Mathieu said.

They stopped talking. Mathieu put his hand in the water
and waggled his fingers. His hand looked pale and silvery,
the blue sky, reflected in the water, cast a halo about it.
Bubbles rose to the surface. A twig, carried downstream
by the current, clung to Mathieu's wrist and whirled
around it. It drifted away, came back, then clung to him.
Mathieu withdrew his hand.

"It's hot," he said.

"Yes," Pinette agreed. "It makes one feel sleepy."

"You feel sleepy?"

"No, but I'm going to try to go to sleep all the same."

Pinette stretched out on his back, his hands clasped behind his head, and shut his eyes. Mathieu thrust a dead
branch into the stream and moved it to and fro. After a
moment Pinette opened his eyes again. "Shit! God damn
it to hell!" He sat up and ruffled his hair with both hands.
"I can't sleep."

"Why not?"

"Too angry!"

"There's no harm in that," Mathieu said. "It shows a
healthy state of mind."

"When I'm really angry," Pinette explained, "I have to
hit something or I choke." He looked up at Mathieu with
curiosity. "Don't *you* feel angry?"

"Yes."

Pinette leaned forward and began to unlace his shoes.
"I never got a chance to fire my rifle," he said bitterly. He
took off his socks. He had the small, soft feet of a child.

They were streaked with dirt. "I'm going to wash my feet."

He dipped his right foot in the water, took it in his hand, and started to rub it. The dirt came away in little rolls. Suddenly he glanced up at Mathieu. "They'll round us up, won't they?"

Mathieu made a movement of the head.

"And they'll take us away to their country?"

"Probably."

Pinette put a fury of energy into rubbing his foot. "If it hadn't been for this armistice, they wouldn't have caught me so easily."

"What would you have done?"

"I'd have raised hell with them!"

"A fire-eater, huh?" said Mathieu.

They exchanged smiles. Suddenly Pinette finished and a defiant look came into his eyes. "You said we made you puke," he recalled.

"I didn't mean you."

"You meant the whole lot of us."

Mathieu was still smiling. "Is it me you'd like to hit?"

Pinette hung his head and said nothing.

"Hit away," said Mathieu. "I'll hit back. That might calm us down."

"I wouldn't like to hurt you," Pinette observed gloomily.

"Too bad."

Pinette's left foot dripped with water and sunlight. Mathieu and Pinette both looked at it. Pinette wriggled his toes.

"What funny feet you've got!" Mathieu said.

"They're small, aren't they? I can pick up a matchbox with my feet and open it."

"Between your toes?"

"Yes."

Pinette grinned; but suddenly a gust of fury shook him and he gripped his ankle violently. "I'd feel better if I'd

killed a God-damned German! I suppose they'll just come
along and mop me up."

"That's about the size of it," said Mathieu.

"It isn't fair."

"It isn't fair or unfair: it's just the way things go."

"It isn't fair: we're paying for what others did—the
fellows in Corap's army, and Gamelin."

"If we'd been in Corap's army, we'd have done the
same."

"Speak for yourself." Pinette flung his arms wide, drew
a deep breath, clenched his fists, throwing out his chest,
and looked at Mathieu arrogantly. "Do I look like the sort
of bastard who can't take it?"

Mathieu smiled. "No, you don't."

Pinette flexed the long biceps of his fair-skinned arms
and seemed for a moment to be glorying in his youth, his
strength, and his courage, silently and for his own benefit.
He smiled, but a light still smoldered in his eyes, and his
brows were drawn together in a frown.

"I would have made them shoot me down on the spot."

"That's easy enough to say."

Pinette smiled and died: a bullet pierced his heart. Dead
but triumphant, he turned to Mathieu. The statue of
Pinette, who had died for his country, said: "I would have
stood until I was shot down." Then the hot stream of life
and anger flowed back into his petrified body. "No one
can blame me; I did everything I was told to. It's not my
fault if they didn't know how to use me."

Mathieu looked at him with a sort of tenderness; Pinette
was transparent in the sunlight, life rose, sank, and
eddied up and down the blue branchings of his veins.
How spare, how healthy, how light he must be feeling!
How could Mathieu have imagined the painless illness
that had begun to gnaw at Pinette, which sooner or later
would bow his young body above the potato fields of
Silesia or which, along Pomeranian motor highways, would

fill him to overflowing with fatigue, heaviness, and melancholy. Defeat is a lesson men must needs learn.

"I didn't ask anyone for anything," said Pinette. "I just did my job; I wasn't against the Heinies: I never even saw the arse of one; I didn't know what Nazism and Fascism meant. As for Danzig, I was called up before I saw the place on a map. Daladier declared war, and Gamelin lost it. What had I got to do with it? Where am I to blame? Did they ask me for my opinion?"

Mathieu shrugged his shoulders. "For fifteen years we've seen it coming. We should have taken steps either to avoid it or to win it."

"I'm not a deputy."

"You had a vote."

"Sure I had a vote," Pinette conceded.

"Who did you vote for?"

Pinette said nothing.

"You see what I mean," said Mathieu.

"I had to serve my hitch in the Army," Pinette explained morosely. "After that I was sick; there was only one election when I could vote."

"And that time did you vote?"

Pinette made no reply. Mathieu smiled.

"Me neither," Mathieu said quietly. "I didn't vote."

The soldier wrung out his shirts in the flowing current. He wrapped them in a red towel and climbed up to the road, whistling.

"Recognize that tune?"

"No," said Mathieu.

"It's *We'll hang out our washing on the Siegfried Line.*"

They laughed. Pinette seemed to have lost something of his tenseness.

"I've worked hard," he said, "and I didn't always eat my bellyful. Then I got this job on the railway and I got married. I had to make a home for my wife, didn't I? She comes from a good family, you know. Things weren't too easy at first. But they settled down later," he added quickly. "A fellow can't be everywhere at once, can he?"

"Of course not," said Mathieu.

"What else could I have done?"

"Nothing."

"I had no time for politics. I came home dead beat, and then there were disputes, and when a man's married, his wife expects him to lay her every night. Am I right?"

"I dare say you are."

"Well?"

"Well, there was nothing else you could do. That's how wars get lost."

Pinette was shaken by another spasm of anger. "You make me puke! Suppose I went in for politics, suppose I gave all my time to that, what difference would it have made?"

"You would have done all you could."

"Did *you* do all you could?"

"No."

"And if you had, would you still say it was you who lost the war?"

"No."

"Well?"

Mathieu did not answer, he heard the singing whir of a mosquito and slapped his hand against his forehead. The whirring stopped. When this war started, I, too, thought of it as a disease. What crap! It's myself, it's Pinette, it's Longin, it's each and every one of us, war made in the image of all of us. Men get the war they deserve.

Pinette sniffled long but kept his eyes on Mathieu. Mathieu decided that Pinette looked very stupid, and a great surge of anger broke over him, filling mouth and eyes: "Enough! I'm through! I'm sick of being the wise guy, the guy who always sees straight!" The mosquito fluttered shrilly over his forehead, derisive as a crown of victory. "If only I could have fought, if only I could have pressed my finger on the trigger, somewhere some German would have fallen. . . ." He raised his hand sharply and smacked his temple; then he lowered it and on his finger saw a small filament of blood, someone bleeding his life away on a stony field, a smack on the temple, a pressure on the trigger, the colored glasses of the kaleidoscope stop dead, blood spreads across the grass. To hell with it! To hell with it! To plunge into blind action as into a forest: action, something that commits one and that one never wholly understands. He said passionately:

"If there were only *something* one could do! . . ."

Pinette looked at him with interest. "What sort of thing?"

Mathieu gave a shrug. "There isn't anything," he said. "Not for the moment."

Pinette put on his socks. His pale eyebrows drew together in a high-pitched frown. "Have I showed you my wife?" he asked suddenly.

"No," said Mathieu.

Pinette sat up, fumbled in the pocket of his blouse, and took a photo from his wallet. Mathieu saw a prettyish woman with a hard mouth and a shadow of a mustache at its corners. Across the picture she had scrawled— "Denise to her Baby-Face, January 12, 1939." Pinette flushed scarlet. "That's what she calls me. I can't get her out of the habit."

"She's got to call you something."

"It's because she's five years older than me," Pinette said with dignity.

Mathieu gave him back the photo. "She's nice."

"She's terrific in bed," Pinette remarked. "You've no idea!" His blush had deepened. With a hint of perplexity he added: "She comes of a good family."

"So you said before."

"Did I?" said Pinette, astonished. "Did I tell you that? Did I tell you that her father was a drawing-teacher?"

"Yes."

Pinette carefully restored the photograph to his wallet. "It's getting me down."

"What's getting you down?"

"It's lousy, to go back home like this." He had crossed his hands on his knees.

"Bah!" said Mathieu.

"Her father was one of the heroes of War I," Pinette said. "Three citations and the Croix de Guerre. He talks about it all the time."

"Well, what of it?"

"Well, that's why it's lousy to go home like this."

"Poor little devil," said Mathieu. "You won't be going home soon."

Pinette's anger had cooled. He shook his head sadly. "I'm so fond of it," he said. "I don't want to go back."

"Poor little devil," Mathieu repeated.

"She loves me," Pinette went on, "but she's not easy to get on with: she thinks she's pretty damned good. And her mother puts on the dog. Don't you believe a man's missus should respect him? If she doesn't, there's no peace in the house."

He got up suddenly. "I've had enough of it here. Are you coming?"

"Where to?" asked Mathieu.

"I don't know. Let's join the others."

"All right," Mathieu said without enthusiasm. He too rose and together they climbed to the road.

"Hullo!" said Pinette. "There's Guiccioli."

Guiccioli, his legs parted and one hand over his brow like the visor of a cap, was looking at them and laughing.

"Boy, did you guys bite!" he cried.

"What do you mean?"

"You poor bastards bit like tarpons!"

"What are you talking about?"

"The armistice!" said Guiccioli, still laughing.

Pinette's expression brightened. "You were kidding us?"

"You said it!" said Guiccioli. "Lequier came along and bored the pants off us asking for news. Well, we gave him the works."

"So it's not true about the armistice?" Pinette said with high satisfaction.

"Armistice, my royal arse!"

Mathieu glanced at Pinette out of the corner of his eye. "What difference does it make?"

"It makes all the difference in the world," Pinette said. "You'll see! You'll see what difference it makes."

4 o'clock

Nobody on the boulevard Saint-German; in the rue Danton nobody. The iron shutters had not even been lowered, the windows glittered: the proprietors had just removed the handles from the doors and gone. It was Sunday. For the last three days it had been Sunday; the whole week now, in Paris, consisted of one day. A ready-made, colorless Sunday, rather stiffer than usual, rather more synthetic, over-marked by silence, and already filled by secretly working rot. Daniel approached a large shop (knitted goods and textiles); the multicolored balls of wool, arranged in pyramids, were in process of turning yellow; they smelt of old age. In the shop next door a display of baby linen and ladies' blouses was fading; white dust, like flour, was accumulating upon the shelves. The plate glass was stained with long white streaks. Daniel thought: "The windows are weeping." Behind the windows was festival: flies were buzzing in the millions. Sunday. When the Parisians returned they would find their dead city motionless beneath the weight of a stagnant Sunday. If they return! Daniel gave free rein to that irresistible desire to laugh which had been with him all morning as he stalked the streets. If they return!

The tiny square of Saint-André-des-Arts lay abandoned in the sunlight, lifeless; black night reigned in the heart of noon. The sun was a fake, a magnesium flare concealing darkness, which in a split second would go out. He pressed his face to one of the big windows of the Brasserie Alsacienne. I lunched here with Mathieu. That had been in February, when Mathieu was on leave. It had been swarming with heroes and angels. After a while he managed to distinguish in the darkness of the interior a number of ambiguous blotches, mushrooms growing in a cellar: they were paper napkins. Where are the heroes? Where are the angels? There were still two iron chairs on the terrace; Daniel took one of them by its back, carried it to the edge of the pavement, and sat down, a gentleman of leisure beneath the military sky, in a white glare that was alive with childhood memories. At his back he could feel the magnetic pressure of silence. He looked at the empty bridge, at the padlocked book-boxes on the quay, at the clock face that had no hands. "They should have smashed all this up a bit," he thought. "A few bombs, just to make us realize what was what." A shadow slipped past the Prefecture of Police, on the farther bank of the Seine, as though on a moving roadway. Paris was not, strictly speaking, empty; it was peopled by little broken scraps of time that sprang here and there to life, to be almost immediately absorbed again into this radiance of eternity. "The city is hollow," thought Daniel. He was conscious, beneath his feet, of the caverns of the subway, and in front, behind, above, of tall cliffs pierced with openings: between heaven and earth thousands of Louis-Philippe boudoirs, Empire dining-rooms, and cosy-corners, echoing to the secret sounds of emptiness. It was enough to make one die of laughing.

He turned sharply: someone had tapped at the window. Daniel stared at it for a long time, but could see only his own reflection. He got up. There was a curious lump in his throat, but he did not feel particularly unhappy: it was amusing to be afflicted with night fears in broad daylight. He walked across to the Saint-Michel fountain and looked at the green bronze dragon. He thought: "There is nothing now that I can't do." He could take down his trousers beneath the glassy stare of all these darkened windows, pull up a paving-stone, and heave it through the plate glass of the Brasserie, he could shout: "Long live Germany!" and nothing would happen. At the most, high on some sixth floor, a frightened face might be pressed to a window-pane, but that would be all; they had lost even the power to be indignant. The respectable gentleman up there would turn to his wife and in a tone of complete detachment would say: "A fellow down there in the square has just taken off his trousers," and she would reply, from the far end of the room: "Don't go showing yourself at the window, you never know what might happen." Daniel yawned. Should he smash the window? Bah! There'd be better things than that to see when the looting began. "I only hope," he thought, "that they put the whole place to fire and sword." He yawned again: he felt himself filled with a sense of vast and pointless freedom. Now and then his joy turned sour within him.

As he moved away, a procession emerged from the rue de la Huchette. "They're traveling in convoy now." It was the tenth he had met that morning. Daniel counted nine individuals—two old women carrying rush baskets, two young girls, three dried-up, gnarled old men with mustaches, and, bringing up the rear, a couple of young women, one of them pale and beautiful, the other superbly pregnant and with the hint of a smile about her lips. They were walking slowly, and not a word was spoken. Daniel coughed and they turned, as one person, to look at him; there was neither sympathy nor condemnation in their eyes, only an incredulous astonishment. One of the two girls leaned toward the other without shifting her gaze from Daniel, she whispered a few words and they both laughed, seeming greatly surprised. Daniel felt himself to be as strange as a chamois bending its slow and virgin stare upon a party of alpine climbers. They passed him by, figures of a fantastic and an outworn age, drowned deep in their solitude. Daniel crossed the road and, at the near end of the Pont Saint-Michel, leaned his elbows on the stone parapet. The Seine was a glitter of sunlight; far away to the northwest smoke was rising above the houses. All at once he found the whole scene intolerable, turned away, retraced his steps, and started to walk up the boulevard.

The procession had vanished. As far as eye could reach, silence and emptiness, an abyss stretching horizontally away from him. He felt tired; the streets led nowhere; without human life, they all looked alike. The boulevard Saint-Michel, but yesterday a long southward spread of gold, seemed now like a stranded whale, belly upwards. Daniel made his feet ring out upon the great, sodden, hollow carcass; he forced a shudder of delight. Out loud he said: "I always hated Paris." In vain: No sign of life save the greenery, the long, leafy arms of the chestnut trees; he had the stale, sickly impression of walking through a forest. The disgusting wing of boredom was already brushing him when, by a lucky chance, he noticed a white and red poster stuck on a billboard. He went up to it and read: "We shall win because we are the stronger." He flung out his arms and grinned with a sense of delight and release: they're running, they're running, they've never stopped running. He raised his head, laughing to high heaven, and drew deep breaths: for twenty years he had been on trial, there had been spies even beneath his bed; every casual passer-by had been a witness for the prosecution or a judge or both; every word he spoke could have been used in evidence against him. And now, in a flash, stampede. They were running, the witnesses, the judges, all the respectable folk, running beneath the sun, the blue sky, and a threat of aircraft over their heads. The walls of Paris were still clamorously extolling their merits and their pride: we are the stronger, the more virtuous, the sacred champions of democracy, the defenders of Poland, of human dignity, or heterosexual love; the wall of steel will be unbreached, we shall hang out our washing on the Siegfried Line. The posters on the walls of Paris were still trumpeting a hymn of triumph that had gone cold. But *they* were running, mad with terror, flinging themselves flat in the ditches, begging for mercy—honorable mercy, needless to say—all is lost save honor, take everything but without offending honor; here is my arse, kick it but leave me my honor, I'll kiss yours if only you will let me have my life. They are running, they are crawling. I, the Criminal, reign over their city.

He walked with his eyes on the ground, he thrilled with pleasure, he could hear the cars swishing past him on the roadway. He thought: "Marcelle's pupping at Dax, Mathieu's probably a prisoner, Brunet's almost certainly got himself bumped off, all the witnesses against me are dead or thinking of other things; it's I who am making a comeback. . . ." Suddenly he said to himself: "*What cars?*" He looked up suddenly, his heart began to thump so violently that he could feel it in his head, and then he saw *them.* They were standing upright, images grave and chaste, fifteen or twenty of them together in long camouflaged trucks, moving slowly toward the Seine, effortlessly gliding, standing stiffly, the inexpressive glances of their eyes resting momentarily on him. And after them came others, other angels, exactly alike, looking at him in precisely the same way. Daniel could hear a military band in the distance, he had a feeling that the sky was suddenly filled with banners, and he leaned for support against a chestnut tree. *Alone* in the whole length of the avenue he was the only Frenchman, the only civilian, and the whole of the enemy army was looking at him. He had no fear, he surrendered with confidence to these myriad eyes, he thought: "Our conquerors!" and was wrapped in happiness. Boldly he returned their stare, taking his fill of their blond hair, of their sun-tanned faces in which eyes showed like glacier lakes, their narrow waists, the unbelievable length of their muscular thighs. He murmured: "How beautiful they are!" He felt no longer earth-bound: they had lifted him in their arms, they were clasping him to their chests and their flat bellies. Something came hurtling down from the sky—the ancient law! Fallen the society that had judged him, erased the sentence; those horrible little khaki soldiers, those champions of man and the citizen, were running for their lives. "What blessed freedom!" he thought, and his eyes grew moist. He was the sole survivor of disaster, the sole *man* confronted by the angels of hate and fury, the angels of extermination whose gaze invested him with the gifts of childhood. "Here are new judges," he thought, "here is the new law!" How ludicrous now seemed, above their heads, the marvels of the gentle heavens, the innocence of the fluffy little clouds. This was the victory of contempt, of violence and bad faith, this was the victory of Earth. A tank moved past him, slow and majestical, covered with branches, scarcely so much as purring. At the back of the tank stood a very young man, his handsome bare arms folded, his blouse thrown loosely about his shoulders, shirtsleeves rolled above his elbows. Daniel smiled at him. For a moment or two the young man looked at him with impassive face, his eyes sparkling, then, suddenly, as the tank drew away, he smiled back. Hurriedly he felt in the pocket of his breeches and threw a small object, which Daniel caught in flight: it was a pack of English cigarettes. So tightly did Daniel clasp it that he could feel the cigarettes snap beneath his fingers. He was still smiling. An intolerable, delicious thrill mounted in him from thighs to temples; he no longer saw very clearly; panting, he said: "Just like butter—they are going through Paris just like a knife through butter." Other faces passed before his dimmed vision, more and more of them, each as beautiful as the last. They have come here with intent to do Evil to us, the Reign of Evil begins. What joy! He longed to be a woman so that he might load them with flowers.

A roaring in the sky, Christ, get down, quick! In a flash the street was empty, a clatter of old tin cans filled it from end to end, a dazzle of steel tore through the sky, they passed between the houses, Charlot, pressing close to Mathieu in the shelter of the barn, shouted: "They're hedge-hopping!" The indolent and greedy gulls made a half-turn above the village, seeking their feeding-ground, then flew off, trailing behind them a metallic din that echoed from roof to roof. Cautiously a few heads rose, men came out from barns, from houses, others jumped from the windows, the place was swarming like a fair-ground. Silence. Silence brooded over them, a hundred all told, sappers, radio men, sound men, telephonists, orderly-room clerks, observers, specialists of every kind except the drivers who had sat waiting at the wheels of their cars since the evening before. They settled down as though in expectation of some show—but *what* show? They sat cross-legged in the middle of the road, which was dead now and without traffic, they sat on the edge of the pavement, on window sills, and others stood leaning against the houses. Mathieu had found a place on a small bench in front of the grocer's shop; Charlot and Pierné joined him. No one spoke. they had come there to be together and exchanged silent looks; they saw themselves as they were: the big fair, the crowd, much too quiet, with a hundred gray faces. The street was an incandescent ribbon burned up by the sun, twisting away under the gutted sky, burning hot to heels and buttocks, but they were careless of the heat.

The general was billeted in the doctor's house: the third window on the second floor was his eye, but to hell with the general. They looked at one another, and what they saw filled them with fear. They were chafing under the imposed delay; no one put the thought into words, but its presence thumped through their chests; they could feel it in arms and legs, like the ache of strained muscles; it droned dully like a top spinning in their hearts. Somebody or other whimpered, like a dog deep in dreams; half awake he murmured: "There are cans of bully-beef in the Q.M. stores." Mathieu thought: "Sure there are, but they've posted M.P.'s at the door," and Guiccioli replied: "Hell, you dope, they've got civilian police guarding the door." Another guy took up the refrain in a drowsy impersonal voice: "It's like the bakery, there's bread there, I saw the loaves myself; but the baker's barricaded his shop." Mathieu, sunk in the same dream, said nothing; he envisioned a piece of steak and his mouth watered. Grimaud, propped on one elbow, pointed to the rows of shuttered windows and said: "What's going on in this dump? Yesterday they were chattering away to us, now they're hiding." The evening before, the houses gaped like oysters on the half-shell, now they were tight shut; within these secret rooms men and women were playing possum, sweating in the shadows, filled with hatred of the French Army.

Nippert said: "It's because we've been beaten that they treat us like lepers." Charlot's stomach rumbled. Mathieu said: "Your stomach's singing." And Charlot replied: "Not singing, it's shouting."

A rubber ball fell in the middle of the group, Latex caught it. A small girl, five or six years old, drew near and stood staring with frightened eyes. "It this your ball?" Latex asked. "Come get it." They all looked at her. Mathieu would have liked to take her on his knees. Latex tried to soften his harsh voice: "Come along! Come! Come sit down here on my knee."

A quiet ripple of voices rose here and there: "Come! Come! Come!" The child stood her ground. "Come along, chickabiddy, come, come along, sweetheart, come!"

"Christ," Latex burst out, "even the kids are scared of us."

The others laughed, they said to him: "It's you who frighten her with your mug!" Mathieu laughed.

Latex went on with his singsong plea: "Come along, my chocolate drop!" Suddenly he lost his temper, he cried: "If you don't come, I'll keep your ball." He held the ball high above his head so that she could see it, then he pretended to be putting it in his pocket. The child started to scream. Everybody scrambled to his feet, everybody began to shout: "Give it to her; you bastard, you're making a kid cry, no, no, put it in your pocket, throw it over the roof." Mathieu stood gesticulating.

Guiccioli, his eyes blazing with rage, pushed him aside and strode over toward Latex.

"For Christ's sake, give it back to her, we aren't savages!"

Mathieu stamped his foot in a white heat of anger. Latex was the first to recover his temper; he lowered his eyes and said: "Pipe down, she'll get her ball." Clumsily he tossed the ball toward the child. It struck the wall and rebounded. The child pounced on it and took to her heels. Peace returned. They all sat down again. Mathieu sat down, too; his anger had died down, but he felt very sad. "We're not lepers," he mused. Nothing else; his mind was nothing but a sounding-board for what they all were thinking. At one moment he was just an emptiness filled with vague forebodings, at another he became just everybody else, his distress faded; the general mood welled sluggishly up in his mind and oozed from his mouth. "We're not lepers."

Latex held out his hands and eyed them mournfully.

"I've six of my own, the oldest child seven, and I've never lifted my hand to any of 'em."

They had sat down again, lepers, foodless, shabby, beneath a peopled sky, against the tall, blind houses oozing hatred. They said nothing; what could they say, they, so many abject vermin dirtying the fair June day? Easy does it! the exterminator will come, they'll spray all the streets with Flytox.

Longin pointed to the shuttered windows and said: "They're waiting for the Heinies to come and take us off their hands."

Nippert said: "Bet your sweet life they'll treat Heinie more friendly than they have us."

And Guiccioli: "Hell, if they must be occupied, better be occupied by the winning side. It's more cheerful and it helps business. All we can do is to bring bad luck."

"Six kids," said Latex, "my oldest is seven, and I've never given 'em cause to be scared of me."

Grimaud said: "They hate us."

The sound of approaching footsteps made them raise their heads, but at once they bowed them again as Major Prat crossed the street between rows of averted eyes. No one saluted him. He stopped in front of the doctor's house. The heads jerked upward again, and the eyes came to a focus on his padded shoulders as he lifted the iron knocker and rapped three times. The door was opened a crack and he slipped through the narrow space into the house. Between five forty-five and five forty-six all the officers of H.Q. Staff walked by, one by one, stiff and embarrassed, through the group of silent soldiers. Every head was lowered as they passed, every head was raised as soon as they had disappeared.

Payen said: "The General's throwing a party."

Charlot turned to Mathieu and said: "What in hell are they up to?"

Mathieu replied: "Oh, shut up!"

Charlot looked at him and said no more.

Ever since the officers had passed, the men looked grayer, drabber, more shriveled. Pierné glanced at Mathieu with anxious surprise. He recognizes his own pallor on my cheeks.

There was a sound of singing, Mathieu gave a start, the singing drew nearer:

> *Tant qu'il y aura de la merde dans le pot*
> *ca puera dans la chambre.*

Thirty fellows or so, without rifles, blouses, or caps, drunk, rounded the corner; they rolled down the street, singing, they seemed both expansive and rancorous; their faces were ruddy with wine and sunlight. Seeing this grayish larva sprawled out on the ground and staring at them from the multi-headed eyes, the soldiers stopped dead and broke off their singing. A bearded giant stepped forward; he was stripped to the waist and black, with bulging muscles and a gold chain around his neck.

"Are you bastards dead?" he asked.

No one answered. He turned his head and spat; he had great difficulty in keeping his balance.

Charlot peered at him shortsightedly, screwing up his eyes. "You don't belong to our outfit?" he asked.

"Your outfit?" asked the bearded man, patting his privates. "Ask this little fellow if he belongs to your outfit. Christ, no! We're another outfit. We couldn't stomach your outfit for shit!"

"Where are you from?"

"From up yonder." He pointed vaguely.

"Had some fun up there?"

"Fun, shit! No, no fun. When things started to stink, the captain pissed off, we did too, but we went the other way, not to meet him."

Behind the hirsute one his pals began to laugh, and two stalwarts among them sang defiantly:

> *Traîne tes couilles par terre,*
> *Prends ta pine à la main, mon copain,*
> *Nous partons à la guerre*
> *A la chasse aux putains. . . .*

Every head was turned toward the general's eye; Charlot made a frightened gesture with his hand. "Take it easy!"

The singers stopped; they stood there, their mouths agape, swaying on their feet. Suddenly they looked very tired.

"Officer bastards in there," Charlot explained, pointing to the house.

"Shit on your officers," bawled the man with the beard. His gold chain twinkled in the sunlight; he looked down at the men seated by the roadside and added: "If they shit on you, boys, just come with us, and they won't any more."

"Come on with us!" the others behind him shouted in rhythm. "With us! With us! Come on with us!"

There was a short silence. The bearded man's look fixed on Mathieu. Mathieu looked away.

"Well, who's coming along? Going, going, gone!"

No one moved. The bearded man concluded contemptuously: "They're not men, they're bastards. Come on, fellows, I don't want to rot here; they make me puke."

The column set off again, the others drawing back to let them pass. Mathieu put his feet under the bench.

> *Traîne tes couilles par terre.*

Every head was turned toward the general's eye. Faces appeared from behind H.Q. windows, but there was no sign of an officer.

> *Nous partons en guerre . . .*

The intruders moved away; no one spoke a word; the song died away. Mathieu breathed freely at last.

Nippert, without looking at his comrades, said: "Well, there's no proof we won't be moving!"

"You're wrong," Longin said. "There's plenty of proof."

"Proof of what?"

"Proof that we won't be moving."

"What makes you think so?"

"There's no gas left."

"There's always gas for officers," Guiccioli said. "The storage tanks are full."

"No gas for our trucks."

Guiccioli laughed wryly. "Of course not!"

"We've been sold down the river!" Longin shouted at the top of his shrill voice. "Sold, sold out to the Germans!"

"Break it up," said Ménard wearily.

"Break it up, peace, brother," Mathieu repeated, "break it up!"

"Take it in your stride!" a telephonist said. "Quit talking about leaving, we'll see what happens. My arse to you!"

Mathieu had a vision of them walking down the road, singing, perhaps even stopping to pick flowers. Somehow it shamed him, but they were all involved in his shame. The prospect was not unpleasant.

"Bastards," Latex said. "He called us bastards, that jerk. And me the father of a family. Did you see the chain that cunt was wearing around his neck?"

"Listen!" said Charlot. "Listen!"

They heard an airplane throbbing overhead; a weary voice murmured: "Down we go, boys. Take cover. Here they are again."

"Tenth time this morning," said Nippert.

"Are you keeping count? I gave that up long ago."

They rose, leisurely leaned back flat against the door and

moved down the passageways. A plane swept over at roof-level, the noise diminished, they came out from under cover, scanning the sky, and sat down.

"Fighter," said Mathieu.

"Kiss my arse!" said Lubéron.

From far away they caught the dry rat-tat-tat of a machine-gun.

"Ack-ack?"

"Ack-ack my arse! That's a fighter firing."

They looked at one another.

"It's not healthy on the road in daylight," said Grimaud. "Not today, anyhow."

They said nothing, but their eyes sparkled and the hint of a smile showed at the corners of their mouths. Presently Longin observed conversationally: "They can't have got very far."

Guiccioli rose to his feet, crammed his hands into his pockets, and bent his knees once or twice for relaxation. He turned to the sky a face empty of expression, but with an evil curl on his lips. "Where are you going?"

"Off for a stroll."

"Where?"

"Over there. I'm going to see what happened."

"Look out for the wops!"

"I'll be all right."

Guiccioli shuffled off. All of them would have liked to go along. Mathieu dared not get up. There was a long silence. The color had returned to their faces, and they looked brightly at one another.

"Jesus, if we could walk the roads the way we did in peacetimes!"

"What did they expect? A hitch-hike back to Paris? Some guys never learn."

"If they could get a free ride, what are we doing here?"

They were silent, nervy and tense; they waited. A thin,

gawky fellow leaned against the grocer's iron shutters, his hands shaking. Guiccioli returned, debonair as ever.

"Well?" Mathieu exclaimed.

Guiccioli shrugged. The others propped themselves up and looked at him with shining eyes.

"Wiped out!" he said.

"All of them?"

"How should I know? I didn't count." He was pale. He was belching through close lips to no avail.

"Where are they? On the road?"

"If you sons of bitches want to know, go and have a look for yourselves!" Guiccioli sat down. A gold chain around his neck shone in the sunlight. Guiccioli raised his hand and played with the chain, then suddenly let it alone. Almost regretfully he said: "I sent the stretcher-bearers down there."

Poor devils! Guiccioli's chain, sparkling in the sunlight, fascinated them. Would someone say: "Poor devils"? The words were on every lip, but who would be hypocrite enough to speak them: "Poor devils"? But would that be hypocrisy? The gold chain sparkled on the brown neck. Cruelty, horror, pity, rancor spread from man to man—a harsh yet comforting feeling. We are a verminous dream, our thoughts thicken, become less and less human; hairy, clawed thoughts that scurry around from head to head; the vermin kingdom is about to inherit the earth.

"Delarue, God damn it! Are you deaf?"

Delarue, I am Delarue. He turned sharply. Pinette was smiling at him from a distance: *he sees Delarue.*

"What gives?"

"Come on, pal!"

Delarue shivered, suddenly naked and alone, a man. *I.* He waved Pinette aside, but already the group had closed its ranks to hem him in; their vermin eyes had banished him; they gazed upon him as if they had never seen him before, as if they were looking out on him through layers

of slime. I'm no better than they are, I've no right to let
them down.

"Come on, fellow."

Delarue rose to his feet. The unspeakable Delarue,
Delarue the scrupulous, Professor Delarue no less, Delarue the school teacher moved slowly across to where
Pinette was waiting. Behind him were two hundred eyes;
his back bristled with fear, and once again, with anguish.
Anguish began very gently, like a caress, and then settled
down, modest and familiar, in the pit of his stomach. It
was nothing—merely a sense of emptiness. Emptiness
within himself and around him. He was moving in an
atmosphere of rarefied gas. Delarue the gallant warrior
took off his cap; Delarue the fighting soldier ran his hand
through his hair, good old Delarue, the dutiful army man,
turned to Pinette with a weary smile.

"What's up?" Delarue asked.

"Are you getting a kick out of those guys?"

"No."

"Then why stay with them?"

"We're all alike, we're all the same," said Mathieu.

"Who is?"

"They and us."

"Well, what of it?"

"So why not stick together?"

Pinette's eyes showed fire. "I'm not like them!" he said
with an upward jerk of the head. "I'm not the same!"

Mathieu was silent.

Pinette said: "Come along with me."

"Where to?"

"Post office."

"Post office? Is there a post office?"

"Sure. A branch office on the outskirts of the village."

"What are you going to do at the post office?"

"Wait and see."

"It's certain to be shut."

"It'll open up for me all right," Pinette insisted, and, linking arms with Mathieu, he led him away.

"I've found a girl," Pinette explained. His eyes shone with feverish excitement; he smiled self-importantly. "I want to introduce you."

"What ever for?"

Pinette gave him a stern look. "You're my pal, aren't you?"

"Sure I am," said Mathieu. "Tell me," he asked, "is this girl of yours the postmistress?"

"She works in the post office."

"I thought you wanted nothing to do with women."

Pinette forced a laugh. "We've got to do something to pass the time if there's no fighting."

Mathieu, turning to look at him, found him insufferably self-complacent. "You're not yourself, pal. Have you fallen for this dame?"

"Well, I could have picked worse!" Pinette crowed. "Wait till you see what she's got up front in the chest department. Boy, her bubs are as sweet a pair of apples as ever I saw. She's an educated kid too—geography, arithmetic, she knows it all!"

"How about your wife?" Mathieu asked.

Pinette's expression changed. "Aw, let her go frig herself!" he said roughly.

They had reached a small, single-storey house. The shutters were closed; the handle had been removed from the door. Pinette knocked three times.

"It's me!" he yelled. Then, turning to Mathieu with a grin. "She's scared of being raped."

Mathieu heard the sound of a key turning in the lock.

"Come in quick," said a woman's voice.

They dived into a smell of ink, paste, and paper. A long counter with a wire grille divided the room into two parts. At the back, Mathieu could make out an open door.

Through this the woman retreated and they could hear her shoot the bolt. For a few moments they were left in the narrow corridor reserved for the public; then the woman reappeared at the little window in the protective wire grille. Pinette leaned forward and pressed his forehead against the wire.

"Keeping us at a distance, eh? That's not kind."

"Ah!" she said, "a girl can't be too careful."

She had a nice voice, deep-toned and warm. Mathieu noticed that her black eyes were shining.

"Are you scared of us?" Pinette asked.

She laughed. "I'm not scared, but I'm not too trusting, either."

"Because I've a pal with me? Hell, you two ought to get on well together; he's in the civil service, same as you; that ought to stop you worrying."

He had assumed a mincing manner of speech and a well-bred smile. "Come on," he urged her, "put one finger through the bars. Just one finger."

She passed one long, thin finger through the grille, and Pinette kissed the tip of it.

"You behave yourself," she warned, "or I'll take it back."

"That wouldn't be polite," he said. "I want my pal to shake hands with you."

He turned to Mathieu. "Allow me to introduce Mademoiselle Won't-Tell-Her-Name. She's a plucky little French girl who could have been evacuated, only she wouldn't leave her post in case she might be needed."

He wriggled his shoulders and smiled, he never stopped smiling. He spoke in a soft singsong, with a faint English accent. "How d'you do, mademoiselle," Mathieu said.

She wiggled the finger she had pushed through the grille, and he clasped it in his hand.

"Are you in the civil service?" she asked.

"I'm a teacher."

"And I'm a postmistress."

Mathieu felt hot and bored; his thoughts were with the dull, gray faces he had left behind.

"Mademoiselle is responsible for all the love letters of the village," Pinette announced.

"Oh, we don't have many love letters here," she said timidly.

"Well, if *I* lived in this dump," Pinette went on, "I'd write love letters to all the girls in the place just so my letters would pass through your hands. That would make you the postmistress of love." He laughed rather wildly. "The postmistress of love! The postmistress of love!"

"That would be a fine mess," she said. "I'd have to work overtime."

There was a long pause. A nonchalant smile still fluttered on Pinette's lips, but there was a tenseness about him, and his eyes darted inquisitively around the room. A penholder hung by a piece of string from the wiring; Pinette took it, dipped it in the ink, and scribbled a few words on a money-order blank.

"There!" he said, holding out the blank to her.

"What's that?" she asked without touching it.

"Take it! You're in charge here: do your job."

She finally took it and read: "Pay to Mademoiselle-No-Name the sum of one thousand kisses."

"Ah," she said, half annoyed, half amused, "now you've spoiled a money order!"

Mathieu was thoroughly fed up. "Well," he said, "I'll leave you here."

Pinette seemed disconcerted. "Not going, are you?"

"I'd better be going back."

"Then I'll go with you," said Pinette hurriedly. "Yes, yes, I'll go with you."

He turned to the girl. "I'll be back in five minutes. You'll open the door again, won't you?"

"Oh, how tiresome you are!" she grumbled. "First you

want to come in, then you want to go out. Why can't you
make up your mind?"

"All right, all right," he said. "I'll stay. But don't forget,
now: it was you that asked me to stay."

"I didn't ask anything."

"Oh yes, you did!"

"No!"

"Oh, hell!" Mathieu muttered between clenched teeth.
"Shit!" He turned to the girl, "Good-by, mademoiselle."

"Good-by," she replied somewhat coldly.

Mathieu went out and walked away, his mind a blank.
It was getting dark. The soldiers were still sitting where
he had left them. He joined the group, and a number of
voices rose from the ground:

"Any news?"

"No news," said Mathieu.

He went back to his bench and sat down between
Charlot and Pierné.

"Officers still with the general?" he asked.

"Yes."

Mathieu yawned; he looked gloomily at the others, only
half visible in the darkness. "*We*," he murmured, but the
word had no meaning for him; he was alone. He tossed
back his head and gazed at the first stars. The sky was as
soft and gentle as a woman; all the love in the world
seemed to have taken refuge in the sky. He blinked. "A
shooting star, fellows! Make a wish."

Lubéron farted, and "That's my wish," he said.

Mathieu yawned again. "Good," he said. "Well, I'm going to turn in. You coming, Charlot?"

"Don't know; we might be moving tonight. Just as well
to be ready."

Mathieu uttered a harsh laugh. "Don't be a God-damned
fool all your life!" he said.

"All right, all right!" said Charlot hastily. "I'll come."

Mathieu went into the barn and flung himself fully

dressed on the hay. He was dropping with sleep, he always felt sleepy when he was oppressed by gloom. A red ball started to spin before his eyes; women's faces were leaning from a balcony, then they, too, started to spin. Mathieu dreamed that he was the sky; he leaned over the balcony and looked down at the earth. The earth was green, with a white belly; it was jumping about like a flea. Mathieu thought: "I mustn't let it touch me." But it stretched out five enormous fingers and gripped Mathieu by the shoulder.

"Get up! Quick!"

"What's the time?" Mathieu asked. He could feel warm breath on his face.

"Ten twenty," said Guiccioli's voice. "Get up quickly, go to the door and take a look, but don't let them see you."

Mathieu sat up and yawned. "What's the matter?"

"Officers' cars waiting in the road a hundred yards off."

"What of it?"

"Do as I say, you'll see."

Guiccioli vanished. Mathieu rubbed his eyes. In a low voice he called out: "Charlot! Charlot! Longin! Longin!"

There was no answer. He rose and tiptoed sleepily as far as the door. It was wide open. A man was hiding in the shadows.

"Who's there?"

"It's me," said Pinette.

"I thought you were busy frigging your dame."

"She's being difficult; I won't make her till tomorrow. Christ! My lips feel stiff with all that grinning."

"Where's Pierné?"

Pinette pointed to a dark entry across the street. "Over there, with Charlot and Longin."

"What are they doing?"

"I don't know."

They waited in silence. The night was cold and clear

in the moonlight. Opposite, in the entry, a confusion of shadows moved vaguely. Mathieu turned his head and looked toward the doctor's house: the general's eye was shut, but a faint light showed under the door. *I am there.* Time, with its great scarecrow future, collapsed. All that was left was a tiny flickering patch of local moments. There was no such thing as Peace or War, France or Germany, only that faint light under a door that might perhaps open. Would it open? Nothing else mattered. Mathieu was deprived of everything now but this tiny scrap of the future. Would it open? A sense of keen adventure flooded his dead heart with light. Would it open? It was important: it seemed to him that if the door opened, all the questions he had asked himself all his life would at last be answered. Mathieu felt that a little shudder of delight was about to start in the pit of his stomach; he felt ashamed. With deliberate care, he said to himself: "We have lost the war." Instantly, the reign of Time was restored; the tiny pearl of the future swelled until it became an immense and sinister vista. The Past and the Future, as far as eye could reach, from the Pharaohs to the United States of Europe. His joy was extinguished, the light under the door was extinguished, the door creaked, swung slowly back, stood open to the night. The shadow in the dark entry quivered; the street crackled like a forest and then was silent. Too late: adventure was dead.

After a moment shapes appeared on the entrance steps; one after another the officers descended. The first to reach the bottom stopped in the middle of the road, waiting for the others, and the street became metamorphosed: a street in a garrison town in 1912 blanketed with snow; it was very late, the general's party had just broken up; handsome as pictures, Lieutenants Sautin and Cadine stood arm in arm; Major Prat laid his hand on Captain Mauron's shoulder; they all threw out their chests, smiled, obligingly posing under the moon's magnesium. (One last exposure, gentlemen; this time the whole group. Thank you.) Major Prat turned sharply on his heels, looked at the sky, and raised two fingers in the air as though bless-ing the village. The general came out, a colonel closed the door gently behind him. Divisional H.Q. staff was present in full strength, twenty officers all told; it was a snowy night, a clear sky; they had danced till midnight, the best of garrison evenings, long to be remembered. The little group started to move very quietly. On the second floor a window opened noiselessly; a white figure leaned out, watching their departure.

"Who ever would have believed it!" Pinette muttered.

The officers sauntered out without the least show of ex-citement, with a smooth solemnity; so much loneliness and so much silence shone upon those statuesque, moon-drenched faces that it seemed a sacrilege to look at them; Mathieu felt at once guilty and cleansed.

"Who would have believed it! Who would have be-lieved it!"

Captain Mauron hesitated. Had he heard? His tall, lithe, stoop-shouldered figure faltered ever so slightly and turned toward the barn; Mathieu could see his eyes glit-tering. Pinette uttered a sound like a growl and made as though to run into the street. But Mathieu snatched Pinette's wrist and held it in an iron grip. For another moment the captain raked the shadows with his gaze, then he turned away and yawned airily, tapping his lips with the tips of his gloved fingers. The general passed by. Mathieu had never before seen him at such close quarters. The general, a stout, imposing-looking man, with a deeply lined face, leaned heavily on the colonel's arm. The or-derlies followed, bearing the officers' kits; a whispering, laughing party of subalterns brought up the rear.

"Officers!" Pinette said almost aloud.

More like gods, Mathieu thought. Gods returning to Olympus after a brief visit to earth. The Olympian procession faded away into the night; a flashlight made a dancing circle over the road, then was extinguished. Pinette turned toward Mathieu; the moonlight illumined the expression of despair on his cheerful face.

"Officers!"

"Yes, officers."

Pinette's lips began to tremble; Mathieu was afraid Pinette might burst into sobs.

"Come on, come on!" said Mathieu. "Come on, angelface. Take it easy."

"If I hadn't seen it with my own eyes I wouldn't believe it," said Pinette. "Well, we've just seen the bottom drop right out of everything."

He gripped Mathieu's hand and pressed it, as though he were determined to hope against hope.

"Perhaps the chauffeurs will refuse to start."

Mathieu shrugged his shoulders. Already the engines were humming, like the pleasant echo of grasshoppers very far away. A moment later the cars started and the sound of the engines was lost. Pinette folded his arms.

"Officers! By God, I begin to believe France is really done for."

Mathieu turned: masses of shadow were moving away from the walls as soldiers crept silently out from alleyways, carriage entrances, and barns. Real soldiers, of a second-line formation, ill-kempt, ill-fed, slipping past the shadowed whiteness of the house-fronts; of a sudden, the street was full of them. So sad were their faces that Mathieu felt a lump in his throat.

"Come along," he urged Pinette.

"Where to?"

"Outside, with the others."

"Oh, hell!" cried Pinette, "I'm going to hit the hay; to hell with talking."

Mathieu hesitated. He was sleepy, his head was splitting, he longed for sleep and the obliteration of all thought. But they looked so downcast, their backs made such a whited huddle in the moonlight, and he felt one of them.

"I am going to talk to them," he said. "Good night!"

He crossed the street and mingled with the crowd. The chalky moonlight shone on faces that seemed to have been turned to stone; no one spoke. Suddenly the sound of motor engines was distinctly heard.

"They're coming back!" Charlot cried. "They're coming back!"

"Don't be a cunt! That was them turning into the main road."

They listened, however, with a vague sense of hope. The purring died away and was lost. Latex sighed: "Well, that's the end."

"Now we're on our own!" Grimaud observed. "Alone at last."

No one laughed. Somebody, in a low, anxious voice, asked: "What happens now?"

There was no answer; they did not give one damn what was going to happen to them; something far different was worrying them—an obscure hurt for which they could find no words. Lubéron yawned. After a long silence he said: "No good hanging about here. Let's turn in."

Charlot made a broad, despairing gesture. "All right," he said, "I'm for hitting the hay; but Christ! it's terrible."

The soldiers looked anxiously at one another. They did not want to separate, but there seemed no point in sticking together.

Suddenly a voice, a voice edged with bitterness, cried: "They never liked us anyhow!"

Its owner was expressing a general thought. Everyone started talking.

"That's right—you said it—they never liked us, never, never! For them the enemy wasn't Heinie, it was but us.

We fought this war together, and now they've gone and left us high and dry."

Mathieu's voice rose amid the general babble: "They never liked us! Never!"

"When I saw 'em go by," Charlot said, "it was such a shock you could've knocked me over with a feather."

A buzz of talk drowned him: that wasn't what they wanted to hear. The abscess had to be drained. Tongues were loosened, talk had become a necessity. No one likes us, no one: the civilians blame us for not defending them, our wives have no pride in us, our officers have left us in the lurch, the villagers hate us, the Heinies are coming up through the darkness. More accurately they should have said: we are the scapegoats, the conquered, the cowards, the vermin, the offscourings of the earth; we have lost the war, we are ugly, we are guilty, and no one, not one solitary being in the whole world has any use for us. Mathieu dared not voice this sentiment, but Latex, behind him, spoke it calmly and unemotionally: "We're pariahs."

There was a sputter of voices; everywhere the word was repeated, harshly, pitilessly: "Pariahs!"

The voices were silent. Mathieu looked at Longin, for no particular reason, but simply because Longin was nearest him, and Longin was looking at him. Charlot and Latex exchanged glances; all those present stared at one another, all those present seemed to be waiting, as though something still remained to be said. Nothing remained to be said, but suddenly Longin smiled at Mathieu, and Mathieu returned his smile. Charlot smiled, Latex smiled; over every face the moon brought to blossom the pallid flowers of a smile.

❁❁❁❁❁❁❁❁❁❁❁❁❁❁❁❁❁❁❁❁❁❁

Monday, June 17

"C OME ALONG," said Pinette. "Come along, let's go."

"No."

"Come on, dope!" Pinette looked at Mathieu and spoke in his meekest and most cajoling tone. "Come on!"

"For God's sake, cut out the crap and leave me alone," said Mathieu.

They were both under the trees in the middle of the square, the village church opposite them, the mayor's office to their right. Charlot sat on the bottom step of the *mairie*, deep in a daydream, a book on his knee. Soldiers sauntered slowly up and down past them, alone or in small groups, not knowing what to do with their freedom. Mathieu's head felt heavy and painful as though he had been drinking.

"You look fed up."

"I am fed up," said Mathieu.

At first there had been the exhausting intoxication of brotherly love; there they were, fellow soldiers, sharing a glow of affection under the light of the moon, and life had seemed worth living at that moment. And then the torches were extinguished; they hit the hay because there was nothing else to do and because they were as yet unused to the claims of mutual affection. Now was the morning after and they felt like committing suicide.

"What's the time?" asked Pinette.

"Ten past five."

"Hell, I'm late."

"Get a move on, then."

"I don't want to go alone."

"Afraid she'll swamp you?"

"It's not that," Pinette said. "That's not it. . . ."

Nippert walked by, deep in secret thought, utterly unconscious of them.

"Take Nippert with you," Mathieu suggested.

"Nippert? Are you crazy?"

Their curiosity aroused by the blank look on Nippert's face and by his jaunty step, they kept their eyes on him as he walked away.

"What's the betting he goes into the church?" Pinette asked. He waited a moment, then, slapping his thigh: "He is going in! He is going in! I win."

Nippert disappeared. Pinette turned quizzically to Mathieu. "I heard there are fifty or more in there, since this morning. Now and then one of them comes out to take a piss and then he goes right back in again. What's cooking? D'you know?"

Mathieu made no reply. Pinette scratched his head.

"I'd like to have a look-see."

"You're late for your date already," said Mathieu.

"To hell with my date!" said Pinette.

Pinette loped away; Mathieu moved close to one of the chestnut trees. Just an untidy bundle left lying by the roadside, that was all that remained of divisional staff headquarters; and there were others like them in all the villages of France; the Heinies would mop them up without bothering to stop. "What in God's name are they waiting for? Why don't they hurry?" Defeat had become a part of every day: it was the sun, the trees, the very air they breathed, and, deep down, that longing for death. Nevertheless he was conscious of a sort of hangover from the previous night, a taste of brotherly love that had gone cold in his mouth. The post orderly advanced toward him, flanked by two cooks; Mathieu looked up at them. In the night, under the moon, they had smiled friendship at him. But all that was a thing of the past; the hard secrecy of their faces seemed to say: "Beware of the madness of the moon and of the ecstasies of midnight; each man for himself, and the Devil take the hindmost; we're not in this world for fun." They, too, were suffering from the morning after. Mathieu took his knife from his pocket and began cutting at the bark of the tree. He felt a need to carve his name somewhere in the world.

"Carving your name?"

"As a matter of fact, I am."

"Ha ha!"

They laughed and walked on. Other soldiers followed close behind them, fellows Mathieu had never seen before. They were unshaven; there was a glitter in their eyes and a strange look on their faces. One of them was limping. They went across the square and sat down on the sidewalk in front of the closed bakery. Gradually, others turned up, and still others, none of whom Mathieu knew by sight, without rifles or puttees, their faces gray, their boots caked with dried mud. Mathieu felt he should have been able to look at them with affection. Pinette, strolling up, scowled at them.

"Well?" asked Mathieu.

"The church is full." With an air of disappointment he added: "They're singing."

Mathieu shut his knife.

"Carving your name?" asked Pinette.

"I was going to," Mathieu said as he slipped his knife back into his pocket. "But it takes too long."

A huge strapping fellow stopped close by them; he

looked tired and shagged out; above his unfastened collar his face seemed a dull blur.

"Hello, you guys," he said unsmiling.

Pinette stared at him.

"Hello," said Mathieu.

"Any officers around here?"

Pinette began to laugh.

"Did you hear him?" he appealed to Mathieu; then turning to the newcomer, he added: "No, bud, you won't find any officers here: this is a republic."

"Oh," said the other.

"What division are you from?"

"Forty-second."

"Forty-second?" Pinette grumbled. "Never heard of it. Where did it hang out?"

"Épinal."

"What you doing farting around here for, then?"

The soldier gave a shrug. Pinette, uneasy, suddenly asked: "It's not coming here, is it, your division, with its officer bastards and the rest of the shit?"

It was the other's turn to laugh. He pointed to four men seated on the sidewalk. "That's our division," he said.

Pinette's eyes sparkled. "Things are pretty hot in Épinal, huh?"

"They were. They must have calmed down by now." He turned on his heel and moved off to join his companions. Pinette stared after him.

"Forty-second Division, hell! Have *you* ever heard of the Forty-second Division? I never have till now."

"That's no reason for high-hatting him," said Mathieu.

Pinette shrugged. "These bastards keep on turning up from God knows where," he said contemptuously. "We don't know where in hell we are."

Mathieu did not reply; he kept his eyes fastened on the scratches on the trunk of the chestnut tree.

"Oh, come on!" said Pinette. "Come on! Let's spend a

day in the country, all three of us. We won't see another soul; it'll be fun."

"Why do you want me to come; I'll only be in the way. When you're out for what you want, you don't need me."

"We won't get down to it right away," Pinette said gloomily. "We'll have to do a little *parley-vous* first." He broke off sharply. "Look over there! Another God-damned stranger."

A soldier, short and stocky, was walking very stiffly toward them. A bloodstained bandage hid his right eye.

"Maybe there's a big battle going on," Pinette suggested in a voice shaken by hope. "Maybe the shit is going to fly!"

Mathieu said nothing.

Pinette shouted to the bandaged man: "Hey, you!"

The man stopped and stared at him out of his lone eye.

"Is the stuff flying around over there?"

The man looked at him without replying. Pinette turned to Mathieu. "I can't get a thing out of the bastard."

The man went on his way. Having taken a few steps, he stopped, leaned his back against a chestnut tree, and slumped to the ground. He sat there, his knees drawn up to his chin.

"He looks pooped out!" Pinette observed.

"Come on," said Mathieu.

They went up to him.

"Feeling lousy, pal, huh?" Pinette asked.

The soldier said nothing.

"Hey, pal, feeling lousy?"

"We've come to give you a hand," Mathieu said to the soldier.

Pinette leaned down to lift him from under the arms, then stood up again. "Nothing doing."

The stranger was still sitting, his eye staring, his mouth agape. He seemed to be smiling gently.

"What do you mean, 'Nothing doing'?"

"Take a look at him."

Mathieu stooped and put his ear to the stranger's chest. "O.K.," he said, "you win."

"Better close his eyes," Pinette suggested.

He did so with his fingertips, an intent look on his face, his shoulders hunched, his under lip protruding. Mathieu looked at him, it was no dead man he saw: the dead mattered no longer.

"Anyone would think you'd been doing that all your life," he remarked.

"Oh, I've seen plenty of stiffs in my time," Pinette answered. "But this is the first one since the war started."

The dead man, with closed eyes, was smiling at his thoughts. How easy it seemed to die! Easy and almost gay. "Why go on living, then?" The whole scene took on a wavering and insubstantial look: the living, the dead, the church, the trees. Mathieu gave a start. A hand had touched his shoulder. It was the tall fellow with the blurred face; from washed-out eyes he stared at the dead soldier.

"What gives?"

"The guy's croaked."

"It's Gérin," the other explained. Then, turning eastward: "Hi, fellows! Hop to it, double quick!"

The four soldiers got up and ran over.

"Gérin's got it!" the man with the blurred face cried. "Jesus! Hell!"

Standing about the dead man, they stared at him suspiciously. "Funny he didn't fall."

"Happens like that sometimes. Some of them die on their feet."

"Sure he's dead?"

"These guys say so."

Simultaneously they leaned over the dead man. One felt for his pulse, another listened to his heart, a third took a mirror from his pocket and held it in front of the

dead lips, just as is always done in detective stories. Then
they straightened up, satisfied.

"Poor bastard!" said the tall man, wagging his head.

Four heads waggled and four voices repeated in chorus:
"Poor bastard!"

A short stout fellow turned to Mathieu. "Fifteen miles
he trudged. If he'd sat on his arse, he'd be living now."

"He didn't want Heinie to get him," Mathieu said by
way of excuse.

"What the hell! The Heinies have ambulances. I talked
to him myself along the road. He was bleeding like a
stuck pig, but you couldn't tell him anything. He *would*
have his way. He wanted to get home, he said."

"Where, home?" Pinette asked.

"Cahors, down south. He was a baker there."

Pinette shrugged. "Well, anyhow, he took the wrong
road."

"Sure!"

They stopped talking and looked down at the dead man
with embarrassment. "What do we do now? Bury him?"

"Nothing else we can do."

They raised him from under the arms and knees. He
was still smiling at them but, minute by minute, he
looked increasingly dead.

"We'll give you a hand."

"Don't bother."

"Yes, we will," Pinette said eagerly. "We've nothing on
hand; it'll help us pass the time."

The tall soldier eyed Pinette sternly. "No," he said, "this
is our job. He was in our outfit, it's up to us to bury him."

"Where will you put him?"

The small, stout stranger nodded toward the north.
"Over there."

Carrying the corpse between them, they started off;
they looked as dead as the corpse.

"A round-trip ticket, huh? Maybe the guy was a Christer," Pinette declared.

They looked at him in amazement; Pinette nodded toward the church. "He ought to find plenty of mumbo-jumbo fellers in there."

The tall soldier raised his hand in a gesture at once vigorous and noble. "No, no, no," he protested. "This is *our* business." He turned and followed the others. They crossed the square and disappeared.

"What was troubling that guy?" Charlot asked.

Mathieu turned. Charlot had laid his book down on the steps beside him and was looking up.

"That guy's trouble? He only croaked, that's all!"

"Jesus, what a mess! I never thought to look; I only saw them carrying him away. Not in our outfit, is he?"

"No."

"O.K., then," he said.

They drew close to the *mairie*, through whose windows emerged shouts and song more bestial than human.

"What goes on in there?" Mathieu asked.

Charlot smiled. "It's a regular whorehouse," he said simply.

"And you can read while—"

"I really can't read very well," Charlot said humbly.

"What is that book there?"

"The Vaulabelle. Remember?"

"I thought Longin was reading it?"

"Longin!" said Charlot ironically. "Oh, I should think so! He's in no state to read now, Longin." He jerked his thumb over his shoulder in the direction of the building. "He's in there, boiled as an owl."

"Longin? Longin tight?"

"Well, go see for yourself if he isn't plastered!"

"What's the time?" asked Pinette.

"Five thirty-five."

Pinette turned to Mathieu. "You won't come along? Sure?"

"Quite sure. I'm not coming."

"O.K., buddy, fuck you!" He looked at Charlot from out of his clear, myopic eyes. "That's what browns me off."

"Why?"

"He's found a piece!" Mathieu explained.

"If you can't take it, pass her on to me," Charlot said.

"To hell with you," Pinette answered. "She loves me!"

"Get yourself out of your own crapper, then." Pinette turned on his heel, with a gesture of imprecation.

Charlot grinned at his retreating back.

"He's the wolf of the French Army."

"Sure," said Mathieu.

"Well, he can have her," said Charlot. "Right now I don't feel a bit like burying the mutton dagger." He looked at Mathieu curiously. "I hear when you're scared, you get a hard on!"

"So what?"

"Not with me: I can't raise a hard on."

"Are you scared?"

"Christ, no. It's just a kind of weight on my stomach."

"I see."

Suddenly Charlot gripped Mathieu's sleeve; he lowered his voice. "Sit down, I've got something to tell you."

Mathieu sat down.

"There's a lot of God-damned fool talk going around," Charlot said in a low voice.

"What sort of talk?" Mathieu asked.

Charlot blushed. "Just a lot of fuck-all."

"Go ahead! What?"

"Well, Corporal Cabel says the Boches are going to cut off our balls." Charlot laughed, but his eyes were still fastened on Mathieu's face.

"Oh, that's a lot of hooey," said Mathieu.

Charlot was still laughing. "I never believe it, see. Sounds like too much of a job for them."

They stopped talking. Mathieu took up the Vaulabelle and thumbed through the pages; he was hoping that Charlot would let him keep the book.

With assumed carelessness Charlot said: "They do that to the Jews, don't they, in their own country?"

"Of course they don't."

"I've heard it said they do," said Charlot in the same tone.

He seized Mathieu by the shoulders. Mathieu could not bear the sight of the naked terror in Charlot's face and he looked down at his knees.

"What will they do to me?" Charlot asked.

"No more than to the rest of us." After a pause Mathieu added: "Tear up your A.G.O. card and throw your dog-tag away."

"I've done that long ago."

"Well then?"

"Look at me," said Charlot.

Mathieu could not bring himself to raise his head.

"Look at me, I tell you!"

"O.K. So what?"

"Do I look like a Jew?"

"No," said Mathieu. "You do not look like a Jew."

Charlot sighed. A soldier stumbled out of the *mairie*, descended three steps, missed the fourth, staggered between Mathieu and Charlot, and collapsed in the middle of the road.

"What the hell goes on!" Mathieu said.

The man propped himself up on his elbows and vomited. Then his head fell back, and he lay there motionless.

"They've been scrounging wine from the Q.M.," Charlot explained. "I saw them go by with a lot of jugs they nicked from somewhere or other, and a great pisspotful of ration booze. Dirty drunken bastards!"

Longin appeared at a window on the ground floor and belched. His eyes were bloodshot, and one side of his face boasted a shiner.

"A fine state you're in!" Charlot shouted to him disapprovingly.

Longin blinked, then, realizing who they were, he raised both arms in a gesture of tragedy. "Delarue?"

"Hello!"

"I'm a God-damned bastard and a disgrace!"

"O.K., bastard, go home!"

"Can't go home under my own steam."

"I'll take you back," said Mathieu. And, clutching the Vaulabelle, he rose.

"You're a swell guy," Charlot said.

"I do what I can."

Mathieu had reached the second step when Charlot shouted after him: "Hi, give me back my Vaulabelle."

"All right, but don't scream so loud." Mathieu was vexed.

He flung the book to Charlot, pushed open the door, found himself in a corridor with whitewashed walls, and stopped dead, in sudden horrified surprise: someone in a sleepy and discordant voice was singing the *Artilleur de Metz*. He recalled how in 1924 he had visited his aged and lunatic aunt at the insane asylum in Rouen; some of the patients had been singing at the windows. On the left, as you entered, there was a notice posted on the wall under a wire screen; he went up to it and read the words: "General Mobilization," and thought: "I was once a civilian." The voice at times slumbered, falling back upon itself, and then was drained in a gurgle, only to awake again with a great cry. "I was a civilian once, but that was long ago." He looked at the two crossed flags at the top of the notice, and suddenly had a vision of himself in an alpaca coat and a stiff collar. He had never worn either, but that was how he envisaged civilians. "I should hate to be a civilian again," he thought. "Anyhow, they belong to a dying race."

He heard Longin shouting: "Delarue!" saw an open door on his left, and went through it. The sun was already low; its long, dusty beams cut the room in two but did not lighten it. A strong smell of wine caught him by the throat, and Mathieu blinked his eyes, seeing nothing at first but a wall map that showed up like a dark square on the white plaster. Then he noticed Ménard seated on top of a small cupboard, his legs dangling over the edge; he was swinging his army boots in the red glow of the evening light. It was he who was singing; there was a wild gleam of gaiety in his eyes as they rolled from side to side above his open mouth. He seemed to have no control over his voice; it was like some huge parasite feeding upon him, sucking up his blood and guts and transforming them into song. He sat there inert, with dangling arms, watching with horrified amazement the vermin issuing from his mouth. Not a stick of furniture; somebody must have made a clean sweep of tables and chairs. A roar of greeting welcomed him:

"Delarue! Hello, Delarue!"

Mathieu lowered his eyes and saw a mass of men. One guy was lying deep in his vomit; another, stretched out his whole length, was snoring loudly; a third was leaning against a wall, his mouth agape like Ménard's, but he was not singing.

"Hi, Delarue! Delarue, hi!"

There were others to his right, not quite so far gone. Guiccioli was sitting on the floor, a canteen full of wine between his spread legs. Latex and Grimaud were squatting tailor-fashion; Grimaud was holding his quart pot by the handle and banging it on the floor in time to Ménard's singing; Latex's hand was hidden up to the wrist in the gaping fly of his trousers. Guiccioli said something that was covered up by the singer's voice.

"What's that you say?" asked Mathieu, curving his hand round his ear.

Guiccioli turned furious eyes on Ménard. "For God's sake, pipe down! You're driving us crazy!"

Ménard stopped singing. "I can't stop it," he said tearfully, and dragged on by his voice, he at once started on *Les Filles de Camaret.*

"He's off again," said Guiccioli, who, not too discontented, looked proudly at Mathieu. "He's feeling merry," he said. "We're all feeling merry and gay: a lot of tramps, bums, and hotheads, we are; a gang of dish-smashers, that's what we are!"

Grimaud nodded approval and laughed. Very carefully, as though speaking a foreign language, he said: "Nothing melancholy about us."

"So I notice," said Mathieu.

"You want a drink?" Guiccioli asked.

In the middle of the room there was a large copper can filled with rough ration wine. Various objects were floating about in it.

"That's a jam can," said Mathieu. "Where'd you find it?"

"No business o' yours," said Guiccioli. "Have a drink or get to hell outta here!"

He expressed himself with difficulty, and he was having trouble keeping his eyes open, but his mood was aggressive.

"No," said Mathieu. "I've just come to get Longin."

"To get Longin? What for?"

"To get some air."

Guiccioli gripped his canteen in both hands and drank. "*I'm* not going to stop you from taking him away," he said. "He does nothin' but talk about his brother, it's enough to make a feller shit his guts out. Remember we're riproarers here; we don't wan' anyone who can't enjoy his wine!"

Mathieu took Longin by the arm. "Come on, pal!"

Longin shook himself free, irritably. "What's the hurry? Gimme time to dress."

"Take all the time you want," said Mathieu. He turned and went to have a look at the cupboard. Through glazed doors he could see large cloth-bound books inside. Something to read. At that moment he would have read anything at all, even the Civil Code. The doors were locked: he tried vainly to open them.

"Smash the glass!" Guiccioli suggested.

"I will not!" Mathieu said angrily.

"Why not? Wait and see if the Heinies are so considerate." He turned to the others. "The Heinies'll burn the whole dump down, and here's Delarue won't smash the cupboard."

They all roared with laughter.

"He's a God-damned bourgeois," Grimaud said contemptuously.

Latex caught hold of Mathieu by the blouse. "Hey, Delarue, come have a look!"

Mathieu turned round. "Have a look at what?"

Latex pulled his penis out of his fly. "Take'n eyeful of that, and tip yer hat. I've made six of them with that."

"Six what?"

"Six kids. And fine kids too! Twenty pounds or more they weighed. I don't know who's feeding them now. But you'll make some more," he went on, bending affectionately over his privates. "You'll make dozens of 'em, y'ole devil, you!"

Mathieu looked away.

"Tip your hat, beginner!" cried Latex in a sudden fury.

"I haven't got a hat on," said Mathieu.

Latex stared round the room. "Six in eight years. Can anyone here do better than that?"

Mathieu turned back to Longin. "Well, are you coming?"

Longin looked darkly at him. "I don't like bein' pushed around," he said.

"I'm not pushing you around, it was you who called me in here."

Longin thrust a fist under his nose. "I don't much like you, Delarue. I never like you!"

"I feel the same way," said Mathieu.

"Good!" said Longin with satisfaction. "Now we can get along fine. First, why shouldn't I drink?" he asked with a suspicious look at Mathieu. "What's the point in my not having a drink?"

"He don't enjoy his liquor," said Guiccioli.

"I'd be even worse off if I didn't drink."

Ménard was singing:

> *Si je meurs, je veux qu'on m'enterre*
> *Dans la cave où y a du bon vin.*
>
> (*If I die, lay me in the cellar,*
> *In the cellar where there's lots of wine.*)

Mathieu looked at Longin. "You can drink as much as you like," he said.

"Whass zat?" Longin asked, disappointed.

"I said," Mathieu shouted, "you can drink as much as you like, for all I care!"

He thought: "I'd better get out of here," but he could not make up his mind to go. When he bent down, he could smell the sticky sweetness of their drunkenness, of their wretchedness. He thought: "But where can I go?" and he felt dizzy. They did not disgust him, these beaten men who were draining defeat to the dregs. If he felt disgust at anyone, it was at himself.

Longin, bending down to pick up his mug, fell on his knees. "Oh, shit!" he exclaimed. He crawled up to the wine can, plunged his arm in the wine up to the elbow, drew out his dripping mug, and bent forward to drink.

The liquor trickled into the tin from the two corners of his trembling mouth.

"Don't feel too good," he said.

"Go and throw up," Guiccioli advised.

"How?" asked Longin. His face was white and he was breathing stertorously.

Guiccioli stuck two fingers down his own throat, leaned sideways, retched, and brought up a small amount of viscous fluid. "Like that," he said, wiping his mouth with the back of his hand.

Longin, still on his knees, passed his mug across to his left hand, and thrust the fingers of his right down his throat.

"Hey!" cried Latex, "you'll vomit in the booze!"

"Give him a push, Delarue," Guiccioli cried. "Quick! Push him!"

Mathieu pushed Longin aside and Longin slumped down on his buttocks without removing his fingers from his mouth. The rest of the party gave him encouraging looks. Longin pulled out his fingers and retched.

"Attaboy! Keep it up!" Guiccioli cried. "Up she comes!"

Longin started to cough and turned scarlet. "Nothing's coming," he protested, still coughing.

"Y're a bastard!" cried Guiccioli in sudden fury. "If yer can't vomit, you shouldn't drink."

Longin felt in his pocket, scrambled to his knees again, and squatted close to the wine can.

"What're you up to?" Grimaud asked.

"Goin' to make myself a liquid compress," Longin explained, withdrawing his wine-soaked handkerchief from the tin. He laid it on his forehead and said with the voice of a small child: "Please, Delarue, will you tie it in back?"

Mathieu took the two corners and fastened them in a knot on Longin's neck.

"Ah!" said Longin, "that's better." The hankerchief lay

like a bandage over his left eye; the red wine trickled down his cheeks and into his neck.

"You look like Jesus Christ Himself!" Guiccioli said, laughing.

"You're right!" said Longin. "I'm the same kind of feller as Jesus." He held out his mug to Mathieu to be refilled.

"Oh, no. You've had enough," said Mathieu.

"Do's I tell yer," cried Longin, "do's I tell yer. Oh God!" he went on plaintively, "I feel awful!"

"For Christ's sake, giv'm something to drink," said Guiccioli, "or he'll be starting in again about his brother."

Longin stared back at him haughtily. "Why shouldn't I talk about my brother if I want to? Who's goin' to stop me?"

"Oh, get the hell outta here," said Guiccioli.

Longin turned to Mathieu. "My brother's at Hoseggor," he explained.

"Isn't he in the army?"

"Hell, no, he's discharged. He an' his little wife go walkin' unner the trees, and sayin': 'Poor Paul's out of luck.' They're hav'n their fun, screwing their heads off and thinking about me all the time. I'll give'm poor Paul, arse and all." He thought for a moment, then "I don't like my brother," he concluded.

Grimaud laughed till the tears came.

"What you got to laugh at?" Longin asked aggressively.

"You want to stop my laughing?" Guiccioli asked indignantly. "Carry on, buddy," he told Grimaud paternally. "Enjoy yourself, son, have a good laugh, have fun, that's what we're here for."

"I'm laughing about my wife," said Grimaud.

"To hell with your God-damned wife," said Longin.

"If you can talk about yer brother, I can talk about my wife."

"What's the matter with your wife?"

Grimaud put a finger to his lips. "Ssh!" he said, and,

leaning across toward Guiccioli, he said confidentially: "My old woman's ugly as a duck's arse."

Guiccioli tried to say something.

"Don't interrupt me!" Grimaud commanded. "Ugly as a duck's arse, there's no two ways about that! Hey, wait a moment," he added, raising himself slightly and stretching his left hand between his buttocks in order to reach his revolver pocket. "I'll show you her face; it'll make you gag."

After a number of vain efforts, Grimaud fell back into his former position. "What the hell! She's ugly as duck's arse, take my word for it. Why should I lie about it? I've nothing to gain by lying."

Longin seemed to be interested. "She is *really* ugly?" he asked.

"I've told you: ugly as duck's arse."

"What's so ugly about her?"

"The whole works. Her tits hang down to her knees, and her arse hangs down to her heels. And you should see her legs; they're enough to make you croak! When she pisses it's—what do you call the things?—it's between parentheses!"

"You better pass her on to me," Longin suggested with a laugh; "sounds like just the woman for me. I never frigged anything but floozies; my brother got all the good numbers."

Grimaud winked slyly. "No, pal, I won't pass her on to you. Because if I do, how can I be sure of getting another? I'm no beauty myself. That's the way it goes," he concluded with a sigh, "that's life. You must put up with what you got."

Ménard burst into song:

> "Et voilà la vie, la vie,
> Que les bons moines ont."
>
> ("Such is the life, the life,
> Led by the jolly monks.")

"Such is life!" Longin agreed. "Such is life! We're just a lot of corpses remembering their lives, and pretty God-damned awful lives they were, too."

Guiccioli flung his canteen at Longin's face. It grazed Longin's cheek and fell into the wine can.

"Pipe down," Guiccioli snarled. "I've had my troubles same as everyone else; but I don't bullshit about them wherever I go. We're out for fun here, see?"

Longin turned despairing eyes on Mathieu. "Gemme out of here," he begged in a low voice, "gemme out of here!"

Mathieu bent down to put his hands under Longin's armpits, but Longin wriggled free like a snake. Mathieu lost patience. "I'm fed up," he said. "Are you coming or aren't you?"

Longin was lying on his back, eying him maliciously. "You'd really like me to go with you, wouldn't you?"

"I don't give a damn. I only want you to make up your mind one way or the other."

"Well, have a drink!" Longin proposed. "There's plenty of time to have a drink while I'm thinking it over."

Mathieu made no reply. Grimaud held out his mug to him. "Here! Take it!"

"No, thanks," said Mathieu, waving the mug away.

"Why aren't you drinking?" Guiccioli asked, flabber-gasted. "There's enough for all; no need to be shy."

"I'm not thirsty."

Guiccioli started to laugh. "He says he's not thirsty! You poor bastard, don't you know we're the gang that drinks, thirsty or not?"

"I don't want to drink."

Guiccioli raised his eyebrows. "Why don't you want to drink like the rest of us? Why?" He looked at Mathieu sternly. "I thought you were a good guy, Delarue; I'm disappointed in you."

Longin propped himself up on one elbow. "Don't y'see he despises us?"

There was a silence. Guiccioli looked quizzically at Mathieu, then suddenly slumped. His eyelids drooped. He smiled miserably and, with his eyes closed, said: "Anyone who despises us had better get the hell out of here. We don't want to keep anybody here against his will, we're all pals here."

"I don't despise anybody," Mathieu replied. He stopped short. "They're drunk and I've not had a drop." This, in spite of himself, endowed him with a superiority that made him ashamed. He was ashamed of the patient voice he had been compelled to adopt in speaking to them. "They got drunk because they can't stand any more." But no one could share their wretchedness unless he shared their drunkenness too. "I ought never to have come here," he thought.

"He despises us," Longin repeated with a dull anger. "He thinks he's in the movies, laughing like hell at a lot of drunks shitting away on the screen!"

"Speak for yourself," said Latex. "I'm not shitting."

"Oh, shut up!" said Guiccioli wearily.

Grimaud looked thoughtfully at Mathieu. "If he despises us, he can go."

Guiccioli began to laugh. "You can go to hell," he bawled. "You can go to hell!"

Ménard, who had stopped singing, slid off the top of the cupboard, stared about him with the look of a trapped beast, then seemed to be reassured, heaved a sigh of relief, and passed out on the floor. Nobody paid any attention to him; all of them gazed blankly straight in front of them and from time to time turned to look angrily at Mathieu. Mathieu was at a loss: what should he do next? He had come here quite innocently, hoping to help Longin. But he should have known that shame and embarrassment would bear him company. Merely because of him, all these pals of his had become self-conscious; he had ceased to speak their language and, without wishing to, he had become both their judge and a witness against them. The sight of the tin, filled with wine and floating filth, gave him a feeling of acute disgust; nevertheless, he blamed himself for feeling as he did. "Who am I to refuse to drink when my pals are drunk?" he thought.

Latex was musingly fingering his groin. Suddenly he turned on Mathieu, his eyes blazing defiance. Then he put his canteen between his legs, and proceeded to dangle his penis in the wine.

"Giving the old man a drink," he explained; "it gives him pep."

Guiccioli guffawed. Mathieu turned aside to meet Grimaud's ironical gaze.

"You're wondering what sort of a joint you've crashed, huh?" Grimaud asked. "You don't know the kind of guys we are, pal. Anything can happen when we're around." He leaned forward and, with a knowing wink, called: "Hey, what about another drink, Latex, you bastard?"

Latex returned the wink. "Sure." He raised his canteen and drank noisily, keeping his eyes on Mathieu.

Longin giggled; everyone was grinning. "They're starting again because of me!" Latex put down his canteen and smacked his tongue against his palate. "That was delicious."

"What the hell!" Guiccioli said. "Aren't we a lotta good fellers? Aren't we? Who says we don't enjoy ourselves?"

"You ain't seen nothin' yet," Grimaud put in. "You ain't seen nothin'." With trembling hands he tried to unbutton his fly.

Mathieu leaned across to Guiccioli. "Give me your canteen," he said calmly. "I want to join in the fun."

"It's fallen into the wine can," Guiccioli replied morosely. "Fish it out for yourself."

Mathieu plunged his hand into the can, felt about in the wine with his fingers, touched the bottom, and brought up the canteen full to the brim. Grimaud's hands ceased to move; he looked at them, then put them in his pockets and stared at Mathieu.

"Good!" said Latex in a friendlier tone. "I knew you couldn't hold out on us."

Mathieu drank. There were lumps of some soft, colorless substance floating about in the wine. He spat them out and refilled the canteen.

Grimaud laughed good-humoredly. "No one can come here, without having a little drink. Just to see us makes a man thirsty."

Guiccioli, his good temper restored, opined that it was better to be the object of envy than of pity.

Mathieu took time to save a fly that was struggling in the wine; then he drank.

Latex looked at him with an appraising eye. "This isn't a binge," he said; "it's suicide."

The canteen was empty.

"I'm finding it hard to get drunk," Mathieu said. He filled the canteen for the third time. The wine was heavy with a curious sugary taste. Suddenly suspicious, "You haven't pissed in it, have you?" he asked.

"Are you nuts?" Guiccioli demanded indignantly. "Do you think we'd waste good booze by pissing in it?"

"Oh hell," said Mathieu, "I don't give a good Goddamn!" Mathieu drained the canteen at a gulp, then drew a deep breath.

"Well," Guiccioli inquired with interest, "feel better?"

Mathieu shook his head. "I haven't got there yet."

He took up the canteen again and was leaning with clenched teeth over the wine can when he heard Longin's mocking voice behind him:

"He wants to show us he can carry his liquor better than we can."

Mathieu swung round. "That's not true! I'm getting drunk just for the fun of it."

Longin sat down again, holding himself very stiffly; his

bandage had slipped down over his nose. Above it
Mathieu could see his eyes, round and staring like the
eyes of an aged hen.

"I don't like you much, Delarue," said Longin.

"You've said that already."

"The boys don't like you much either," Longin continued. "You scare them off because you're educated, but
don't think for a minute they like you."

"Why should they like me?" Mathieu asked between
his teeth.

"You're always different from anybody else," Longin
went on. "Even when you get fried, you don't do it like
us."

Mathieu, puzzled, looked at Longin; then, turning
round, he flung the canteen through the glass front of
the cupboard.

"I can't get drunk," he shouted. "I *can't*. Don't you see
I can't?"

No one breathed a word. Guiccioli removed a large
fragment of glass that had fallen on his knees and laid it
on the floor. Mathieu went up to Longin, firmly took his
arm, and pulled him to his feet.

"What the hell goes on?" Longin protested. "What have
I done? Piss off in your own pot, high-hat!"

"I came here to take you away," said Mathieu, "and I'm
going to."

Longin struggled violently. "Lemme alone, I tell you!
For Christ's sake, lemme alone or I'll beat the hell out of
you."

Mathieu attempted to drag him from the room. Longin
raised his hand and tried to poke his fingers into Mathieu's
eyes.

"You fucking bastard!" Mathieu said. He let go of
Longin in order to give him two easy hooks to the jaw.
Longin went limp and spun round; Mathieu caught him

before he fell, and hoisted him onto his shoulders like a sack of coal. "You see," he said, "I can be tough too if I want to."

He hated the lot of them. He went out and down the stone steps with his burden. Charlot burst out laughing as he passed.

"What's biting you, brother?"

Mathieu crossed the road and parked Longin against a chestnut tree. Longin opened one eye, tried to say something, and vomited.

"Feel better?" Mathieu asked.

Longin vomited again.

"Feel fine!" he gasped between belches.

"I'm off," said Mathieu. "When you're through with your vomiting, try and get some sleep."

By the time Mathieu reached the post office he was out of breath. He knocked at the door. Pinette opened, a look of rapture on his face.

"Ah!" he said. "So you decided to come after all."

"Yes," said Mathieu, "at long last."

The postmistress loomed out of the shadows behind Pinette.

"Mademoiselle isn't afraid of me any more," Pinette said. "We're going for a stroll in the fields."

The girl glowered at him. Mathieu smiled. He thought: "She's not very friendly," but he felt utterly indifferent.

"You stink of booze," said Pinette.

Mathieu laughed without replying. The postmistress put on a pair of black gloves, turned the key twice in the door, and the three of them set out. She took Pinette's arm, Pinette took Mathieu's. They passed a number of soldiers who greeted them.

"We're off for a Sunday walk!" Pinette shouted.

"With no officers around, every day is Sunday!" they answered.

A moonlight silence in the glare of the sun. Crude plaster effigies set in a circle about deserted spaces *will tell to generations yet unborn what men once were.* Sooty tears streaked the faces of tall white ruins. To the north-west a triumphal arch, to the north a Roman temple; southwards a bridge led to still another temple; water lay stagnant in a fountain's basin, a stone knife stood pointing toward the sky. Stone, imitation stone made from the sugar-loaves of history; Rome, Egypt, the Stone Age: that was all that remained of a celebrated site. He repeated: "All that remains," but the edge had gone from his pleasure. Nothing is more monotonous than catastrophe; he had begun to get used to it. He leaned against the iron railings, happy still, but tired, with the taste of summer's dry heat in his mouth: he had been walking all day; his legs could scarcely carry him, but he felt the need to go on walking all the same. What else to do in a dead city but walk? "I deserve a little luck," he said to himself. Precisely what sort of luck did not matter, so long as some flower suddenly blossomed at the corner of some street for him alone. But there was nothing. The desert stretched all around him; tiny flickers of sunlight from the windows of palaces, small objects, black and white, pigeons and im-memorial birds turned to stone as a result of feeding on statues. The only gay note in this mineral landscape was the Nazi flag flying over the Hôtel de Crillon.

Oh! le pavillon en viande saignante sur la soie des mers et des fleurs arctiques.

Oh, the banner bleeding like meat over the silk of arctic seas and flowers.

In the middle of the blood-red rag, a circle, white as that of the magic lantern shining on the sheets of child-hood; in the middle of the circle a knot of black serpents, Monogram of Evil, my emblem. A red drop kept forming in the folds of the standard, detached itself, fell on the macadam of the street: Courage lay bleeding. He murmured: "Courage lies bleeding!" But the idea seemed less amusing than it had the day before. For three days he had spoken to nobody, and his pleasure had grown hard; fatigue had momentarily clouded his vision, and he wondered whether he had not better go home. No, he couldn't do that: my presence is needed *everywhere*. He must walk. The sonorous rending of the sky brought him relief: the airplane glittering in the sunlight brought him relief; the dead city had found another observer, it could parade its myriad dead faces for other eyes. Daniel smiled: it was for him that this airplane was searching among the tombs. It is for me, for me alone, that it is there. He wanted to rush into the middle of the square and wave his handkerchief. Let them drop their bombs! That would bring resurrection; the city would reverberate with a tumult of hammers striking anvils just as in the days when it had labored. Lovely weeds would sprout, encroaching upon its walls. The airplane passed; all around Daniel a silence of planets was once more formed. He must walk, walk without ceasing over the surface of this cooling planet.

He resumed his walk, dragging his feet; the dust whitened his shoes. He gave a start: standing with his face pressed to a window, a general, idle and victorious, his hands behind his back, was perhaps observing this native wandering aimlessly through the museum of Parisian antiques. The windows all about him were now so many German eyes; he threw back his head and walked with jauntiness, swaying his hips in a faintly comical manner. "I am the warden of the Necropolis, the watchman of the cemetery." The Tuileries, the Quai des Tuileries; before crossing the street Daniel looked right and left from force of habit, but he could see nothing save the long tunnel of greenery. He was about to cross the Sol-

férino Bridge when sudddenly he stopped, his heart
thumping: his stroke of luck! A little tremor ran all the
way up his body from his hams to the nape of his neck;
his hands and feet went cold; he stood perfectly still,
holding his breath. All his life found refuge in his eyes:
with his eyes he devoured the slim young man who, in all
innocence, turned his back and leaned over the water.
"The miraculous meeting!"

Had the evening breeze spoken his name or had the
clouds printed its syllables boldly across the mauve and
lavender firmament, Daniel could not have been more
deeply stirred, so evident was it that this youth had been
placed there for him; that the boy's long, broad hands,
blossoming from silken sleeves, spoke the vocabulary of
Daniel's own secret language: "he is mine by deed of
gift." The boy was tall and smooth, with tousled blond
hair and rounded shoulders, almost feminine in shape; his
hips were narrow, his rump was firm and fleshy, his ears
exquisitely fashioned. He might be nineteen years old, or
twenty. Looking at his ears, Daniel thought: "The miraculous meeting," and he felt almost afraid. Like certain
insects at the threat of danger, every fiber of his body
feigned death: "for me the worst danger is beauty." His
hands grew cold and colder; metallic fingers encrusted
the back of his neck. Beauty, most treacherous of snares,
lay in ambush for him with a smile of connivance and an
invitation to enjoyment; it beckoned to him, as though it
had been awaiting him. What deception: that proffered
soft neck awaited nothing and no one: it caressed itself
against the collar of its coat; those warm, white thighs one
could guess under the gray flannel trousers were a private
pleasure. The river fills this youth's vision, he is living in
the flow of the river, he is lost in solitary and unaccount-
able thought, like a palm tree; he belongs to me, yet he
does not know it. A wave of anxiety swept over Daniel
like nausea; for a second he swayed dizzily: the boy, a

tiny and distant figure, called to him from the abyss; beauty was summoning him; Beauty, my Destiny. He thought: "Everything is about to blossom again. Everything: hope, wretchedness, shame, madness." Then suddenly he remembered that France was screwed up: *"Anything goes!"* From the pit of his stomach a warmth rose gratefully through him to his fingertips; his weariness was effaced, the blood throbbed at his temples: "We are the sole visible representatives of the human species, the only survivors of a vanished nation; it is inevitable that we should speak to each other: what could be more natural?"

He took a step toward the stranger, whom he had already baptized "the Miracle." He felt young and sound, big with the exciting revelation he was bringing to this innocent. Almost at once he stopped short: he had just noticed that the Miracle was trembling in all his limbs, now leaning backwards with a convulsive movement, now pressing his belly to the balustrade, leaning forward above the river.

Vexed, Daniel thought: "Silly little twerp!" This boy was not worthy of this extraordinary moment, he was not actually and fully a party to this meeting, his mind, which should have been vacant for the tidings of joy, was distracted by childish fancies. "Silly little fool!"

Suddenly the Miracle raised his right foot in an odd, clumsy movement as though to climb over the parapet. Daniel was ready to leap forward when the boy turned, uncertain, his leg still raised. The boy saw Daniel, and what Daniel saw was a pair of smoldering eyes set in a face of chalk. For a moment the boy hesitated, his foot dropped to the ground, scraping the stone as it did so, then he started walking off nonchalantly, his hand brushing the edge of the parapet. So you want to kill yourself, do you?

On the moment Daniel's sense of wonder froze. So that was all: just a dirty terror-stricken lad unable to pay the

price of his own tomfoolery. A wave of lust stiffened
Daniel in his most private parts; he followed the boy with
the predatory lust of a hunter. His very exultation had
gone cold; he felt delivered, cleansed, filled with the joy
of evil. Deep within him he would prefer matters to take
their course, but he enjoyed bearing a grudge against the
youngster: you want to kill yourself, you silly little twerp?
Is it as easy as all that? Wiser people than you haven't
succeeded.

The youth seemed to sense that somebody was following him; he strode forward like a horse pacing, stiff, self-
conscious exaggeration in his movements. Halfway across
the bridge he suddenly noticed his right hand trailing
along the parapet. His hand rose, stiff and prophetic, at
the end of his arm, he forced his hand down, crammed it
into his pocket, and walked on, hunching his shoulders.
"Something *fishy* here," Daniel thought, "that's how I like
them." The young man began to walk faster; Daniel did
likewise. A harsh smile rose to his lips. "My boy is suffering, he wants to get the job done but he can't because I
am behind him. Go on, go ahead, I won't leave you." At
the far end of the bridge the boy hesitated, then turned
down the Quai d'Orsay. As he reached the point where a
flight of steps descends to the river bank, he stopped,
turned impatiently toward Daniel, and stood waiting. Delighted, Daniel glimpsed an exquisite pale face, a short
nose, a small, weak mouth, proud eyes. With hypocritical
modesty he lowered his own eyes, slowly drew near,
passed the boy without looking at him, and then, a few
steps farther on, glanced back over his shoulder. The boy
had disappeared. In a leisurely fashion Daniel leaned
over the parapet and saw him on the river bank, absorbed
in contemplation of a mooring-ring that he was medita-
tively kicking. The first thing to do, Daniel decided, was
to get down there as swiftly as possible without being
noticed. Fortunately there was another way down twenty

yards ahead, a narrow iron ladder, concealed by a but-
tress. Slowly and noiselessly Daniel made his way down:
he was enjoying himself madly. At the bottom of the
ladder he flattened himself against the wall. The boy,
standing on the edge of the bank, was looking at the
water. The Seine, greenish, with sulphurous reflections,
flowed on, carrying with it dark and flabby objects; to
dive into that evil stream was not a tempting prospect.
The boy bent down, picked up a stone, and let it fall into
the water; then he relapsed into his morbid brooding.
Nothing doing today; in five minutes' time he'll be like a
pricked bubble. Ought I to let things take their course?
Stay hidden, wait until he has tasted the very lees of his
humiliation, and then, when he has turned away, burst
out laughing? Pretty risky: he might develop a permanent
loathing for me. On the other hand, if I suddenly fling
myself on him as though saving him from a watery grave,
he'll be grateful to me for thinking him capable of such
an act, even though he may protest, for form's sake, and
especially for sparing him the necessity of making up his
mind.

Daniel passed his tongue over his lips, drew a deep
breath, and jumped out from his hiding-place. The young
man, startled, swung round; he would have fallen had not
Daniel seized him by the arm.

He said: "I—"

At the same moment he took note of Daniel and seemed
to pull himself together; the look of fright in his eyes gave
place to one of rage. It's *somebody else* he's terrified of.

"What do you want?" he asked haughtily.

Daniel could not answer him at once: desire caught him
by the throat and checked his speech.

"Young Narcissus!" he said, bringing out the words with
difficulty, "young Narcissus!" After a moment's pause he
added: "Narcissus leaned over a bit too far, young man:
and he fell into the water."

"I'm not Narcissus," said the youth, "I've got a sense of balance, and I don't need your help."

He's a student, thought Daniel. He put his question with brutal directness: "Were you contemplating suicide?"

"Are you crazy?"

Daniel started to laugh, and the boy flushed.

"Leave me alone," he said gloomily.

"In my own good time," Daniel said, tightening his grip.

The young man lowered his handsome eyes, and Daniel jumped back just in time to avoid a kick. So that's his little game, he thought, regaining his balance. Kicking out wildly, without so much as looking at me. He was delighted. Both of them were breathing heavily; not a word passed between them. The boy kept his head down, and Daniel noted with admiration the astonishing silkiness of his hair.

"So that's it? Kicking, eh? A woman's trick!"

The boy moved his head from side to side as though in a vain effort to raise it. After another moment he said, with studied roughness: "Get the hell out of here."

There was more of mulishness than assurance in his voice, but he had managed to raise his eyes and now stared Daniel straight in the face with a frightened insolence. Then his gaze slid sideways and Daniel could contemplate at his ease the handsome, vulnerable face. "Pride and weakness," he thought. "And bad faith. A little bourgeois face overwhelmed by an abstract melancholy; charming features, but with no generosity." At the same moment a kick on the calf made him grimace with pain.

"You God-damned young fool! I've half a mind to put you across my knee and give you a good spanking."

The boy's eyes glittered. "You just try!"

Daniel started to shake him. "Suppose I do? Suppose I feel like taking your trousers down here and now, who's going to stop me?"

The boy blushed scarlet and began to laugh. "I'm not afraid of you."

"We'll soon see about that!" said Daniel. He gripped the back of the young man's neck and tried to force his head forward.

"No! No!" cried the boy in tones of despair. "No! No!"

"Are you going to try to kick me again?"

"No, let me go."

Daniel let him straighten up. The boy kept quiet; all the fight had gone out of him. "A young horse that's already felt the bit; someone has already broken him in for me, I see. A father? An uncle? A lover? No, not a lover; later he'll revel in it, but just for the moment he's virgin."

"So you wanted to kill yourself," he said, still maintaining his grip. "Why?"

The boy remained mulishly silent.

"Sulk as much as you please," said Daniel. "What does it matter to me? You've bungled it this time, at any rate."

The boy was smiling to himself; there was something at once knowing yet indeterminate in his expression. "This is just marking time," thought Daniel, thoroughly put out. "I must get out of this dead end." He gave his victim a violent shake. "What are you grinning at?"

The young man looked him straight in the eyes. "You'll have to let me go sooner or later."

"True enough," said Daniel, "so I'll do it now." He let go of him and put his hands in his pockets. "Well?" he asked.

The boy made no attempt to move. He was still smiling.

"He's laughing at me," thought Daniel. He added aloud: "Listen, I am an excellent swimmer. I've already saved two persons, one of them in a high sea."

The boy gave a girlish giggle, mocking and sly. "It seems to be a mania with you," he said.

"Maybe it is," said Daniel. "Perhaps it is a mania. Jump in!" he added, spreading his arms. "Go on, jump in if that is how you feel. I'll let you swallow a good big mouthful, you'll see how you like it. Then I'll take my clothes off at my leisure, I'll dive into the water, I'll give you a clout over the head, and I'll fish you out more dead than alive." He started to laugh. "You should know that when people have failed to bring off a suicide, they seldom indulge in a second attempt. Once I've brought you round, you won't feel like trying it again."

The boy took a step forward as though to strike Daniel. "What right have you to speak to me like that?"

Daniel continued to laugh. "Ha ha! What right? You may well ask!" Suddenly he gripped his wrist. "So long as I am here you can't kill yourself, even if you die wanting to. I have the power of life and death over you."

"But you won't always be there," said the boy with an odd look.

"That's where you are wrong!" said Daniel. "I shall *always* be there." He had a little thrill of pleasure: he had caught a sudden flash of curiosity in the lovely hazel eyes.

"Suppose I do want to kill myself, what's that got to do with you? You don't even know who I am."

"Just a little mania of mine, as you said yourself," Daniel replied jovially. "I happen to have a passion for preventing people from doing what they want to do." A look of kindliness came into his eyes. "Are things really as bad as all that?" he asked.

The boy made no reply. He was doing all he could to keep from crying. Daniel felt so moved that tears came into his own eyes. Fortunately, the youngster was too much concerned with his own feelings to notice. For a few seconds more Daniel managed to control his longing to stroke the boy's hair; then his right hand came out of his pocket independently of his will and rested for a moment, with the fumbling uncertainty of a blind man, on the golden head. He snatched it back as though he had touched fire. "Too soon! That was a mistake." The boy

shook his head vehemently and walked a few paces along
the bank. Daniel waited, holding his breath. "Too soon,
you fool, much too soon." In a sudden spurt of self-
punishing anger he completed his thought: "If he makes
off now, I'll let him go." But at the first sound of sobs, he
ran to him and took him in his arms. The boy yielded
without a struggle.

"You poor dear!" said Daniel, overcome by emotion,
"You poor dear!"

He would have given his right hand to be able to console him or to share his fit of weeping. After a second or
so, the boy raised his head. He was no longer crying, but
two tears were trickling down his delicate cheeks; Daniel
would have liked to lick them off, to drink them down, to
feel in his mouth the salty taste of this grief. The young
man looked at him distrustfully.

"How was it you happened to be there?"

"I was just passing by," said Daniel.

"Aren't you in the army?"

Daniel heard the question with no sense of pleasure. "I
am not interested in their war." He hurried on: "Look
here, I'll make you a proposition. Are you still determined
to kill yourself?"

The boy said nothing, but a dark, obstinate look came
into his face.

"All right," said Daniel, "just you listen to me. I found
it amusing to frighten you, though, in point of fact, I've
nothing whatever against suicide so long as it is the fruit
of mature reflection. I take a sort of sporting interest in
your death, since you are a perfect stranger to me. I see
no reason why I should stop you from killing yourself if
you have valid reasons for doing so."

He saw with pleasure that the color had ebbed from the
young man's cheeks. "You were feeling safe," he thought.

"Take a look at this," he went on, displaying the thick
bezel of his ring. "Inside there I carry a poison that brings

sudden death. I wear this ring always, even at night, and if I found myself in a position that my pride found intolerable—"

He stopped talking, and unscrewed the bezel. The boy stared at the two brown capsules with a distrust full of repulsion.

"Tell me your motives. If I decide they are valid, one of these pills is yours; anyway it's better than a cold bath. Would you like me to give it to you now?" he asked, as though he had suddenly changed his mind.

The boy passed his tongue over his lips without speaking.

"Do you want it? It is yours for the asking; you can swallow it in my presence and I'll not leave you." He took the young man by the hand. "I'll hold your hand and close your eyes."

The boy shook his head. "What proof have I got that it really is poison?" he asked with an effort.

Daniel's laugh was young and gay. "You're afraid it's just a laxative? Swallow it and see."

The boy made no reply. His cheeks were still pale and the pupils of his eyes were dilated, but he gave Daniel a sidelong smile that was at once sly and coquettish.

"You don't want it, then?"

"Not immediately."

Daniel screwed up the bezel of his ring. "Just as you like," he said coldly. "What's your name?"

"Must I tell you my name?"

"Yes, your given name."

"Well, if I must—Philippe."

"All right, Philippe," said Daniel, putting his arm through the young man's, "since you want to talk about yourself, you'd better come home with me."

He pushed him toward the steps and hurried him up them. At the top they turned along the embankment, arm in arm. Philippe obstinately kept his eyes lowered; he had started to tremble again, but he made no effort to keep a distance between himself and Daniel, whose leg he brushed with his own at every step. Smart suède shoes, almost new, but bought at least a year ago, a well-cut flannel suit, a white tie, a blue silk shirt. The boy's whole turnout was Montparnasse, vintage 1938; his hair was carefully disarranged; his whole appearance reeked of narcissism. "Why isn't he in the army? Probably too young; still, he may be older than he looks; childhood is prolonged in boys with dominant parents." Obviously it wasn't poverty that drove him to suicide.

As they passed the end of the Henri IV Bridge, Daniel suddenly shot a question at him:

"Was it because of the Germans that you wanted to kill yourself?"

Philippe looked surprised and shook his head. He was as pretty as an angel. "I'll help you," thought Daniel with passion, "I'll help you." He longed to save Philippe, to make a man of him. "I'll give you everything I have, you shall know all that I know."

The markets were dark and empty; gone was their old familiar smell. But the city looked wholly different. An hour ago it was the end of the world, and Daniel had felt himself to be a character in history. Now the streets were slowly becoming themselves again, and Daniel was at the heart of a prewar Sunday, at that turning-point of the afternoon when the promise of a brand-new Monday begins to emerge from the death-agonies of the week and of the sinking sun. Something was about to begin: a new week, a new love-adventure. He threw back his head and smiled: a window blazed with the scarlet of the last light—an omen. The exquisite smell of crushed strawberries suddenly filled his nostrils—another omen. In the distance a shadow crossed the rue Montmartre at a run—yet a third omen. Each time that fortune brought him face to face with a boy of angelic beauty, heaven and earth in-

dulged in knowing winks. He felt weak with desire and
caught his breath with every step; but he had become so
used to walking silently in the company of the unsuspect-
ing young that he had grown to love for its own sake the
long-drawn-out patience of the pederast. "I am watching
you, you are naked in the hollow of my gaze, I possess
you though we are not touching, through the medium of
sight and smell, giving nothing of myself in return." He
leaned the better to breathe the fragrance of that bent
neck and was suddenly brought up short by a strong
smell of naphthalene. At once he straightened his back,
feeling his passion cool and conscious of a little flutter of
amusement; he adored such alternating moods of thrill
and aridity, he adored the exacerbation. Let's see if I'm
a good detective, he thought with a flicker of gaiety. A
young poet wants to throw himself into the river on the
day the Germans enter Paris; why? I have but one clue
to the problem, but it is a capital one: his suit smells of
naphthalene, so he hasn't been wearing it recently. Why
should he change his clothes in order to commit suicide?
Because he could no longer wear those he had on yesterday. Ergo, it was a uniform, which would have given him
away and led to his being taken prisoner. He's a soldier.
But what is he doing here? If he was on duty at the Ministry of Information or at the Air Ministry, he would have
gone off to Tours with the others days ago. Well then,
what? Well, it's clear. The whole thing is clear. He
stopped and pointed to an entry.

"Here we are."

"I'm not going any farther," said Philippe suddenly.

"What?"

"I'm not going in."

"You'd rather be picked up by the Germans?"

"I just don't want to," Philippe said, staring at his feet.
"I've nothing to tell you, and I don't know you."

"Oh, so that's it?" Daniel observed. "So that's it!"

He took the boy's head between his hands and raised it by force. "You know nothing about me, but I know all about you," he said. "I could tell you your whole story."

Staring fixedly into Philippe's eyes, he went on: "You were with the northern armies. The men panicked and you scampered away. Later, I suppose, you couldn't find your outfit again, so you came home. You found your family gone, so you put on a suit of civvies and made a beeline for the Seine with the idea of drowning yourself. It's not that you're particularly patriotic, but you can't bear the feeling that you're a coward. Am I right?"

The boy stood there motionless, but his eyes had grown round and large. Daniel's mouth was dry; he could feel anguish flooding through him like a tide. He repeated his question with more violence than assurance in his voice:

"Am I right?"

Philippe uttered a faint groan, and his body went limp. Anguish died away. Daniel caught his breath in a spasm of joy; his heart was hammering madly in his chest.

"Come on upstairs," he said in a low voice. "I know a cure."

"A cure for what?"

"For your troubles. I can teach you a lot of things."

Philippe looked exhausted but relieved. Daniel pushed him into the entry. He had never dared to bring home with him the young professionals whom he used to pick up in Montmartre and Montparnasse. But today the concierge and most of the tenants were fleeing along the roads between Montargis and Gien; today was a special occasion.

They climbed the stairs in silence. Daniel put the key into the lock but kept his grip on Philippe's arm. He opened the door and stood aside for the other to pass.

"Come along in."

Philippe entered like someone only half awake.

"The door opposite—that's the living-room." He turned

his back on the boy, shut the front door, locked it, and put the key in his pocket. He found Philippe standing in front of the bookshelves, gazing with lively interest at the statuettes.

"These are marvelous."

"Not bad," said Daniel, "not at all bad. The great thing about them is that they're *genuine*. I bought them from the Indians."

"And that?" Philippe asked.

"That's the portrait of a dead child. In Mexico, when anyone kicked the bucket, they used to call in the painter of corpses, who proceeded to paint a lifelike portrait of the dead man. This is an example of what sort of work they did."

"You've been to Mexico?" Philippe asked, a faint note of respect in his voice.

"I lived there for two years."

Philippe gazed ecstatically at the disdainful and pallid face of the lovely child which, with the serious, self-sufficient expression of an initiate, stared back at him from the remote distances of death. There's a resemblance between them, Daniel mused: both of them are fair, both of them are insolent and pale, the one within the picture, the other outside it, the young creature who had sought to die and the young creature who had died in fact looked at each other. The only thing that separated them was death: nothingness, the flat surface of the canvas.

"It's marvelous!" Philippe repeated.

Suddenly an immense weariness swept over Daniel. He heaved a deep sigh and collapsed into an armchair. Malvina jumped onto his knee.

"There, there," he said, stroking her.

"Be a good little cat, Malvina, be a beautiful little cat." He turned to Philippe and in a feeble voice said: "There's whisky in the liqueur cabinet. No, to your right, that small

Chinese cupboard. You'll find glasses there, too. You must be the daughter of the house and do the necessary."

Philippe filled two glasses, handed one to Daniel, and remained standing in front of him. Daniel emptied his drink at one gulp and felt more cheerful.

"If you were a poet," he said suddenly, using the more formal *vous* instead of the familiar *tu*, "you'd realize what an extraordinary meeting ours was."

The boy uttered an odd, provocative little laugh. "How do you know I don't realize it?" He looked Daniel full in the face. Since he had entered the room, a complete change had come over his expression and his whole way of behaving. He is the type who fears the head of the household, the paterfamilias, Daniel thought with annoyance; he is not frightened of me now because he realizes that I'm not one. Deliberately he assumed an air of uncertainty.

"I'm just wondering," he said, as though pondering a problem, "whether you really interest me."

"You might better have asked yourself that question earlier," Philippe remarked.

Daniel smiled. "It's never too late. If I find you a bore, I can turn you out."

"You needn't bother to do that," Philippe replied. He turned toward the door.

"Stay where you are," said Daniel. "You know perfectly well that you need me."

Philippe smiled with an air of easy laziness and sat down on a chair. Poppæa brushed past him. He caught her and lifted her onto his knee. She made no protest. He stroked her gently, voluptuously.

"That's a point in your favor," said Daniel with no little surprise. "It's the first time she's ever allowed that."

Philippe indulged in a self-satisfied smile. "How many cats have you got?" he asked, dropping his gaze.

"Three."

"That's a point in *your* favor."

He scratched Poppæa's head; the cat purred. He's a great deal more at his ease than I am, thought Daniel; he knows that I like him. Then, in order to break down his visitor's self-possession, he asked abruptly: "How did it all happen?"

Philippe spread his knees and let Poppæa go. The cat jumped to the floor and fled.

"Well, since you've guessed the truth, there's no more to be said."

"Where were you?"

"In the Département du Nord. A village called Parny."

"And afterwards?"

"Nothing happened afterwards. We held on for two days and then the tanks and airplanes took a hand."

"Both at the same time?"

"Yes."

"Were you frightened?"

"Not a bit. Or perhaps fear isn't what you expect it to be." His face had assumed a hard, old look. He stared before him with an expression of weariness. "The other guys ran; I ran with them."

"And then?"

"I walked, then I jumped a truck; later still I walked some more. I got here the day before yesterday."

"What did you think while you were walking?"

"I didn't think."

"Why did you wait until today to kill yourself?"

"I wanted to see my mother again," Philippe explained.

"And she wasn't here?"

"No, she wasn't here." He raised his head and looked at Daniel with sparkling eyes. "If you think I'm a coward, you're barking up the wrong tree," he said in a clear, sharp tone.

"Really? Then why did you run away?"

"I ran because the others ran."

"Still, you did want to kill yourself."

"Well, yes; the idea did cross my mind."

"Why?"

"It would take too long to explain."

"What's the hurry?" said Daniel. "Have some more whisky."

Philippe poured himself out a glass. There was color in his cheeks now. He giggled. "If I had only myself to think of, I wouldn't in the least mind being a coward," he said. "I am a pacifist. What does military virtue amount to? Lack of imagination, that's all. The really brave guys, when it came to fighting, were the hicks and louts and bruisers, guys who were little better than brutes. I had the misfortune to be born into a family of heroes."

"I see," Daniel said. "Your father, I suppose, was a regular officer."

"A reserve officer, but he died in 1927 as a result of the first war: he was gassed a month before the Armistice. His glorious death gave my mother a taste for that sort of thing, so she married again in 1933, this time a general."

"It looks as though she woulα be disappointed," Daniel observed. "Generals have a way of dying in their beds."

"Not this one," Philippe objected with hatred in his voice. "He's a regular Bayard: he makes love, he kills, he prays, and never thinks at all."

"Is he at the front?"

"Where do you suppose he is? He's the kind of mug who would work a machine-gun single-handed or charge the enemy at the head of his men. You can rely on him to get his soldiers mowed down to the last man."

"I can imagine him, black, hairy, with a large mustache."

"Exactly," said Philippe. "Women adore him because he smells like a goat."

They looked at each other and laughed.

"You don't seem to care for him much," Daniel suggested.

"I hate him!" Philippe answered. He blushed and stared fixedly at Daniel. "I have an Œdipus complex," he went on. "The regular case-book type."

"Is it your mother you're in love with?" Daniel asked with incredulity.

Philippe made no reply. He had the self-important air of a victim of destiny.

Daniel leaned forward. "Isn't it more likely you're in love with your stepfather?" he asked quietly.

Philippe gave a start and turned scarlet; then, looking Daniel straight in the eyes, he burst out laughing. "That's rich!" he said.

Daniel joined in the laughter. "Well, but look here," he said, "it was because of him that you wanted to kill yourself."

Philippe continued to laugh. "Nonsense! Absolutely not."

"Then who was the cause of it? You made a beeline for the Seine because you lacked courage, yet you proclaim that you detest courage. You're afraid he'll despise you."

"I'm afraid my mother may despise me," Philippe corrected.

"Your mother? I'm sure she'd understand."

Philippe bit his lips but said nothing.

"When I touched you on the shoulder you were terrified," said Daniel. "I suppose you thought it was the general, eh?"

Philippe jumped to his feet, his eyes shining. "He—he struck me."

"When?"

"Less than two years ago. Ever since, I've had a feeling he was always behind me."

"Have you ever dreamed that you were lying naked in his arms?"

"You're crazy," Philippe cried with genuine indignation.

"Anyway, it's certain the thought of him is an obsession with you. You go down on all fours, the general rides you, he puts you through your paces like a mare. Never are you yourself: sometimes you think with him, sometimes against. You don't really care a damn about pacifism, you'd never have given it a thought if your stepfather wasn't a soldier." Daniel rose and took Philippe by the shoulders. "Do you want me to make you a free man?"

Philippe broke away, went on suspiciously: "How can you do that?"

"I told you, I have much to teach you."

"Are you a psychoanalyst?"

"Something of the sort."

Philippe shook his head. "Assuming that what you say might be true," he argued, "why should you interest yourself in me?"

"I have a passion for the human soul," Daniel said with a smile. Then, with emotion, he added: "Yours should be exquisite, if only we could rid it of all its frustrations."

Philippe said nothing, but he seemed flattered. Daniel paced the floor, rubbing his hands. Then with an air of gay excitement he said: "We must begin by liquidating all moral values. Are you a student?"

"I was," said Philippe.

"Law?"

"Literature."

"So much the better. In that case you will be able to understand what I am going to say. Systematic doubt, eh? Rimbaud's deliberate disorganization. We must set about complete destruction, but not in words: in deeds. Everything you have borrowed from others will go up in smoke. What remains will be the essential you. Do you agree?"

Philippe looked at him, questioning.

"Given the state of mind you're in," Daniel went on, "what risk can you possibly run?"

Philippe shrugged. "None."

"Good," Daniel said, "I adopt you here and now. We'll start on the journey to hell right away. But, for heaven's sake," he added with a sharp look, "no transference business with me."

"I'm not a hopeless fool," Philippe protested with an answering glance.

"When you reach the stage of throwing me away like an old glove," Daniel said, his eyes still fixed on the young man's face, "the cure will be complete."

"Don't worry," said Philippe.

"Like an old glove!" Daniel repeated with a laugh.

"Like an old glove!" Philippe repeated.

They were both of them laughing. Daniel refilled Philippe's glass.

"Let's sit down over there," the girl said suddenly.

"Why over there?"

"It looks nice and soft."

"Oho!" Pinette observed. "So young ladies in the post office like things soft." He took off his blouse and flung it on the ground. "Here, park your softness on my blouse."

They settled down in the long grass at the edge of a wheatfield. Pinette, clenching his left fist, kept a watch on the girl out of the corner of his eye; then he put his thumb in his mouth and pretended to blow. His biceps began to swell as though inflated by a pump, and the girl gave a little laugh.

"Feel it."

She placed a timid finger on Pinette's arm. As she did so, the muscle disappeared and Pinette made a noise like air escaping from a balloon.

"Oh!" she said.

Pinette turned to Mathieu. "What do you think Mauron would say if he saw me sitting by the side of the road in my shirtsleeves?"

"You can't see Mauron for dust," Mathieu said. "He's still running."

"That's all right by me," Pinette commented; "I won't chase the bastard!" Then, leaning toward the girl: "Mauron's our captain," he explained. "He's busy taking a fresh-air cure."

"A fresh-air cure?" she repeated.

"He finds it healthier." With a chuckle, he said: "We're our own masters now; there's no one to give us orders, we can do as we like. If you want to, we can go to the school-house and sleep in the captain's bed; the whole village belongs to us."

"Not for long," Mathieu said.

"All the more reason to make hay while the sun shines."

"I'd rather stay here," said the girl.

"Why? Haven't I just said there's no one to stop us?"

"There are still a few people left in the village."

Pinette stared at her arrogantly. "I was forgetting," he said, "you are a civil servant; you have to watch your step. You're different from us; we don't have to bother about any one." He grinned knowingly at Mathieu. "We're homeless and roofless, and faithless and lawless, that's what we are, just birds of passage. *You* have to stay put, but we are on the wing, here today and gone tomorrow, a gang of gypsies, eh? Wolves and beasts of prey. Big, bad wolves, that's us!" He broke off a blade of grass and began to tickle her chin. His eyes fixed on her, still smiling, he sang:

"Who's afraid of the big bad wolf?"

The girl blushed, smiled, and chimed in:

"Not us! not us! not us!"

Pinette was delighted. "Hey, darling," he went on, an absent-minded look in his eyes, "hey, darling, pet, pretty pet, Miss Pretty Pet!"

Suddenly he stopped. The sky was red, the earth cool and shadowy with blue. Under his hands, under his buttocks, Mathieu felt the swarming, tangled life of grass and soil and insects, a vast expanse of rank moist hair, crawling with lice. To feel it against his palms was naked agony. Cornered! Millions of men cornered between the Vosges and the Rhine, robbed of all possibility of existing as men. This flat forest of living things would still be there when they were dead; it was as though the world had no room for anything but fields and grass and a sort of impersonal ubiquity. Beneath his hands the earth was as tempting as suicide—the grass and the dense darkness with which it overlay the soil, the shackled thoughts creeping earthbound through this shadowy dusk, the spider beside his foot, motionless, until of a sudden it spread its giant's legs and vanished. The girl sighed.

"What's the matter, baby?" Pinette asked.

She made no answer. Her small face, the face of a respectably brought-up young woman, was feverishly flushed. She had a long nose, a thin mouth, and a lower lip that projected slightly.

"What's the matter? Come on, tell me what's the matter?"

She remained silent. A hundred yards or so from them, silhouetted between sun and field, four soldiers moved like vague shadows in a golden mist. One of them stopped and turned toward the east. In the glare he seemed to be insubstantial, not black and solid but mauve, rather, against the red glow of the setting sun. He was bareheaded. The man behind bumped into him and gave him a push. Their torsos seemed to drift like ships upon the surface of the wheat. A third man loitered at their heels, his arms raised; behind him a laggard was slashing with a switch at the growing crops.

"Come on!" Pinette said. He held the girl's chin in his hand and stared into her face: her eyes were brimming with tears. "Not very cheerful company, are you?" He tried to put a soldier's roughness into the words, but lacked the necessary assurance. When she spoke, the phrase she used, slipping from her child's mouth, seemed wan and faded:

"I can't help it," she said.

He drew her to him. "Come now, you mustn't cry." Then, laughing, "*We're* not crying, are we?" he asked.

She let her head droop against Pinette's shoulder and he stroked her hair; there was a look of pride on his face.

"They'll take you away," she said.

"Pooh!"

"They'll take you away," she repeated, crying.

Pinette's face hardened. "I'm not asking for pity."

"I don't want them to take you away."

"Who told you they would take us away? You'll see how Frenchmen can fight; you'll have a ringside seat."

She gazed at him with wide, dilated eyes, her fear so intense that she left off crying. "You mustn't fight."

"Fiddlededee!"

"You mustn't fight, the war's over."

There was amusement in the look he gave her. "Ha!" he said. "Ha ha!"

Mathieu averted his eyes, he wanted to go away.

"We've only known each other since yesterday," the girl went on. Her lower lip was trembling, her long face drooped. She had the noble, sad, and frightened look of a horse. "Tomorrow," she concluded.

"Oh, between now and tomorrow—" Pinette said.

"Between now and tomorrow there's only one night."

"Precisely, one night," said Pinette, winking. "Time enough for a little fun."

"I don't want any fun."

"You don't want any fun? Do you really mean you
don't want any fun?"

She looked at him without answering.

"Are you unhappy?" he asked.

She continued to look at him, her mouth half open.

"Because of me?" he asked. He leaned across her with
a look of tenderness on his face, a rather haggard tenderness. Almost at once he drew back, his lips twisted in an
unpleasant sneer.

"Come on," he said, "come on, baby, don't take it so
hard: there'll be others. There's as good fish in the sea as
ever came out of it."

"I'm not interested in the others."

"You won't talk like that when you see them. They're
strange fellows, you know. Well set up! With broad shoulders and narrow hips!"

"Who are you talking about?"

"The Heinies, of course!"

"They're not men at all."

"Choosy, aren't you?"

"For me, they're just a lot of beasts."

Pinette gave her an impersonal sort of smile. "That's
where you're wrong," he said quietly. "They're fine-looking
fellows and good soldiers. They're not up to French stand-
ards, but they're good soldiers."

"So far as I'm concerned, they're just beasts," she repeated.

"I wouldn't be too sure about that," he said, "because
if you start talking like that, you'll look like a fool when
you have to change your tune. They're conquerors, and
don't you forget it. You can't stand out against a he-man
bruiser who's just won a war. You'll have to go through
the mill like the others; there's something about them,
you know, and it'll get you. Just ask the Paris girls if I'm
not right! They're having a hell of a good time in Paris,

this very moment, lots of fun, lying on their backsides, their legs in the air."

Suddenly she shook herself free of him. "You disgust me," she said.

"What's biting you, baby?" asked Pinette.

"I'm French!" the girl said.

"The women of Paris are French too, but it's all the same in the long run."

"Leave me alone," the girl said. "I want to go away."

Pinette's face paled; he sneered.

"Don't be angry with him," Mathieu said. "He was kidding you."

"He went too far. What does he take me for?"

"It isn't very pleasant to lose a war," Mathieu said gently. "It takes time to get used to the idea of being conquered. You don't know how nice he really is, he's a lamb."

"Ha!" said Pinette. "Ha ha!"

"He's jealous," Mathieu went on.

"Of me?" the girl asked, tractable again.

"Sure! He's thinking of all the men who'll try to make up to you while he's away breaking stones somewhere."

"Or eating dandelion roots," Pinette put in, still laughing.

"I won't have you getting yourself killed," she cried.

Pinette smiled. "You're talking like a woman, like a little girl, like a teeny-weeny little girl," he concluded, and he began tickling her.

"Behave yourself!" she said, wriggling. "Oh, do behave yourself!"

"Don't you worry about him," Mathieu said, irritated. "Everything will take place quietly, and besides we have no ammunition, you know."

At one and the same moment, both turned to look at Mathieu with an expression of dislike and a sort of numb frustration as though he had prevented them from making love. Mathieu stared at Pinette without sympathy. After a moment Pinette dropped his head and began tugging moodily at a tuft of grass between his legs. A number of soldiers sauntered along the road. One of them carried a rifle; he played the fool, pretending it was a candle.

"Very, very funny!" said a dark, stocky little fellow with knock-knees.

The other took the barrel of his rifle in both hands, swung the weapon like a golf club, and slogged with the butt at a stone, which he sent flying about twenty feet. Pinette regarded their antics with a frown.

"Some of 'em getting out of hand already," he remarked.

Mathieu made no comment. The girl had taken Pinette's hand and was playing with it on her lap.

"You're wearing a wedding ring," she said.

"This the first time you've noticed it?" Pinette asked, half closing his hand.

"I noticed it before, all right. Are you married?"

"Why else would I wear a wedding ring?"

"I see," she said sadly.

"Just watch me!" Pinette said. He pulled at his finger, grimacing, wrenched off the ring, and flung it into the growing grain.

"Oh, you shouldn't have done that!" said the girl, scandalized.

He took up a knife from the table, Ivich was bleeding: he drove it into the palm of his hand, acting, acting, little gestures of trivial destruction that get you nowhere; and I took it all as a fine manifesto of freedom. He yawned.

"It was gold?"

"Yes."

She leaned forward and kissed him lightly on the lips.

Mathieu got up, then sat down again. "I'm off," he announced.

Pinette looked at him uneasily. "Oh, don't go yet."

"You don't want me."

"Stay awhile longer!" said Pinette. "You've got nothing to do."

Mathieu smiled and pointed at the girl. "She's not particularly anxious for me to stay."

"She? Of course she is, she likes you." Pinette leaned over her; there was a note of eagerness in his voice. "He's my pal. You like him, don't you?"

"Yes," said the girl.

She hates me, thought Mathieu; but he stayed. Time was standing still: it quivered and eddied above the russet plain. He knew that if he made any sharp sudden movement, he would feel it in his bones, like the twinge in an old rheumatic joint. He stretched himself on his back. The sky, the sky, pink and empty; if only one could fall headlong into the sky! But there was nothing he could do about it; we are earthbound creatures, and that is the root of all our troubles.

The four soldiers whom he had seen moving slowly along the edge of the field, had turned at its far end in order to regain the road. They were strung out in single file. They were men from an engineer outfit; Mathieu did not know them. The corporal, walking ahead of the others, looked like Pinette; like Pinette he was in his shirtsleeves and he had opened his shirt over his hairy chest. Behind him came a dark, sun-tanned fellow, his blouse thrown loosely about his shoulders; he was holding a wheatstalk in his left hand and was extracting the grain with his right. Raising it to his mouth, he stuck out his tongue and licked up the small golden seeds with pecking movements of his head. The third, taller and older than the rest, kept running his fingers through his fair hair. All of them walked forward slowly, dreamily, with the easy carriage of civilians. The blond man who had been fidgeting with his hair dropped his hands, passing them gently over his neck and shoulders as though enjoying the feel of a body that had suddenly emerged into the sunlight from its shapeless military chrysalis. Almost at the same moment they stopped, still in single file, and stood looking at Mathieu. Under those which belonged to a different age of the world's history, Mathieu felt as though he had melted into the grass; he was a meadow exposed to the fixed stare of animals.

The dark fellow said: "I've lost my belt." His voice did nothing to break the charm of the relaxed, inhuman world; the sounds it uttered were not words but just part of the rustle that made up the silence. A similar rustle came from the lips of his fair-haired companion:

"Don't worry, the Heinies would have taken it away from you."

A fourth man arrived noiselessly; he stopped and looked up, his face reflecting the sky's emptiness. "Hey!" he called. He stooped, picked a poppy, and stuck it in his mouth. As he straightened up again, he noticed that Pinette was holding the girl tight against him. He started to laugh. "Been pretty hot, huh?"

"You said it, pal," Pinette acknowledged.

"But it's cooling off now, eh?"

"Could be!"

"About time, too."

The four heads nodded; the intelligence conveyed by their gesture was peculiarly French. Then, intelligence faded; all that remained was a sense of immense leisure, and the heads continued to nod. "For the first time in their lives," thought Mathieu, "they know what it is like to rest."

They were resting from forced marches, from inspections, from maneuvers, from drilling, from furloughs, from waiting, from hoping; they were resting from the war and from a weariness more ancient still: from peace. Amid the growing crops, at the forest's edge, on the outskirts of the village, other small groups were resting too: processions of convalescent troops were roaming the countryside.

"Hey, Pirard!" the corporal shouted.

Mathieu turned his head. Pirard, Captain Mauron's orderly, a sly, brutish peasant from Brittany, stopped by the side of the road to piss. Mathieu looked at him with surprise: the man's earthy face was flushed by the setting sun, his eyes were dilated; gone was his habitual expression of distrust and shiftiness. For the first time, perhaps, he was seeing the signs written across the sky and the mystic circle of the sun. A clear stream of water jetted from between hands that looked as though they were lost in the opening of his fly.

"Hey, Pirard!"

Pirard gave a start.

"What are you doing?" the corporal asked.

"I'm taking a breath of air," Pirard said.

"You're pissing, you bastard! Can't you see there's ladies here?"

Pirard looked down at his hands, seemed surprised, and hastily buttoned up his trousers.

"I did it without thinking," he said.

"Don't mind me," said the girl.

She snuggled up against Pinette's chest and smiled at the corporal. Her skirt was above her knees; it never occurred to her to pull it down: all was innocence in this new world. They looked at her legs, but with a sort of gentle and astonished melancholy: they were angels, the expression of their faces was without emotion.

"Well, so long," said the dark-haired man, "we'll be off about our business."

"We're out on a jaunt to try to raise an appetite," the tall fair man said with a laugh.

"Here's wishing you a good one!" Mathieu said.

They laughed: everyone knew there was nothing to eat

in the village; the spare rations in the Q.M. stores had been looted early that morning.

"That's the least of our troubles."

None of them moved; they had stopped laughing now, and a flicker of uneasiness showed in the corporal's eyes. It was as though they were afraid to say good-by. Mathieu was half inclined to ask them to sit down.

"Come on, men," the corporal said, the calm authority of his tone somewhat overdone.

They started off again toward the road. Their departure tore a sudden hole in the coolness of the evening, through which trickled a few drops of time. The Germans took a leap forward; five steel fingers closed about Mathieu's heart. Then the bleeding stopped, time once again coagulated, and the scene reverted to a park in which angels were sauntering at their ease. "How empty it all is!" Mathieu thought. Some vast, brooding figure had made off, leaving Nature in charge of a few second-line soldiers. *A voice runs beneath the sun of an older world: Pan is dead,* and some such dereliction was what they felt now. But what was it that had died this time? France? Christendom? Hope? Quietly the earth and the fields had reverted to their pristine uselessness; on the surface of these meadows that they could neither cultivate nor protect, men were now but so many parasites. The world seemed made anew, yet all about the evening stood the black fringes of the coming night, and in the depths of that night a comet would strike the earth. Were they going to be bombed? It might not be long before some such ceremony might occur. Was this the first day of the world or the last? The wheat, the poppies, now growing dark as far as eye could see, the whole prospect, seemed caught in a simultaneous crisis of birth and death. Mathieu let his eye roam over this peaceful ambiguity; he thought: "It is the paradise of despair."

"Your lips are cold," Pinette said as he leaned over the girl, kissing her. "Do you feel cold?" he asked her.

"No."

"Do you like me to kiss you?"

"Yes, very much."

"Then why are your lips cold?"

"Is it true they rape the women?" she asked.

"You're crazy."

"Kiss me!" she said passionately. "I don't want to think about anything any more." She took his head between her hands and fell back upon the grass, pulling him down upon her.

Very quietly Mathieu rose and moved away. As he crossed the field, he caught a glimpse of one of the angels sauntering along the road, which still shone white between the dark stains of the poplars. The couple lay hidden in the dark grasses. Soldiers passed, carrying bunches of flowers, One of them, as he walked, raised the bouquet he carried to his face, buried his nose in the flowers, and breathed in, with their fragrance, his idleness, his pain, and that sense of superfluity which nothing seemed to justify. The corrosion of the night lay on flowers and faces; in the darkness they all looked alike. "I am like them," Mathieu mused. He walked on a little way, saw a star come out, and brushed past a shadowy stroller who was whistling. The man turned his head; Mathieu saw his eyes, and they exchanged a smile—one of those smiles he had seen yesterday, a smile of friendship.

"It's chilly," said the man.

"Yes," Mathieu answered, "it's getting cold."

There being nothing more to say, the other moved on. Mathieu looked after him. Must men lose everything, even hope, he wondered, before you could read in their eyes all that they might gain? Pinette was busy making love; Guiccioli and Latex were lying dead drunk on the floor of the mayor's office; along the roads, solitary angels walked at leisure with only their pain for company. "No one needs me." He sat down at the edge of the road because he knew nowhere else for him to go. Night entered into him through mouth and eyes, through nose and ears. He was no one now, he was nothing now—nothing but misery and darkness. The thought of Charlot came to him and he jumped to his feet; he thought of Charlot alone with his fear, and he felt ashamed. All the time I was indulging in romantic melancholy among those drunken swine while Charlot was alone and humble and afraid, and I might have helped him.

Charlot, bending over his book, was seated just where Mathieu had left him. Mathieu went up to him and ruffled his hair.

"You're ruining your eyes."

"I'm not reading," Charlot protested. "I'm thinking." He had raised his head, and there was the hint of a smile on his thick lips.

"What are you thinking about?"

"About my shop. I wonder whether it's been looted."

"That's not very likely," Mathieu assured him. He pointed to the darkened windows of the *mairie*. "What's going on in there?"

"I don't know," Charlot answered. "There hasn't been a sound for some time."

Mathieu sat down on a step. "Not feeling too good, eh?"

Charlot smiled sadly. "Was it because of me you came back?" he asked.

"I was feeling bored. I thought you might feel inclined for a little company. I certainly need it."

Charlot shook his head but said nothing.

"Would you like me to go away?" Mathieu asked.

"No," said Charlot, "I don't mind you being here. But you can't help me. What can you say? That the Germans aren't savages? That a fellow must keep his courage up?

I know all that crap!" Sighing, he put the book down beside him with great care. "If you aren't a Jew," Charlot
said, "you can't possibly understand." He laid his hand on
Mathieu's knee and added, almost apologetically: "It's not
me that's frightened, it's my race deep down in me. There's
nothing I can do about that."

Mathieu was silent. They sat there side by side, saying
nothing, the one without any hope, the other powerless to
help, both waiting for the darkness to descend upon them.

It was the hour at which objects overflow their contours
and fuse together in the fluffy shades of evening; the windows slid with motionless movement into the dusk; the
room was a pinnace adrift, the whisky bottle an Aztec
god. Philippe was a long, gray weed, powerless to
frighten; love was much more than love, and friendship
was not quite friendship. Daniel, invisible in the shadows,
was talking of friendship; he was no more than a calm,
warm voice. He paused for breath and Philippe took advantage of the silence to say: "How dark it is! Don't you
think we might turn on the lights?"

"If the current isn't cut off," Daniel said dryly.

Daniel rose to his feet with an ill grace: the moment
was come when he must submit to the ordeal of light. He
opened the window, leaned out above the emptiness below, and breathed in the violet fragrance of the silence.
How often, in this same place, I have longed to escape,
and have heard the sound of mounting steps trampling
upon my thoughts!

The night was gentle and mild; the flesh of night, so
often wounded by the darkness, had healed. A virgin
night, deep and profound, a lovely night with never a
man to be seen, an exquisite blood orange without a seed
in it. Regretfully he closed the shutters and turned the
switch; the room leaped from the shadows, the various
objects took on a familiar identity. Philippe's face pressed

against Daniel's eyes. Within the focus of his vision, Daniel felt the movement of this magnified head, precisely defined, freshly severed, disconcerted; its two bewildered eyes held his own fascinated as though he were seeing it for the first time. "I've got to play a cautious game," he thought. Conscious of a feeling of embarrassment, he raised his hand as though to dissipate a phantasmagoria; then he pinched the lapel of his coat between his fingers and smiled: he dreaded being unmasked.

"What are you staring at me like that for? Do you think I'm handsome?"

"Very handsome!" Philippe said in a colorless voice.

Daniel turned to the mirror and, not without pleasure, studied his dark, handsome face. Philippe, his eyes lowered, was sniggering behind his hand.

"You're giggling like a schoolgirl."

Philippe stopped.

Daniel insisted: "What are you giggling at?"

"Nothing special."

The boy was half drunk with wine, suspense, weariness. Now is the moment, Daniel thought, he is ripe for plucking. Provided he treated the whole thing *as a joke*, a sort of schoolboy prank, Philippe would sink down on the divan and suffer himself to be petted, to be kissed behind the ear; any resistance he put up would dissolve in helpless laughter. Sharply Daniel turned his back on him and strode across the room: too soon, much too soon, I mustn't make a fool of myself! He might easily run away in the morning and kill himself, unless he tries to kill *me*. Before turning toward Philippe, Daniel buttoned his jacket and smoothed it down over his thighs, the better to conceal the evidence of his state.

"Well, that's that!" he said.

"Well?" said Philippe.

"Look me in the eye."

Daniel stared hard at the boy and nodded with satisfaction. "You're no coward," he said slowly, "I'm convinced of that." He extended a forefinger and tapped Philippe on the chest. "You wouldn't run away because you were panicked? Come, that's not the sort of thing you'd do. You just turned your back on the whole rat race; you left them to settle it without you. Why should you get yourself killed for the sake of France, eh? Why indeed? You don't care a damn about France, do you? You don't care a damn, you young scamp!"

Philippe nodded; Daniel resumed pacing up and down the room.

"You're through with all that," he said with nervous gaiety. "The game's up, you're washed up with all that! Well, you've had a stroke of luck that never came my way when I was your age. Still," he added hastily, waving his hand, "I'm not referring to our meeting. Your luck was a *historical* coincidence: you want to undermine bourgeois morality, don't you? Well, here are the Germans to lend you a helping hand. They'll make a clean sweep of the board; you'll see respectable householders crawling to lick the conquerors' boots and inviting them to kick their fat arses; you'll see your stepfather grovel in the dust. He's the man who was really beaten in this war, and will you have a chance to crow over him!"

He laughed till the tears came. "Oh, what a spring cleaning there's going to be!" he said. Then, swinging round toward Philippe, "You'll have to learn to love them," he finished.

Philippe, startled, asked: "Who?"

"The Germans. They are our allies."

"Love the Germans? But—I don't know them."

"We'll get to know them, never fear. We shall dine with the *Gauleiter*, with the field-marshal. They'll drive us around in their great black Mercedes cars while Parisians go on foot."

Philippe stifled a yawn; Daniel, shaking him by the

shoulders, said with intense seriousness: "You've got to love the Germans. That will be the first of your intellectual and spiritual exercises."

The boy showed no sign of enthusiasm. Daniel let him go, flung out his arms, and, with mock solemnity, *"Voici venir le temps des assassins!"* he declaimed. *"Behold the era of assassins comes."*

Philippe yawned for the second time; Daniel could see his pointed tongue.

"I'm sleepy," Philippe said apologetically. "I haven't shut my eyes for two nights."

Daniel was half inclined to show anger, but he, too, felt exhausted, as always after each new encounter. Desire for Philippe had left him with a sensation of heaviness in the region of the groin. He longed suddenly to be alone.

"I'll leave you to yourself, then," he said. "You'll find some pajamas in the chest of drawers."

"Thanks all the same," the boy answered feebly, "but I ought to be getting home."

Daniel smiled at him. "Just as you choose; but you risk meeting a patrol and God knows what they'll do to you: you're as pretty as a girl, and all Germans are homosexual. Besides, even if you do get home safely, you'll only find what you're running away from. Aren't there photographs of your stepfather on the walls? Doesn't the room reek of your mother's scent?"

Philippe seemed not to have heard. He made an effort to get up but fell back on the divan. "Haah," he said in a drowsy voice. Then he looked at Daniel with a puzzled smile. "I think it would be better if I stayed here."

"Good night, then."

"Good night," said Philippe with another yawn.

Daniel crossed the room. As he passed the fireplace he pressed on a panel, and one of the bookshelves turned on itself, revealing a row of yellow-bound books.

"That," he said, "is the Inferno. Later on, you must read all these books: they're full of you."

"Of me?" said Philippe, not understanding.

"Well, of case documents about people like you."

He readjusted the shelf and opened the door. The key was still on the outside. He tossed it across to Philippe. "If you're afraid of ghosts or burglars, you can lock yourself in," he said mockingly. Then he shut the door behind him, groped his way in the darkness to the far end of his bedroom, switched on the reading-lamp, and sat down on his bed. Alone at last! Six hours of walking the streets and four more hard at it playing the part of Mephistopheles. I'm all in! He sighed with the sheer pleasure of solitude, with pleasure at the thought that there was no one to hear him; he moaned softly: "My testicles ache." Delighted that no one could see him, he pulled a mournful face. Then he smiled and stretched himself out as though in a lovely hot bath: he was accustomed to these long fits of desire in the abstract, to these futile and furtive erections; he knew from experience that he would suffer less if he lay down. The lamp threw a round patch of light on the ceiling; the pillows felt cool. Motionless, dead, smiling, Daniel lay there at rest. "Peace, perfect peace; I have locked the front door; the key is in my pocket. Besides, he's dropping with fatigue; he won't wake up till midday. A pacifist! Really! On the whole, though, I haven't got much out of the adventure yet. There must be some weak spot on which I can play if only I can find it." With the Nathanaels and the Rimbauds Daniel was on his own ground, but he found the younger generation disconcerting. "What an extraordinary mix-up—narcissism and social theories— it just doesn't make sense." All the same, by and large, things hadn't gone too badly: he had the boy safe there under lock and key. If the worst came to the worst, he could always play the card of systematic debauching. It flattered the victim, and it usually worked. "Sooner or later, I'll get you," he thought, "and then I'll put your principles through the mangle, dear angel-face. Social theories! You'll see what will become of them!"

The coldly calculated enthusiasm in which he had been indulging lay heavy on his stomach. What he needed was a good strong dose of cynicism to clear his emotional bowels. "If I can keep him for a good long time, I'm in luck: I need a quiet life, with a little bit of relaxation always on tap when I feel like it. I'm through with the old racketing round with Graff and Toto, with my 'aunt' from Honfleur, with Marius and 'Sens Interdit': I'm through with hanging round the Gare de l'Est on the look out for squalid little soldiers on leave with their smelly feet; I'm going to settle down (*my days of Terror are over!*)." He sat up on the bed and began to undress. This time, he decided, it was going to be a serious attachment. He felt sleepy, he was calm. He got up to fetch his pajamas, clearly conscious that he felt calm. "It's extraordinary that I'm not all on edge," he thought. At that precise moment he got the feeling that there was somebody behind him. He swung round. There was nobody, but the calmness of his mood was shattered, rent in two. "Just the same old business over again!" He knew it all backwards, he could foresee precisely what would happen, he could reckon minute by minute the years of misery that lay ahead, the daily toll of long, long years heavy with boredom and hopelessness, and, at the end of them, the squalid, inevitable end: it was all there. He looked at the shut door, he breathed heavily. "This time," he thought, "it'll be the end of me," and in his mouth he could taste the bitterness of the agonies still to come.

"It's a real first-class blaze!" said an old man.

Everybody was out on the road, soldiers, old men, and girls. The schoolmaster pointed with his stick toward the horizon. Perched on its ferrule was the glow of an artificial sun, of a ball of fire dimming the pale dawn. Roberville was burning.

"It's a real first-class blaze."

"You bet!"

The old men stood, their hands behind their backs, rocking a little on their feet, and saying "Sure is!" and "You bet!" in their deep, calm voices. Charlot dropped Mathieu's arm.

"It's awful!" he said.

"That's what always happens to us country folk," one of the veterans replied. "When it isn't war, it's hail or frost. There's no peace anywhere for country folk."

The soldiers were petting the girls in the darkness and making them giggle. Behind him Mathieu could hear the shouts of urchins playing in the abandoned alleys of the village. A woman came forward; she was holding a baby in her arms.

"Did the French start the fire?" she asked.

"Get wise, Ma," Lubéron said, "it's the Heinies."

One of the old men shook his head, incredulous. "The Heinies?"

"Yes, Heinies, Boches!"

The old man seemed unconvinced. "We had the Boches here in the other war and they didn't do much harm; they're decent fellows."

"Why should we Frenchmen go and do a thing like that?" Lubéron demanded indignantly. "We're not a lot of savages."

"Why should *they* have done it? What'll they do for billets now?"

A bearded soldier raised his hand. "Probably some of our bastards have been playing the fool and firing at 'em. One man dead is enough for the Heinies to burn down a whole village."

The woman turned to him with a worried look. "And what about you?" she asked.

"How d'you mean, what about us?"

"You're not going to play the fool?"

The soldiers laughed. "Don't you worry your head about that," one of them said with conviction. "We know what's good for us."

They exchanged conspiratorial looks under cover of their laughter. "Oh yes, we know what's good for us!"

"We're not likely to go hunting for trouble, right on the eve of peace."

The woman stroked her child's head. "Is it really going to be peace?" she asked in quavering tones.

"Yes, it's peace all right," said the schoolmaster with conviction. "It's peace. That's what we've got to remember."

A ripple passed through the crowd. Mathieu could hear a confused medley of almost happy voices behind him.

"It's peace, it's peace!"

They watched Roberville burning and kept repeating: "The war's over; it's peace." Mathieu looked at the road: Two hundred yards ahead it emerged from the darkness, flowed, a white, glimmering stream, to his feet, and passed beyond, to lap against the houses with their closed shutters: a lovely road, a road of adventure and danger, a road on which there was no turning back. It had recaptured the untamed wildness of the rivers of antiquity; tomorrow it would float into the village bearing ships filled with murderers. Charlot sighed and Mathieu silently pressed his arm.

"There they are!" said a voice.

"What do you mean?"

"The Heinies, I tell you, there they are!"

There was movement in the darkness. Scattered skirmishers, their rifles under their arms, were emerging one by one from the dark waters of the night. They advanced slowly, cautiously, ready to open fire.

"There they are! There they are!"

Mathieu felt himself jostled, pushed about. The crowd swayed around him with an uncertain but ample movement.

"Hey, boys, let's get the hell out of here!" cried Lubéron.

"Are you crazy? They've seen us. All we can do is wait for 'em."

"Wait for 'em? They'll shoot!"

A great sigh of hopelessness rose from the crowd. The schoolmaster's thin voice cut through the stillness: "You women move to the rear! You men, drop your rifles if you have them. Put your hands up."

"You bastards," Mathieu exclaimed, beside himself with anger, "can't you see they're French?"

"French . . ."

There was a pause, a marking time, and then someone said defiantly: "French? Where from?"

They were French, right enough, fifteen men under the command of a lieutenant. Their faces were set and grimy. The village folk lined the edges of the road and looked at them with unfriendly eyes as they approached. French they might be, but they were from a strange and dangerous country. With rifles. In the dead of night. Frenchmen creeping out of the shadows, out of the war, bringing the war with them into this village to which peace had already come. French. From Paris, they might be, or Bordeaux, only a degree less harmful than Germans. They came on between twin hedges of hostile apathy, looking at nobody; the expression on their faces was one of pride. The lieutenant gave an order and they halted.

"What division do you belong to?" he asked.

The question was addressed to nobody in particular. It was met by silence, and he repeated it.

"Sixty-first," said a surly voice.

"Where are your officers?"

"They beat it."

"What do you mean?"

"They scrammed!" the soldier explained with obvious satisfaction.

The lieutenant drew his lips together and pressed his inquiry no further. "Where is the *mairie*?"

Charlot, always willing to oblige, stepped forward. "On the left, at far end of the street. You have about a hundred yards to go."

The officer swung round suddenly and looked him up and down. "Is that the way you speak to an officer? Have you forgotten how to stand at attention? Would it choke you to say 'sir'?"

For a few moments no one spoke. The lieutenant was looking hard at Charlot. The men crowded about Mathieu were looking at the lieutenant. Charlot straightened up.

"I beg your pardon, sir."

"That's better." The lieutenant looked contemptuously at the circle of faces, motioned with his hand, and the little group of soldiers moved on without a word. The men of the Sixty-first watched the darkness swallow them up.

"I thought we were through with officers," Lubéron said with an effort.

"Through with officers?" came a voice, bitter and exacerbated. "You don't know officers; they'll frig us to the very end."

One of the women asked suddenly: "They won't start any of their fighting here, will they?"

There was laughter in the crowd, and Charlot said good-humoredly:

"Not on your life, Ma; they're not crazy."

Silence once more: every face was turned to the north. Roberville, isolated, out of reach, already legendary, was burning, as ill luck would have it, in a foreign country, on the other side of the frontier. Brawling, slaughter, fire, destruction—well, that's just too bad for Roberville, but that can't happen to us. Slowly, nonchalantly, men began to drift away from the crowd and move toward the village. They had better get their beauty sleep so as to be fit when the Heinies turned up at dawn.

"What rubbish!" Mathieu thought.

"Well," said Charlot, "I'm off."

"Going to turn in?"

"Seems to be the general idea."

"Want me to come with you?"

"Don't bother," said Charlot, yawning.

He moved off and Mathieu was left alone. "We're slaves," Mathieu thought, "no more nor less than slaves." But he felt no anger at his companions, it wasn't their fault. They had served ten months at hard labor; now there had been a transfer of authority, and they were about to pass into the hands of German officers; they would salute the *Feldwebel* and the *Oberleutnant*. It wouldn't make much difference; the officer caste is international, their sentence at hard labor would go on, that was all there was to it. "It's at myself that I feel angry," he thought, but he resented doing so, because it was a way of setting himself up above the rest. To be indulgent to others and severe with oneself was just another trick of pride. At once innocent and guilty, too severe, yet too indulgent, impotent yet responsible, part of the general whole yet rejected by each individual, perfectly lucid yet utterly deceived, enslaved yet sovereign, I'm just like everybody else.

Somebody clutched his arm. It was the girl from the post office. Her eyes were blazing.

"Stop him if you're his friend!"

"Eh?"

"He wants to fight on. Stop him!"

Pinette appeared behind her, pale, his eyes dead, with a sinister grin.

"What do you want me to do, dear?" Mathieu asked her.

"I've just told you, he wants to fight, I heard him say so. He went to the captain and told him he wanted to fight."

"What captain?"

"The one that went by with his men."

Pinette chuckled, his hands clasped behind his back.

"That was no captain, he was a lieutenant."

"Is it true that you want to fight on?" Mathieu asked him.

"You make me sick, the whole lot of you!" he answered.

"You see!" the girl said. "You see! He said he wanted to fight. I heard him."

"But who said there's going to be any fighting?"

"Didn't you see them? They've got murder in their eyes. He"—she pointed to Pinette—"look at him, he frightens me, he's a monster!"

Mathieu shrugged his shoulders. "What do you want me to do?"

"Aren't you his friend?"

"That's just why I can't do anything."

"If you're his friend, you ought to tell him that he has no right to get himself killed." She clung to Mathieu's arm. "He has no right to!"

"Why not?"

"You know perfectly well."

Pinette's smile was cruel and insensitive. "I'm a soldier, it's my job to fight; that's what soldiers are for."

"Then you shouldn't have come after me!" She seized him by the arm and added in a trembling voice: "You belong to me!"

Pinette shook himself free. "I don't belong to anyone."

"Yes, you do!" she insisted, "you belong to me!" She turned on Mathieu, passionately summoning him to her aid. "*You* tell him! Tell him that he has no right to get himself killed! It's your duty to tell him that."

Mathieu said nothing. She advanced upon him, her face ablaze. For the first time Mathieu saw her as desirable.

"You call yourself his friend and you don't care whether he gets hurt or not!"

"Certainly I care."

"You think it's a fine thing for a kid like him to stand up to a whole army? It's not as if he could do any good! You know perfectly well that no one's going to fight now."

"I know," said Mathieu.

"Then why don't you tell him?"

"Because he hasn't asked me for my opinion."

"Henri, I implore you, ask him what he thinks: he's older than you are, he must know."

Pinette raised his hand to refuse her request, but an idea occurred to him and he let his arm fall to his side, screwing up his eyes with a sly expression that Mathieu had never seen in them before.

"You want me to discuss with him what I mean to do?"

"Yes, since you don't love me enough to listen to me."

"All right, then, I will. But you beat it first."

"Why?"

"I'm not going to talk to him in front of you."

"But why?"

"Because! This isn't a woman's business."

"It's *my* business, since it concerns you."

"Hell!" he said, exasperated, "you give me a pain in the balls." He nudged Mathieu in the ribs.

"There's no need for you to go away," Mathieu said quickly; "we'll go a few steps down the road; you wait here."

"Oh yes, and then you won't come back."

"You're crazy!" Pinette said. "Where do you think we're going? We'll be within twenty yards of you, you can see us the whole time."

"And if your friend tells you not to fight, you'll listen to him?"

"Sure," said Pinette. "I always do what he tells me."

She clung to Pinette's neck. "Swear you'll come back, even if you decide to fight? Even if your friend advises you to? Anything would be better than not seeing you again. Will you swear?"

"All right, all right."

"Say that you swear! Say: 'I swear.'"

"I swear," said Pinette.

"And you," she said to Mathieu, "swear you'll bring him back to me?"

"Of course."

"Don't be gone long," she said, "and don't go far."

They went a few yards up the road in the direction of Roberville. Trees and bushes mottled it with shadow. After a moment Mathieu turned his head: the girl from the post office was standing where they had left her, tense and upright, almost obliterated by the night, trying to make them out in the darkness. Another step and she would vanish altogether. At that very moment her voice came to them:

"Don't go too far, I can't see you!"

Pinette began to laugh. He made a funnel of his hands and shouted back to her: "Oho! Ohoho! Ohohoho!"

They walked on. Pinette was still laughing.

"She wanted me to believe she was a virgin; that's what all the trouble's about."

"Ah!"

"That's her story anyhow. I can't say I noticed it myself."

"Some girls are like that; you think they're lying and then you find they really are virgins."

"Says you!" Pinette chuckled.

"It does happen."

"Oh, yeah? Even if it does happen, it would certainly be a funny coincidence if it happened to me."

Mathieu smiled but said nothing; Pinette jerked his head up.

"Look here, you know! I didn't force her. When a girl's serious, she can always keep a guy at a distance. Take my wife, for instance: we both wanted it bad, but there was nothing doing before we got spliced." He clinched his words with a movement of the hand. "Cross my heart! That little piece had ants you know where; I was just doing her a favor."

"What if you've knocked her up?"

"Me?" said Pinette, flabbergasted. "You don't know what you're talking about! I'm one of your careful sort. My wife wouldn't have one because we were too poor, so I got in the habit of watching my step. Oh no," he said, "no. She's had her fun, I've had mine; we're quits."

"If it really was the first time," Mathieu said, "it would be unusual if she had much fun."

"Well then, that's just too bad!" Pinette answered curtly. "In that case it's her own fault."

They were silent. After a moment Mathieu raised his head and tried to see Pinette's face in the darkness.

"Is it true they're going to put up a fight?"

"Yes."

"In the village?"

"Where else do you suggest?"

Mathieu's heart contracted. Then, suddenly, he thought of Longin vomiting under the tree, of Guiccioli sprawling on the floor, of Lubéron watching Roberville burning, and saying: "This means peace!" He laughed angrily.

"What are you laughing at?"

"I was thinking of the boys," said Mathieu, "and of what a hell of a surprise they've got coming to them."

"You said it!"

"Is the lieutenant willing to take you on?"

"If I've got a rifle. He said: 'Come along if you have a rifle.'"

"Your mind's made up?"

Pinette laughed savagely.

"It's—" Mathieu began.

Pinette swung round on him. "I'm of age. I don't need any advice."

"Good," said Mathieu. "Well, let's go back."

"No," said Pinette, "let's go on."

They walked on a few steps. Suddenly Pinette said: "Hey, jump into the ditch!"

"What?"

"Do as I say—jump!"

They jumped, scrambled up the bank, and found themselves in the middle of a wheatfield.

"There's a path over there to the left that leads back to the village," Pinette explained.

Mathieu stumbled and fell on one knee. "What's all this damned nonsense about?" he asked.

"I just can't stand the sight of her now," Pinette answered.

They could hear a woman's voice coming from the direction of the road. "Henri! Henri!"

"She sticks to me like a leech!" Pinette said.

"Henri! Don't leave me!"

Pinette seized Mathieu by the arm and pulled him down. They lay in the wheat. They could hear the girl running along the road. A wheat ear rasped Mathieu's cheek; some small animal scuttled away between his hands.

"Henri! Don't leave me! You can do whatever you like, but don't leave me, come back! Henri, I won't say a thing, I promise, but please come back, don't leave me like this! Henri-i-i-i-i! Don't go away without giving me a kiss!"

She passed close by them, panting.

"Lucky the moon's not up yet," Pinette whispered.

The smell of the earth was strong in Mathieu's nostrils; earth lay soft and damp beneath his hands. He heard Pinette's hoarse breathing and thought: "They're going to fight in the village." The girl cried out to them twice more, her voice hoarse with anguish; then suddenly she turned on her heel and started to run back the way she had come.

"She loves you," said Mathieu.

"Oh, to hell with her!" replied Pinette.

They got up. Away to the northeast Mathieu could see, just above the line of the wheat, a ball of flickering fire. *One man dead is enough for the Heinies to burn down a whole village.*

"Well, what about it?" Pinette challenged him. "You can console her, can't you?"

"She gets on my nerves," said Mathieu. "Besides, I'm not particularly interested in tail just now. But still, it was wrong of you to hump her if you meant to drop her like a hot brick."

"Oh, shit!" said Pinette. "With you, a feller's always in the wrong."

"There's the path," said Mathieu. They walked for a while.

Pinette said: "Look, the moon!"

Mathieu, looking up, saw a second fire on the horizon, this time a blaze of silver.

"We'll make a nice bunch of corpses!" Pinette remarked.

"I don't think they'll get here before tomorrow morning," Mathieu said. A moment later, without looking at Pinette, he added: "You'll be killed to the last man."

"That's war," Pinette said hoarsely.

"You've got it wrong," said Mathieu. "It ceases to be war."

"No armistice signed yet."

Mathieu took Pinette's hand and squeezed it gently; it was icy. "Are you sure you want to get bumped off?"

"I don't want to get bumped off; I want to bump off a couple of God-damned Germans."

"The two things go together."

Pinette withdrew his hand without replying. Mathieu wanted to speak. "He's going to die for nothing," he mused, and the idea stuck in his throat. But suddenly he felt cold, and he remained silent. "What right have I to stop him? What have I to offer him?" He turned his head, looked at Pinette, and began to whistle softly. Pinette was far out of his reach, marching blindly through the darkness of his last night on earth, marching but not advancing; he had already reached his destination; his birth and his death had swung full circle and met. He was marching under the moon, with the imminent sun already shining on his wounds. Over and done with was Pinette's pursuit of Pinette; now he was wholly himself, a Pinette entire, close-packed in the final reckoning. Mathieu sighed and silently took his arm, the arm of a young subway employee, a noble, gentle, brave, and tender youth who had been killed June 18, 1940. Pinette smiled at him; from the depths of his past Pinette smiled at him; Mathieu saw the smile and felt utterly alone. I can break the shell that separates us only if I wish for myself no other future than his, no other sun than that on which tomorrow he will look for the last time. In order to share his time and his very minutes, I would have to will to die the same death.

Very slowly he said: "It's I, really, who ought to go to the slaughter in your place. After all, I have so much less reason for living."

Pinette looked at him happily; once again they had become almost contemporaries. "You?"

"I have been on the wrong track ever since the word go."

"Oh, well," said Pinette, "all you need do is to come along with me. We can wipe the slate clean and start again."

Mathieu smiled. "You can wipe the slate clean, but you can't begin again," he said.

Pinette put his arm about Mathieu's neck. "Delarue, my dear old pal," he said passionately, "come with me. It'll be wonderful having you, you know, the two of us; I don't know the other guys."

Mathieu hesitated. To die, to enter into the eternity of a life that was already dead, to die together. . . . He shook his head. "No."

"Why not?"

"I don't want to."

"Scared?"

"No, it just seems God-damned stupid, that's all."

To cut one's own hand with a knife, to throw away one's wedding ring, to shoot off a rifle at the Heinies—so what? To smash, to destroy, that was no solution; to act on mere impulse was not freedom. If only I could be *humble!*

"Why is it God-damned stupid?" Pinette asked irritably. "I want to bump off a Heinie; there's nothing so God-damned stupid about that."

"You can bump off a hundred, but we've lost the war just the same."

"I shall save my honor!"

"In whose eyes?"

Pinette walked on silently with lowered head.

"Even if they put up a monument to you," said Mathieu, "even if they laid your ashes under the Arc de Triomphe, would that be worth the burning of a village?"

"Let it burn," said Pinette. "That's war."

"There are women and children in it."

"There's nothing to stop them from running off into the fields. Ah," he said with a face like an idiot's, "the sooner the better!"

Mathieu laid his hand on his shoulder. "You love your wife as much as all that?"

"What's she got to do with it?"

"Isn't it for her sake you want to bump off your Heinies?" asked Mathieu.

"Don't give me that bullshit!" Pinette shouted. "All you do is turn round in a circle raping fleas and buggering ants. If that's all an education does for a guy, I'm glad I'm not educated."

They had reached the first houses of the village. Suddenly Mathieu started to shout in his turn. "I'm fed up!" he cried. "I'm fed up! Fed up!"

Pinette stopped and stared at him. "What's biting you?"

"Nothing," said Mathieu, dumbfounded at his own behavior. "I'm going mad."

Pinette shrugged his shoulders. "I want to look in at the schoolhouse," he said. "The rifles are in the classroom."

The door was open; they went in. Soldiers were sleeping on the tiled floor of the entry. Pinette took his flashlight from his pocket; a little circle of light showed on the wall.

"In there."

Rifles were lying about in piles. Pinette took one of them, looked it over by the light of his torch, put it down, and took another, which he examined with care. Mathieu felt ashamed of the way he had yelled; the essential thing is to wait and to keep one's brain clear. To save oneself for a good opportunity. Flying off the handle doesn't help. He smiled at Pinette.

"You look as though you were choosing a cigar."

Pinette, satisfied at last, slung one of the rifles across his shoulder. "This'll do. Let's get going."

"Give me your flashlight," said Mathieu.

He shone the beam over the rifles. There was something tedious about the look of them, something administrative, like so many typewriters. It was difficult to believe that one could kill a man with things like that. He bent down and picked one up at random.

"What are you doing?" Pinette asked with surprise.

"Can't you see?" Mathieu answered. "I'm taking a rifle."

"No!" said the woman, and slammed the door in his face.

He stood there on the steps, his arms dangling; he wore the cowed look that came over him when he could no longer bully someone. "Old witch!" he muttered, loud enough for me to hear but not loud enough for her to hear, too. No, my poor Jacques, not "old witch," anything but that. Look down with those blue eyes of yours, look down between your feet, where justice, that lovely masculine toy, lies shattered; come back to the car with that step of yours which is so infinitely melancholy. It's up to God to settle accounts with you, but you'll manage to come out on the right side at the Day of Judgment. (He went back to the car with that step of his which was so infinitely melancholy.) No, not "old witch"; he should have found a different epithet, he should have said "old carp," "old cow," "old so-and-so," but not "old witch." You envy him his knowledge of slang; no, if he had said nothing at all, these people would have opened their doors to us then, would have given us their bed, their linen, their very shirts. He would have sat down on the edge of the bed, with his great hand on the red counterpane, he would have blushed and said: "They take us for man and wife, Odette," and I should have said nothing. He would have gone on: "I'll sleep on the floor," and I should have said: "Nonsense, it can't be helped, a night's soon over, what does it matter? We'll sleep in the same bed. Come, Jacques, come, seal up my eyes, crush my thoughts, be the man in occupation, lie heavy upon me, be exigent, possessive, don't leave me alone with him. He was coming now, descending the steps, so transparent, so foresee-able, that he was like a memory. You will sniff, with a

lift of the right eyebrow; you will drum with your fingers
on the hood, you will look me through and through—but
it was *his* sniff, *his* lift of the eyebrow, *his* searching and
pensive look. There he was, leaning over her, a drifting
presence in the deep, animal darkness which she seemed
to be, she stroking him with her fingertips, he a drifting
shade, unsubstantial, old, a thing of habit. I can see
through him the vague, solid mass of the farmhouse, the
road, the prowling dog; everything is new, everything
except him. He is not a husband at all, he is merely a
general idea; I call to him, but he gives me no help. She
smiled at him because you must always smile at them; she
offered him the sweet tranquillity of nature, the confident
optimism of a happy woman; but deep down she was
melting into the darkness, liquefying, merging into the
vast femininity of the night where, somewhere in her
heart, Mathieu lay concealed. He did not smile, he rubbed
his nose, with a gesture that he had borrowed from his
brother. She gave a start. What have my thoughts been
doing? I must have been dozing on my feet, it's too soon
yet for me to be an old and cynical woman, I've been
dreaming. The words sank back into the dark obscurity
of her throat, all was forgotten, nothing remained on the
surface but a flow of shared and tranquil generalities. She
asked her question cheerfully.

"Well?"

"Nothing doing! They say they have no barn but I saw
it with my own eyes, over there, on the other side of the
yard. Do I look like a highwayman?"

"After fourteen hours on the road," she said, "I don't
suppose we are a very reassuring sight."

As he looked at her with careful scrutiny, she felt her
nose gleam like a lighthouse beneath his gaze. He's going
to tell me that my nose is shiny.

He said: "You've got pouches under your eyes, poor
darling; you must be all in."

With a quick movement she took her compact from her bag and examined herself mercilessly in the mirror. I look a perfect sight! In the light of the moon her face seemed as though covered with black splotches. I don't mind looking ugly, but I can't stand being dirty!

"What do we do now?" Jacques asked uncertainly. She had taken out her powder-puff and was dabbing at cheeks and eyes.

"That's for you to say," she said.

"I was asking you."

Catching at the hand that held the powder-puff, he kept it and imprisoned it with smiling authority. "I was asking your advice, for once I was asking your advice, poor dear, and you know perfectly well that if I told you what I thought, you wouldn't take the slightest notice of it." But he had to have other people's ideas to criticize in order to find out what he was thinking himself. She said the first thing that came into her head.

"Let's drive on; perhaps we will find more friendly people."

"No, thank you! Once is enough for me. How I hate peasants!" he said violently.

"Why shouldn't we drive all night?"

He stared at her. "All night?"

"We could reach Grenoble tomorrow morning, we could rest at the Bleriots'. Then we could start off again in the afternoon and sleep at Castellane. We should be in Juan by the day after tomorrow."

"Not on your life!" Then very seriously he added: "I am far too tired. I should fall asleep at the wheel and we would land in the ditch."

"We could take turns driving."

"Darling, the sooner you realize that I'll never let you drive at night, the better. With your shortsightedness, it would be sheer murder. The roads are packed with carts, trucks, and cars, driven by people who never handled a steering-wheel in their lives and who just started off wildly in a panic. No, you need a man's nerves for this kind of job."

Shutters were flung open; a head appeared at a window.

"Oh, shut up, will you? We're trying to get some sleep," a rough voice shouted. "For God's sake, go somewhere else and talk!"

"Many thanks, monsieur," Jacques replied with biting irony, "you are very polite and most hospitable."

He flung himself into the car, slammed the door, and started up the engine, making as much noise as possible. Odette looked at him out of the corner of her eye: much better say nothing; he's doing fifty at the very least, without lights, because he's afraid of the airplanes; luckily the moon is full. She was thrown against the door.

"What are you doing?"

Scarcely slowing down, he had swung the car round into a side road. They drove on for a while, then he braked sharply and brought the car to a standstill, some distance up the road, under a clump of trees.

"We're going to sleep here."

"Here?"

He said nothing, but opened the door and got out. She followed him. It was almost chilly.

"How about sleeping in the open?"

"No."

Looking regretfully at the soft, dark grass, she bent down and touched it as though it had been water.

"Oh, Jacques, it would be lovely out here. We could bring a cushion and rugs from the car."

"No," he repeated, and added with determination: "We'll sleep in the car; there's no knowing who's prowling the roads in times like these."

She watched him walking up and down, his hands in his pockets. His step was young and jaunty. The wind was playing a devil's tattoo in the trees. Jacques seemed compelled to keep time to it. The face he turned to her was old and worried; there was a shifty look in his eyes: something was wrong; it was almost as though he were ashamed. He turned back toward the car. The youth and magic of the leafy music seemed to possess him, to have run into his feet, so that he moved with an air of gaiety. He hates sleeping in the car. Whom is he punishing, himself or me? She felt guilty, though she did not know of what.

"Why are you looking so sore?" he asked. "Here we are, on the open road, headed for adventure. You ought to be satisfied."

She looked down. I never wanted to come away, Jacques; the Germans don't bother me, I wanted to stay in my own home. If the war lasts, we shall be separated from him, we shan't know whether he is alive or dead. What she actually said was:

"I am thinking of my brother and of Mathieu."

"At this moment," Jacques said with a sour smile, "Raoul is in bed at Carcassonne."

"But Mathieu isn't. . . ."

"You'd better get this into your head," Jacques said with a flare of temper, "my brother is in a second-line formation, so he's in no danger. The worst that can happen to him is to be taken prisoner. In your eyes all soldiers are heroes, but that is where you are wrong, my dear. Mathieu is pushing a pen in some headquarters or other; he is having an easier time than if he were out of the battle zone altogether, probably a much easier time than we're having at this moment. He's got what the army calls a soft job, and very glad I am for his sake."

"It's not much fun being a prisoner," Odette said without raising her eyes.

He turned a solemn look upon her. "Don't put things into my mouth that I never said! Mathieu's fate causes me

a great deal of anxiety. But he is strong and he is resourceful. Oh yes he is, a great deal more resourceful than you
think, for all his moony, happy-go-lucky ways. I know
him much better than you do; all that perpetual hesitation of his is largely put on, it's all part of the character he
has built up for himself. Once they get him, he'll manage
to find an easy job; I can just see him acting as secretary
to a German officer or working as a cook. Yes, a cook!
That would fit him like a glove!" He smiled and repeated
with relish: "A cook, yes, just the very thing for him! If
you really want to know what I think," he went on confidentially, "I think a spell in a prison camp will do a lot to
steady him. He'll come back a different man."

"How long will it last?" asked Odette, her heart in her
mouth.

"How should I know?" With a wag of the head he
added: "But I can tell you this: the war, so far as I can
see, can't last very long. The next objective of the German
Army will be England—and the Channel is narrow."

"But the British will put up a fight," Odette protested.

"To be sure they will!" He threw out his arms in a
gesture of despondency. "But whether we should want
them to or not, I really don't know."

What ought we to want? What ought I to want? When
the war started, it all seemed so simple: what they ought
to want, she had thought, was a victory, on the 1914
model. But apparently nobody shared her views. She had
smiled cheerfully, as she had seen her mother do when
the Nivelle offensive began in 1917; she never wearied of
saying, "Of course we shall win! We must say to ourselves
all the time that we just *can't not* win." But she had hated
herself for talking like that because she loathed war, even
a victorious war. People had shaken their heads and said
nothing, almost as though she were lacking in tact. So she
had given up talking about the war at all, she had tried to
make herself as little conspicuous as possible. She had

heard a great deal of argument about Germany, England, and Russia, but she never really began to understand what it was that people wanted. "If only he were here, he would explain it to me," she thought. But he wasn't here, he didn't even write to her. In nine months he had sent Jacques only two letters. What does he think? He must know, he must understand. But what if he didn't? Suppose no one understood. On a sudden impulse, she looked up: she longed to see in Jacques's face that expression of comfortable certainty which still had the power, at times, of calming her; she longed to read in his face the assurance that everything would be all right, that there were solid reasons for hope of which she knew nothing. Hope of what? Was it true that an Allied victory could profit nobody but the Russians? She scrutinized his too familiar features and saw him suddenly as someone new and strange: eyes darkened by anxiety; a hint of arrogance in the corners of the lips, but the sulky arrogance of a child caught doing what it ought not to do. "Something is wrong; he doesn't feel comfortable." Ever since they had left Paris, he had not seemed quite himself, he had been sometimes over-violent, sometimes over-gentle. How frightening it was when men produced that impression of being obsessed by a sense of guilt!

He said: "I'm dying for a smoke."

"Haven't you any cigarettes left?"

"No."

"Here," she said. "I've got four."

They were De Rezskes; he made a face, but took one suspiciously.

"Straw!" he said, slipping the packet into his pocket.

At the first puff Odette smelled the fragrance of tobacco; the longing to smoke caught her by the throat. For a long time now, even after she had ceased to love him, she had liked to feel thirsty when he drank, hungry when he ate, drowsy when she saw him sleeping. Such feelings were reassuring: it was as though he laid hold of her desires, sanctified them, and satisfied them in a fashion more virile, more moral, more definite than her own. But now . . .

She laughed softly. "Give me just one."

He looked at her as though he did not understand, then he raised his eyebrows. "Sorry, my darling; that was a purely automatic reflex." He took the cigarettes from his pocket.

"You can keep the packet," she said, "I only want one."

They smoked in silence. She was afraid of herself, as she recalled the violent, irresistible desires that had swept her off her feet when she was a young girl. Perhaps that was all going to start over again. He coughed two or three times to clear his throat. There is something he wants to say to me, but he's taking his time, as usual. She went on patiently smoking. He will approach his subject like a crab, sideways. He was sitting very straight and upright; there was severity in the look he turned on her.

"Well, my dear?" he said.

She smiled at him vaguely, it seemed to be the only thing to do. He laid his hand on her shoulder.

"This is a pretty kettle of fish."

"Yes," she said, "it certainly is."

His eyes were still fixed on her. He crushed out his cigarette against the running-board of the car and put his foot on it; then he moved closer to her and, as if to overcome any possible resistance, said vehemently:

"We were running absolutely no risk."

She made no reply, and he went on, his voice quiet but insistent: "I feel sure the Germans will be on their best behavior; they'll be particularly careful about that."

It was just as she had always thought. But she could read in Jacques's eyes the answer he wanted her to make. She said: "But you can never be sure, can you? Suppose they burned Paris to the ground and put everyone to the sword!"

He shrugged. "Why should they? How like a woman to suggest such a thing!" He leaned close to her and began patiently to explain: "Listen to me, Odette, and try to understand: once the armistice is signed, Berlin will certainly want France to take her place as one of the partners in the Axis. It may even be counting on our prestige in America to keep the United States out of the war. Do you see my point? In a word, we may be beaten, but we've still got a card up our sleeve. It may even be that our political bigwigs," he added with a low chuckle, "may have an important part to play, if they can rise to the occasion. Good. Well, in view of all that, it's incredible that the Germans should, by a display of useless violence, risk unifying French opinion against them."

"I agree," she said, but her nerves were on edge.

"Ah!" He looked at her, biting his lip. He seemed to be so thoroughly put out that she added hastily: "Still, you can never be sure, can you? Suppose they're fired on from windows."

Jacques's eyes flashed. "If there had been any danger, I would have stayed; I made up my mind to leave because I was sure there was none."

She remembered how he had come into the drawing-room, his quiet, tense manner, the way his hand had trembled when he lit a cigarette, the deliberate way in which he had said: "Pack your things, Odette; the car is downstairs, and we're leaving in half an hour." What was he getting at now? He gave an unpleasant little laugh as he said by way of conclusion: "It might have looked rather like abandoning one's post."

"But you had no post."

"I was warden in charge of our block," he said, and waved away any possible objection. "It may sound silly,

I know, and I took on the job only because Champenois insisted. All the same, even in that I might have been useful. Besides, we ought to set an example."

The look she gave him was devoid of sympathy. Yes, yes, *yes*, of course you ought to have stayed in Paris, and don't count on me to say you oughtn't. He sighed.

"Well, what's done is done. Life would be too easy if men were never confronted by a clash of duties. But I'm boring you, darling. These are masculine scruples."

"I think I can understand them."

"Naturally, my dear child, naturally." There was something lonely and virile in his smile. He took her wrist, and a note of reassurance came into his voice. "Nothing much could happen to me. At the very worst, they might send all men of military age to Germany. Well, what of it? Mathieu is in the same boat, though, of course, he hasn't got this cursed heart of mine. Remember when that damned fool of an army doctor turned me down?"

"Yes."

"How wild I was! I'd have done anything to get in. Don't you remember? Don't you remember how angry I was?"

"Yes."

He sat down on the running-board of the car, rested his chin in his hands, and stared straight in front of him.

"Charvoz stayed," he said without shifting his gaze.

"Really?"

"He stayed. I ran into him this morning at the garage; he looked surprised that I was going."

"It's different for him," she said automatically.

"That's true," he said bitterly. "He's a bachelor."

Odette was standing beside him on his left; she could see the glint of his scalp through the thinning hair. So that's it! she thought.

His eyes were unfocused. "There was no one I could have trusted to look after you," he muttered.

She stiffened. "What?"

"I said there was no one I could have trusted to look after you. I didn't dare let you go off to your aunt's alone."

"Are you trying to tell me," she asked in a trembling voice, "that you left on my account?"

"It was a case of conscience," he replied. He looked at her affectionately. "You'd been so nervous these last few days; I was frightened about you."

Amazement kept her silent. Why did he have to say that? Why did he feel obliged to?

With a sort of nervous gaiety he went on: "You kept the shutters closed, we lived all day long in darkened rooms, you began hoarding food, there were boxes of sardines all over the place. And I think Lucienne was a very bad influence; you weren't the same after one of her visits. She is frightened out of her wits, besides being as gullible as they make 'em, and only too ready to swallow cock-and-bull yarns about rape and mutilations."

I won't say what he wants me to say. I won't. What is there left for me if I despise him? She took a step backwards. He fixed a steely glare on her; it was as though he were saying: "Come on, out with it. Out with it!" Once again beneath that eagle stare, beneath that husband's scrutiny, she felt guilty. Perhaps he did think I wanted to go, perhaps I did seem frightened, perhaps I was frightened without knowing it. What is the truth? Until now it has always been what Jacques said; if I stop believing in him, in whom can I believe? Lowering her head, she said:

"I didn't want to stay in Paris."

"You were frightened, weren't you?" he asked in a tone of kindly indulgence.

"Yes," she said. "I was frightened." When she raised her head again, he was smiling.

"Well, there's not much harm done," he said. "A night

under the stars—not perhaps quite suited to our time of life, but we're still young enough to find it rather attractive." He stroked the back of her neck. "Remember Hyères, in '36? We slept in a tent; it's one of the happiest memories of my life."

She said nothing; she had gripped the handle of the door and was clinging to it with all her strength. He choked back a yawn.

"It's terribly late; how about turning in?"

She nodded assent. Somewhere a night-bird called, and Jacques laughed.

"Nothing if not rural!" he said. "You lie on the floor of the car," he added with affectionate concern. "That way you'll be able to stretch out your legs a little. I'll sleep in the driving seat."

They got back into the car. He locked the right-hand door and pushed the catch on the other.

"You all right?"

"Yes, perfectly all right."

He took out his revolver and examined it with amusement. "This is a situation that would have delighted my old pirate of a grandfather," he said; then gaily: "There's something of the sea-rover in all the members of my family."

She remained silent. He turned in his seat and touched her chin.

"Give me a kiss, darling."

She felt his warm, open mouth pressing against her own. He just touched her lips with his tongue, as in the old days, and she shuddered. At the same moment she felt his hand creeping under her arm and caressing her breast.

"My poor Odette," he said tenderly, "poor little girl, poor darling child."

She flung herself back. "I'm simply dropping with sleep."

"Good night, sweetheart," he said with a smile.

He turned round, folded his arms over the wheel, and dropped his head on his hands. She remained seated, rigid, filled with a sense of oppression, and watching him. Two deep breaths—not yet; he was still fidgeting. She could think of nothing while he sat there still wakeful, with that picture of her in his mind. I've never been able to think while he was close to me. Ah, now he's off! He had uttered his three familiar grunts. She relaxed slightly. He's no better than an animal. He was sleeping, the war was sleeping, the whole world of men was sleeping, engulfed in that head of his. Upright in the darkness, with the chalky patches of the two windows on either hand, deep in a pool of moonlight, Odette kept her vigil. A memory came back to her from the distant past. I was running along a little pinkish road; I was twelve years old, I stopped, my heart beating with a sense of uneasy happiness; I said out loud: "I am indispensable." She repeated the words: "I am indispensable," but indispensable to what, she did not know. She tried to think about the war, and it seemed to her that she was on the point of discovering the truth. "Is it a fact that victory will profit nobody but the Russians?" Suddenly she gave up the attempt, and her joy was turned to a feeling of disgust. I don't know enough about it.

She wanted to smoke. I don't really want to; it's just nerves. The desire grew and grew, distending her breasts, a peremptory and conquering desire, as in the days of her uncontrolled girlhood. He put the packet in his coat pocket. Why should he smoke? In his mouth the taste of tobacco must be so terribly boring, so terribly ordinary. Why should he smoke rather than I? She leaned over him. He was breathing regularly. She slipped her hand into his pocket and took out the cigarettes; then, very quietly, she pushed back the catch of the door and slipped out of the car. The moon seen through the leaves, the puddles of moonlight on the road, the freshness of the night air, the cry of a night-bird—all these things are *mine*. She lit a cigarette. The war is asleep, Berlin is asleep, Moscow, Churchill, the Politburo, our statesmen, all are asleep. There is no one to see *my* night; I am indispensable. Those cans of food were for the soldier boys I adopted. It was suddenly borne in on her that she loathed tobacco; she took two more pulls at her cigarette, then threw it away. She could not think why she had wanted to smoke. The leaves rustled softly, the countryside creaked like a floor; the stars were wild animals. She felt frightened. He was sleeping and she had rediscovered the mysterious world of her childhood, a forest of questions to which there was no answer. It was he who knew the names of the stars, the exact distance of the earth from the moon, the number of persons living in this part of France, their history, their employments. He is asleep; I despise him and I know nothing about anything. She felt lost in a world of which she could make no use, in a world created *to be seen* and *touched*. She ran back to the car; she wanted to wake him now at once, to wake Science, Industry, and the Moral Code. She touched the handle, she leaned on the door, and through the glass glimpsed a large open mouth. What's the use? she wondered. She sat down on the running-board and began to think, as she did every night, of Mathieu.

The lieutenant ran up the dark stairs. They ran and twisted at his heels. He stopped in the pitch darkness, pushed open a trapdoor with the back of his neck, and they were dazzled by a silvery radiance.

"Follow me!"

They jumped into a cold, clear sky that was full of memories and faint sounds.

A voice said: "Who goes there?"

"It's me," said the lieutenant.

"Atten-*tion!*"

"At ease."

They were on a square platform at the top of the church tower. It had a roof supported on four pillars, one at each corner. Between the pillars ran a stone parapet about three feet high. All about them was sky. The moon cast the shadows of one of the pillars on the floor.

"Well," asked the lieutenant, "everything all right here?"

"O.K., lieutenant."

Three men stood facing him. All of them were tall and thin; all of them had rifles. Mathieu and Pinette felt shy and kept well behind him.

"Do we hang on here, sir?" one of the chasseurs asked.

"Yes," said the lieutenant. "I've put Closson and four of his fellows in the *mairie;* the rest will be with me in the schoolhouse. Dreyer will be responsible for keeping contact."

"What are our orders, sir?"

"Open fire as you see fit. You can use up every scrap of ammunition."

"What's that, sir?"

The sound of muffled voices and shuffling feet rose towards them from the street. The lieutenant smiled.

"Those are our charming friends from headquarters staff; I've had to put them away in the cellar over at the *mairie*. They'll be a bit crowded, but it's only for one night: tomorrow morning the Boches will take delivery when they've finished with us."

Mathieu looked at the chasseurs. He felt ashamed for his companions, but not a flicker showed on any of the three faces.

"Look!" the lieutenant said, "at twenty-three o'clock the inhabitants of the village will assemble in the square. Don't fire on them. I'm sending them off to spend the night in the woods. Once they're out of the way, open fire on anyone who crosses the street. And don't leave the church on any account: if you do, we'll fire on you."

He moved toward the trapdoor. The chasseurs looked Mathieu and Pinette up and down in silence.

"Lieutenant—" said Mathieu.

The lieutenant turned round. "I'd forgotten about you fellows. They want to be in on the show," he explained to the others. "They've got rifles and I've given them ammunition. Do what you can with them. If their shooting's too bad, you'd better divide their ammo up among yourselves."

There was friendliness in the way he looked at his men. "Good-by, boys," he said.

"Good-by, lieutenant," they answered politely.

For a second he hesitated, shaking his head; then he moved backwards down the first few steps and let the trapdoor fall. The three men on the roof looked at Mathieu and Pinette with neither sympathy nor curiosity. Mathieu took two steps backward and leaned against a pillar. His rifle embarrassed him: either he handled it with excessive unconcern or else he held it before him like a candle. Finally, with great care, he laid it on the ground. Pinette joined him. Both of them stood with their backs to the moon. The three chasseurs, on the contrary, stood square in its light. The same black stubble stained their chalky faces; all of them had the same fixed stare of birds of the night.

"It's as formal as a social call, isn't it?" Pinette said.

Mathieu smiled. The chasseurs did not smile at all.

Pinette went close to Mathieu and whispered in his ear: "They don't seem to care for us much."

"You said a mouthful!" said Mathieu.

They felt too much embarrassed to say more. Mathieu leaned over the parapet looking at the dark, billowy foliage of the chestnut trees beneath him.

"I'm going to have a word with 'em," said Pinette.

"Take it easy."

But Pinette was already strolling across toward the others. "My name's Pinette. This dope here's Delarue." He stopped and waited. The tallest of the three nodded, but furnished no information. Pinette cleared his throat. "We've come up here to do a little fighting," he said.

Still no reply. The tall, fair man scowled and turned his head away. Pinette, disconcerted, hesitated.

"What you want us to do?"

The tall, fair man was leaning with his back to the wall; he yawned. Mathieu noticed that he was a corporal.

"What you want us to do?" asked Pinette again.

"Nothing."

"What do you mean, nothing?"

"Nothing for the moment."

"How about later on?"

"You'll be told."

Mathieu smiled at them. "We're as popular here as the clap, huh? You guys'd rather be alone?"

The tall, fair man looked at him thoughtfully; then he turned to Pinette. "What's your job?"

"Subway employee."

The corporal gave vent to a bark of laughter, but there was no sign of amusement in his eyes.

"You think you're a civilian already, huh? Just you wait a bit."

"Oh, you mean my job in the army?"

"Yes."

"I'm an observer."

"And him?"

"Telephonist."

"Second-line troops?"

"Yes."

The corporal studied him attentively, as though he found some difficulty in bringing his mind to bear on him.

"What's wrong with you? You look hefty enough."

"Bad heart."

"Ever shot a man down?"

"Never," said Mathieu.

The corporal turned to his companions. All three shook their heads.

"We'll do our best," said Pinette in a choky voice.

There was a long silence. The corporal looked at them and scratched his head. Presently he heaved a sigh; he seemed to have made up his mind. He straightened up and said abruptly:

"My name's Clapot. I give orders around here. These two men are Chasseriau and Dandieu. You fellows just do what they tell you; we've been in action for the last two weeks and we know pretty much what the hell gives."

"Two weeks?" Pinette repeated incredulously. "How did that happen?"

"We were covering your retreat," Dandieu replied.

Pinette blushed and hung his head. Mathieu felt his jaws contract. Clapot explained in a more conciliatory tone.

"A delaying action."

They looked at one another, but not a word more was said. Mathieu felt ill at ease; he thought: "We'll never be one with them. They've been fighting for two weeks on end while we were hotfooting it like hell down the roads. We can't be their buddies just by joining them for the last fireworks. We can never be one with them. Our pals are down there in the cellar, wallowing in filth and shame; we belong with them and now we've abandoned them at the last moment from pride." He leaned over; he could see the black houses, the glittering ribbon of the road. "My place is down there, my place is down there," and he knew in his heart that he would never again be able to go down from the tower. Pinette was sitting astride the parapet, probably just in order to keep up his spirits.

"Get down off there!" Clapot ordered. "You'll give our position away."

"The Germans are a long way off."

"What do you know about it? Get down, I tell you."

Pinette, vexed, jumped down onto the roof. Mathieu thought: "They'll never accept us as equals." Pinette was getting on his nerves; he kept moving about, and talking when he should have remained in the background, closed his big mouth, and let the others forget about him. Mathieu gave a jump as an enormous explosion, muffled and heavy, went off close to his ear. A second explosion followed, a third; there was a clamor of bronze as the roof quivered under his feet. Pinette laughed nervously.

"Don't get scared, feller; that's just the clock striking."

Mathieu, stealing a glance at the chasseurs, noticed with satisfaction that they, too, had jumped.

"Twenty-three o'clock," said Pinette.

Mathieu shivered. He was cold, but the feeling was not unpleasant. He was high up in the sky, above the roof tops, above the men in the village; he felt cold, and it was dark. "No, I shall never go down again. I wouldn't go down for anything in the world."

"There go the civilians."

They were all leaning over the parapet. Through the leaves Mathieu could see black animals moving about; it was as though he were looking down into the bottom of the sea. In the main street doors were being opened noiselessly; men, women, and children were creeping out. Most of them carried bundles or suitcases. Small groups were forming in the roadway; they appeared to be waiting for something. Then the groups melted together into a single procession, which moved off slowly in a southerly direction.

"Like a funeral," said Pinette.

"Poor devils!" said Mathieu.

"Don't worry about them," said Dandieu dryly. "They'll

find their shacks waiting for 'em when they get back. The Germans don't often burn down whole villages."

"How about that?" Mathieu nodded toward Roberville.

"That was different: we weren't the only ones shooting; the villagers joined in."

Pinette started to laugh. "Not at all like here! These bastards here shitting with fright."

Dandieu looked at him. "You fellows weren't fighting. After all, it's not up to civilians to start a scrap."

"Who's fault was it?" Pinette asked in a fury. "Who's fault was it we didn't fight?"

"God knows!"

"It was the officers' fault! It's the officers who lost the war."

"Don't go bawling out the officers," Clapot warned. "You've no right to do that."

"Do you expect me to praise them?"

"You've no call to talk against the officers to us," Clapot went on resolutely. "Because you can take it from me that except for one lieutenant—and it was no fault of his, either—all our officers stuck by us to a man."

Pinette, trying to explain, waved his arms at Clapot, then dropped them to his side. "It's no good," he said dejectedly, "we'll never understand each other."

Chasseriau looked inquiringly at Pinette. "What in Christ's name did you come here for?"

"I told you; we came to do a little fighting."

"But why? You didn't have to."

Pinette laughed in a foolish, duncelike sort of way. "Oh, I don't know. To have some fun."

"You'll get your fun all right!" Clapot said harshly. "Take my word for it."

Dandieu broke into a pitying laugh. "Did you hear them? They came here to pay us a little call, to have some fun, to find out what a nice little scrap looks like. They wanted to score up a nice little target, like at pigeon-shooting. And they weren't even forced to!"

"And you, you chump," Pinette asked, "who forced you to fight?"

"That's different; we're chasseurs."

"What of it?"

"If you belong to the chasseurs, you fight." He shook his head. "If it weren't for that, you wouldn't catch me shooting men just for the fun of it."

Chasseriau was staring at Pinette with mingled surprise and repulsion. "Haven't you got it into your thick head that you're risking your skin?"

Pinette's only reply was a shrug.

"Because if you have," Chasseriau went on, "you're an even bigger fool than you look. It don't make sense to risk your skin if you're not forced to."

"We were forced to, all right," Mathieu said suddenly. "We were forced to. We were fed up and we didn't know what to do." He pointed down at the schoolhouse. "For us it was either the church tower or the cellar."

Dandieu seemed to be impressed; some of the harshness went out of his expression.

Mathieu pursued his advantage. "What would you have done in our place?" he inquired.

None of the chasseurs answered. Mathieu pressed his point: "What would you have done?"

Dandieu shook his head. "I might have chosen the cellar. Fighting's not much fun. You'll see."

"Perhaps not," Mathieu admitted, "but it's not much fun to be cooped up in a cellar when others are fighting."

"I don't suppose it is," said Chasseriau.

"Yes," Dandieu had to admit. "A fellow in that fix can't feel very proud of himself."

They seemed less hostile now. Clapot looked at Pinette with a kind of surprise, then turned away and went over to the parapet. The expression of feverish hardness had gone; his face showed a certain vague gentleness. He stared out into the mild darkness, at the childlike and legendary countryside, and Mathieu could not determine whether the mildness of the night was reflected in his face or whether the loneliness of his face was reflected in the night.

"Hi! Clapot!" Dandieu called.

Clapot straightened up. He was once more the alert specialist.

"What's the matter?"

"I'm going to mosey round down there; I think I saw something."

"O.K."

Just as Dandieu lifted the trap, a woman's voice came up to them from below:

"Henri! Henri!"

Mathieu leaned out over the street. A few laggards were scuttling about aimlessly, like frightened ants. He could see, close to the post office, a small patch of shadow.

"Henri!"

The expression of Pinette's face darkened, but he said nothing. Some women had taken the post-office girl by the arm and were trying to lead her away. She was struggling with them and shouting: "Henri! Henri!" She broke free, rushed into the post office, and slammed the door.

"A hell of a muck-up!" Pinette muttered. He scraped the stone of the parapet with his nails. "She ought to have gone with the others."

"Sure," said Mathieu.

"She'll get herself in trouble."

"Whose fault will that be?"

There was no reply. The lid of the trapdoor rose.

"Give me a hand!"

They pulled the trap back; Dandieu emerged from the

darkness. He was carrying two straw mattresses on his back.

"See what I've found!"

Clapot smiled for the first time: he seemed overjoyed. "That's a bit of luck," he said.

"What are you going to do with those?" Mathieu asked.

Clapot looked at him with surprise. "What do people usually use mattresses for? To string beads with?"

"You're going to sleep?"

"We're going to have some chow first," Chasseriau answered.

Mathieu watched them busying themselves round the mattresses, taking cans of bully-beef from their haversacks. Don't they realize they're going to be killed?

Chasseriau had discovered a can-opener; with quick, precise movements he opened three cans. Then they all sat down and took their knives from their pockets.

Clapot glanced at Mathieu over his shoulder. "You two hungry?" he asked.

It was two days since Mathieu had last eaten; his mouth was filled with saliva. "Not me," he said.

"How about your pal?"

Pinette made no reply. He was leaning over the parapet, his eyes fixed on the post office.

"Come on, have some chow," Clapot said; "there's plenty for all of us."

"The guys who do the fighting have a right to eat," Chasseriau declared.

Dandieu rummaged about in his haversack and produced two cans, which he offered to Mathieu. Mathieu took them and tapped Pinette on the shoulder. Pinette gave a start.

"What is it?"

"This is for you; go ahead and eat!"

Mathieu took the can-opener that Dandieu offered him,

applied it to the edge of the can, and pressed hard; but
the blade slipped over the metal without penetrating it,
jumped out of the groove, and struck his left thumb.

"Clumsy!" said Pinette. "Hurt yourself?"

"No," said Mathieu.

"Give it here." Pinette opened the two cans and they
ate in silence, standing close to one of the pillars: they
were too shy to sit down. They dug into the meat with
their knives and pecked the pieces off the points. Mathieu
munched conscientiously, but his throat felt paralyzed:
he could taste nothing and he found it difficult to swallow. Seated on the mattresses, the three chasseurs were
concentrating on the food; their knives gleamed in the
moonlight.

"To think we should be quietly eating our chow in the
belfry of a church," said Chasseriau dreamily.

In the belfry of a church. Mathieu looked down. Under
their feet was the fragrance of spices and incense, coolness, and the stained-glass windows feebly shining in the
shadows of the faith. Under their feet was confidence and
hope. Mathieu felt cold; he looked at the sky, breathed
the sky, thought with the sky. He was naked on a glacier,
at a great height; far below him lay his childhood.

Clapot had thrown his head back, his eyes were fastened
on the sky as he ate.

"Pipe that moon," he said in a low voice.

"What's that?" Chasseriau asked.

"The moon! Isn't it bigger than usual?"

"No."

"Ah, I thought it was." Suddenly he lowered his eyes.
"Hey, you two, come and eat with us. Men don't eat
standing."

Mathieu and Pinette hesitated.

"Come on, come on!" Clapot urged.

"Let's go," said Mathieu to Pinette.

They sat down. Mathieu could feel Clapot's warmth

against his hip. They were silent: this was their last meal and it was sacred.

"We've got some rum," Dandieu announced. "Not much, just enough for a snifter all round."

He passed his canteen, and each man put his lips where the last had drunk. Pinette leaned over to Mathieu.

"It looks like they've adopted us."

"Yes."

"They're not bad guys. I like 'em."

"So do I."

Pinette straightened up with sudden pride; his eyes were shining. "We would've been like them if we'd been told what to do."

Mathieu looked at the three faces and nodded.

"Am I right?"

"Could be," said Mathieu.

For the last few moments Pinette had been looking at Mathieu's hand; finally he touched his elbow. "What's the matter? You bleeding?"

Mathieu looked down; there was a ragged gash in his left thumb. "That must've been the can-opener," he said.

"And you let it bleed, you fathead?"

"I didn't feel anything," said Mathieu.

Pinette was delighted. "What would you do if I wasn't here?" he grumbled.

Mathieu looked at his thumb, surprised that he had a body. He was conscious of nothing, neither of the taste of food nor of that of alcohol, not of the pain in his hand. It's as though I was made of ice. He laughed.

"Once at a night club I had a knife—" He broke off.

Pinette was looking at him with surprise. "Go on."

"Oh, nothing. I'm unlucky with sharp instruments."

"Give me your hand," Clapot said.

Taking a roll of gauze and a blue bottle from his pack, he poured some of the burning liquid on Mathieu's thumb and bound it up. Mathieu moved it as he might a puppet and smiled down at it: all this trouble to prevent blood from flowing too soon!

"There you are!" Clapot said.

"That's swell!" Mathieu answered.

Clapot looked at his watch. "Time to hit the hay, fellers: it's close to midnight."

They bunched round him.

"Dandieu," he said, jerking his thumb at Mathieu, "he'll be on guard with you."

"O.K."

Chasseriau, Pinette, and Clapot lay down side by side on the mattresses. Dandieu took a blanket from his pack and laid it over the three of them. Pinette stretched luxuriously, winked roguishly at Mathieu, and closed his eyes.

"I'm going over there," Dandieu told Mathieu. "You stay where you are. If you hear any movement, don't do a thing without telling me first."

Mathieu settled down in his corner and raked the countryside with his eyes. It occurred to him that he was going to die and the idea of such a thing appealed to him as highly comic. He looked at the dark roofs, at the mild, phosphorescent gleam of the road between the blue trees, at all the sumptuous uninhabitable land, and he thought: I am going to die for nothing. A faint sound of snoring made him start; he turned: the lads were already asleep. Clapot his eyes shut, looking younger, was smiling blissfully. Pinette, too, was smiling. Mathieu bent over him and looked down at his face. He thought: "What a shame!" Dandieu, at the other end of the platform, was leaning forward, his hands on his thighs like a goal-keeper in a soccer game.

"Hi!" said Mathieu in a low voice.

"Hi!"

"Goal-keeper, eh?"

Dandieu turned toward him in surprise. "How did you know?"

"It's obvious." And, "Were you good?" he added.

"With luck I might have been a pro."

They exchanged a wave of greeting and Mathieu returned to his post. He thought: "I am going to die for nothing," and he was filled with self-pity. For a brief moment memories rustled about him like leaves in the breeze. *All* his memories: "I was in love with life." An uneasy question stirred at the back of his mind: "Had I any right to abandon my pals? Have I any right to die for nothing?" He stood up and rested his hands on the parapet; he shook his head angrily. "I'm fed up! To hell with the guys down there, to hell with everybody. I'm through with remorse, hesitations, mental reservations. No one has the right to judge me, no one is thinking about me, no one will remember me, no one can make up my mind for me." He had reached a decision without remorse, with full knowledge of the facts. He had made up his mind, and, on the instant, his scrupulous and sensitive heart went tumbling down through the branches. No more sentiment for him: all that was over now. "Here and now I have decided that all along death has been the secret of my life, that I have lived for the purpose of dying. I die in order to demonstrate the impossibility of living; my eyes will put an extinguisher upon the earth and shut it down forever."

The earth raised its topsy-turvy face to the dying man; the foundering sky swept across him with all its stars. But Mathieu kept watch without so much as deigning to pick up these useless gifts.

Tuesday, June 18, 5.45 a.m.

L OLA!"
      She awoke, as she always did, with a sense of loath-
ing, and, as always, crept back into the shell of her putrid
flesh.

"Lola! Are you asleep?"

"No," she said. "What's the time?"

"Five forty-five."

"Five forty-five? And my little tough guy's awake, eh?
That's something new for a change."

"Come to me," he said.

No, she thought, I don't want him to touch me.
"Boris—"

My body disgusts me; even if it doesn't disgust you,
it's a swindle, it's rotten, and you don't know it. If you
did know, it would fill you with horror.

"Boris, I'm tired."

But already he had taken her by the shoulders; he was
heavy upon her. . . .

Finally she felt cold and at peace. I am too old, much
too old, she thought. These antics seemed grotesque to
her, and gently she pushed him from her.

"Get off me."

"What?" He raised his head and looked at her in surprise.

"It's my heart," she explained. "It's beating too hard and you're suffocating me."

With a smile he stretched out beside her and lay there on his stomach, his face in the pillow, his eyes shut, a comic little pucker at the corner of his mouth. She propped herself on her elbow and looked at him. So used to the sight was she, he had become such a habit, that she could no longer observe him, any more than she could see her own hand. I felt nothing. And yesterday when he came into the courtyard, looking as pretty as a girl, I felt nothing. Nothing at all, not even the old feverish dryness in my throat, not even the old bushy heaviness at the pit of my stomach. Gazing at the too familiar face, she thought: I am alone. How often she had taken that little head in her hands and pressed it, that little head which had secreted so many sly thoughts; in those days she had fought, questioned, begged, so eager was she to open it like a pomegranate and lick out the contents. Then at last the secret had emerged, and, as in a pomegranate, all she had found was a few drops of sugary liquid. She gazed at him with rancor; she was angry at him for failing to stir her deeply. She looked at the bitter lines about his mouth: if he lost his gaiety, what was left? Boris opened his eyes and smiled at her.

"I'm idiotically happy just to be here with you, you dear old wizard."

She returned his smile. Now it's I who have a secret, and try to get it out of me! He sat up, drew back the sheet, and studied Lola's body attentively; he brushed her nipples lightly with his hand; she felt embarrassed.

"Just marble," he said.

She thought of the unclean beast proliferating in the fastness of her body, and the blood rushed to her cheeks.

"I'm proud of you," said Boris.

"Why?"

"Because you laid the guys at the hospital flat on their arses!"

Lola chuckled. "Didn't they ask you what you could see in an old bag like me? Didn't they take me for your mother?"

"Lola!" said Boris reproachfully. Then he laughed, moved by some memory, and for a moment he looked young again.

"What are you laughing at?"

"I was thinking of Francillon. His girl's a loose little fish though she's not yet eighteen. He said to me: 'I'll swap with you any time.'"

"That was very polite of him," said Lola.

A thought drifted like a cloud across Boris's face, and his eyes darkened. She looked at him, but there was no friendliness in her look. Sure, you've got your little troubles like everyone else, sure, sure. If I told him mine, what would he do? What would you do if I said: "I've got a tumor of the womb; I've got to have an operation, and at my age it can be dangerous." You'd open those great whore's eyes of yours and you'd say: "It's not true!" "Yes it is," I'd reply, and you'd say that it couldn't be, that things of that kind can be cured with drugs and X-ray treatment, that I was exaggerating. I'd say: "It wasn't to get my money that I went back to Paris, I went to see Le Goupil, and he was quite definite about everything." You'd tell me that Le Goupil is a fool, that he's the last person in the world I should have consulted, you'd protest and deny, you'd dart your head this way and that like a trapped animal, and then at last, when you were cornered, you'd stop talking and you'd look at me tragically, resentfully."

She raised her bare arm and took hold of Boris by the hair.

"Lie down, rough-neck! Lie down. Tell me what's the matter."

"Nothing's the matter," he said, but his face belied his words.

"That's odd. You don't usually wake up at five o'clock in the morning."

He said again, without conviction: "Nothing's the matter."

"I see," she said. "You have something to tell me, but you want me to pull it out of you like a midwife."

He smiled and laid his head on her breast, just below the shoulder. He took a deep breath and said: "How sweet you smell!"

She shrugged her shoulders. "Are you going to talk or aren't you?"

He shook his head, as though terrorized. Silent, she lay there on her back. All right, don't talk! It doesn't matter to me. He speaks to me, he screws me, but I shall die alone. She heard Boris heave a sigh and turned her face toward him. He had a sad, set expression on his face, an expression she had never seen before. She thought, unenthusiastically: "Now, I suppose, I've got to start worrying about you." She would have to question him, to spy on him, to draw conclusions from the way he looked, just as in the old days of her jealousy, she would have to work away at him until at last he told her what he had been dying to tell her all along. She sat up.

"Give me my dressing-gown and a cigarette."

"Why a dressing-gown? You're nicer as you are."

"Give me my dressing-gown. I'm cold."

He rose, brown and naked. She looked away. He took the dressing-gown from the foot of the bed and held it out to her. She slipped it on. After a moment's hesitation he put on his trousers and sat down on a chair.

"You've found some pure sweet virgin you want to marry? Is that it?"

He looked so completely dumbfounded that she blushed.

"All right, all right," she said.

There was a brief silence. "What are you going to do when they discharge you?" she went on.

"I'm going to marry you," said he.

She took a cigarette and lit it. "Why?" she asked.

"I've got to be respectable. I can't take you with me to Castelnaudary unless you're my wife."

"What the hell are you going to do at Castelnaudary?"

"Earn my living," he said sternly. "I'm not kidding you: I'm going to be a teacher."

"Why Castelnaudary?"

"You'll see," he said, "you'll see. Castelnaudary is a must."

"Are you trying to tell me that I shall be addressed as Madame Serguine, that I shall have to dress up and call on the headmaster's wife?"

"They call him the principal there," said Boris. "Yes, that is what you will do. And at the end of the school year I shall have to make a speech at commencement."

"Hm!" said Lola.

"Ivich will come to live with us," Boris went on.

"She can't stand me."

"Perhaps not, but that is how it's going to be."

"Does she want it?"

"Yes. She can't stand living with her in-laws; it's driving her nuts. You'd hardly recognize her."

Silence. She watched him out of the corner of her eye. "So it's all arranged, is it?" she asked.

"Yes."

"And what if I don't like the arrangement?"

"Oh, Lola, how can you say that?"

"Naturally, you think I shall jump at the chance of living with you," said Lola.

She fancied that she caught a gleam in Boris's eye.

"You're not serious, are you?" asked Boris.

"Perfectly serious," she said. "You're just a little rough-neck and rather too certain of your power to charm."

The gleam vanished. He looked at his knees, and Lola noticed that his jaws were moving.

"You like the idea of that kind of life?" she asked.

"I'd like anything so long as I could live with you," said Boris politely.

"You used to say you couldn't bear the thought of being a teacher."

"What else can I do now? The whole trouble is," he went on, "that while I was fighting I didn't bother my head with problems. But now I spend all my time wondering what I'm fit for."

"You wanted to write."

"I never thought seriously of writing: I've nothing to say. You see, I never believed I should come out of this business alive, I've been caught on the wrong foot."

Lola looked at him attentively. "Are you sorry the war's over?"

"It isn't over," said Boris. "The English are carrying on, and within six months the Yanks will be in it."

"Anyway, it's over for you."

"Yes," Boris agreed, "it's over for me."

Lola was still looking at him. "For you and for all Frenchmen," she said.

"Not for all of them!" he remonstrated fiercely. "Some of them are in England and they'll fight on to the end!"

"I see," said Lola. She drew at her cigarette, then dropped the butt on the floor. Very quietly, she said: "Is there any way you could get over there?"

"Oh, Lola!" said Boris, with admiration and gratitude in his voice. "Yes, there is a way."

"What way?"

"A plane."

"A plane?" she repeated without understanding.

"There's a little private airfield near Marignane, between two hills. A military plane landed there about a fortnight ago because of engine trouble. It's being repaired."

"But you can't handle a plane."

"I've got some pals who can."

"Who are they?"

"One of them's Francillon, the guy I introduced to you. Then there's Gabel and Terrasse."

"Did they suggest you go with them?"

"Yes."

"Well?"

"I refused." The words came tumbling out of his mouth.

"I see: you refused, but it wasn't final. You said to yourself: I'll break it gently to the old girl?"

"No," he said.

He gazed at her tenderly. It was not often that his eyes had so melting a look. There was a time when I'd have killed myself for a look like that.

"You may be an old bit of nonsense with nothing in the top story," he said, "but I can't leave you in the lurch. You'd do all sorts of ridiculous things if I weren't there to keep an eye on you."

"When are we going to get married?" Lola asked.

"Whenever you like," he said indifferently. "All that matters is that we should be married by the beginning of term."

"That's in September, isn't it?"

"No, October."

"Good," she said. "We've plenty of time."

She rose from bed and started pacing up and down the room. There were cigarette ends on the floor, stained with lipstick. Boris bent down and picked them up with a stupid expression on his face.

"When are your pals starting?" she asked.

Boris carefully arranged the cigarette ends on the marble top of the bedside table. "Tomorrow evening," he told her without turning round.

"As soon as that!" she said.

"Yes, they've got to be quick about it."

"As soon as that!"

She walked to the window and opened it. She looked at the swaying masts of the fishing boats, the empty wharves, the pink sky, and she thought: Tomorrow evening. There was one more cable to cut, and only one. As soon as that was broken, she would turn round. Well, tomorrow evening is as good as any other time, she thought. The first golden gleams of sunrise lay on the idle sea. Far off Lola could hear a ship's siren. She waited until she felt truly free, then she turned toward him.

"Go if you want to," she said. "I'm not holding you back."

She got the words out with difficulty, but once they were spoken, she felt empty and relieved. She looked at Boris and thought, without knowing why: Poor boy, poor boy!

Boris had jumped to his feet. He went to her and took her by the arm. "Lola!"

"You're hurting me," she protested.

He dropped his hand, but the look he gave her was suspicious. "Won't it make you unhappy?"

"Yes," she said, "it'll make me unhappy, but I'd rather have it that way than see you a school teacher at Castelnaudary."

He seemed slightly reassured. "You couldn't live there any more than I could?" he asked.

"No more than you could," she said.

His shoulders drooped, he hung his arms. For the first time in his life he seemed to feel that his body was an embarrassment. Lola was grateful to him for not showing his joy openly.

"Lola!" he said. He stretched out his hand and touched

her shoulder. She wanted to tear that hand away from her shoulder, but she kept a tight hold on herself. She was smiling at him. She could feel the weight of his hand and already he was hers no longer, he was in England; already they faced each other as dead persons.

"I'd refused, you know," he said in a trembling voice. "I'd refused!"

"I know."

"I'll be true to you," he said. "I won't sleep with any other woman."

She smiled. "My poor boy."

He was in the way. She could have wished that the next evening had already come. Suddenly he struck his forehead.

"*Merde!* Hell!"

"What's the matter now?" she asked.

"I can't go! I can't go!"

"Why not?"

"Ivich! I told you she wanted to live with us."

"Boris!" said Lola in a fury, "if you won't stay for my sake, I forbid you to stay for Ivich's!" But her anger was something that belonged to a time already dead. "I'll look after Ivich," she said.

"You'll take her with you?"

"Why not?"

"But you can't stand her!"

"What's that got to do with it?" said Lola. She felt horribly tired. She said: "Either get dressed or go back to bed. You'll catch cold."

He took a towel and began to rub his body. He seemed bewildered. How odd, she thought: he's just made a decision that will affect his whole life. She sat down on the bed. He was rubbing away vigorously, but his face was gloomy.

"What's wrong?" she asked.

"Nothing," he said. "Everything's grand. What a sweat I got into!"

She rose to her feet with difficulty, grabbed his hair, and forced his head up. "Look at me. What's wrong?"

Boris turned his face away. "It's only that I think you're rather strange."

"What do you mean, strange?"

"You don't look very much put out at the idea of my going, I feel rather shocked."

"So you feel shocked, do you?" Lola repeated. "You actually feel shocked?" And she burst out laughing.

6 a.m.

Mᴀᴛʜɪᴇᴜ grunted, sat up, and rubbed his head. A cock crowed, the sun was warm and cheerful, though still low.

"Fine day," said Mathieu.

No one replied. They were all kneeling behind the parapet. Mathieu looked at his wrist watch and saw that it was six o'clock. He heard a distant, rhythmic rumbling. He crawled on all fours over to his companions.

"What is it? A plane?"

"No, it's them. Motorized infantry."

Mathieu hoisted himself up till he could see over their shoulders.

"Don't be a damned fool," said Clapot. "Keep well down; they've got glasses."

Two hundred yards before reaching the first houses, the road made a bend to the west, disappeared behind a grassy knoll, ran between the high buildings of a flour mill, which masked it, and entered the village at an angle, from the southwest. Mathieu could make out motor vehicles, very far away, which seemed not to be moving. He thought: "Here come the Germans!" and he felt frightened—frightened in an odd, almost religious way, a sort of sacred horror, such as is inspired by the supernatural. Thousands of foreign eyes, the eyes of supermen and insects, were raking the village. Mathieu was overwhelmed by a frightful realization: they *will see* my dead body.

"They'll be here any minute now," he said in spite of himself.

The others didn't answer. After a moment, in slow, solemn tones, Dandieu said: "No use opening fire at that range."

"Get back," Clapot ordered.

The four of them withdrew and sat down on one of the mattresses. Chasseriau and Dandieu looked exactly like two dried prunes, and Pinette was doing his best to resemble them: they had the same dirty faces and the same large, gentle eyes with no depth to them. "My eyes are like a doe's," Mathieu thought. Clapot was squatting on his heels; he talked back to them over his shoulder:

"They'll halt just outside the village and send in motorcyclists for a look-see. Whatever you do, don't fire on them."

Chasseriau yawned; the same sweetish and nauseous yawn distended Mathieu's mouth. He tried to fight against his fear, to find some little warmth in anger. To himself he said: "Christ! we're fighting men, aren't we? We're not victims!" But his anger was not *genuine*. He yawned again. Chasseriau looked at him with sympathy.

"The waiting is always the toughest part," he said. "You'll feel better later on, you'll see."

Clapot, still squatting on his heels, turned and faced them. "There's only one order," he said: "to defend the schoolhouse and the mayor's office; they mustn't get near either of them. The guys down there will give us the high sign. As soon as they start shooting, we can open up as much as we like. Remember, while they hold out, our job's only to cover them."

They looked at him with obedient and attentive faces.

"And after that?" asked Pinette.

"Clapot shrugged his shoulders. "Oh, after that—"

"I don't think they'll hold out long," said Dandieu.

"You never can tell. They may have a light field piece; it's up to us to stop them bringing it into action. We won't have a clear field of fire, but neither will they, because the road enters the village at an angle."

He got onto his knees again and crawled to the parapet. Screened by a pillar, he looked out over the countryside.

"Dandieu!"

"Eh?"

"Come over here."

He gave his directions without turning his head. "We'll face 'em, Dandieu, you and I. Chasseriau, you watch the right flank, and you, Delaruc, the left. Pinette, you'd better get round to the other side in case they try a turning movement."

Chasseriau dragged one of the mattresses to the parapet facing west. Mathieu took the blanket and dropped to his knees.

"I've got to turn my back on those bastards in the cellar," Pinette complained angrily.

"You've nothing to bellyache about," said Chasseriau. "I'll have the sun shining smack in my eyes."

Flattened against his pillar, Mathieu looked straight down at the *mairie;* by craning his head slightly to the right, he could see the road. The square was a deep pit filled with poisonous shadow, a trap; it made him feel sick to look at it. In the chestnuts the birds were singing.

"Watch your step!"

Mathieu held his breath. Two motorcyclists, dressed in black and wearing helmets, were dashing along the road: two supernatural messengers. He tried in vain to make out their faces: they had none. Two slim figures, four long, parallel legs, a pair of round, smooth heads with neither eyes nor mouths. They came on to an accompaniment of mechanical spasms with the stiff nobility of the figures that move forward on old-fashioned clocks when the hour strikes. The hour was just about to strike.

"Hold your fire!"

The motorcyclists made the round of the square, their exhausts roaring. Some sparrows flew off, but otherwise nothing stirred: the stage décor of a square was playing dead. Mathieu, fascinated, thought: "They're Germans." They caracoled past the *mairie*, riding immediately beneath him; he could see their great leather paws trembling on the handlebars; then they turned into the main street. A moment later they reappeared, sitting very upright, screwed to their jolting saddles; at top speed they whizzed back along the road by which they had come. Mathieu felt pleased that Clapot had told them not to fire: to him they seemed invulnerable. The birds circled for another moment or two, then flew back into the trees.

Clapot said: "It's our turn soon."

There was a screaming of brakes, car doors slammed, Mathieu heard steps and the sound of voices: a wave of nausea washed over him like the oncoming of sleep; he had to struggle to keep his eyes open. Through half-closed lids he looked down at the road and felt in a conciliatory mood. If we went down now and threw away our rifles, they'd crowd round us; perhaps they'd say: "Comrades of France, the war's over." The steps drew nearer. They've done nothing to us, they're not thinking of us, they wish us no harm. Suddenly he shut his eyes; hatred was about to spout to the skies. They'll see my dead body, they'll kick it out of their way. He was not afraid of death, he was afraid of hatred.

At last! A sharp crackling sounded in his ears, he opened his eyes: the road was silent and deserted. He tried to believe he had been dreaming. No one had fired, no one. . . .

"The fucking idiots!" Clapot muttered.

Mathieu gave a start. "Who?" he asked.

"The bastards in the *mairie*. They opened up too soon. They must have been scared as hell or they'd have let them come on."

Mathieu's gaze painfully retraced the road, slipping over the cobbles and the tufts of grass in the cracks between them, until it came to the corner of the street. No one. Silence; *a village in August; the men are in the fields.* But he knew that from behind those walls were men planning his death. They're trying to do us as much damage as possible. He foundered in a sea of syrupy kindliness; he loved the whole world, Frenchmen, Germans, Hitler. In a soggy dream he heard shouts, followed by a violent explosion and the clatter of broken glass; then the firing started again. He gripped his rifle to keep it from falling.

"That grenade fell short," Clapot muttered.

The firing was continuous now; the Heinies were using their rifles. Two more grenades exploded. If it could only stop, just for a moment, so I could get a grip on myself. But the cracking and banging and din of explosions went merrily on; inside his head a cogwheel kept turning ever more quickly; each cog was a rifle-shot. Christ! Suppose I turn out to be a coward! That would be the last straw! He turned and looked at his buddies: squatting on their heels, their faces pale, their eyes hard and shining, Clapot and Dandieu were watching. Pinette had his back to him; his neck was stiff and rigid, his shoulders were jerking. Pinette was in the throes of St. Vitus's dance or a fit of uncontrollable laughter; his shoulders kept jerking. Mathieu, taking shelter behind a pillar, cautiously poked his head out. He managed to keep his eyes open, but he could not bring himself to look at the *mairie;* he gazed toward the south, where all was empty and calm. That way lay Marseille and the sea. There was another explosion, followed by a dry rattling on the tiles of the clock tower. Mathieu screwed up his eyes, but the road still

streaked by beneath him. The objects he descried swept
along, a blurred mass, and dwindled out of sight; this was
all a dream. The pit grew deeper, it seemed to hypnotize
him; *all was a dream.* A wheel of fire kept turning, turning, like the spinning disk at a waffle booth. He was about
to wake up in bed when he noticed a toad crawling into
battle. For a moment, with complete indifference, Mathieu
watched the squat creature; then the toad became a man.
With extraordinary clarity Mathieu saw the two creases
on the shaven back of his neck, his green blouse, his belt,
his soft, black leather boots. "He must have got here
across the fields; now he's crawling towards the *mairie* to
throw his grenade." The German was working his way
forward with knees and elbows; his right hand, which he
held aloft, grasped a stick topped by a cylinder of metal,
like a small saucepan.

"But—" Mathieu stuttered, "but, but—"

The road stopped streaking by, the road came to a dead
stop. Mathieu jumped to his feet and buried his rifle in
the pit of his shoulder; a hard look came into his eyes. He
stood there, a foursquare object in a world of foursquare
objects, with an enemy at the business end of his rifle,
and he calmly aimed at the man's stomach. A momentary
grin of superiority stretched his lips: the famous German
Army, the army of supermen, the army of locusts, was
summed up in this poor devil, who looked touching because he was so wrong-headed, so bogged down in igno-
rance and error, so absorbed in what he was doing; the
poor bastard had all the comic intentness of a small child.
Mathieu was in no hurry, he kept his eye on his man, he
had plenty of time. The German Army is *vulnerable.* He
fired. The man gave a funny little jerk, then fell on his
stomach, throwing his arms forward, like somebody learning to swim. Mathieu, amused, fired again; the poor
wretch swam two or three strokes more, then dropped his
grenade, which rolled on the roadway without exploding.

He lay quite still, inoffensive and grotesque, smashed. "I've soothed *him*," Mathieu said in a low voice, "I've cooked *his* goose." He looked at the dead man and thought: "They're just like everyone else!" He felt happy as a lark.

He was aware of a hand on his shoulder: Clapot was taking a look at the job done by this amateur. Clapot stared at the squashed insect, nodding his head, then turned round.

"Chasseriau!"

Chasseriau crawled toward them on his knees.

"Keep an eye on this side," Clapot ordered.

"I don't need Chasseriau," Mathieu objected, vexed.

"They'll try to pay us back for that one," said Clapot. "If they attack in strength, you'll be overrun."

There was a burst of machine-gun fire. Clapot raised his eyebrows.

"Hullo!" he said, going back to his own post, "things are beginning to warm up."

Mathieu turned to Chasseriau. "I rather think we're giving the Heinies a headache!" he said excitedly.

Chasseriau said nothing. He had a heavy, animal, almost sleepy look.

"You notice how long they're taking?" asked Mathieu in a strained voice. "I'd have thought they'd settle with us in two shakes of a duck's tail."

Chasseriau looked at him in astonishment, then glanced at his wrist-watch. "Only three minutes since the motorcyclists rode by," he said.

Mathieu's excitement collapsed; he laughed. Chasseriau stared straight ahead; Mathieu, viewing his dead soldier, continued to laugh. For years he had tried in vain to act; one after another he had been robbed of action as fast as he had determined to act; he had been about as firm as a pat of butter. But this time no one had cheated him. He had pressed a trigger, and, for once, something had happened, something definite. The thought made him laugh louder than ever. His ears were deafened by shouts and by the din of explosions, but he scarcely heard them; he looked with satisfaction at his dead man. He thought: "I bet the bastard felt that all right! He knew what was happening to him, he understood!" *His* dead man, *his* handiwork, something to mark *his* passage on the earth. A longing came to him to do some more killing: it was fun and it was easy; he would have liked to plunge all Germany into mourning.

"Look out!"

A fellow was creeping along the wall, holding a grenade in his hand. Mathieu took careful aim at this strange, delectable creature. His heart was thumping against his ribs.

"Shit, piss, and corruption!"

He had missed him. The thing he had fired at bunched up, became a bewildered human being who looked about him without understanding. Chasseriau fired. The man slackened like a spring, straightened up, sprang into the air, winding up for the throw, and hurled his grenade; then he crumpled up on his back in the middle of the road. At the same moment there was a crash of broken glass. In a blinding flash Mathieu saw a number of shadowy figures twisting and writhing on the ground floor of the *mairie;* then everything went black; there were yellow spots in front of his eyes. He felt furious with Chasseriau.

"Shit!" he repeated with rage. "Hell! Hell!"

"Shut up," said Chasseriau. "Anyhow, he missed: the boys are up on the second floor."

Mathieu blinked his eyes and shook his head to get rid of the yellow spots which were dazzling him. "I'm blinded," he said.

"It'll pass," said Chasseriau. "Just plug that fellow I dropped if he makes a move."

Mathieu leaned forward; he could see somewhat better now. The Heinie was lying on his back, his eyes wide open, his legs twitching. Mathieu raised his rifle.

"Don't be a damned fool!" said Chasseriau. "Don't waste ammunition!"

Mathieu lowered his rifle sullenly. "The bastard may make a getaway," he thought.

The door of the *mairie* was flung open. A man appeared on the threshold and advanced with a sort of grandeur in his movements. He was naked to the waist: he looked like an anatomical model. His face was dark red as though it had been flayed, the skin hung from it in flakes. Suddenly he started to scream. Twenty rifle-shots rang out simultaneously. He tottered, pitched forward, and collapsed on the steps.

"That wasn't one of ours," said Chasseriau.

"No," said Mathieu, in a voice strangled with rage, "he was one of ours, a guy called Latex."

His hands were trembling, his eyes hurt him. Tremulously he repeated: "Latex he was called. He had six kids."

Then suddenly he leaned over the parapet and aimed straight at the wounded man, whose great eyes seemed to be fixed on him.

"You're going to pay for that, you dirty bastard."

"You're going berserk!" Chasseriau warned. "Didn't I tell you not to waste ammo?"

"Oh, go to hell!" said Mathieu.

He was in no hurry to shoot. If the swine can see me, he won't enjoy what he sees. He leveled his sights on the man's head and fired. The head burst, but the man was still twitching.

"Swine!" Mathieu shouted. "Swine!"

"Look out, for Christ's sake! Look out! To the left!"

Five or six Germans had just come into view. Chasseriau and Mathieu both opened fire, but the Germans were employing different tactics. They had taken cover behind the corners of the houses and stood there, apparently waiting.

"Clapot! Dandieu! Come over here!" Chasseriau shouted. "There's something screwy going on."

"I can't move," said Clapot.

"Pinette!" Mathieu yelled.

Pinette made no reply. Mathieu dared not turn round. "Look out!"

The Germans had started to run. Mathieu fired, but they were already across the road.

"Christ!" said Clapot. "There are some Boches under the trees. Who let 'em get by?"

No one answered. The ground under the trees was alive with men. Chasseriau took a pot shot.

"It'll be one hell of a hard job to get them out of there."

The men in the schoolhouse had started shooting; the Germans under the trees were returning their fire. The *mairie* was silent. Smoke was billowing very low over the road.

"Don't shoot into the trees!" Clapot shouted. "It's a waste of ammo."

At that moment a grenade exploded against the second floor of the *mairie*.

"They're climbing the trees," said Chasseriau.

"If they do, we'll get 'em," Mathieu answered.

He peered into the dense foliage, saw a lifted arm, and fired. Too late: the *mairie* went up in smoke, the windows of the second floor were wrenched from their frames; for a second time Mathieu was blinded by the same horrible yellow flash. He fired at random and heard the sound of large, ripe fruits, tumbling from branch to branch; he had no idea whether the men were falling or climbing down.

"The *mairie's* out of action!" Clapot reported.

They held their breath, listening. The Germans kept up their fire, but there was no reply from the *mairie*. Mathieu shuddered. Dead men. Joints of bleeding meat on the staved-in floors of empty rooms.

"It's not our fault," Chasseriau said. "They were too many for us."

Suddenly great clouds of smoke billowed up from the second-floor windows. Through the smoke Mathieu could see red and black flames. Someone in the *mairie* shrieked in a shrill, feminine, impersonal voice. Mathieu suddenly felt he was going to die. Chasseriau fired.

"You're crazy!" Mathieu told him. "Why keep firing at the *mairie?* Who's wasting ammo now?"

Chasseriau kept his rifle leveled at the windows of the *mairie;* he fired three times into the flames.

"It's that poor bastard screaming. I can't stand it."

"He's still screaming," said Mathieu.

They listened, frozen with horror. The voice grew weaker.

"That's that! It's all over."

But even as Mathieu spoke, the inhuman noise started again, a vast, solemn noise creeping up the scale to a high shrillness. Mathieu, too, began shooting at the windows, but with no result.

"He won't die!" said Chasseriau.

Of a sudden the screaming stopped.

"Phew!" said Mathieu.

"He's through!" Chasseriau said. "Finished, burnt to a crisp."

There was no sign of movement now either under the trees or in the street. The sun laid a patina of gold over the burning front of the *mairie.* Chasseriau looked at his watch.

"Seven minutes," he said.

Mathieu turned and twisted in the flames, a blazing torch, he was choking. He had to clasp his hands to his chest and move them slowly downward to his stomach to convince himself that he was unscathed.

Clapot's voice rose sharply: "There are some of 'em on the roofs."

"On the roofs?"

"Right opposite; they're firing at the schoolhouse. Hell and shit, can you see what they're doing?"

"What?"

"They're bringing up a machine-gun. Pinette!" he shouted.

Pinette crawled back toward them.

"Come over here! The guys in the schoolhouse are in for a spraying."

Pinette, raising himself on hands and knees, stared at them vacantly. His face was ashen gray.

"Anything wrong?" Mathieu asked.

"Nothing wrong," Pinette answered dryly, dragging himself toward Clapot, then kneeling by the parapet.

"Give 'em the works!" Clapot ordered. "Shoot into the street to distract attention. We'll look after the machine-gun.

Pinette said nothing, but started to shoot.

"Do better'n that, for Christ's sake!" cried Clapot. "You can't shoot if you shut your eyes!"

Pinette gave a start; he seemed to be making a violent effort to control himself. A little color had come back into his cheeks. He was aiming with his eyes wide open. Clapot and Dandieu, beside him, were firing continuously. Clapot uttered a shout of triumph.

"That's done it!" he cried. "That's done it! We've silenced them."

Mathieu strained his ears: the noise of the machine-gun had stopped. "Yes," he said, "but the boys down there have stopped firing."

The schoolhouse was silent. Three Germans who had been hiding under the trees raced across the road and flung themselves against the door of the schoolhouse. It flew open. They rushed in, and reappeared a moment later, leaning from the second-floor windows, gesturing and shouting. Clapot fired and they vanished. A few moments later Mathieu, for the first time since morning, heard the whine of a bullet. Chasseriau looked at his watch.

"Ten minutes," he said.

"Yes," said Mathieu, "this is the beginning of the end."

The *mairie* was burning, the Germans occupied the schoolhouse; it was as though France had been defeated a second time.

"Shoot! For Christ's sake, shoot!"

A few Germans showed themselves cautiously at the far end of the street. Chasseriau, Pinette, and Clapot fired at them. The heads disappeared.

"This time they've caught on."

Once more there was silence, a long silence. Mathieu thought: "What are they up to?" In the empty street lay four dead men; a little farther on, two more: the sum total of what we've been able to do. Nothing for it but to finish the job and get polished off. What difference has all this made to the Germans? It has merely put their time-table out by ten minutes.

"Our turn now," said Clapot suddenly.

A small, squat monster was moving toward the church. It glittered in the sun.

"*Schnellfeuerkanon*," muttered Dandieu between his teeth.

Mathieu crawled toward them. They were still firing, though there was no one to be seen. The gun seemed to be moving independently of human aid. They were firing from a sense of duty, because there was still some ammunition left. Their faces had a calm, tired beauty, the faces of their last hour.

"Back!"

A big man in shirt-sleeves appeared suddenly on the left of the gun. He made no attempt to take cover, but gave his orders quietly, with one arm raised. Mathieu straightened up suddenly: the little figure with its bare throat inflamed him with desire.

"Back, and keep down!"

The gun's maw rose slowly in the air. Mathieu had not moved; he knelt there aiming at the *Feldwebel*.

"Hear what I said?" Clapot shouted.

"Shut up!" grumbled Mathieu.

Mathieu fired first. The butt of his rifle drove back against his shoulder; at the same moment there was a huge detonation like the amplified echo of his own shot. Everything went red before his eyes, then he heard a long-drawn-out muffled sound of tearing linen.

"They missed us!" Clapot exclaimed. "They're aiming too high!"

The *Feldwebel* was writhing on the ground, his legs in the air. Mathieu looked at him with a smile. He was about to finish him off when two soldiers appeared on the scene and carried him away. Mathieu worked himself backwards, still on his knees, and lay down beside Dandieu.

Clapot already had the trapdoor open. "Come on, down with you!"

Dandieu shook his head.

"There are no windows on the floor below."

They looked at one another.

"We must use up our ammo," said Chasseriau.

"Got much left?"

"Two magazines."

"How about you, Dandieu?"

"One."

Clapot let the trap fall again. "You're right," he agreed, "we must use it up."

Behind him Mathieu heard the sound of rasping breath; he turned. Pinette, pale to the lips, was breathing with difficulty.

"You been hit?"

Pinette looked at him with a wild expression. "No."

Clapot stared attentively at Pinette. "If you want to go down, lad, nobody's going to stop you. It's a matter of ammo with us, you know; we've got to use it up."

"Hell!" said Pinette. "Why should I go down if Delarue's staying?" He dragged himself to the parapet and started to fire.

"Pinette!" Mathieu shouted.

Pinette did not answer. Bullets were whining over them.

"Let him alone," said Clapot. "It'll give him something to do."

The gun fired two shots in rapid succession; they heard a dull shock above their heads, and a shower of plaster rained down on them from the ceiling. Chasseriau took out his watch.

"Twelve minutes."

Mathieu and Chasseriau crawled to the parapet. Matheiu squatted down beside Pinette, with Chasseriau on his right, standing and leaning forward.

"Not bad, twelve minutes," Chasseriau commented. "Not at all bad."

The air about them screamed, hurtled, and struck Mathieu full in the face: it felt hot and heavy like the flick of a damp rag. Mathieu collapsed in a sitting-position. He was blinded by blood; his hands were red to the wrists. He rubbed his eyes, mingling the blood on his hands with that on his face. Chasseriau was sitting on the south side parapet, headless; blood was spouting and bubbling from his neck.

"I can't stand it," said Pinette, "I can't stand it!"

He jumped up, ran to Chasseriau, and struck him full on the chest with the butt of his rifle. Chasseriau swayed and tumbled over the parapet. Mathieu, seeing him fall, felt no emotion. This was no more than the beginning of his own death.

"Independent fire!" shouted Clapot.

The square was suddenly alive with soldiers. Mathieu went back to his post and resumed firing. Dandieu was firing close by.

"It's a massacre!" said Dandieu with a laugh. He dropped his rifle, which fell into the street. He crumpled up on top of Mathieu, with the words: "Good lad! Good old pal!"

Mathieu pushed him away with his shoulder. Dandieu fell backwards, and Mathieu went on firing. He was still firing when the roof fell on top of him. A beam struck him on the head. He dropped his rifle and fell. "Fifteen minutes!" he thought in a fury; "I'd give anything just to hold on for fifteen minutes!" The butt of a rifle was jutting from a pile of splintered wood and broken tiles; he seized it: it was sticky with blood, but still loaded.

"Pinette!" shouted Mathieu.

Pinette did not answer. The ruins of the roof obstructed the whole north side of the platform; the trapdoor was blocked by a heap of beams and rubble; an iron bar was hanging from the yawning rent in the ceiling. Mathieu was alone.

"Christ!" he said out loud. "No one can say we didn't hold out for fifteen minutes."

He made his way to the parapet and stood there firing. This was revenge on a big scale; each one of his shots wiped out some ancient scruple. One for Lola, whom I dared not rob, one for Marcelle, whom I ought to have ditched, one for Odette, whom I didn't want to screw. This for the books I never dared to write, this for the journeys I never made, this for everybody in general whom I wanted to hate and tried to understand. He fired, and the tables of the law crashed about him—Thou shalt love thy neighbor as thyself—bang! in that bastard's face—Thou shalt not kill—bang! at that scarecrow opposite. He was firing on his fellow men, on Virtue, on the

whole world: Liberty is Terror. The *mairie* was ablaze,
his head was ablaze; bullets were whining around him,
free as the air. The world is going up in smoke, and me
with it. He fired; he looked at his watch: fourteen minutes
and thirty seconds. Nothing more to ask of fate now except one half-minute, just time enough to fire at that
smart officer, at all the Beauty of the Earth, at the street,
at the flowers, at the gardens, at everything he had loved.
Beauty dived downwards obscenely, and Mathieu went
on firing. He fired: he was cleansed, he was all-powerful,
he was free.

Fifteen minutes.

PART TWO

NIGHT, starlight; a red glow in the northern sky—
doubtless some hamlet ablaze. Eastward and west-
ward, long flashes of heat, winking sharp and spasmodic:
enemy guns. "Enemy guns everywhere, and tomorrow
they'll get me."

He entered the sleeping village; he crossed a square,
drew up to a house at random, and knocked in vain; then
he pressed the latch gently and the door opened. He went
in, closed the door behind him; all was blackness. A
match. He was in a corridor, a mirror shone vaguely out
of the darkness. He looked at himself in it. "I need a
shave," he thought. The match went out.

He saw a staircase leading downwards on his left. He
groped his way toward it. The staircase turned, Brunet
turned with it; he was conscious of a vague, diffused light,
he turned once more: the cellar. It smelled of wine and
mushrooms. Some barrels, a heap of straw. A bulky man
in nightshirt and trousers was sitting on the straw beside
a half-naked blonde who held a child in her arms. They
looked up at Brunet, their three mouths open, gaping
with fear. Brunet went down the remaining stairs; the

man was still looking at him. Brunet went on. Suddenly the man said: "My wife is sick."

"What of it?" asked Brunet.

"I didn't want her to spend the night in the woods."

"Why tell *me* that? I don't give a good God-damn," Brunet answered. He was in the cellar now.

The man looked at him defiantly. "What do you want, anyhow?"

"I want to sleep here," said Brunet.

The man pulled a face; he was still staring hard.

"You a warrant officer?"

Brunet did not reply.

"Where are your men?" asked the other suspiciously.

"Dead," Brunet replied, moving over to the pile of straw.

"What about the Germans?" the man asked. "Where are they?"

"Everywhere."

"They mustn't find you here," the man said.

Brunet took off his blouse, folded it up, laid it on one of the casks.

"Hear what I said?" shouted the man.

"I heard," Brunet said.

"I've got a wife and kid: I don't want to pay for any of your nonsense!"

"Take it easy," said Brunet. He sat down.

The woman looked at him with hatred. "There are some Frenchmen up there who are going to fight; you ought to be with them."

Brunet looked at her. She pulled her nightdress up over her breasts; she shouted: "Get out of here! Get out of here! You've lost the war, and now you're going to get us killed into the bargain!"

"Calm down," Brunet told her. "All you need do is wake me when the Germans arrive."

"What'll you do then?"

"Give myself up."

"Dirty bastard!" said the woman, "the boys up there are going to get killed!"

Brunet yawned, stretched, and smiled. He had been fighting for a week without sleep and almost without food. Twenty times he had been within an ace of staying where he lay, for good and all. No more fighting for him, now; the war was lost and he had work to do. A lot of work. He lay down on the straw, yawned, and fell asleep.

"Get out!" the man called, "here they are."

Brunet opened his eyes; he saw a large red face, he could hear the cracking of rifles and the thud of explosions.

"They were here?"

"Yes. There's a scrap going on. You can't stay here."

The woman had not moved. She was looking at Brunet with a savage glare, holding her sleeping child in her arms.

"I'll beat it," Brunet said. He got up, yawned, went over to where there was a ventilating-shaft, routed about in his haversack, from it took a fragment of mirror and a razor. The man stared at him with loutish indignation.

"You're not going to shave?"

"Why not?" asked Brunet.

The man's face was red with fury. "I tell you they'll shoot me if they find you here."

"I won't take but a minute," Brunet told him.

The man took hold of his arm and tried to push him out. "I won't have it! I've got a wife and a kid; if I'd known, I wouldn't have let you come in."

Brunet shook himself free. He looked with disgust at that great hulk of flesh which seemed so determined to go on living, which would live on under every regime, humble, muddleheaded, close-fisted, of use to no one. The fellow made a rush at him. Brunet flung him against the wall. "You keep quiet, or there'll be trouble!"

The man said nothing. He was breathing heavily and rolling his drink-sodden eyes. He seemed to be gathering himself for a spring. He gave off a strong smell of death and dung. Brunet started to shave, without soap or water; his skin smarted. Beside him the woman sat shivering with terror and hatred. Brunet hurried. "If I'm too long about it, she'll go mad." He put his razor back in the haversack; the blade'll do for two more shaves. "There now, I'm through. Not worth making all that fuss."

The man still said nothing. The woman screamed: "Get out, you dirty beast, you filthy coward, you'll get us all shot!"

Brunet put on his blouse; he felt clean, fresh, and stiff. His face was red.

"Get out! Get out!"

He raised two fingers in farewell. "Many thanks," he said.

He climbed the dark staircase and crossed an entrance hall. The front door was wide open. Outside, the white cascade of the day, the lunatic stammer of machine-guns; the house was dark and cool. He walked over to the door: he must make a plunge into that surf of light. A small square, the church, the war memorial, piles of manure in front of the houses. Between two blazing buildings the main road looked pink in the morning sun. The Germans were there, thirty men or so, all busy, workmen on the job; they were firing on the church with a *Schnellfeuerkanon* and being shot at from the tower; the place looked like a builder's yard. In the middle of the square, beneath the cross-fire, French soldiers in shirt-sleeves, their eyes red with sleep, were tiptoeing along, with short, hurried steps, like so many competitors filing past the judges at a beauty contest. Their pale hands were raised above their heads, and the sun played antics between their fingers. Brunet looked at them, he looked at the church tower. To his right a large building was in flames; he could feel the heat on his face. "Hell!" he said, and went down the three steps into the street. It was all over: he was taken. He kept his hands in his pockets; they felt as heavy as lead.

"Put 'em up!" A German was pointing his rifle straight at him. He flushed, his hands rose slowly until they were in the air above his head: they shall pay for that with blood. He joined the Frenchmen and tripped along with them. It's just like a movie, nothing looks real, those bullets can't kill anyone, the gun's firing blank shells. One of the Frenchmen dropped a curtsy and fell; Brunet stepped over him. Without hurrying, he turned the corner of the brown house and emerged on the main road at the same moment as the church tower collapsed. No more Heinies, no more bullets, the movie was over, he was in the open country, he put his hands back in his pockets. All around him were Frenchmen. A crowd of little Frenchmen in khaki, unwashed, unshaved, their faces blackened with smoke, laughing, joking, talking together in low voices, a bobbing sea of bare heads and service caps and not a helmet among them. There were recognitions and greetings: "Saw you at Saverne in December. Hello, Girard, how goes it? Takes a defeat, don't it, to bring old pals together? Is Lisa O.K.?" A single German soldier, with a bored look and his rifle slung, was in charge of this herd of the undersized vanquished; he matched his long, slow stride to the patter of their progress. Brunet pattered with the rest, though he was as tall as the Boche and as smoothly shaved.

The pink road wound between stretches of grass; there was not a breath of air, only the stifling stillness of defeat. The men smelt strong, they chattered away, and the birds sang. Brunet turned to his neighbor, a large, kindly-looking fellow who was breathing through his mouth.

"Where does this lot come from?"

"From Saverne. We spent the night in farmhouses."

"I came on my own," said Brunet. "All this is a damned nuisance, I thought the village was deserted."

A young, fair-haired fellow with a sun-tanned face was walking along a couple of files from him. He was stripped to the waist and had a great bleeding scab between his shoulder blades. Behind Brunet a vast hubbub developed, the normal, everyday sound of shouts and laughter and boots scrabbling on the surface of the road; it sounded like the noise of wind in the trees. Brunet turned his head: by this time the number of men behind him had run into thousands; mopped up from here, there, and everywhere, from the fields, from the hamlets, from the farms. Brunet towered head and shoulders above the rest, a solitary landmark in the undulating sea of heads.

"I'm Moulu," said the big man, "from Bar-le-Duc." He added with pride: "I know this part of the country."

At the side of the road a farm was burning; the flames looked black in the sunlight. A dog was howling.

"Hear that pooch?" Moulu said to his neighbor. "They shut him up inside."

The man he was speaking to hailed, obviously, from the north; he was blond, medium-sized, with a skin like milk; he bore a strong resemblance to the Heinie in charge of them. He frowned and looked at Moulu with his large blue eyes.

"What's that?"

"The dog. He's inside."

"Well, what of it?" said the northerner; "it's only a dog."

"Ouah! Ouah! Ouah! Ouah!" This time it was not the dog howling, but the young fellow with the naked back. Someone was dragging him along with one hand clamped over his mouth. Brunet had a glimpse of his large, pale, frightened face with its lashless eyes.

"Charpin don't seem too good," said Moulu to the northerner.

The northerner stared at him. "Eh?"

"I said your pal Charpin don't seem too good."

The northerner laughed, displaying very white teeth. "He's always been kind of peculiar."

The road began to climb. All about them was a delicious smell of sun-warmed stone and wood-smoke; behind them the dog was howling. They reached the top of the hill; the road began to descend steeply.

Moulu jerked his thumb in the direction of the interminable column. "Where's all this mob from?" He turned to Brunet. "How many would you say there are?"

"I don't know. Maybe ten thousand, maybe more."

Moulu looked at him incredulously. "Do you mean to say you can tell that just by looking at 'em?"

Brunet thought of the 14th of July, of the 1st of May, when they used to have fellows posted along the boulevard Richard-Lenoir to estimate the numbers demonstrating, timing their progress past a given point. The crowds on those occasions had been silent and hot; to stand among them was stifling. This crowd was noisy, but cold and dead. He smiled.

"I'm used to crowds," he said.

"Where are we going?" the northerner asked.

"Search me!"

"Where are the Heinies? Who's in charge of this gang?" The only Heinies they saw amounted to about ten whom they passed along the road. The herd slid down the hill as though propelled by its own weight.

"This is crazy!" Moulu said.

"You bet it is," Brunet agreed, "it's crazy." It was crazy; there were enough of them to overwhelm the Germans, to strangle them and then make off across the fields. But what good would that do? On they trudged straight ahead, as the road took them. Awhile back they had been at the bottom of the hill, in a kind of cup; now they were climbing, they felt hot.

From his pocket Moulu took a bundle of letters held together by a rubber band and for a while turned it over and over in his great clumsy fingers. Sweat made stains on the paper, causing the violet ink to run. Then he took off the elastic band; he started to tear the letters up methodically, without rereading them, and scattered the fragments with the movement of a man sowing seed. Brunet followed their eddying progress with his eyes; most of them fell, like showers of confetti, on the men's shoulders, and from there to their feet; there was one that fluttered for a moment and then settled on a tuft of grass. The blades bent slightly, upholding it like a canopy. There were other pieces of paper all along the road, torn, crumpled up, rolled into balls; they lay in the ditches, among the broken rifles and dented helmets. Where the writing was round and elongated, Brunet could make out an occasional sentence: eat well, don't expose yourself, Hélène has come with the children, all my love, darling. The road was one long, dirtied love-letter. Small flabby monsters crouched low on the ground, watching the gay convoy of defeated men with sightless eyes—gas-masks.

Moulu nudged Brunet with his elbow and pointed to one of them. "Lucky we didn't have to use 'em."

Brunet said nothing; Moulu looked about for someone else to confide in. "Hey! Lambert!" A man in front of Brunet turned his head. Moulu silently pointed to a gas-mask and they both began to laugh; others near them joined in. They were filled with hatred of the parasitic grubs that had once filled them with terror, yet that they had had to care for and keep efficient. Now they lay beneath their feet, smashed and useless; the sight of them was a further reminder that the war was over.

Peasants who had come as usual to the fields to work leaned on their spades as they watched the men pass. Lambert was in a gay mood and shouted to them: "Morning, daddy! We're the boys they drafted!" Ten voices, a hundred, repeated with a kind of defiance: "We're the boys they drafted, we're the boys they drafted! We're all going home!" The peasants said nothing; they seemed not even to have heard.

A youth with blond, frizzled hair, who looked as though he came from Paris, asked Lambert: "How long d'you think it'll be?"

"Pretty soon," said Lambert, "pretty soon, Goldilocks."

"Really think so? Are you sure?"

"Look for yourself. Where are the guys who ought to be guarding us? If we were real honest-to-God prisoners, we'd be watched more carefully than this."

"Why did they capture us, then?" Moulu asked.

"Capture? They didn't capture us; they've just put us aside so we won't get in the way while they're advancing."

"Even so," Goldilocks sighed, "it might be quite a while."

"Are you crazy? Why, they can't run fast enough to keep up with us fellows!" He was as merry as a cricket and laughing all the while. "Nothing for old Fritz to do: just a pleasure jaunt in the country with a nice little skirt in Paris, a drink or two at Dijon, and a bowl of bouilla-baisse at Marseille. Marseille'll be the end. Damn it all, they can't go beyond Marseille: that's where the sea starts. When they get there, they'll turn us loose. We'll be home by the middle of August."

Goldilocks shook his head. "That means two months. It's a long time."

"You're in a thundering hurry. They got to mend the railroad tracks, haven't they?—so's to get the trains running."

"They can keep their trains, for all I care," Moulu said. "If that's all we're waiting for, I'd do it on my flat feet!"

"Hell, not for me! I've been walking for the last two weeks and I've had my bellyful, I want to take things easy."

"How about having a tumble with your girl?"

"What'll I use? I've done so much foot-slogging, I haven't anything left inside my pants. I want to sleep, and alone."

Brunet listened to them, he looked at the backs of their necks, he thought what a lot of work there was for him to do. Poplars, poplars, a bridge over a stream, more poplars.

"Makes a fellow thirsty," said Moulu.

"It's not the thirst I mind," said the northerner, "it's the hunger: I haven't had a bite since yesterday."

Moulu was sweating profusely as he jogged along, panting; he took off his blouse, put it across his arm, and unbuttoned his shirt. "Anyhow, a guy can take off his coat now," he said with a grin, "we're free."

There was a sudden halt; Brunet bumped into Lambert's back. Lambert turned round; he had a fringe of beard under his chin, and sharp little eyes under thick-growing black brows.

"Why can't you look where yer going, clumsy? Haven't you got eyes in yer face?" He looked at Brunet's uniform with an insolent expression. "Noncoms are finished. No one's giving orders now—we're all just regular fellers."

Brunet returned his look, but without anger, and the man said no more. Brunet found himself wondering what his job in civilian life might be. Was he a small shopkeeper? A clerk? Middle-class anyhow. There must be hundreds of thousands like him, with no feeling for authority and no sense of personal cleanliness. There'd have to be iron discipline.

"What are we stopping for?" asked Moulu. Brunet made no reply. Another lower-middle-class product; there was not much difference between him and the other except that he was stupider: not easy material to work on. Moulu heaved a sigh of contentment and began to fan himself. "Perhaps we've got time to sit down." He put his haversack by the roadside and squatted on it.

The German soldier came up and turned his long,

handsome, expressionless face toward them, with a vague look of sympathy in his blue eyes. Speaking slowly and carefully, he said: "Poor French, war is over. You go home. You go home."

"What's he say? What's he say? That we're going home? You're damned right we're going home! Hear that, Julien, he says we're going home. Ask him when. Ask him when we're going home."

"Give us the low-down Heinie, when are we going home?" Their attitude to him was at once servile and familiar. He might represent the army of the victors, but he was only a foot-slogger.

The German, still with his blank stare, repeated:

"You go home, you go home."

"But *when*, eh?"

"Poor French, you go home."

The column started to move again, poplars, poplars. Moulu groaned; he was hot, he was thirsty, he was tired, he wanted to stop, but no one could check this plodding progress because there was nobody in command. Someone grunted: "My head's splitting," and trudged on. The talk began to flag, there were long spells of silence; the same thought was in every mind: "Surely we're not going on walking like this all the way to Berlin?" And they walked; each man, pushed along by the man behind, followed the man ahead. A village, on the square a pile of hemets, gas-masks, and rifles.

"Poudroux," said Moulu, "I came through it yesterday."

"So did I," said Goldilocks, "yesterday evening; in a truck I was. The people were all out on their doorsteps, they didn't look too pleased to see us." They were there now, on the doorsteps, their arms folded, silent: women with black hair, black eyes and black dresses, and old men, all staring. Confronted by these spectators, the prisoners straightened up, their faces became peaked and cynical, they waved their hands, they laughed and shouted: "Hello,

ma! Hello, pa! We're the guys they drafted, the war's over,
so long!" They passed with their greetings, ogling the girls,
smiling provocatively, but the spectators said nothing,
they just looked. Only the grocer's wife, a fat, good-natured creature, murmured: "Poor boys!"

The man from the north smiled gleefully. "Good thing
we're not where I come from," he said to Lambert.

"Why?"

"They would be throwing furniture at us."

A water-trough; ten men, a hundred, broke from the
ranks in their eagerness to drink. Moulu was one of them;
he leaned down clumsily, greedily; they slaked their weariness; their shoulders moved spasmodically; the water ran
over their faces. The German guard seemed not to notice
them: they could have stayed in the village had they been
brave enough to face the inhabitants' hostile eyes. But they
made no effort to do so; one by one they came back,
hurrying as though they feared to miss their places in the
line. Moulu ran like a woman, knock-kneed. They jostled
one another, laughing and shouting, shameless and provocative as a crowd of "fairies," their mouths gaping with
merriment, their eyes abject like the eyes of beaten dogs.

Moulu wiped his lips. "That was good," he said. He
looked at Brunet with astonishment. "Aren't you thirsty?
Aren't you thirsty?"

Brunet shrugged his shoulders without answering. A
pity this mob wasn't surrounded by five hundred soldiers
with fixed bayonets, prodding the laggards and bashing
the chatterers with their butts: that would wipe the grins
off their faces. He looked to the right, to the left, he
turned his head, seeking amid this forest of lost, hysterical
features twisted into masks of irrepressible gaiety for
someone like himself. Where were the comrades? Not hard
to tell a Communist when you see him. Oh, for one face,
one hard, calm face, the face of a man! But no: under-

sized, nimble, mean, they sloped along, their ferrety muzzles pressing ever onwards, the facile mobility of their race showing through the dirt, twitching their mouths like the mouths of puppets, compressing or dilating their nostrils, wrinkling their foreheads, making their eyes sparkle; they were no good for anything but to appraise, to draw fine distinctions, to argue and judge and criticize, to weigh the pros and cons, to savor objections, to demonstrate, to draw conclusions—an interminable syllogism in which each one of them was a term. On they slouched, obedient, argumentative, unworried: the war was over; they had seen no fighting; the Germans didn't appear to be a bad lot. They were unworried because they imagined they had summed up their new masters, and they were intent on hoarding the fruits of their intelligence—that specifically French *article de luxe*—so that they could later use it to advantage with the Heinies to buy a few trivial concessions. Poplars, poplars, the sun blazing down on them: noon.

"That's them!" Gone suddenly all sign of intelligence, a groan of delight rose from the whole concourse, not a cry, not even a murmur, but, rather, a sort of wordless, passive reflex of admiration, like the gentle susurration of leaves under a shower of rain. "That's them!" Back and forth the words passed from man to man like a rumor of good news: that's them! that's them! The ranks crowded together, jostling into the gutter, a shudder went through the long caterpillar: the Germans were moving down the road, in cars, in tractors, in trucks, freshly shaven, rested, tanned, handsome, calm faces, remote as Alpine pastures, they had eyes for no one, but sat there staring southward, driving into the heart of France, upright and silent, getting a free trip, foot-slogging on wheels, that's what I call a war, look at them machine-guns, oh! and the mobile artillery, all A-1 stuff! No wonder we lost the war! They

were delighted that the Germans should be so strong.
They felt themselves by so much the less to blame. "Unbeatable, no use shitting yourself, unbeatable!"

Brunet looked at the defeated mob filled with wonder
and admiration, and he thought: "This is the material.
Pretty poor stuff, but that can't be helped, it's all I have.
One can always work on what is at hand and there must
be one or two in the crowd who will respond to treatment.
The German column had gone by, the human caterpillar
had crawled off the road onto what had been a basketball
court, which they swarmed over like an ooze of black
pitch, they sat and lay about with old newspapers from
the month of May spread over their faces like big hats to
keep off the sun. The whole place looked like a racetrack
or like the Bois de Vincennes on a Sunday.

"What've we stopped for?"

"I don't know," said Brunet.

The sight of all these men stretched on their backs got
on his nerves, he had no wish to sit down, but realized
that he was being merely stupid, no use despising them,
that was the surest way of bungling the job; besides, there
was no knowing how far they would have to go, he had to
husband his strength; he sat down. Behind him first one
German, then another, sauntered past; they grinned at him
in friendly fashion, saying with kindly irony: "Where are
the English?" Brunet looked at their soft black leather
boots, but said nothing, and the Germans took themselves
off; all but one lanky *Feldwebel* who stayed behind and
said in tones of reproachful melancholy: "Where are the
English? Poor Frenchies, where are the English?" No one
answered him; he stood there shaking his head.

As soon as the Heinies were at a safe distance, Lambert
gave his answer between his teeth: "Search me! But
wherever they are, you'll have to run fast to get the English out of your hair."

"You don't say!" Moulu interjected.

"What's that?"

"Perhaps the English *will* get in Heinie's hair," Moulu explained, "but just at the moment he's in theirs good and proper, and not so far away either."

"Who says so?"

"It's a sure thing, you silly dope! It's easy for them to talk big when they're tucked away in their island, but just you wait until the Heinies cross the Channel! If we French couldn't hold out, it's a damn sure thing the Limeys won't win the war."

Where are the comrades? Brunet felt lonely. Never in the past ten years had he felt so alone. He was hungry and thirsty, he was ashamed to be hungry and thirsty.

Moulu turned to him. "They're going to give us some chow."

"Really?"

"Seems the *Feldwebel* said so. There's going to be an issue of bread and canned horse."

Brunet smiled: he knew they were not going to be fed, but they had to talk about it; they would never get enough of talking about it.

Suddenly some of the men got up, then others, then they were all on their feet, they were starting off again. Moulu was furious. "Who gave the order to move?" he grumbled. No one answered, and Moulu shouted: "Don't budge, boys, they're going to give us some chow."

Blind and deaf, the convoy scrambled back onto the road. The march was resumed. A forest; sunlight filtering pale and red through the leaves; three abandoned 75's still pointing threateningly to the east; the men seemed happy because there was shade; a regiment of German pioneers filed past. Goldilocks looked at them with a faint smile, it amused him to watch their conquerors from between half-closed lids, to play with them like a cat with a mouse, to play with them from the heights of his superiority. Moulu gripped Brunet's arm and shook it.

"There! Over there! See that gray chimney over there?"

"What about it?"

"That's Baccarat." He stood on tiptoe and made a funnel of his hands. "Hey, boys, Baccarat!" he shouted. "Pass the word along; we're getting into Baccarat!"

The men were tired, they had the sun in their eyes; apathetically they repeated: "Baccarat, Baccarat," but they didn't care a damn.

"Baccarat?" Goldilocks asked Brunet, "isn't that where they make lace?"

"No," said Brunet, "glass."

"Ah!" said Goldilocks in a vaguely respectful tone. "Ah! Ah!"

The town looked black under the blue sky, gloom settled down on the faces. "Feels odd to see a town again," somebody said in a flat voice. They passed down a deserted street; smashed glass lay on the road and the sidewalk. Goldilocks laughed and jerked his thumb. "There you are," he said, "Baccarat glass."

Brunet raised his head: the houses were undamaged, but all the windows had been blown out; behind him a voice repeated: "Funny to be in a town." A bridge; the column halted; millions of eyes were turned toward the river: five naked Heinies were splashing around in the water, uttering little shouts; twenty thousand gray-faced sweating Frenchmen, stifling in their uniforms, stared at bellies and buttocks that for ten months had been secure behind a rampart of guns and tanks but were now exposed to view with a quiet insolence in their fragility. So that was it: their conquerors were just so much vulnerable white flesh. A sigh, low and eloquent, swept through the ranks. Without the slightest feeling of anger, they had watched the progress of a victorious army perched on its triumphal chariots, but the sight of these naked Boche swine playing leapfrog in the water was an insult. Lambert leaned over the parapet, looked at the river, and murmured: "It must be fun." It was not so much a wish as a dead man's regret. Dead, forgotten, wrapped in the shroud of war now over and done with, the crowd of prisoners moved on, parched, hot, choked with dust.

A gate swung open with a squeal of hinges, around them were high walls; at the far end of a huge courtyard, through the quivering heat, Brunet saw a barracks building with all the shutters closed. He moved forward, somebody bumped into him from behind, he turned. "No need to push, there's plenty of room for all of us." He passed through the gate. Moulu laughed with relief.

"Well, we're through with it for today." Through with the world of civilians and conquerors, with poplars and rivers glittering in the sun; they were going to bury their filthy old war between these walls, they were going to stew in their own juice, unseen of the outer world, isolated and alone. Brunet moved on, pushed from behind, he moved on to the farthest limit of the courtyard, he stopped at the foot of a long gray cliff. Moulu nudged him: "Militia barracks." A hundred pairs of closed shutters, a flight of three steps leading to a padlocked door. To the left of the steps, a couple of yards from the main building, stood a low brick breastwork about three feet high and six feet long. Brunet went across and leaned against it. The courtyard was filling up, a continual stream of men was packing the first arrivals tight, forcing them against the wall of the building; on and on they came. Suddenly, the gates swung to and closed. "Home at last," said Moulu.

Lambert eyed the gate and said with satisfaction: "There's a pisspotful of guys who couldn't get in; they'll have to spend the night outside."

Brunet shrugged his shoulders. "It makes no difference whether you sleep in a street or a courtyard."

"Oh yes, it does!" said Lambert.

Goldilocks nodded approval. "At least *we're* not outside," he explained.

Lambert went one better: "We're in a house without a roof."

Brunet swung round; standing with his back to the barracks, he made a survey of his surroundings: opposite, the courtyard stretched down a gentle slope to the outer wall, on the top of which two watch-towers had been built, a hundred yards apart; for the moment they were empty. A row of posts had been freshly set up to support a curtain of barbed wire and rope that divided the yard into two unequal parts. The smaller of these—a relatively narrow strip of ground between the outer wall and the posts —was unoccupied. The main body of prisoners was crowded together in the other, between the posts and the building. The men looked ill at ease, as though they were temporary visitors; no one dared to sit down. They still had their haversacks and various odd bundles in their hands; sweat ran down their cheeks; the typical French intelligence had left their faces; the sun shone in their vacant eyes; they had taken refuge from the past and from the immediate future in a sort of uncomfortable, provisional, and minor death. Brunet refused to admit to himself that he was thirsty; he had put his haversack on the ground and was standing with his hands in his pockets, whistling.

A sergeant gave him a military salute. Brunet smiled without returning the salute.

The sergeant came up to him. "What are we waiting for?"

"I've no idea."

The man was tall, thin, and tough-looking. Self-importance gave his large eyes a dull look; there was a line of mustache across his bony face; his movements had something violent and staccato about them, clearly the result of training. "Who's in charge?" he asked.

"Who do you suppose? The Heinies."

"I mean in our lot. Who's responsible among us?"

Brunet laughed in his face. "God knows."

The sergeant's eyes expressed a mixture of suspicion and reproach: what he wanted was to be second-in-command, to combine the intoxicating satisfaction of obeying with the pleasure of giving orders; but Brunet had no intention of assuming control; he had ceased to command when the last of his men had fallen. He had other things to think about now.

The sergeant showed signs of impatience. "Why are these poor devils being kept hanging about on their feet?"

Brunet said nothing. The sergeant gave him a furious look and resigned himself to the necessity of taking charge. He drew himself to his full height, made a megaphone of his hands, and shouted: "Sit down, all of you! Pass the word along." Faces were turned uneasily in his direction, but nobody moved. "Sit down, all of you!" the sergeant repeated. "The whole lot of you!"

A few men sat down, looking half-asleep; voices echoed the message: "Down, all of you." A ripple went through the crowd; there was a general subsidence. The cry eddied above their heads, everyone sat down; it traveled to the far end of the courtyard, rebounded from the wall, and returned mysteriously distorted: "Everyone up, stay on your feet, wait for orders."

The sergeant looked at Brunet uneasily: somewhere, over by the gate, he had a rival. Some of the men jumped to their feet, hugging their haversacks and looking about them with hunted eyes. But most of them remained seated, and gradually those who had got up sat down again. The sergeant contemplated the result of his labors and uttered a self-satisfied laugh.

"It's only a matter of issuing orders."

Brunet looked at him and said: "Sit down, sergeant." The sergeant blinked. Brunet repeated: "Sit down: that's an order!"

The sergeant hesitated, then sank to the ground between

Lambert and Moulu; he sat with his arms around his
knees, gazing up at Brunet, his mouth half-open.

Brunet explained: "I stand because I'm a brevet officer."
Brunet didn't want to sit down: he felt a cramp in his
calves creeping up his thighs, but he didn't want to sit
down. Before his eyes were thousands of backs and
shoulder-blades, twitching necks and jerking shoulders;
the whole crowd seemed to have caught the fidgets. He
watched it sweltering and shimmering; without either
boredom or pleasure he thought: "This is my material.
They're just waiting, rigid, expectant; they don't even
seem to be hungry any more: the heat must have affected
their stomachs. They're afraid and they're waiting. What
are they waiting for? An order, a catastrophe, or just nightfall? It wouldn't much matter what, so long as it took
them out of themselves."

A fat reservist raised a white face and nodded in the
direction of one of the watch-towers. "Why aren't there
any sentries up there? What's their little game?" He
paused for a moment, the sun flooding his upturned eyes;
then he shrugged, and said in a voice that combined
criticism with disappointment: "Same trouble with them
as with us: too much organization."

Brunet, the only man on his feet, looked at the skulls;
he thought: "There are comrades somewhere in this
crowd but they'll be as hard to find as needles in hay-
stacks; it'll take time to get them together." He looked up
at the sky, at a plane showing black against it, then lowered his eyes and turned his head. To his right he noticed
a big fellow who had not sat down—a corporal; he was
smoking a cigarette. The airplane passed overhead with
shattering din; the crowded faces, upturned, then lowered,
passed from black to white, like a field bursting into
flower; in place of hard, black heads, thousands of large
camellias broke into blossom. Spectacles glittered like
scraps of glass in a flowerbed. The corporal had not

moved. His broad shoulders were stooped; he was staring at the ground between his feet. With a little thrill of pleasure Brunet noted that he was freshly shaved. The corporal turned, and now it was he who studied Brunet. He had large, heavy, deeply shadowed eyes; but for a broken nose, he would have been almost handsome. Brunet thought: "I've seen that face before." But where? He could not remember; he had seen so many faces. He left off trying to remember; the point was not really important, and, anyhow, the man seemed to have no recollection of him. Suddenly Brunet cried: "Ha!" and the other raised his eyes. But Brunet was still not satisfied. He had no wish to make a pal of the fellow, it was only that the fellow had remained on his feet and was freshly shaved and clean.

"Come over here," Brunet said with no especial eagerness. "If you want to keep standing, you can lean against this low wall." The man stooped, picked up his bundle, and followed Brunet, stepping over the recumbent bodies. He was thickset, but a little fat.

"Howya, pal."

"Howya," said Brunet.

"This spot is O.K. for me," said the man.

"You alone?" Brunet asked.

"My men are all dead," the man replied.

"So are mine," said Brunet. "What's your name?"

"What's that?" asked the man.

"I said: 'What's your name?'"

"Oh. Schneider. What's yours?"

"Brunet."

They relapsed into silence. Why on earth did I pick up this fellow? He's going to be a nuisance. Brunet looked at his watch: five o'clock. The sun was invisible now behind the buildings, but the sky was as oppressive as ever; not a cloud, not the suspicion of a breeze, a dead sea. There was no sound of voices. All around Brunet men were try-

ing to sleep, their heads buried in their arms, but uneasiness was keeping them awake. They sat up, they
sighed or began to scratch.

"Hi!" said Moulu. "Hi!"

Brunet turned. Behind him a dozen or so officers were
marching along in charge of a German sentry, keeping
close to the wall.

"So there's some of *them* about still!" Goldilocks muttered between his teeth. "They didn't all make a get-
away!"

The officers, silent, eyes averted, moved on. The men
laughed in an embarrassed way and deliberately turned
from them as they passed. It was as though officers and
men were afraid of one another. Brunet caught Schneider's
eye and they exchanged a smile. From the ground came
a little splutter of angry voices: the sergeant was having
words with Goldilocks.

"Every God-damned one of them," Goldilocks was saying, "in cars and trucks. The whole shitty lot of 'em beat
it and left us holding the baby!"

The sergeant folded his arms. "I don't like to hear men
talking like that, it's bad."

"It only proves how right the Boches were," replied
Goldilocks. "They said when they nabbed us, the French
Army, they said, is an army without a leader!"

"And what about the other war, didn't the leaders win
that?"

"They weren't the same leaders."

"Of course they weren't the same! The point is they had
different troops."

"So it was us that lost the war? Us, the second line? Is
that what you mean?"

"That's what I mean," the sergeant explained, "I mean
that you farted away in face of the enemy and you handed
them France on a silver platter."

Lambert, who had been listening in silence, turned

scarlet and leaned toward the sergeant. "See here, pal, how come *you're* here if *you* didn't fart off? I suppose you think you died on the field of honor and are just waking up in paradise? Hell, I think they caught you because you couldn't run fast enough."

"I'm not your pal: I'm a sergeant and I'm old enough to be your father. If you want to know, I didn't piss off: they got me because I had no ammunition left!"

Men were crawling toward them from all sides; Goldilocks called them to witness. "Did you guys hear him?" Goldilocks guffawed. Everyone laughed. Goldilocks turned on the sergeant. "O.K., pop, O.K., you shot down twenty parachutists and stopped a God-damned tank all by your God-damned self. I could say just the same. Who can prove me a liar?"

The sergeant, his eyes blazing, pointed to a faded patch on his blouse. "Military Medal, Legion of Honor, Croix de Guerre—I won 'em in 1914, before you were born. Do they prove me a liar?"

"Where's your ribbons?"

"I tore 'em off when the Germans came."

A loud shout rose from the men around him, who lay on their stomachs, curled up like seals; they barked, they yelped, their faces were suffused with passion. The sergeant sat, cross-legged, dominating the lot of them, one man against a mob.

"Listen, you God-damned hero," someone shouted, "why in hell should I feel like fighting when the radio kept on bawling that Old Man Pétain had asked for an armistice?"

And another: "I suppose you'd have wanted us to get bumped off while the generals were pulling a fast one with the Fritz generals in one of them historic châteaux?"

"Why not?" the sergeant countered angrily. "Soldiers are supposed to get killed in a war, aren't they?" Indignation kept his audience silent for a moment. He took advantage of the pause to add: "I saw it all coming a long time ago, I only had to look at you, the boys of 1940, the skulkers, the pretty boys without an ounce of fight in them. No one could so much as say a word to you; the captain had to come, cap in hand, before you'd listen to him: 'Sure, I'm very sorry, I hope you don't mind, but would you be so very kind as to go on K.P.?' Just you wait, I thought, one of these days there'll be a bust-up and what'll the little tough guys do then? The fat'll be in the fire then all right, I said. All the little ninnyhammers asking for leave; when all the fuss about leave started, I knew the game was up. You little bastards were too spunky; the army had to send you home to get your babes to suck some of it off you! Did *we* have leave in '14?"

"Of course you did! Sure you did."

"How d'you know that, kid? Where in hell were you?"

"I wasn't there, but my old man was, and he told me all about it."

"Your old man must have fought the war at Marseille, because we had to wait two years and then some before we got any leave at all. One guy might strike it lucky and then, when the next come along, all leave was suspended. Like to know how much time I spent at home in fifty-two months of war? Twenty-two days. Yes, twenty-two days, my boy, put that in your pipe and smoke it. At that, some said I had all the luck."

"All right, all right," said Lambert, "we don't want to hear the story of your life."

"I'm not telling you the story of my life, I'm just explaining how we won our war and you lost yours."

Goldilocks' eyes were ablaze with anger. "Since you're so smart, maybe you'll explain why you lost the peace."

"The peace?" the sergeant exclaimed in astonishment.

There was a babble of voices. "Yes, the peace, the peace! It was you lost the peace!"

"You were the veterans, huh?" said Goldilocks. "Well, what did you do to make sure your kids were safe? Did you make Germany pay? Did you disarm Germany? What about the Rhineland? And the Ruhr? And the war in Spain? And Abyssinia?"

"And what about the Treaty of Versailles?" a lanky fellow with a head shaped like a sugar loaf challenged. "Did I sign that?"

"I suppose you think I signed it!" The sergeant grinned with vexation.

"Who the hell signed it if it wasn't you, you old fool! You voted, didn't you? *I* didn't; I'm twenty-two and I've never voted yet."

"What does that prove?"

"It proves that you voted like a' cunt and got us ear-high in a tub of shit. You had twenty years to prepare for this war or to avoid it, and what did you do? Don't think I'm not as good as you, pal; if I'd had good leaders and the right weapons, I'd have fought as well as you ever did. But what did I have to fight *with?* Just you tell me that! Why, I didn't even have enough ammo."

"Whose fault was it, then?" the sergeant asked. "Who voted for Stalin? Who went on strike just because he was bored, just because he wanted to raise hell with the boss? Who insisted on wage raises? Who refused to work overtime? What about all the cars and bikes that were never turned out? Who was it thought only about nooky and skirts and holidays with pay and Sundays in the country and youth hostels and the movies? You little bastards took it easy. I worked every day of my life, and that goes for Sundays too!"

Goldilocks, flushing beet-red, crawled over to the sergeant and yelled in his face: "Just you say I didn't do my bit! Just you say it again! I'm the son of a widow, I am, and I left school at eleven to support my mother." If pushed, he didn't care a damn about having lost the war, but he wouldn't tolerate being told he had slacked at his work.

Brunet thought: "I might be able to make something of him."

By this time the sergeant himself was on all fours, and the two men were bawling at each other, their faces only a few inches apart. Schneider leaned forward as though about to interfere; Brunet touched him on the arm.

"Leave 'em alone; it keeps 'em busy."

Schneider did not insist; straightening up, he cast an odd look at Brunet.

"Come on," said Moulu, "pipe down! Why raise hell about it!"

The sergeant sat down again with a little laugh. "You're right, there!" he said. "It's too late to start fighting now. If he wanted a rough-house, the Germans were there."

Goldilocks, too, shrugged and settled back into his former position. "You make me sick!" he said. There was a long silence. They sat side by side; Goldilocks began pulling up blades of grass and amused himself by plaiting them; the others waited a moment, then crawled back on all fours to their former positions. Moulu stretched out and grinned.

"All that sort of thing is nonsense," he said in conciliatory tones, "sheer nonsense!"

Brunet thought of the comrades losing battle after battle, going on with teeth clenched from defeat to defeat until the day of final victory. He looked at Moulu. "I don't know that kind of guy." He felt the need to talk to somebody; Schneider happened to be there, so he talked to him. "You see, it wasn't worth interfering."

Schneider said nothing. Brunet laughed. "That sort of thing's nonsense," he said, imitating Moulu. Still Schneider said nothing, his heavy, handsome face noncommittal. The sight of it irritated Brunet, and he turned his back; he hated passive resistance.

"I could do with a bite to eat," said Lambert.

Moulu jerked his thumb at the open space separating

the outer wall from the posts. His voice when he spoke was low and fervent, his words were a poem: "That's where the chow will come from. The gates will open, the trucks will drive through, and the Heinies'll throw us bread over the wire."

Brunet looked at Schneider out of the corner of his eye. He laughed. "You see?" he said, "there's no point in getting excited. Defeat and war are unimportant; food's the important thing!"

A flash of irony showed in Schneider's half-closed eyes. "What have they been doing to you, pal?" he asked sympathetically. "You don't seem to like 'em much."

"Nothing," Brunet replied curtly. "Just hearing them is enough for me."

Schneider looked down at his right hand, which he kept half-clenched, and stared at his nails. In his loud, carefree voice he said: "It's difficult to help people when you don't like 'em!"

Brunet frowned. They often used to print my mug in the *Huma* and it's easy to recognize. "Who said I wanted to help 'em?"

"We ought all to help one another."

"Sure we ought," Brunet said. He was annoyed at himself, first because he should never have lost his temper, but chiefly because he should not have allowed this uncooperative idiot to see that he had lost it. He made an effort to control himself, smiled, and said: "I haven't got anything against *them.*"

"Against whom, then?"

Brunet gave Schneider an appraising look. "Against those who made fools of them," he said.

Schneider's laugh had an unpleasant sound. "Who made fools of *us*, you mean," he amended. "We're all in the same boat."

Brunet felt his former irritation stirring again, but kept a strong hold on his temper. "If you prefer it that way," he said good-humoredly, "but *I* never had any illusions, you know."

"Nor did I," said Schneider, "but what difference does that make? Fooled or not, here we are."

"So what? Here is as good as anywhere else, isn't it?" He was quite calm now. He thought: "My place and my work lie wherever there are men."

Schneider was looking toward the gate; he said no more. Brunet looked at him without antipathy. "What sort of a chap is he? An intellectual? An anarchist? What was his job in civilian life? Too much fat; he looks as though he'd let himself go a bit, but he holds himself well; I might be able to make use of him."

The evening light was showing pink and gray on the walls, on the black town, which was out of sight. The men's eyes had a fixed stare; they were looking through the walls at the town, thinking of nothing, moving scarcely at all. The vast patience of the soldier had descended upon them with the dusk; they were waiting. They had waited for letters, for leave, for the German attack, and this was their way of waiting for the end of the war. The war was over and still they waited. They were waiting for the trucks loaded with bread, for the German sentries, for the armistice; they were waiting just so that they might have a tiny patch of future before them; they were waiting so as not to die.

Far away in the falling night, in the past, a church bell sounded. Moulu smiled. "Hey, Lambert! Perhaps that's the armistice."

Lambert began to laugh; the two men exchanged a knowing wink. "I did hear there was going to be a regular blow-out," he explained.

"That'll be for when peace is declared," said Moulu.

The thought made Goldilocks laugh. "On the day peace is declared," he said, "I'm going to get so plastered I won't sober up for two weeks!"

"Not for two weeks! Not for a month!" came in a clamor of voices. "We'll be dead to the world then, by God!"

One by one, with infinite patience, we shall have to destroy their hopes, prick their illusions, make them realize the hideous condition of their lives, see it naked and unadorned as it really is, disgust them with everything and everyone, beginning with themselves. Only then . . .

This time it was Schneider who looked at him, as if he were reading his thoughts. A hard look. Brunet returned his look.

"That'll be difficult," said Schneider. Brunet waited, his eyebrows raised. Schneider said again: "That'll be difficult."

"What'll be difficult?"

"To give us a sense of solidarity. We're not a class; we're little more than a herd. Not many workmen; just peasants and middle-class riffraff. We haven't even got jobs; we're just human beings in the abstract."

"Don't you worry," said Brunet in spite of himself. "We'll have jobs all right."

"Oh, I know all about that, but like slaves. That's not the kind of work that frees a man, and we'll never be anything but make-weights. What common action can you ask of us? A strike gives the strikers a sense of their power. But even if every French prisoner folded his arms and did nothing, it wouldn't make two cents' worth of difference to the German economy."

They looked at each other coldly. Brunet thought: "So you have recognized me. Well, so much the worse for you; I shall keep an eye on you." A sudden hatred flared in Schneider's face, then quickly died out. Brunet did not even know against whom the hatred was directed.

There was a cry of surprise and delight. "A Heinie!" "Where? Where?" Everyone looked up. A soldier had just appeared on top of the left-hand watch-tower, wearing a helmet, holding a tommy gun, and with a grenade stuck in his boot top. He was followed by another with a rifle. "About time they did something about us," said a voice. The feeling of relief was general. They were back at last in the world of men with its laws, its routine, its rules, and its regulations; they were back in some sort of human society. All heads turned toward the other tower. It was still empty, but the men waited confidently, as they might have waited for a post-office window to open or the de luxe Blue Train to pass.

A helmet showed at wall-level, then two: two helmeted monsters who carried a machine gun, which they set up on its tripod and leveled at the prisoners. No one was frightened; the prisoners settled down: the sight of the sentries standing on the wall gave assurance that nothing would happen that night, no order would come to wake the assembled men and turn them out again on the road; they felt secure. A tall strapping fellow wearing steel-rimmed spectacles had taken a breviary from his pocket and was reading it, muttering to himself.

"He's on the prowl," thought Brunet, but anger slid over him without penetrating. He felt at peace. For the first time in fifteen years he was aware of time moving slowly, of a day ending in a fine evening without there being anything for him to do. The sense of leisure, forgotten since childhood, welled up in him. Stuck there on top of the wall was the sky, pink-flushed, quite close, unusable. He looked at it shyly, then looked at the men lying at his feet, shifting restlessly, whispering, unmaking and remaking their packs: emigrants on a ship's deck. "It's not their fault," he thought, and he wanted to smile at them. His feet ached; he sat down beside Schneider and unlaced his boots. He yawned; his body felt as useless as the sky. He said: "It's beginning to get chilly." Tomorrow he would set to work.

By this time the color of the earth was gray. He heard a

sound as of something softly rattling, a tight, irregular sound. He listened, tried to make out the rhythm and amused himself with the thought that it might be Morse. Suddenly, a thought came to him: "Somebody's teeth are chattering." He sat up; in front of him he could see a naked back covered with black scabs. It belonged to the man who had been making a noise on the march. He crawled over to him. The man had gooseflesh.

"Hullo!" said Brunet. The man made no reply. Brunet took a sweater from his knapsack. "Hey, feller!" he said again and touched the naked shoulder. The man started to yell. He turned round and looked at Brunet. He was panting, his nose was running, the snot was dribbling into his mouth. Brunet saw his face for the first time, the face of a handsome young man. His cheeks looked blue and his eyes were deeply sunk; there were no lashes to his lids. "Take it easy, old man," said Brunet quietly. "I just want to give you this sweater." The man took the sweater. He looked frightened. He put it on obediently and sat motionless, his arms outstretched. The sleeves, which were too long, reached to the tips of his fingers. Brunet laughed. "Turn 'em up." The man made no reply. His teeth were still chattering. Brunet took him by the arm and rolled up the sleeves.

"It's timed for tonight," said the man.

"Really?" said Brunet. "What's timed for tonight?"

"The hecatomb," said the man.

"That's all right, then," said Brunet. He felt in the man's pocket and brought out a dirty, bloodstained handkerchief. He threw it away, took his own handkerchief, and held it out to the man. "Meanwhile, wipe your nose."

The man did so, stuffed the handkerchief into his pocket, and began to jabber. Brunet stroked his head as he might have done an animal's. "You're quite right," he said.

The man grew calmer, his teeth ceased to chatter.

Brunet turned to the other men near him. "Anyone know this guy?"

A small, dark fellow with a bright face raised himself on his elbows. "It's Charpin," he said.

"Keep an eye on him," said Brunet. "He may try to do something silly."

"I'll keep an eye on him," said the small man.

"What's your name?" asked Brunet.

"Vernier."

"What's your line?"

"Used to be a printer in Lyon."

A printer! What a piece of luck! I'll have a word with him tomorrow.

"Good night," said Brunet.

"Good night," said the man.

Brunet went back to his place. He sat down and started to reckon up his resources. Moulu—a small shopkeeper almost for certain; not much to be got out of him, nor out of the sergeant, an incorrigible old fool. Lambert, a grumbler, disintegrated for the moment under the impact of his own cynicism; it might be possible to win him over later. The man from the north, a hobbledehoy, utterly negligible. Brunet had no use for hobbledehoys. Goldilocks? A man of the same stamp as Lambert but with more intelligence and a worker's self-respect. Still, for the moment, he too was completely at sea. The printer? Probably a young Communist. Brunet glanced across at Schneider, who sat motionless, his eyes wide open, smoking. "I'll have to see about him."

The priest had laid aside his breviary and was talking. Three young men were lying close to him, listening with expressions of pious familiarity. He's got three of 'em already; he works faster than I do, at least in the early stages. Guys like him are lucky, thought Brunet; they can work openly, and on Sundays they can say Mass.

Moulu heaved a sigh. "They won't come tonight."

"Who won't come tonight?" asked Lambert.

"The trucks. It's too dark." He laid his head on his knapsack.

"Look here," said Lambert, "I've got a groundsheet. How many of us are there?"

"Seven," said Moulu.

"Seven," said Lambert, "it'll hold all of us." He spread his groundsheet in front of the steps. "Anyone got blankets?" Moulu produced one, the man from the north and the sergeant two more; Goldilocks had none, nor had Brunet. "It don't matter," said Lambert, "we'll manage."

A face emerged from the darkness, showing a timid smile. "If you'll let me lie on your groundsheet, I'll share my blankets."

Lambert and Goldilocks eyed the intruder coldly. "No room for you, pal," said Goldilocks; and Moulu added in a more friendly voice:

"We're in our own crowd, see?"

The smile vanished, swallowed up by the darkness. A group had formed in the middle of this nondescript mob, a perfectly casual group, without the bond of friendship or any real element of solidarity. But already it was closing its ranks against outsiders; Brunet was part of it.

"Come over here," Schneider urged, "we'll both lie down together under my blanket."

Brunet hesitated. "I don't feel particularly sleepy just now."

"Nor do I," said Schneider.

They sat side by side while the others rolled themselves in their blankets. Schneider was smoking, concealing his cigarette in the palm of his hand because of the sentries. He brought out a pack from his pocket and held it out to Brunet.

"Cigarette? You'd better go behind the wall to light it so they can't see you."

Brunet longed for a smoke, but he refused. "Not at the

moment. Thanks all the same." He wasn't going to play the schoolboy like a kid of sixteen. To disobey the Germans in little things was to some extent to recognize their authority. The first stars came out. From far away on the other side of the wall drifted the sound of music. There was no sweetness in it, it was the music of their conquerors. Sleep rolled like a tide over twenty thousand exhausted bodies, and each body was a wave. The dark surf moved like a sea. Brunet began to feel that he had had enough of doing nothing; a lovely sky was all right to look at for a while, but he might just as well go to sleep. He turned to Schneider with a yawn, and suddenly his eyes hardened; he sat up. Schneider was off his guard. His cigarette had gone out and he had not relit it; it was dangling from his lower lip as he stared gloomily at the sky. This was the moment to find out more about him.

"You from Paris?" Brunet asked.

"No."

Assuming an air of frankness, Brunet said: "I live in Paris, but Combloux's my home town, near Saint-Étienne." Silence.

After a moment Schneider said regretfully: "I'm from Bordeaux."

"Ah!" said Brunet. "I know Bordeaux well. A fine town, but a bit on the gloomy side, eh? You work there?"

"Yes."

"What at?"

"What at?"

"Yes."

"I'm a clerk. Clerk in a law office."

"Ah," said Brunet. He yawned. He must find some way of getting a look at Schneider's Army card.

"And you?" Schneider asked.

Brunet gave a start. "Me?"

"Yes."

"Traveling salesman."

"What do you sell?"

"Oh, anything that happens along."

"I see."

Brunet settled himself along the base of the low wall and curled up. In a scarcely audible voice, as though he were taking toll of the day before going to sleep, he said: "Well, here we are."

"Yes, here we are," said Schneider in the same voice. "Here we are."

"A regular muck-up," said Brunet.

"I agree."

"Well, if we had to be beaten," said Brunet, "it's just as well we got beaten quickly: there's less bloodshed that way."

Schneider laughed. "Don't worry, they'll bleed us by installments; it's all the same in the long run."

Brunet glanced at him. "You're a bit of a defeatist, aren't you?"

"I'm not a defeatist, but I know defeat when I see it."

"What defeat?" asked Brunet, "defeat, my arse!" He broke off, expecting Schneider to protest. But he was wrong. Schneider merely sat and stared blankly at his boots, the cigarette stub still hanging from the corner of his mouth. Brunet had gone too far to stop; he must develop his idea, but it was *no longer* the same idea. If only the fool had asked a few questions, Brunet would have harpooned him; the thought of talking gave him no pleasure now, his words would just slide off this great indifferent lump of flesh without penetrating. "It's just chauvinism that makes the French think they've lost the war. They always believe they're the only people in the world; then, when their invincible army gets it in the neck, all the stuffing goes out of 'em." A little nasal sound came from Schneider. Brunet decided to go ahead willy-nilly. "This war's only just begun," he went on. "In six months we'll be fighting from the Cape to Bering Strait."

Schneider laughed. "*We?*" he said.

"Yes, we Frenchmen," said Brunet. "We'll continue the war in other fields. The Germans will try to militarize our industry. That's something the proletariat can and must stop."

Schneider showed no reaction; his athletic body lay there inert. Brunet did not like the way things were shaping; heavy, disconcerting silences were his own specialty; he had been maneuvering so as to fight on his own ground, he had been trying to make Schneider talk, and now it was he who had been compelled to do the talking. It was his turn now to be silent.

Schneider still said nothing. This sort of thing might go on for a long time. Brunet began to grow uneasy; the fellow had got either too much or too little in his head. Not far from them somebody began to yap feebly. This time it was Schneider who broke the silence. He spoke with a kind of heat:

"Hear that? The guy thinks he's a dog!"

Brunet shrugged. This isn't the moment to get sentimental over a chap who is having a bad dream; I've no time to waste.

"Poor devils!" said Schneider in a deep voice thrilling with passion. "Poor devils!" Brunet remained silent. Schneider continued: "They'll never go home. Never." He turned to Brunet and there was hatred in his eyes.

"Hey! Don't look at me like that," said Brunet with a laugh; "it's not my fault!"

Schneider, too, began to laugh; his expression softened and the fire died out of his eyes. "You're right, it's not your fault."

Silence fell between them. An idea occurred to Brunet. Leaning toward Schneider, he said in a low voice: "If that's how you feel, why don't you try to escape?"

"Bah!" said Schneider.

"Are you married?"

"I've got a couple of kids too."

"Don't you get on with your wife?"

"I? Why, we're a pair of turtle-doves!"

"Well, then?"

"Bah!" Schneider repeated. "Are *you* going to escape?"

"I don't know," said Brunet. "I'll have to think about it." He tried to get a look at Schneider's face, but the yard was wrapped in darkness, it was impossible to see anything save the watch-towers outlined against the sky. "I think I'll go to sleep," Brunet said with a yawn.

"Same here," said Schneider. They stretched out on the groundsheet and pushed their knapsacks against the wall. Schneider spread his blanket and they both rolled themselves into it. " 'Night," said Schneider.

" 'Night." Brunet turned on his back, rested his head on his knapsack, and kept his eyes open. He could feel the warmth of Schneider's body and guessed that Schneider too was lying with his eyes open. He thought: "I would get mixed up with a guy like that!" Which of them, he wondered, had really been maneuvering the other?

Every now and then between the clumps of stars a little falling brilliance streaked the sky. Schneider moved noiselessly under the blanket and whispered: "You asleep, Brunet?" Brunet said nothing; he was waiting. A moment passed, and then he heard somebody breathing audibly through his nose: Schneider was asleep.

Brunet kept his watch in solitude, the one spot of living light among these twenty thousand patches of darkness. He smiled, closed his eyes, and let himself relax: two Arab women were laughing in the little wood. "Where is Abd-el-Krim?" The elder of the two replied: "I wouldn't be surprised if he was at the clothing store." And there indeed he was, sitting quite calmly in front of a tailor's bench, shouting: "Murder! Murder!" He was tearing the buttons from his blouse, and each button, as it came away, made a dry, explosive sound and gave off a flash.

"Behind that wall, quick!" said Schneider.

Brunet sat up and scratched his head. The night seemed unfamiliar and full of noises. "What's up?"

"Hurry! Hurry!"

Brunet threw back the blanket and flung himself flat behind the little wall next to Schneider.

A voice was moaning: "Murder!" Someone cried out in German and a machine gun barked dryly. Brunet risked a peep over the wall. By the light of flashes he could see a world peopled by stunted trees all raising their twisted, knotted branches to the sky. His eyes hurt him, his head felt empty. He said: "Suffering humanity!"

Schneider dragged him back. "Suffering humanity, my arse! They're busy murdering us!"

"Shooting us down like dogs," said the sobbing voice. "Like dogs!"

The machine gun had ceased firing. Brunet passed his hand over his eyes; he was fully awake by now. "What's happening?"

"I don't know," said Schneider. "They opened fire twice; the first time probably in the air, but the second they meant business." All around them the jungle was rustling: What is it? What's up? What's happened? Self-appointed leaders replied: "Don't talk, don't move, lie still!"

The towers rose black against the milky sky, within them were men awake and watchful, their fingers on the triggers of machine guns. Brunet and Schneider, kneeling behind the wall, could see far off the round eye of a flashlight. Swung by an invisible hand, it came nearer, it swept with its light the expanse of gray, flattened grubs. Two harsh voices were speaking German. The torch flashed straight in Brunet's face, so that he was blinded and shut his eyes. A voice with a strong accent asked: "Who was it just shouted?"

"I don't know," Brunet replied.

The sergeant rose to his feet and stood there, very straight under the beam of the electric light, at once mannerly and distant. "One of the soldiers has gone mad, he started to cry out, his companions took fright and got up, and then the sentry fired."

The Germans did not understand. Schneider spoke to them in German. They grunted and then in their turn began to speak. Schneider turned to the sergeant. "They say, find out whether anyone's been wounded."

The sergeant straightened up, put his hands to his mouth in a precise, rapid gesture, and shouted: "Report casualties!"

From all sides weak voices rose in reply. Suddenly two searchlights came into action. They shed a snowstorm of fairy radiance that passed over the supine crowd. Some Germans crossed the yard carrying stretchers. A number of French Medical Corps orderlies joined them.

"Where is this madman?" the German officer asked in a tone of command. Nobody answered, but the madman was in full view, standing up, his lips white and trembling, and tears running down his cheeks. The soldiers surrounded him and led him away; he made no attempt to resist, but went with them. His eyes had a dazed look and he was wiping his nose with Brunet's handkerchief. All around men sat up, looking at the man who was sharing their suffering but carrying it to the bitter end. There was a feeling in the air of death and defeat.

The Germans disappeared. Brunet yawned. The light kept stabbing at his eyes.

"What are they going to do with him?" asked Moulu. Brunet shrugged his shoulders. Schneider merely said: "The Nazis don't like madmen."

Figures were moving about with stretchers. Brunet said: "I think we can go to sleep again." They lay down. Brunet uttered a laugh; in the very spot where he had been lying, there was a hole in the groundsheet—a hole with charred edges. He pointed to it. Moulu's face was green, his hands were trembling.

"Oh!" he said. "Oh! Oh!"

Brunet smiled at Schneider. "I really think you saved my life," he said.

Schneider did not return the smile; he was looking at Brunet with a serious and perplexed expression. "Yes," he said slowly, "I saved your life all right."

"Many thanks," said Brunet, and rolled himself in the blanket.

"I'm going to lie down behind that wall," said Moulu.

Suddenly the searchlights went out, the forest creaked, crackled, rustled, whispered. Brunet sat up, his eyes full of sunlight, his head full of sleep. He looked at his watch: seven o'clock. The men were busy folding the ground-sheets, rolling up their blankets. Brunet felt dirty and clammy; he had sweated during the night and his shirt was glued to his back.

"Christ!" said Goldilocks, "do I stink!"

With an expression of gloomy interrogation Moulu looked at the closed gates. "Another day and no chow!"

Lambert opened a peevish eye. "Have a heart."

Brunet got up, glanced round the yard, saw a group of men clustered about a hosepipe, and joined them. A fat fellow, stripped to the buff, was being sprayed; he was squealing like a woman. Brunet took off his clothes, waited his turn, and received a hard, icy jet of water on his back and front. Then he put on his clothes again without drying himself, took hold of the hose, and played it on the next three men. The bathing found but few patrons, the men preferred their sweat.

"Who's next?" Brunet asked. No one answered; he dropped the hose in a temper. He thought: "They've no self-respect." He glanced about him; that pretty well summed up the whole lot of them. The job he had on his hands would not be easy. He flung his blouse over his arm to hide his stripes and approached a group who were chatting together in low voices; here was a good opportunity to find out how the land lay. Nine chances to one they were talking about food. Not that he minded; food was a good subject to start off with, a simple, concrete, and actual theme. When a guy is hungry, there's something to work on. But they were not talking about food. A tall, thin man with red eyes recognized him.

"You're the fellow who was next to the loony one, aren't you?"

"That's me," said Brunet.

"What did he do, exactly?"

"He yelled."

"Is that all? Hell! Grand total: four dead and twenty wounded."

"How do you know?"

"Gartiser told us."

Gartiser was a thickset fellow with flabby cheeks and a morose, self-important expression.

"You a medical orderly?" asked Brunet.

Gartiser nodded: yes, he was a medical orderly, and the Heinies had taken him to the stables behind the barrack block, where he had had to look after the injured. "One of them croaked in my arms."

"It's lousy to croak like that just one week before going home."

"One week?" Brunet inquired.

"Oh well, a week, two weeks if you like. They'll have to send us home because they can't feed us."

"What about the guy who went mad?" Brunet asked.

Gartiser spat between his feet. "Better not talk about him."

"Why not?"

"They tried to make him keep quiet, one of them put his hand on his mouth and got bitten. Jesus, you should've seen 'em! All shouting and jabbering their lingo until you couldn't hear yourself speak; then they edged him into a corner of the stables and started hitting him with their fists and hitting him with their rifle butts; they were having a hell of a good time beating him up. Some of our fellows egged them on; they said that if it wasn't for that son of a bitch, nothing would have happened. He wasn't nice to look at when they finished with him; his face was all mashed up, and one eye dangling out of it. Then they put him on a stretcher and carried him away, I don't know where to, but they must have gone on having their fun with him because I heard him yelling up to three o'clock this morning." From his pocket he took a small object wrapped in a piece of newspaper. "Look at that." He unfolded the paper. "It's one of his teeth. I picked it up this morning where he fell down." Very carefully he rolled up his package again, returned it to his pocket, and said: "I'm keeping it as a souvenir."

Brunet turned away and moved slowly toward the steps. Moulu cried after him:

"Heard the results?"

"What results?"

"Of last night's fun. Twenty dead and thirty wounded."

"Christ!" said Brunet.

"Not bad," said Moulu, smiling as though he took a vague sort of pride in the news, "not bad at all for a first night."

"What do they want to waste ammo for?" Lambert asked. "They can get rid of us easy enough by letting us starve; they've begun to already."

"They're not going to let us starve," said Moulu.

"What do you know about it?"

Moulu smiled. "Just you keep an eye on the gate same as I'm doing; it'll take your mind off your worries, and that's the way the trucks will come in."

The sound of an engine drowned his voice. "Pipe the

plane!" shouted the man from the north. An observation plane flew over them at a hundred and fifty feet, black and shining; it swooped over the yard and made a sharp left turn, twice, three times. Twenty thousand faces gazed at it, following its every movement; the whole crowd turned when it turned.

"I guess they'll start dropping bombs on us now," Curly said with assumed indifference.

"Bomb us?" Moulu exclaimed. "Why?"

"Because they can't feed us."

Schneider, narrowing his eyes and screwing up his face against the sun, looked at the airplane. "They're more likely to be photographing us," he said.

"Who?" asked Moulu.

"War correspondents," Schneider explained laconically.

Moulu's heavy jowl turned purple, his fear changed abruptly to anger; all of a sudden he stood up, stretched his arms heavenwards, and began to shout: "Stick out your tongues at 'em, pals, stick out your tongues at 'em! The bastards are taking our pictures!"

Brunet was amused. A wave of anger swept over the crowd. One soldier was shaking his fist; another, his shoulders arched and his stomach stuck forward, placed his little finger in the fly of his trousers and jerked his thumb upward like a sexual organ. The man from the north went down on all fours, lowered his head and displayed his backside to the sky. "Let 'em photograph that!"

Schneider looked at Brunet. "They've got guts, you see," he said.

"Pooh!" said Brunet. "It doesn't prove a thing!"

The plane flew off into the sun.

"Well, I'll see my mug in the *Frankfurter Zeitung*," said Moulu.

Lambert, having disappeared, returned in a great state of excitement. "Say, you guys, it seems we can set ourselves up cheap and comfortably."

"What you mean?"

"There's a lot of furniture behind the barracks, mattresses, crocks, water jugs, all to be had for the asking; but we'll have to move carefully because we must pinch them on the sly." He looked round him with shining eyes. "What about trying it?"

"O.K.," said Curly, jumping up. Moulu did not move.

"Come on, Moulu," said Lambert.

"No," said Moulu. "I'm taking it easy; I'm not moving till I've had something to eat."

"Keep an eye on things here, then," the sergeant said, rising and following the others.

When they reached the corner of the building, Moulu shouted after them feebly: "You're wasting your strength, you poor muckers!" He heaved a sigh, looked sternly at Schneider and Brunet, and added in a whisper: "I shouldn't even raise my voice."

"Coming?" Schneider asked.

"What good is a water jug?" Brunet asked.

"Oh, to wash your feet in."

Beyond this barrack block there was another yard and a long single-storied building with four doors—the stables. In one corner, piled anyhow, were old box and spring mattresses, cots, rickety cupboards, tables teetering on a single leg. The men milled round the accumulated rubbish. One of them came back across the yard carrying a mattress, another with a wicker dress-stand. Brunet and Schneider made the round of the stables and came upon a grassy hillock.

"Shall we climb up there?" asked Schneider.

"All right." Brunet felt uncomfortable. What was the fellow after? Did Schneider want to make a friend of him? I'm a bit too old for that. On top of the hillock they saw three graves newly filled.

"See?" said Schneider. "They didn't kill any more than three."

Brunet sat down on the grass beside the graves. "Lend me your knife," he said. Schneider passed it to him; Brunet opened it and began to rip off his stripes.

"That's silly," said Schneider. "Noncoms don't have to work." Brunet shrugged his shoulders without answering, put the pieces of braid in his pocket, and got up.

They went back into the main yard. The men were making themselves comfortable. A handsome fellow with an impudent face was lolling backwards and forwards in a rocking-chair; in front of a tent that had been set up, two fellows had dragged a table and a couple of chairs; they sat there celebrating their victory by playing cards. Gartiser was squatting cross-legged on a Persian bedside rug marked all over with burns.

"This reminds me of the Flea Market," Brunet observed.

"Or an Arab bazaar," said Schneider. Brunet went up to Lambert. "What have you got?"

Lambert looked up proudly. "Plates," he said, pointing to a pile of chipped and blackened dishes.

"What are you going to do with them? Eat 'em?"

"Leave him alone," said Moulu; "maybe it'll hurry up the chow."

The morning dragged on. The men relapsed into their former torpor; some tried to sleep, others lay on their backs, their faces to the sky, their eyes open and staring; they were hungry. Curly kept tearing up handfuls of grass from between the cobbles and chewing it; the man from the north took out his knife and whittled away on a piece of wood. One group lit a fire under a rusty saucepan. Lambert rose to watch them, but came back looking disappointed. "Nettle soup," he announced, and dropped down between Curly and Moulu. "No nourishment in it."

The German sentries were relieved. "They're going off to eat," the sergeant commented with a vacant look.

Brunet sat down next to the printer. "Did you sleep well?" he asked.

"Not badly," said the printer. Brunet looked at him with approval; he had a neat, clean appearance; there was a certain gaiety in his eyes. Two chances out of three.

"Tell me, I meant to ask you before: were you working in Paris?"

"No," said the printer, "in Lyon."

"Where?"

"At the Levrault Press."

"Oh, Levrault," said Brunet. "I know the place. You fellows put on a good strike there in 1936, a fine well-organized strike." The printer laughed proudly. Brunet asked: "Did you know a guy called Pernu? He was there then."

"You mean Pernu the union delegate?"

"That's the man."

"Sure, I knew him!"

Brunet got up. "Let's take a walk, there's something I want to talk to you about." When they were in the farther yard, Brunet faced him squarely. "Are you a member of the party?" The printer hesitated. Brunet said: "I'm Brunet, of the *Huma*."

"So that's who you are?" said the printer. "I thought you were."

"Have you got any pals here?"

"Two or three."

"Tough?"

"Tough as hell. But I lost sight of 'em yesterday."

"Try to find them again," said Brunet, "and let me meet them; we've got to organize a cell." Brunet went back to where he had been sitting beside Schneider and gave him a quick, furtive look. Schneider's face was calm and inexpressive.

"What's the time?" Schneider asked.

"Two o'clock," said Brunet.

"Look at that dog," said Curly. A large black dog was

crossing the yard, its tongue hanging out of its mouth. The men watched it curiously.

"Where's it come from?" the sergeant asked.

"I don't know," said Brunet. "Probably from the stables."

Lambert leaned on his elbow, following the dog with appraising eyes. As though speaking to himself, "Dog meat isn't so bad as people say," he ventured.

"Ever eaten any?"

Lambert made no answer; he sketched an irritable gesture, then lay down again apathetically on his back. The two men playing cards in front of the tent left their hands on the table and rose with a careless air. One of them was carrying a groundsheet under his arm.

"Too late," said Lambert. The dog disappeared behind the barracks. They followed it without sign of hurry and in turn were lost to sight.

"Will they get him or won't they?" asked the man from the north. A moment later the two men reappeared; they carried a bulky object wrapped in the groundsheet, as they might carry a hammock. As they passed Brunet a drop fell on the cobbles, a red drop.

"Poor material," said the sergeant. "That groundsheet is meant to be waterproof." He wagged his head. "Typical, ain't it?" he grumbled. "How could we hope to win the war?"

The two men tossed their load into the tent. One of them crawled in after it on all fours while the other set off in search of wood for the fire.

Curly sighed. "Well, two guys will live through the war, huh?"

Brunet dropped off to sleep, then suddenly awoke with a start at the sound of Moulu shouting: "Here's chow!" The gate swung open slowly. A hundred men were on their feet. "Here's a truck!" The truck drove in, camouflaged with flowers and branches over its hood, a moving

pageant of spring. By now, the number of men standing
had risen from a hundred to a thousand. The truck turned
into the space lying between the outer wall and the barrier. Brunet rose and was promptly elbowed, pulled,
pushed, and almost carried against the barbed wire. The
truck was empty. A Heinie, stripped to the waist, sat
indolently in the back of the truck watching the surging
crowd. He had a brown skin, fair hair, and long, delicate
muscles; he looked like a wealthy clubman, like one of
the young swells who ski, half-naked, at St. Moritz. Much
to his amusement, a thousand pair of eyes were turned on
him; he smiled at the spectacle of these famished night-
prowling animals pressing against the bars of their cage
the better to see him. Leaning back, he asked the sentries
in the watch-tower something; they answered with a
laugh. The crowd, watching the movements of its master,
waited in a sort of daze, growling with impatience and
with delight. The Boche bent down, took a loaf of bread
from the floor of the truck, drew a knife from his pocket,
opened it, sharpened it against his boot, and cut off a
slice. Someone behind Brunet began to pant. The Boche
raised the slice to his nose and pretended to sniff at it
ecstatically, his eyes half-closed. The animals growled. A
wave of anger gripped Brunet at the throat. The German
took another look at them, grinned, raised the slice, held
it flat between his thumb and his first finger, and sent it
spinning toward them like a quoit. But—perhaps on purpose—he had aimed too low; the bread fell between the
truck and the posts. Some of the men were already crawling on the ground under the wire. The sentry on the
watch-tower barked an order and covered them with his
tommy gun. The men stood there pressed against the
fence, their mouths open, a mad look in their eyes.

Moulu, wedged against Brunet, muttered: "There's going to be trouble; I wish I was out of all this." The pressure of the crowd crushed him against Brunet; he tried

in vain to free himself. "Get back!" he shouted, "get back, you fools! Can't you see we'll have last night all over again?" The German in the truck cut a second slice and sent it spinning toward them; it turned over in the air and dropped among the lifted faces. Brunet was caught in a vast surge of bodies; he felt himself jostled, pushed about and beaten; he saw Moulu swept away in an eddy, his hands raised like those of a swimmer in water.

"The swine!" he thought. "The swine!" He wanted to hit the men around him with his fists, he wanted to kick them. A second slice of bread fell, a third, as the prisoners fought to get at them. A tall bruiser broke away from the mob, a piece of bread clutched in his hand. The crowd caught him, hemmed him in, he crammed the slice into his mouth whole, pushing it forcefully with the palm of his hand in order to ram it down his gullet. They let him go, and he moved slowly away, rolling his anxious eyes.

The Heinie was enjoying himself; he kept sending the slices right and left, sometimes making feints to fool the crowd. A piece of bread fell at Brunet's feet. A corporal saw it and made a dive, bumping against Brunet as he did so. Brunet seized him by the shoulders and held him tight while the mob rushed on the bread lying in the dust. Brunet deliberately put his foot on the scrap of bread, grinding it into the ground. But ten hands laid hold of his leg, forced it away, and scraped up the dirty crumbs. The corporal struggled furiously; another piece of bread had just bounced off his boot. "Let me go, you bastard! Let me go!" Brunet maintained his grip; the man tried to hit him, but Brunet parried with his elbow and exerted all his strength to contract his arms; he was enjoying himself. "You're choking me!" the man said in a weak voice. Brunet went on squeezing. He could see above him the white scud of bread; he squeezed and squeezed; he was enjoying himself. The man in his arms had abandoned any attempt at resistance.

"All over!" said a voice. Brunet glanced over his shoulder. The Heinie was shutting his knife. Brunet opened his arms; the corporal swayed, took two steps sideways in an effort to regain his balance, fixed Brunet with a glare of brutish hatred, and started to cough. Brunet grinned. The man eyed his breadth of shoulder, hesitated, finally muttered: "Bastard!" and turned away.

Slowly the crowd dispersed, disappointed, and by no means proud of the scene just enacted. Here and there one who had been luckier than the rest munched shamefacedly, hiding his mouth with his hand and rolling his eyes like a naughty child. The corporal stood leaning against one of the posts. A slice of bread was lying in the coal dust between the truck and the wire; his eyes were fixed on it. The German jumped down from the truck, went along the wall, and opened the door of a small hut. The corporal's eyes were gleaming; he stood there watching. The sentries turned away, and at once he went down on all fours and started to creep under the wire, his hand outstretched. There was a shout. One of the sentries raised his rifle. The corporal tried to crawl back, but the other sentry motioned to him to stay still, and there he waited, white in the face, his hand still extended, his rump in the air.

The German of the truck had by this time returned. Without the slightest sign of hurry he sauntered up to the wire, pulled the man to his feet with one hand, and with the other struck him as hard as he could. Brunet laughed till he cried. A voice behind him said quietly: "You don't seem particularly fond of us." Brunet gave a start and turned. It was Schneider. There was a silence. Brunet's eyes were on the corporal, whom the Heinie was now pushing toward the hut with hard kicks.

In a colorless voice Schneider said: "We're hungry."

Brunet shrugged. "Why do you say 'we'?" he inquired. "Don't tell me *you* took part in that scramble?"

"Of course," Schneider replied. "I behaved like everybody else."

"That's not true," said Brunet, "I was watching."

Schneider shook his head. "I didn't manage to get a bit, but that's not the point."

Brunet, his eyes lowered, was grinding scraps of bread into the ground with his heel. A strange sensation made him look up suddenly; at the same moment the glint in Schneider's eyes went dim, as though a light had been extinguished; there was nothing now in his face but a sort of apathetic anger that gave it a heavy look.

"I know we're greedy," Schneider said, "we're cowardly and servile. Is that our fault? Everything's been taken from us—our jobs, our families, our responsibilities. No man can be brave unless he's got something to do; without that he just dreams. We've got *nothing* to do, not even our livings to earn; we don't count any longer. We live in a dream; if we are cowards, it's in a dream world. Give us work and you'll see us wake up quickly enough."

The Heinie had emerged from the hut; he was smoking. The corporal limped along behind him, carrying a spade and a pick.

"I've got no work to give you," said Brunet, "but a man can at least behave properly even without any work to do."

Schneider's eyelids twitched open, then fell again; he smiled. "I would have thought you were more of a realist. No one's going to object to your behaving properly, but what difference is it going to make? It won't help anyone and it will serve no purpose except to give you a feeling of personal satisfaction, unless," he added ironically, "you believe in the value of good example."

Brunet looked at Schneider coldly. He said: "You've recognized me, haven't you?"

"Yes," said Schneider, "you're Brunet of the *Huma*. I've seen your photo often."

"Did you use to read the *Huma*?"

"Occasionally."

"Are you one of us?"

"No, but I'm not against you."

Brunet pulled a face. They walked back slowly toward the steps, picking their way over the recumbent bodies. The men, exhausted by the violence of their desire and of their disappointment, had once more lain down. Their faces were livid and their eyes glittered. Close to their tent, the card-players had begun a new game. Ashes and bones lay beneath the table. Brunet glanced at Schneider out of the corner of his eye; he was trying to catch again the familiar something that had struck him on the previous evening. But he had been looking at the large nose, the general layout of the face, for too long; the vividness of the first impression had gone dim.

"I suppose you know," he muttered between his teeth, "what happens to a Communist if the Nazis get him." Schneider smiled, but said nothing. Brunet added: "We give short shrift to babblers."

Schneider's smile never left his lips. "I'm no babbler," he said.

Brunet stopped dead; so did Schneider. Brunet asked: "Do you want to work with us?"

"What are you planning to do?"

"I'll tell you, but only when you've answered my question."

"Why shouldn't I?"

Brunet tried to read the expression on the large, smooth, rather soft-looking face. Still staring at Schneider, he said: "It's not going to be easy, you know, just going on day after day."

"I've nothing to lose," said Schneider, "and anyhow it'll be something to do." They sat down again. Schneider stretched himself at full length, his hands behind his head. He shut his eyes and said: "No, that doesn't worry me much. What does worry me is that you don't seem to be particularly fond of us."

Brunet, too, lay down. What, precisely, *was* this fellow? A sympathizer? Hm! "Well," he thought, "it's your funeral. I'm not going to let you go." He slept and woke again; it was evening. He dropped off again. When next he woke, it was night; then the sun was up once more. He sat up, looked about him, wondered where he was, remembered. His head felt empty. Goldilocks was sitting up too. There was something dazed and sinister about him; his arms were dangling between his spread knees.

"Not feeling too good?" asked Brunet.

"I'm feeling lousy. Do you think they're going to give us anything to eat this morning?"

"I've no idea."

"Are they going to let us starve?"

"I doubt it."

"I'm bored," Goldilocks yawned. "I'm not used to doing nothing."

"Go and get a wash then."

The blond looked at the hosepipe without enthusiasm. "It'll be cold!"

"Come on!"

They got up. Schneider was still sleeping, Moulu was sleeping, the sergeant was lying on his back, his eyes wide open, chewing his mustache. All over the ground were thousands of eyes, thousands of open eyes, and others slowly opening under the warm influence of the sun.

Goldilocks was unsteady on his feet. "Hell! I can't even stand now, I'll just melt away!" Brunet unrolled the hose, fixed it to the tap, and turned the water on. He felt heavy. Goldilocks had stripped; he was hard and hairy, with great lumps of muscle. His flesh reddened and contracted under the stream of water, but his face remained gray.

"My turn, now," said Brunet. Goldilocks took hold of

the hose. "It weighs a ton!" he said. He let it drop, then picked it up again. He directed the jet on to Brunet, swayed on his feet, and suddenly let the hose fall to the ground. "Too much for me," he said.

They put on their clothes again. Goldilocks remained for some time sitting on the ground, holding a puttee in one hand. He looked at the water spreading between the stones, he seemed fascinated by the muddy streamlets. He said: "We're losing our strength." Brunet turned off the tap and helped the other to his feet; he led him back toward the steps.

Lambert was awake; he grinned at them. "You can't walk straight, you look as though all the stuffing had been knocked out of you."

Goldilocks collapsed on the groundsheet. "I'm all in," he muttered, "you won't catch me doing that again." He stared at his great hairy hands, which were trembling. "No reaction."

"Come for a stroll," said Brunet.

"Not on your life!" He rolled himself in his blanket and closed his eyes. Brunet moved off in the direction of the farther yard; it was deserted. Thirty times round at the double. At the tenth circuit his head began to feel dizzy; at the nineteenth, he had to lean against a wall, but he kept at it; he felt compelled to master his body. He finished the total and stopped, completely out of breath. His heart seemed to be beating inside his head, but he felt happy. "The body is made to obey. I'll do that every day; I'll work it up to fifty." He did not feel hungry. He was glad that he didn't feel hungry. "My fifth day of fasting, and I'm still in pretty good form." He went back into the main yard.

Schneider was still asleep, his mouth wide open. All the men were lying down, motionless, speechless; they looked like corpses. Brunet would have liked a word with the printer, but the printer was still sleeping. Brunet sat down, his heart still thumping. The man from the north began to laugh. Brunet looked around. The man from the north went on laughing, his eyes fixed on the stick he was carving; he had already scratched a date on it and was busy cutting a flower design with the point of his knife.

"What's biting you?" Lambert asked. "Do you think this is funny?"

The man from the north never stopped laughing. Without raising his eyes, "I'm laughing," he explained, "because I haven't taken a crap for three days."

"What's wrong with that?" Lambert asked. "You've got nothing in you to make you crap."

"Some do, though," Moulu remarked. "I've seen 'em."

"They're the lucky ones," said Lambert, "they're the guys that brought some rations along."

The sergeant sat up. He tugged at his mustache and looked at Moulu. "What about those trucks of yours?"

"They'll come all right," said Moulu, "they'll come." But his voice lacked conviction.

"They'd better hurry, then," said the sergeant, "or they won't find anyone here."

Moulu's eyes were still fixed on the gate. There was a gurgling liquid sound. Moulu apologized. "It's my stomach," he said.

Schneider had waked up. He rubbed his eyes, smiled, and murmured: "Coffee . . ."

"And rolls," said Curly.

"I'd rather have a bowl of soup," said the man from the north, "with a little red wine in it."

"Anyone got a cigarette?" the sergeant asked. Schneider held out his pack, but Brunet restrained him with a look of annoyance; Brunet did not approve of acts of individual generosity.

"Much better share them all round."

"O.K.," said Schneider. "I've got a pack and a half."

"I've got one," said Brunet. He took it from his pocket and laid it on the groundsheet.

Moulu took a tin box from his knapsack and opened it. "Seventeen left."

"That all?" Brunet asked. "Have you got any, Lambert?"

"No," said Lambert.

"That's a lie," said Moulu, "you had a whole pack last evening."

"I smoked 'em all during the night."

"You couldn't have!" said Moulu. "I heard you snoring."

"Have it your own way," said Lambert. "I don't mind giving the sarge one if he's got none, but I'm damned if I share them all round. They're mine, aren't they? I can do what I like with 'em, can't I?"

"Lambert," Brunet said, "you can take your groundsheet and piss off if you like, but if you're going to stay here, you've got to develop the team spirit and get used to sharing things. Hand over those cigarettes!" Lambert shrugged and peevishly threw a pack onto Schneider's blanket.

Moulu counted the cigarettes. "Eighty. That works out at eleven each and three over to draw lots for. Shall I hand 'em round?"

"No," said Brunet. "If you do that, some of the guys will smoke them all up by this evening. I'll keep 'em. You'll get three a day for three days and two on the fourth. O.K.?" The others nodded. They realized vaguely that they were tacitly acknowledging one of their number as leader. "O.K.?" Brunet repeated. They don't really care a damn; all they're interested in is eating.

Moulu shrugged and said: "O.K." The others signified their approval with nods. Brunet gave each man three cigarettes and put the rest in his knapsack. The sergeant lit one of his, took four puffs, stubbed it out, and put it behind his ear. The man from the north tore one open and put the tobacco in his mouth. "It makes you feel less hungry," he explained, chewing. Schneider had said nothing; he had been the heaviest loser in the deal, but he said nothing. Brunet thought: "He may turn out to be a good recruit." Brunet let his mind run on Schneider and then on something else. What was it, he wondered suddenly, he was thinking about and could not remember? He sat there awhile staring at nothing, playing with a handful of pebbles; then he got up heavily. The printer was now awake. "Well?" Brunet asked.

"I don't know where they are," said the printer. "I've been round the yard three times and I can't find 'em."

"Try again," said Brunet; "don't lose heart." He sat down, looked at his watch and said: "That can't be right. What time do you make it, fellows?"

"Four thirty-five," said Moulu.

"Then I *am* right." Four thirty-five and I've done nothing; I thought it was ten a.m. He felt as though someone had been filching time from him. And that printer who can't find his pals. . . . Everything is in slow motion here, hesitating, delayed, complicated; it'll take months to get anything going.

The sky was a crude blue, the sun struck at them with violence. Gradually the heat diminished, the sky grew pink. Brunet looked at the sky, his mind busy with the thought of gulls. He felt sleepy, his head was buzzing, he was not hungry. He thought: "I've not felt hungry all day." He fell asleep, dreamed that he was hungry, and woke up. Still he was not hungry, he was conscious only of a slight feeling of nausea and of a burning circlet around his skull. The sky looked blue and gay, the air was cool. From far away came the hoarse sound of a rooster crowing. The sun was hidden, but its beams made a golden haze above the wall; the yard was still streaked with long, violet shadows. The rooster fell silent. Brunet thought: "How quiet everything is!" For a moment he felt as though he were alone in the world. He sat up with difficulty. The others were there, all around him, thousands of men, motionless and supine. He could almost believe that he was on a battlefield. But all the eyes were wide open. He could see heads thrown backward, matted hair, eyes fixed in a watchful glare. He turned to Schneider and saw that his eyes, too, were fixed.

"Schneider!" he said quietly. "Schneider!" Schneider made no reply. Far away, Brunet could see a long, slobbering snake, the hosepipe. He thought: "I've got to have a wash." His head felt heavy, he had the sensation that it was dragging him backwards; he lay down again, he seemed to be floating. "I've got to wash." He tried to get up, but his body would no longer obey him. His legs and arms were without substance, he could no longer feel them, it was as though they lay beside him like independent objects. The sun peeped over the wall. "I've got to wash." It made him angry to think that he was just another corpse among all these open-eyed corpses. He began to fidget, sorted out his limbs, forced himself forward. At last he was on his feet, his legs were shaky, he was sweating. He took a few steps; he was afraid he might fall. He went up to the printer. "Hello!" he said. The printer sat up and looked at him oddly. "Hello!" said Brunet. "Hello!"

"Not feeling too good?" said the printer. "Why don't you sit down?"

"I'm all right," said Brunet, "I'm feeling fine. I'd rather stand." He was none too sure that if he sat down he would be able to get up again. The printer remained sitting; he looked alive and fresh, his dark eyes shining in his pleasant, girlish face.

"I've found one of 'em," he said excitedly. "A guy called Perrin, a railwayman from Orléans. He's lost his pals and is looking for 'em. If he finds 'em, they'll come along, all three of 'em, at noon."

Brunet looked at his watch: ten o'clock. He wiped the sweat from his forehead with his sleeve. "Good," he said. He felt he wanted to say something more, but did not know what. He stood there for a moment swaying above the printer and repeating: "Good! That's fine!" Then effortfully he resumed his walk. His head was burning; He let himself fall heavily on the groundsheet. He thought: "I haven't had a wash."

Schneider was lying on one elbow, his head propped on his hand, eying him anxiously. "Not feeling well?"

"I'm perfectly well," Brunet said irritably. He took out a handkerchief and spread it over his face because of the sun. He did not exactly feel sleepy, but his head seemed empty and he felt as though he were going down in an elevator. Someone coughed above him. He whipped away the handkerchief. It was the printer, with three other men. Brunet looked at them in surprise. In a thick voice he said: "Is it noon already?" Ashamed to have been caught napping, he tried to sit up. He remembered that he was not shaved, that he was just as dirty as the rest of them. He made a violent effort and scrambled to his feet. "Hello," he said.

The newcomers looked at him with curiosity. They were the sort of fellows he liked, tough, clean, and hard-eyed. Good tools. They were looking at him. "I'm their only hope," he thought, and felt better. He said: "Let's take a little walk." They followed him. Turning the corner of the barrack block, he went to the far end of the other yard, looked about him, and smiled at them.

"I know who you are," said a swarthy man with a shaven head.

"And I'm sure I've seen you somewhere," said Brunet.

"I came to see you in 1937," said the swarthy man, "my name's Stephen; I was in the International Brigade."

The others, too, gave their names: Perrin from Orléans, Dewrouckère, a miner from Lens. Brunet leaned against the wall of the stables. He looked at them, noting, without pleasure, that they were young. He wondered whether they were hungry.

"Well," said Stephen, "what do you want us to do?"

Brunet kept his eyes on them; he could not remember what he had meant to say; not a word did he utter. He could see the astonishment in their eyes. At last he unclenched his teeth. "Nothing. For the moment there's nothing we can do except pick out the men we can count on and keep in touch with 'em."

"Would you like to come in with us?" Perrin asked. "We've got a tent."

"No," Brunet said briskly, "we'd better stay as we are. Collect as many good guys as you can, try to find out something about what the others are thinking. And no propaganda. Not yet."

Dewrouckère frowned. "I know what they're thinking," he said. "Of nothing. Their minds are on their bellies."

Brunet felt his head swelling. He half closed his eyes and said: "Things may change. Any priests in your sector?"

"Yes, in mine," said Perrin, "and they're acting pretty funny, too."

"Leave 'em alone," said Brunet. "Don't let 'em know what you're up to. And if they try to softsoap you, don't frighten 'em off. Got it?" They nodded, and Brunet said: "We'll meet again tomorrow at noon."

They looked at him with a hint of hesitation in their manner. He said with a slight irritation: "Get going. I'm staying here." They moved off. Brunet kept his eyes on them, waiting until they turned the corner. He was not steady on his feet, he might fall at any moment. He thought: "Thirty times around the courtyard at the double." He took two steps, swaying; anger brought the blood to his face. It was as though a hammer were beating inside his head: thirty times, and now. He wrenched him-

self free of the wall, advanced three yards, and fell flat
on his stomach. He rose again and collapsed, cutting his
hand. Thirty times round, every day. He clung to an iron
ring embedded in the wall; he managed to stand on his
feet. Then he started off at a jog-trot. Ten times, twenty
times; his legs were trembling; each stride he took was
like a fall, but he knew that if he stopped he would col-
lapse. Twenty-nine. After the thirtieth circuit, still running, he rounded the corner of the building and slowed
down only when he was back in the main yard. He
stepped over the prostrate bodies and reached the steps.
No one had moved; they looked like so many dead fish,
floating stomach-upwards. He smiled. The only man there
on his feet. "What I've got to do now is shave." He took
up his knapsack, went over to a window, extracted his
razor, propped his fragment of mirror on the sill, and began to give himself a dry shave. The pain made him half
close his eyes. He dropped the razor, bent to pick it up,
and knocked over the mirror, which shattered at his feet.
He sank to his knees. This time he *knew* that he could
not get up again. He crawled back to his place on all
fours and rolled over on his back, his overworked heart
thumping in his chest. At each beat a point of fire bored
into his skull.

Without a word, Schneider lifted Brunet's head and
laid a blanket, folded into four, behind his neck. Clouds
were drifting across the sky; one of them looked like a
nun, another like a gondola. Somebody pulled at his
sleeve. "Get up! We're going to move!" He got to his feet
without understanding and was pushed toward the steps;
the door was open. Prisoners in an unbroken flow were
being swallowed up inside the barrack building. He could
feel himself going upstairs, he wanted to stop, but he was
being pushed from behind. A voice said: "Go on up!" He
missed a step and fell, his hands flung forward.

Schneider and the printer each took one arm and carried him. He tried to free himself, but he was not strong enough. He said: "I don't understand."

Schneider laughed quietly. "You need food."

"No more than you do."

"You're bigger and heavier than us," the printer said. "You need more food."

Brunet was beyond speaking. They hoisted him up to the attic floor. A long, dark corridor ran through the building from end to end; on each side were cubicles, separated from one another by latticework. They went into one of them. Three empty crates, that was all. No window. There was a skylight to each two or three cubicles. One of these, in the box next to theirs, admitted a slant of light that cast shadows from the great wooden bars obliquely upon the floor. Schneider spread his blanket on the floor, and Brunet subsided on it. For a moment he saw the printer's face bending over him. "Don't stand there," Brunet told him; "find somewhere for yourself farther off; we're meeting at noon tomorrow."

The face vanished and a dream began. The shadows of the bars crept slowly across the floor, slipped, bending, over the prostrate bodies, scaled the crates, bent and bent again, and then grew dim; darkness scaled the walls. Through the bars the skylight looked like a bruise, a pallid bruise, a black bruise, which turned suddenly to a bright and mocking eye. The bars resumed their progress, turning and turning around; the darkness turned like the lamp of a lighthouse; the beast was in its cage. For a moment men scurried, then disappeared. The ship drifted from the shore with all the convicts dead from hunger in their cages. A match sputtered; on one of the crates a label in red letters said, at an angle: FRAGILE. There were chimpanzees in the next cage, pressing their inquisitive faces to the bars, they had sad and wrinkled eyes, monkeys have sadder eyes than any animal except man. Something had happened, Brunet wondered what. A catastrophe?

What catastrophe? Perhaps the sun had turned cold? A voice sounded from the back of the cages: "Some evening I'll tell you the loveliest things." A catastrophe, everyone is screwed up. What catastrophe? What will the party do? There was the cool delicious taste of pineapples on Brunet's tongue, a young, rather gay, childish taste; he was chewing pineapple, he was munching the sweet resilient fibrous substance of pineapples, when did I last eat pineapple? I used to love pineapple, it was like a defenseless wood, wood stripped of its bark; he chewed. The youthful yellow taste of tender wood rose softly again from the back of his throat as the sun might rise hesitantly, it spread over his tongue, there was something it *sought to say*, what was it this synthetic soft-drink sun wanted to say? I used to love pineapple, oh, a long time ago, in the days when I loved skiing, the mountains, boxing, little sailboats, women. Fragile. What is fragile? We are all fragile. The savor, on the tongue, twists, turns like a solar whirlpool, an ancient taste, forgotten, I have forgotten, *the sun swarming in the leaves of chestnut trees, a shower of sunlight upon my forehead, I was in the hammock reading, the white house behind me, behind me Touraine, I loved the trees, the sun, and the house, I loved the world and happiness, oh, long ago.*

He moved. There's something I've got to do, there's something I've got to do now. He had arranged an urgent meeting, with whom? With Krupskaia. He fell back: Fragile. What have I done with my loves; they said to me: You do not love us enough. They had me, they stripped me, *a young tender shoot, sticky with sap,* when I get out of here I'll eat a whole pineapple. He half sat up, an urgent meeting; then, again, fell back into calm childhood, in a park, *part the grasses and you will see a sun; what have you done with your desires?* I have no desires, I am a piece of stripped wood, the sap is dead; the monkeys clinging to the bars were looking at him with their feverish eyes, something had happened. He remembered, he started up, he shouted: "The printer, has the printer come?" No one answered. He fell back into sticky sap, into SUBJECTIVITY, we have lost the war and this is where I am going to die, Mathieu was leaning over him whispering: you didn't love us enough, you didn't love us enough; the monkeys were chattering and laughing, slapping their thighs: you loved nothing, no, nothing at all!

The shadows made by the bars circled slowly across his face, darkness, sunlight, darkness; he found it amusing. I am a member of the party, I love the comrades; I have no time to waste on others, there's someone I've got to meet. "Some evening I'll tell you lovely things, some evening I'll tell you that I love you." He was sitting up, he was breathing hard, he was looking at them. On Moulu's face, turned to the ceiling, was an angelic smile, a cool shadow was stroking his face, creeping down his cheek, the sunlight was making his teeth shine. "Hey! Moulu!" Moulu was still smiling. "D'you hear 'em?" he asked, without moving.

"Do I hear what?" asked Brunet.

"The trucks."

He could hear nothing; he felt terrified of the huge wave of desire that suddenly swept over him, a desire to live, a desire to love, a desire to caress white breasts. Schneider was lying on his right; he called to him for help: "Ho! Schneider!"

"This is a bad business," said Schneider in a weak voice.

"You'll find the cigarettes in my knapsack. Three a day." Slowly his buttocks slid along the flood; he found himself lying with his head thrown back, he stared at the ceiling: I do love them, of course I love them, but *they've got to serve,* what is the nature of my desire? The body, the mortal body, a forest of desires, on each branch a bird, they serve Westphalian ham on wooden plates, the knife cuts into the meat, when one draws it out, one can smell, still sticking to it, the faint odor of damp wood, they had me, I am no more than a desire, we are all of us lying in excrement and this is where I am going to die. What desire? Somebody lifted him, somebody sat him up, Schneider made him swallow some soup. "What's that?"

"Barley broth."

Brunet started to laugh; that was what it was, just that. This immense, guilty desire was nothing but hunger. He slept, somebody woke him, he had some more soup. He could feel it burning in his stomach; the bars circled, the voice was silent; he said: "Someone was singing."

"Yes," said Moulu.

"He's stopped now."

"He's dead," said Moulu. "They took him away yesterday."

More soup, and this time with bread. He said: "That's better." He sat up without help, he smiled; childhood, love, "subjectivity," all that was nothing—just a dream brought on by weakness. Lightheartedly he put a question to Moulu: "So the trucks did come, after all?"

"Yes," said Moulu, "they came." He was scraping away with his pocket-knife at a lump of bread, scooping bits out of it. He was carving it into a shape. Without looking up, he said: "A piece of left-over bread, it's moldy. If you eat the blue part, it gives you cramps, but some of the crust's all right." He held out a slither of bread to Brunet and stuffed another into his large mouth; he said proudly: "Six days without chow. I was going nuts."

Brunet laughed; he was thinking of "subjectivity." "Me too," he said. He fell asleep, and was wakened by the sun; he still felt weak, but he was able to get up. "Has the printer been here asking for me?" he inquired.

"We haven't been paying much attention to visitors these last few days."

"Where's Schneider?" asked Brunet.

"I don't know."

Brunet went out into the corridor. Schneider was talking to the printer; both of them were laughing. Brunet looked at them with irritation.

The printer came up to him and said: "Schneider's found a job for us." Brunet turned to Schneider. He thought: "He gets his foot in everywhere."

Schneider was smiling; he said: "We've been getting around a little these last few days; we've found some new pals."

"Hm!" Brunet said dryly. "I'd better give 'em the once-over." He went downstairs, Schneider and the printer at his heels. In the yard he stopped, screwing up his eyes against the dazzle. It was a beautiful day. Men were seated on the steps, quietly smoking; they looked thoroughly at home, like men resting after the week's work; now and then one of them would nod his head and say something, at which all the rest nodded. Brunet looked at them angrily; he thought: "That's it! They've settled down." The yard, the watch-towers, the outer wall *belonged to them*, there they sat at their own front door, gossiping with rustic wisdom about every little thing that went on in the village. "What can you do with guys like that? They've got a passion for ownership; you could throw 'em in the hoosegow and in three days you wouldn't know whether they were prisoners or owned the prison."

Others were walking about by twos and threes, carrying themselves smartly, chatting, laughing, turning this way and that: bourgeois taking a stroll. Officer cadets passed by in fancy uniforms, looking at nobody, and Brunet could hear their refined voices: "No, old man, I beg your pardon, they did not file a petition in bankruptcy; there was a question of their filing a petition, but the Bank of France took a hand in the nick of time." In the middle of one group, two men in spectacles were playing a game of chess on their knees; a little bald fellow was reading, and frowning over his book; now and then he laid it down and excitedly referred to an enormous volume. Brunet passed behind him; the volume was a dictionary. "What are you up to?" Brunet asked. "Learning German."

Round the hosepipe several naked men were shouting, shoving one another and laughing. Leaning against one of the posts, Gartiser, the Alsatian, was speaking in German to a German sentry, who nodded agreement. It had needed only a mouthful of bread! A mouthful of bread and this sinister yard, where a beaten army had been lying at its last gasp, had been transformed into a seaside resort, a solarium, a fairground.

Two men, stripped to the skin, were lying on a blanket, tanning themselves in the sun. Brunet felt like kicking their golden buttocks. Burn down their towns, their villages, drag them into exile, and they'll fight tooth and nail to build up again their squalid, poverty-stricken contentment; and that was the material he'd got to work with! He turned his back on them and went into the other yard.

He stopped dead in amazement: backs, thousands of backs, the tinkle of a bell, thousands of bowed heads. "Good God!" he said.

Schneider and the printer began to laugh. "Just a little surprise for you. It's Sunday!"

"So that's it!" said Brunet, "Sunday, of course!" He could scarcely believe his eyes. What stubborn idiocy! They had turned out a synthetic Sunday, like all the Sundays they had ever known in towns or countryside, just because they had seen on a calendar that it was Sunday. In the other yard it was a village Sunday, a country main-street Sunday; here it was a church Sunday. It only needed a movie house. He turned to the printer: "No film this evening?"

The printer smiled. "The priests are putting on a show."

Brunet clenched his fists; he thought about the priests, he thought: "They've been working overtime while I've been sick. One ought never to get sick."

Shyly the printer said: "It's a lovely day."

"Sure," said Brunet between his teeth. "Sure, a lovely day. A lovely day all over France: torn and twisted railroad tracks glinting in the sun, and golden sunlight on the yellowing leaves of uprooted trees, water gleaming at the bottom of bomb craters, dead men turning green in the fields, their upturned bellies chanting pæans under a cloudless sky. Have you forgotten so soon?"

The men were made of rubber. Their heads were raised, the priest was talking. Brunet could not hear what he was saying, but he saw his red face, his gray hair, his steel-rimmed spectacles, and his broad shoulders; he recognized him: it was the fellow with the breviary whom he had noticed on the first evening. He moved closer. A few paces from the preacher, the mustached sergeant, his eyes shining and a humble look on his face, was listening with passionate intensity:

". . . that many of you are believers, but I know also that there are others who are listening to me out of curiosity, out of a wish to learn or merely to kill time. You are all of you my brothers, my very dear brothers, brothers in arms, brothers in God, and it is to all of you that I am speaking now, Catholics, Protestants and atheists, because the Word of God is for all men. The message I bring you on this day of mourning, which is also the Lord's day, may be summed up in these three simple words: 'Do not despair!' For to despair is not only to sin against God's loving mercy, even those of you who are unbelievers will agree with me that despair is self-slaughter and, if I may so describe it, moral suicide. No doubt, my dear brothers, there are men among you who have been led astray by a sectarian education, who have been taught to see in the wonderful events of our history no more than a succession of accidents without meaning and without cohesion. Such men will go from this place saying that we were beaten because we lacked tanks, because we

lacked airplanes. Of them our Lord has said that they have
ears but they hear not, eyes have they, but they see not,
and doubtless when the divine wrath was loosed upon
Sodom and Gomorrah, there were in those wicked cities
sinners so hardened as to say that the rain of fire that reduced their cities to ashes was only the result of an atmos-
pheric disturbance or a meteorite. Oh, my brothers, were
not those men sinning against themselves? For if it was
only by accident that the lightning struck Sodom, then is
there no work of man's hands nor product of his patience
and his industry that may not, without rhyme or reason,
be reduced to nothingness by blind forces. Why, if that is
so, should men build? Why sow their fields? Why raise
families? Today we are vanquished and imprisoned, hu-
miliated in our legitimate pride of country, suffering in
our bodies, without news of our dear ones. And why? Is
it without design that all these things have happened?
Does their origin lie only in the interplay of mechanical
forces? If that be true, my brothers, then I say unto you:
despair, for there can be nothing more productive of
despair and nothing more unjust than to suffer for no
reason. But I, too, my dear brothers, would ask a question of these daring and emancipated thinkers: Why was
it that we lacked tanks? Why was it that we lacked guns?
No doubt they will answer: Because we did not produce
enough of them. And those words suddenly reveal to us
the countenance of that France of sinfulness which, for a
quarter of a century, has been forgetful of its duty to
God. Why did we not produce enough? Because we did
not work. And whence, my brothers, came this wave of
idleness which has descended upon us as once the locusts
descended upon the land of Egypt? Because we were a
nation divided by internal quarrels. The workers, led by
cynical agitators, had grown to detest their employers;
the employers, blinded by selfishness, cared nothing about
satisfying even the most legitimate of claims; our busi-

nessmen were eaten up with jealousy of our public functionaries, the functionaries lived like the parasite mistletoe
upon the oak; our elected representatives in the Chamber,
instead of discussing affairs of state calmly, with only the
general interest in mind, spent their time in brawling and
hurling mutual insults so that at times they actually came
to blows. And what, my very dear brothers, was the cause
of all this discord, of all this conflict of interests, of all
this degradation of public conduct? The cause of it was
that a sordid materialism had spread through the country
like an epidemic. And what is materialism if not a turning
away from God? A materialist holds that man is born of
the earth and that to the earth he will return; his sole
concern is with his worldly interests. This, then, I say to
our skeptics: You are right, my brothers: we lost the war
because we lacked *material*. But your argument is only in
part correct, because it is a *materialistic* argument; it is
because you are materialists that you were beaten. It was
France, the eldest daughter of the Church, that inscribed
in her annals the dazzling succession of her triumphs; it is
France without God that has been laid low in 1940."

He stopped. The men were listening in silence, their
mouths open; the sergeant was nodding approbation.
Brunet turned his eyes to the priest and was struck by
his air of triumph. His gleaming eyes darted hither and
thither over his audience, his face was red. He raised his
hand and resumed his sermon with something almost gay
in his passionate utterance:

"And so, my brothers, let us abandon the idea that our
defeat was the effect of chance. It is at the same time our
punishment and our fault. Not by chance, my brothers.
Chastisement: that is the good news I bring to you today." He paused again and gazed at the faces bent toward
him in rapt attention so as to judge of the effect he had
produced. Then, leaning forward, he continued in a more
persuasive tone: "That it is harsh and unpleasing news, I

agree, but it is good news. When a man believes that he is the innocent victim of a catastrophe and sits wringing his hands, unable to understand what has happened to him, is it not good news for him to be told that he is expiating his own fault? And that is why I say unto you: rejoice, my brothers! Rejoice in the deep abyss of your suffering, for where there has been sin, there, too, is expiation; there, too, is redemption. I say unto you again: rejoice, rejoice in the house of your Father, for there is yet another reason why you should rejoice. Our Lord, who suffered for all men, who took our sins upon Himself, who suffered, and still suffers, that He may expiate them, our Lord has chosen you. Yes, all of you, peasants, workers, men of the middle class, none of whom are wholly innocent, though certainly not the most guilty, you He has chosen to fulfill an incomparable destiny: as He suffered for us, so has He ordained that you shall suffer that you may redeem the sins and the faults of that France which God has never ceased to love and which He has punished with a heavy heart. It is for you, my brothers, to choose: either you may groan and tear your hair, saying: Why should these miseries have fallen upon me? Upon me rather than upon my neighbor who was rich and wicked, upon me rather than upon the politicians who have led my country to destruction? But if you do that, then is there no meaning in anything, all you can do is to die in rancor of heart and in hatred. On the other hand, you can say we were as nothing, and now are we chosen out from all men to suffer, to make of ourselves a willing sacrifice, to endure martyrdom. In that case, while a man raised up by Providence, a worthy follower of those men whom the Lord has always given to France when she found herself on the brink of destruction . . ."

Brunet tiptoed away. He found Schneider and the printer leaning against the wall of the barrack. He said: "He knows his job!"

"I'll say he does!" said the printer. "He sleeps near me at night and nobody gets a chance when he starts talking; he's got the boys just where he wants 'em!"

Two men passed close to them, one of them tall, thin, with a long face and spectacles, the other small, fat, with a disdainful expression on his lips. The tall one was talking in tones of sweet reasonableness: "He spoke very well. Very simply. And he said things that needed to be said."

Brunet started to laugh. "God in heaven!" They all walked on a little way. The printer was looking at Brunet with trusting eyes. "Well?" he asked.

"Well?" echoed Brunet.

"What did you think of that sermon?"

"There was good in it as well as bad. In a sense he's doing our work for us. He explained that captivity wasn't going to be a bed of roses, and I rather think he'll keep that stop out: it's to his interest as well as to ours, that he should do so. So long as these mugs think they're going to see their best girls at the end of a month, there's no doing anything with them."

"Ha?" The printer's handsome eyes were wide open, his face was gray.

Brunet went on: "To that extent you might make use of him. What you want to do is to get some of the boys away on the q.t. and say: 'You heard the chaplain. He said things are going to be pretty tough.'"

"And you think they will be for long?" the printer asked with an effort.

Brunet turned hard eyes on him. "You believe in Santa Claus?" The printer swallowed hard, but said nothing. Brunet turned to Schneider and continued: "I'm surprised, though, to find 'em coming to heel so quickly; I thought they'd wait and see. That sermon of his was a blatant political program: France, the eldest daughter of the Church, and Pétain, the leader of the French. It's

enough to make a fellow crap!" He turned on the printer
sharply. "What do the boys around you think of him?"

"They like him."

"Do they?"

"They've not got much against him. He shares everything he has, but he doesn't let you forget it. He always
seems to be saying: 'I'm giving you this for the love of
God.' Personally, I'd rather not smoke at all than take his
butts, but I'm the only one."

"Is that all you know about him?"

"Well," said the printer as though excusing himself, "I
only see him at night."

"Where does he hide in the daytime?"

"In the infirmary."

"Do you mean to tell me there's an infirmary here?"

"Yes, in the other building."

"Is he a medical orderly?"

"No, but he's a buddy of the major in charge; he plays
bridge with him and two wounded officers."

"He does, does he?" said Brunet. "And what do the boys
say about that?"

"They don't say nothing; they're inclined to think it's
true, but they'd rather not know for certain. I got it from
Gartiser, who's an orderly."

"Good, that's something you can give 'em to chew on.
Ask them how they like the idea of the priest always hob-
nobbing with the officers."

"O.K."

Schneider had been looking at them for the last few
minutes with an odd smile. "The other building is where
the Heinies hang out," he said.

"Ah!" said Brunet.

Schneider turned to the printer; he was still smiling.
"Your line's pretty clear: here's a priest who leaves his
own pals high and dry and prefers to make up to the
Heinies."

"As a matter of fact," said the printer without much conviction, "I don't believe he sees much of the Heinies."

Schneider shrugged his shoulders in assumed impatience; Brunet had a feeling that he was up to some game or other. "You got the right to go into the German building?" Schneider asked the printer, who shrugged and said nothing. Schneider voiced his triumph: "You see, I don't care a damn what his intentions may be; he may be sincere in his wish to save France. But *objectively* he's a French prisoner who spends his days in the company of the enemy. That's what the boys ought to know."

The printer, out of his depth, turned to Brunet. Brunet had resented Schneider's tone, but did not wish to give him the lie. "You want to go cautiously," he said. "It's no use trying to discredit him all at once. Besides, there are about fifty of his sort here and you can't take 'em all on single-handed. What you want to do is drop a few hints, like: the chaplain thinks it'll be longer than we think before we get home, and he ought to know because he's in with the officers and has long chats with the Boches. The great thing is to let them realize gradually that he isn't really one of them, see?"

"Yes," said the printer.

"Do any of our bunch see much of the padre?"

"Yes, one of 'em."

"A sharp guy?"

"Pretty keen."

"Tell him to string him along, then, to make believe he's convinced, we need an informer." He leaned against the wall, thought for a moment, and then said to the printer: "Go get some of our guys. Two or three. The newer ones."

As soon as they were alone, Brunet said to Schneider: "I'd rather have waited a little; in a month or two the boys'll be ripe. But these padres hold too strong a hand. If we don't start in at once, they'll get a head start on us. You still feel the same about coming in on the job?"

"What, exactly, is the job?" asked Schneider.

Brunet frowned. "I thought you wanted to work with us. Changed your mind?"

"I haven't changed my mind," said Schneider. "I'm asking you what you're going to work at."

"Well," said Brunet, "you heard the priest, didn't you? He's not by any means a lone performer; in a month from now they'll be thick on the ground. But that's not all. It wouldn't surprise me at all if Heinie managed to scrape together two or three Quislings from our crowd and got them to try to win us over. Before the war we could have put up a strong organized front against them, the party, the unions, the vigilance committee. Here we've got nothing. Our job is to build *something*. Naturally, it may mean having to put up with a lot of palavering and I've never liked that much, but we've no choice. Our immediate objective, then, must be to sift out the healthy elements, organize them, and get some sort of clandestine counter-propaganda going. The two main themes must be: that we refuse to recognize the armistice, and that democracy is the only form of government we are prepared to accept under present conditions. Useless to go further than that; we must move cautiously in the early stages. It's up to me to collect any members of the Communist Party who may happen to be around. But they're not the only ones; there are the Socialists, the Radicals, and, generally speaking, all the fellows who can be vaguely classed as belonging to the Left, sympathizers like you."

Schneider produced a wintry smile. "You mean the softies."

"Let us rather say the lukewarm." Brunet added hastily: "Not that a guy can't be both lukewarm and honest. I'm not quite sure that I know how to speak their language, but you won't have that difficulty, because it's the language you speak yourself."

"O.K.," said Schneider. "What it comes to, I take it, is

to some extent reviving the spirit of the old Popular Front?"

"That might not be altogether a bad thing," said Brunet.

Schneider nodded. "So that's to be my job," he said; "but—are you quite sure it's *yours*?"

Brunet looked at him in astonishment. "Mine?"

"Oh," said Schneider, as though the matter were one of complete indifference to him, "so long as you're sure—"

"Explain yourself," said Brunet. "I don't like veiled hints."

"But there's nothing to explain. All I meant to say was: what's the party up to? What orders has it issued, what directives? I suppose you've been kept informed."

Brunet looked at him with a smile. "I wonder whether you really see the situation as it is. The Germans have been in Paris for the last two weeks, the whole of France is topsy-turvy; many of the comrades are dead or captured, others have gone heaven knows where with their divisions, to Pau, to Montpellier; others are in the jug. If you really want to know what the party is up to at this moment, the answer is that it's busy reorganizing."

"I see," said Schneider without enthusiasm. "And you're just trying to make contact with any comrades who happen to be here. Fine."

"That's about the long and short of it," said Brunet, as though anxious to bring the discussion to an end. "If you're in agreement—"

"Of course I'm in agreement, my dear fellow," said Schneider. "All the more so since it has nothing to do with me. I'm not a Communist. You tell me that the party is reorganizing, and that's all I want to know. Still, if I were in your place, I should want to know—" he fumbled in the pocket of his blouse as though feeling for a cigarette, but after a moment withdrew his hand and let his arm hang loosely against the wall. "What is to be the basis of this reorganization? That's what really matters." Without looking at Brunet, he went on. "The Soviets are allies of Germany."

"That's where you're wrong," Brunet burst out impatiently. "They signed a non-aggression pact, of an entirely provisional nature. Just think for a moment, Schneider: what else could they have done after Munich? . . ."

Schneider heaved a sigh. "Oh, I know," he said, "I know everything you're going to say. You're going to tell me that the Soviets had lost all confidence in the Allies and were temporizing until they felt strong enough to declare war on Heinie. Isn't that it?"

Brunet hesitated. "Not exactly," he said. "My own view is that they're quite convinced that Germany means to attack them."

"But you do believe that they did all they could to postpone the event for as long as possible?"

"I imagine so."

"In that case," said Schneider slowly, "in your place I wouldn't feel too sure that the party will take up a strong position against the Nazis. They might be afraid of injuring the Soviets if they did." The look he turned on Brunet was full of uncertainty. It expressed melancholy and a lack of incisiveness; he had difficulty in keeping his eyes focused.

Brunet turned away with a movement of impatience. "Don't pretend to be more stupid than you are," he said. "You know perfectly well that it's not a question of the party's official position. Since 1939 it's been an illegal organization, and any action it takes must be under cover."

Schneider smiled. "Under cover, yes, but what does that mean? Will it, for instance, go on printing *L'Humanité* in secret? Besides, look here, of every ten thousand copies circulated, at least a hundred will fall into German hands; that's inevitable. With luck, an underground organization can conceal the source of its literature, the place where it's printed, the editorial offices, and so on, but not the literature itself, because pamphlets and that sort of stuff are printed to be distributed. I should say that in three months the Gestapo will know every detail of the party's political program."

"What if they do? They can't hold the Russians responsible."

"What about the Comintern?" asked Schneider. "Do you really think that Ribbentrop and Molotov have never discussed the Comintern?" He spoke without aggressiveness, his tone perfectly neutral. All the same, there was something suspect in his unspectacular insistence.

"What's the use of indulging in armchair strategy?" said Brunet. "What Ribbentrop and Molotov may have talked about I have no idea, I wasn't hidden under the table. All I know—because the evidence is there for everybody to see—is that contact between the U.S.S.R. and the party has ceased."

"You really believe that?" asked Schneider. Then, after a moment's pause, he continued: "But even if it has ceased today, it will be re-established tomorrow. There is always Switzerland."

Mass was now over. Soldiers were drifting past, silent and with their minds elsewhere. Schneider lowered his voice. "I'm quite sure that the Nazis hold the U.S.S.R. responsible for the activities of the C.P."

"Suppose they do," said Brunet, "what of it?"

"Let's assume," said Schneider, "that, in order to gain time, the U.S.S.R. muzzles the Communists of France and Belgium."

Brunet gave a shrug. "Muzzles! What extraordinary ideas you have about the relations between the U.S.S.R. and the C.P.! Don't you know that the C.P. contains cells and that those cells are made up of people who discuss and who vote?"

Schneider smiled and patiently continued: "I've no wish

to hurt your feelings. Let me put things a little differently. Suppose that the C.P., anxious not to make difficulties for the U.S.S.R., decides to muzzle itself."

"Would there be anything new about that?"

"Not much. After all, it's what you did at the outbreak of the war, isn't it? But since then the position of the U.S.S.R. has deteriorated. If England should capitulate, Hitler would have his hands free."

"The U.S.S.R. has had time to prepare. She is braced for the shock."

"Are you sure of that? The performances of the Red Army this last winter were not particularly brilliant, and you said yourself that Molotov was temporizing."

"If the relations between the U.S.S.R. and the C.P. are as you describe them, the comrades will know in good time all about the preparations of the Red Army."

"The comrades in Paris, yes; but what about you? It's *you* who are working *here.*"

"What are you getting at?" Brunet said, his voice rising. "What are you trying to prove? That the C.P. has turned fascist?"

"No, but that the Nazi victory and the German-Soviet Pact are two realities with which the C.P. has got to come to terms, however little the party may like them. The point is that you've no sort of an idea *how* it'll come to terms with them."

"Are you suggesting that I should sit still and twiddle my thumbs?"

"I'm not suggesting anything of the kind," Schneider protested. "Surely, one can talk things over." He paused, then, rubbing his great nose with his forefinger, continued: "The C.P. is no more in sympathy with the capitalist democracies than the Nazis are, though for other reasons. So long as it was possible to imagine an alliance between the U.S.S.R. and the Western democracies, you took as your platform the defense of political liberties against fascist dictatorship. You know even better than I do that those political liberties are illusory. Today the democracies are on their knees, the U.S.S.R. has drawn closer to Germany, Pétain has seized power. It is now within the framework of a fascist society, or of one with fascist sympathies, that the party has to carry on its work. And here are you, without leaders, without a political slogan, without contact, without news, reverting, on your own initiative, to that old and outworn platform. We were talking just now of the spirit of the Popular Front; but the Popular Front is dead, dead and buried. In 1938, given the historical context, it had a meaning; today it has none. Look out, Brunet, or you'll find yourself working in the dark." His voice had become suddenly edged; he broke off sharply and continued more quietly: "That was why I asked whether you were sure what your job was."

Brunet began to laugh. "Come now," he said, "there's nothing very terrible about that. What we've got to do is to get the boys together to try to neutralize the priests and the Nazis, and then just wait and see. We'll find out soon enough what's got to be done."

Schneider nodded approval. "That's right," he said, "that's right."

Brunet looked him straight in the eyes. "It's you I'm worried about," he said, "you seem such a pessimist."

"Oh, me!" said Schneider with an air of indifference. "If you really want to know, my opinion is that nothing we can do will be of the slightest importance politically. The situation is abstract, and we are without responsibility. Those of us who are lucky enough to get home, eventually, will find society organized anew, with its own hierarchies and its own myths. There's nothing we can do to influence the future one way or the other. Still, if we can succeed in keeping up the boys' morale, if we can save them from despair, if we can give them something to live for here—no matter how illusory that something may be—the necessary effort is well worth making."

"That's the spirit!" said Brunet. A moment later he added: "As this is my first day out, I'm going to take a walk. So long."

Schneider raised a hand in farewell and strolled away.

A negative type, an intellectual; why on earth did I get mixed up with him? An odd sort of fellow, sometimes so warm and friendly, at others cold as ice, almost cynical. Where have I seen him before? Why does he say *the* comrades in talking of the party members, and not *your* comrades, as I'd have expected him to do. I must manage to get a look at his Army card.

In the Sunday atmosphere of the yard the men looked as though they were out for the afternoon; on all their scrubbed and freshly shaven faces was the same expression of absence. They were waiting for something, and the fact of waiting had conjured into being, outside the confining wall, a whole garrison town, with its gardens, its brothels, and its cafés. In the middle of the yard somebody was playing a harmonica, and couples were dancing. The phantom town had grown till its roofs and treetops were higher than the prison wall and seemed reflected in the blind faces of these ghostly dancers.

Brunet made a half turn and moved into the farther yard. Here the scene was different: the temporary church had been dismantled, and the men were playing prisoner's base, shouting and running like lunatics. Brunet climbed the little hillock behind the stables and had a look at the graves; he felt at ease. Someone had scattered flowers on the trodden earth and planted three small crosses in a row. He sat down between two of the graves. There, beneath him, were the dead laid at full length; they had

attained to peace; some day it would come to him too,
innocence. He unearthed an old sardine can, empty and
rusty, and threw it away.

It was Sunday, the day of the week devoted to picnics
and visiting the cemetery. I was walking on a hill, and
below me, in a town, children were playing prisoner's
base; their shouts came up to me. Where was that? He
had forgotten. He thought: "It's true enough that I've got
to work in the dark." But what alternative was there? To
do nothing? His natural vigor revolted against the idea;
how could he go home at the end of the war and say to
the comrades: "Here I am, I just worked away at keeping
alive"? A fine thing that would be! How about trying to
escape? He looked at the walls. They were not so high
as to make an attempt impossible; it would only be a
matter of reaching Nancy. "The Poullains would hide me."
But there were the three dead men beneath him, there
were the children shouting in the timeless afternoon. He
laid his hands palm-downward on the cool earth; he would
not, he decided, escape. Elasticity, that was what was
needed. He must get the lads together so that, little by
little, they would take him as the focus of their confi-
dences, of their hopes for the future; then he must urge
them to denounce the armistice and he must always remain ready to modify his instructions so as to keep in step
with the turn of events.

"The party won't leave us in the lurch," he thought.
"the party *can't* leave us in the lurch." He lay down at full
length, in the same posture as the dead, there above the
dead. He looked at the sky; he got up. Slowly he descended
the little hill, feeling very much alone. Death was all about
him like a smell, like the fag end of a Sunday afternoon;
for the first time in his life he was conscious of a vague
sense of guilt: guilt because he felt lonely, guilt because
he was alive and capable of thought; guilt because he was
not dead. Beyond the walls were houses, dark, dead,

houses with dead eyes, an eternity of stone. This babble
of the Sunday crowd had been mounting skyward since
the beginning of time. It was only he that was not eternal;
but eternity was upon him like a fixed stare. He walked.
When he returned in the dying light, he had been walking
all day, there had been something he had had to kill, but
whether it had been killed he did not know. When one
doesn't care a damn for anything, one gets moods; it is
inevitable that one should. The corridor up on the attic
floor smelt of dust, the cages gave off a droning sound,
Sunday was dragging slowly to its end.

The ground looked like a sky pricked with shooting
stars; the men were smoking in the darkness. Brunet
stopped dead. Addressing nobody in particular, he called
out: "Be careful with those cigarettes; we don't want the
whole place to go up in flames." The men groaned and
grumbled under the impact of this voice striking down on
them from above. Brunet became silent; he felt at a loss,
in the way. He moved on a few steps. A red star leaped
into life and rolled lazily down to his feet; he put his foot
on it. The night was mild and blue; the windows stood out
clearly against the darkness, they had the purplish color
of specks that float before the eyes when one has been
staring too long at the sun. He could not find his own
cage.

"Hey! Schneider!" he shouted.

"Here I am," came a voice, "over here!" He retraced
his steps. A man was singing very quietly, to himself:
"*Sur la route, la grand' route, un jeune homme chantait.*"
Brunet thought: "How they love the dusk!"

"Over here," called Schneider, "keep on as you're going
another few steps, that's right." He went into the cage,
looked at the skylight through the tracery of bars, thought
of a gas jet springing into life in the blue darkness. He sat
down in silence, his eyes still on the skylight. What had
happened to the gas jet?

All around him was a sound of whispering. In the morning these men shouted, but at night they murmured, because they loved the evening. Peace came on velvet pads at nightfall in this great dark box, peace and the dead years; it was almost possible to believe that they had loved their lives.

"What I used to like," Moulu was saying, "was to take off my collar and settling down with a pint of wine. Just about now is the time I'd be having a drink at the Cadran Bleu and watching the people go by."

"The Cadran Bleu?" asked Goldilocks. "Where's that?"

"Gobelins—corner of the avenue des Gobelins and the boulevard Saint-Marcel."

"You mean somewhere near the Saint-Marcel movie?"

"Couple of hundred yards away; I know it like the back of my hand. I hang out just opposite the Lourcine barracks. After work I'd go home for a bite, and then I'd walk off again, usually to the Cadran Bleu, sometimes to the Canon des Gobelins. But at the Cadran Bleu there's a band."

"Used to be some pretty good shows at the Saint-Marcel."

"Don't I know it! There was Trenet, there was Marie Dubas. I've seen her there in the flesh; she used to drive a small car, a funny little affair."

"I used to go there myself," said Goldilocks. "I live over Vanves way. Many's the time I've walked home on my flat feet when it was a fine night."

"A pretty long hike, that."

"Oh, well, we were young in those days."

"It's not the beer I miss," said Lambert, "but the red wine. I could knock off a couple of quarts a day in my time, and even three if I'd got a thirst on. What you say to a nice bottle of Médoc now?"

"Three quarts!" said Moulu. "That's pretty good going!"

"Just about suit me!"

"I can't manage more'n one myself, it turns acid on me."

"You ought to stick to white."

"Ah, now you're talking!" Moulu exclaimed. "White's my drink."

"You ought to see the old girl I live with. Sixty-five she is, but she can still take her kilo of red every day without turning a hair. But of course it's red wine she takes." He broke off and sat there, dreaming of the past. The others were dreaming too; very quietly they listened to the voices that spoke for all of them, making no effort to interrupt.

Brunet thought of Paris, of the rue Montmartre, of a little bar where he'd been in the habit of taking a glass of white wine, well laced, after leaving the *Humanité* office.

"On a Sunday like this," the sergeant was saying, "I'd have been off with my old woman to my garden. It's about fifteen miles out of Paris, a little beyond Villeneuve-Saint-Georges. I grow wonderful vegetables there."

From beyond the bars a hoarse voice chimed in approvingly: "The soil is good all around there."

"We'd be thinking of making for home about now," said the sergeant, "or a bit earlier maybe, when the sun started going down; I don't much care for biking after the dark. The old lady'd have a bunch of flowers on the handle-bars, and I'd have a stack of vegetables on the carrier."

"I wasn't keen about going out on Sundays myself," said Lambert. "Too many people in the streets. Besides, I worked Mondays and it was pretty far to the Gare de Lyon."

"What the hell do you do at the Gare de Lyon?"

"I work in the information office, that big building just outside the main entrance. Any time you're thinking of taking a little trip, just let me know; I'll see you get a seat, even on short notice. There's always a way to fix things like that."

"I couldn't stand staying at home," said Moulu, "it gave me the willies. I'm on my own, see?"

"Quite often I didn't go out even on Saturdays," said Lambert.

"How'd you manage when you wanted a girl?"

"Got 'em to come round to my place."

"To your place?" said Goldilocks in astonishment. "Didn't your old lady have something to say to that?"

"No, she used to get us a meal and then go off to the pictures."

"Ah, well trained, she must have been!" said Goldilocks. "Very different from mine. Why, she'd give me a smack over the ear if she caught me with a girl, even when I was eighteen."

"Still live with her?"

"Not now, I've got a little place of my own." He stopped speaking for a moment, then went on: "Night like this I wouldn't have gone out either. I'd have stayed in and had a piece of tail."

There was a long silence. Brunet sat listening to them; he felt ordinary, he felt eternal. Almost shyly he said: "I'd have been in a bar on the rue Montmartre at this hour, taking a glass of spiked white wine with my pals." No one said anything. Someone started singing "*Mon cabanon*" at the top of his voice. "Who's that?" Brunet asked Schneider.

"Gassou, he's a tax collector from Nîmes." The voice sang on. Brunet thought: "Schneider didn't say a word about how he used to spend Sunday."

He awoke with a start. In his ears was the sound of a long, melodious call. What was it? White showed on the skylight frame, and on the white ceiling the bars cast shadows. Three o'clock in the morning. Vines were a sea of foam under the sprayed sulphur of the moon. The *Allier* nuzzled past its tufted islands, and at the Pont de Vau-Fleurville the vinedressers stood stamping their feet as they waited for the three-o'clock train. Brunet lay wondering happily what it could have been. He started suddenly because somebody whispered: "Ssh! Listen!" *I am not* in my bed at Mâcon, *this is not* the summer vacation.

Again, that long, impersonal call: three drawn-out whistles that slowly died away. Something was happening. The great attic was filled with rustlings; the huge beast moved its length across the floor; from the depths of this ageless night came the voice of the lookout man, "A train! A train! A train!" So that was it: the first train. Something was undoubtedly beginning: the night, till then abstract, was taking on substance and life; the night was beginning to sing. Everyone started talking at once. "The train! The first train! The track has been repaired. You've certainly got to hand it to the Germans, they know how to get a move on, they always have been good workers. Well, it's in their own interest, isn't it? They got to get things going again; at this rate, just you see, France, how things are going to hum. Where's it going? Nancy? Paris perhaps; try to find out whether there are any prisoners on it, prisoners going home."

Out there the train was rolling onward over the makeshift track and the great dark building was all agog. Brunet thought: "It's a munitions train." He tried, for caution's sake, to turn his back on his childhood; he tried hard to see in imagination the rusty rails, the tarpaulins, a waste of iron and steel; but he could not. Women were sleeping under the dimmed blue light of ceiling lamps in a pervasive smell of wine and sausages; a man was smoking in the corridor, and the darkness, pressed against the windows, reflected the image of his face. Tomorrow morning, Paris. Brunet smiled and lay down again, wrapped snugly in his childhood, under the whispering glimmer of the moon; tomorrow, Paris.

He was dozing in the train with his head on a soft, bare shoulder and he awoke in a silken radiance, Paris! He looked to his left without moving his head: six bats were clinging to the wall by their feet, their wings drooping like skirts. He was now wide awake: the bats resolved themselves into the shadows cast by hanging blouses. Moulu, of course, had kept his on; I must make him take it off when he goes to bed and change his shirt; otherwise we'll all be crawling with lice. Brunet yawned; another day. What was it that had happened in the night? Oh yes, the train.

He started up, threw back the blanket, and sat down. His body felt like wood, a zigzag pattern of stiffness, a pleasing woodenness in muscles that had gone numb; he felt as though the hardness of the floor had passed into the very substance of his flesh. He stretched and thought: "If I get out of this mess, I'll never sleep in a bed again."

Schneider was still asleep, his mouth open and a look of distress on his face. The man from the north had an angelic smile; Gassou, his hair tousled, his eyes red, was picking crumbs of bread from his blanket and eating them. Now and then he opened his mouth and rubbed the end of his tongue with his finger, to get rid of a scrap of wool or fiber that had been stuck to the bread. Moulu was scratching his head in a puzzled manner; the lines of his face were accentuated by streaks of coal dust; he looked as though he had been making a night of it. I must find some way of making him wash. Goldilocks was blinking; his face expressed gloom and bewilderment.

Brunet leaned over the man from the north and shook him. The man from the north groaned and opened his eyes. "Calisthenics!" said Brunet. "Ugh!" said the man from the north. He got up and took his blouse. They went down into the stable yard.

In front of one of the sheds, the printer, Dewrouckère, and the three chasseurs were waiting for them. While he was still some distance away, Brunet shouted: "Everything all right?"

"Everything fine! Hear the train in the night?"

"Yes, I heard it," said Brunet irritably. But his feeling

of annoyance quickly subsided: these men were young, clean, full of vigor; the printer was wearing his cap set sideways with a jaunty air. Brunet smiled at them. It started to drizzle. On the far side of the yard a crowd of men were waiting for Mass. Brunet noticed with pleasure that it was smaller than it had been on the first Sunday. "Did you do what I told you?"

Dewrouckère, without replying, opened the door of the shed; he had spread some straw on the ground. Brunet was conscious of a damp smell of stables. "Where did you get it?"

Dewrouckère smiled. "There's ways."

"Good," said Brunet, and he looked at them with eyes of friendship. They went in and undressed, keeping on only their pants and socks. Brunet pushed his feet into the soft, crisp straw; he felt satisfied. He said: "Let's get started."

The men stood in a row, their backs to the door. Brunet, facing them, went through the movements by number. They copied him. Their breath came through their closed lips with a hissing sound. Brunet looked at them approvingly as they squatted on their heels, their hands behind their heads, well set-up fellows, with young, taut muscles. Dewrouckère and Brunet were stronger than the rest, but the muscles of all of them stood up in hard, round balls. The printer was too thin; Brunet looked at him with a certain amount of anxiety. Suddenly an idea came to him; he stood up and shouted: "Stop!" The printer seemed pleased at the order; he was breathing hard. Brunet went up to him. "You're too thin."

"I've lost twelve pounds since the 20th of June."

"How d'you know that?"

"There's a set of scales in the hospital."

"You've got to put them on again," said Brunet; "you're not eating enough."

"Well, but how can I?"

"There's a perfectly simple way," said Brunet; "we'll each give you some of our rations."

"I—" began the printer. Brunet stopped him.

"I'm doctor here and I order you extra food. O.K.?" He turned to the others.

"O.K.," they said.

"Good. From now on you'll come round to our bunks every morning and collect it. As you were!"

They bent and rotated their bodies from the waist. At the end of a few moments, the printer began to sway on his feet. Brunet frowned. "What's wrong now?"

The printer smiled apologetically, "It's a bit tough."

"Don't stop," said Brunet; "whatever you do, don't stop." The trunks of their bodies turned like wheels, the men flinging their heads skywards, then dropping them between their legs, up, down, up, down. *Enough!*

They lay down on their backs to go through the abdominal exercises. We'll finish up with the back-throw; they like that, it makes them think they're wrestling. Brunet was conscious of his laboring muscles, of a long, dragging weariness in the groin. He was happy; this was the one good time of the day. The black rafters swung back and down, the straw seemed to jump to meet his face; he caught its yellow smell, his fingertips touched it well in advance of his toes. "Get going!" he said. "Put all you have into it."

"That catches you," one of the chasseurs said.

"So much the better. Get on! Get on!" He stood up. "Your turn now, Marbot."

Marbot had done some wrestling before the war. By profession he was a masseur. He approached Dewrouckère and seized him by the waist. It tickled and Dewrouckère, giggling, let himself fall backwards on his hands. Now it was Brunet's turn; he felt a warm grasp on his thighs and flung himself backwards. "No, no!" said Marbot; "don't tighten up like that! It's suppleness, not strength, that does it." Brunet felt the strain on his legs, his muscles cracked; he was too old for this sort of thing, too muscle-bound. He could only just touch the ground with his fingers. He got up, feeling pretty pleased with himself, all the same, and sweating; he turned round and began to hop.

"Stop!" He turned round sharply. The printer had fainted. Marbot laid him gently on the straw; with a faint hint of reproach he said: "It was too much for him."

"Nonsense," said Brunet, on edge. "He's not used to it, that's all." By this time the printer had opened his eyes; he was pale and breathed with difficulty. "How are you, old man?" said Brunet affectionately.

The printer smiled at him with complete trust. "I'm all right, Brunet, I'm all right. I'm sorry I—"

"Cut it out," said Brunet; "you'll be all right when you get some more food in you. That's enough for today, boys. A shower and then a run around!"

Still in their pants, with their clothes under their arms, they raced away to the hosepipe. They threw their clothes on a groundsheet, rolled them up into a watertight bundle, and took a shower in the falling drizzle. Brunet and the printer seized the hose and played it on Marbot. The printer shot a worried look at Dewrouckère, cleared his throat, and said to Brunet! "I'd like a word with you."

Brunet turned to him, still keeping hold of the nozzle; the printer lowered his eyes. Brunet felt slightly irritated: he disliked feeling that he could intimidate people. He said shortly: "Three this afternoon in the yard."

Marbot dried himself with a scrap of khaki shirt and dressed. He said: "Hey, boys; something's going on!" A great swarthy-looking fellow was holding forth in the middle of a group of prisoners. "That's Chaboche, the secretary," said Marbot in great excitement. "I'm going over

to see what's doing." Brunet watched him walk away:
the silly ass hadn't waited to put his puttees on and he
carried them off one in each hand.

"What do you think it's all about?" the printer asked.
He spoke in an impersonal sort of way, but his voice be-
trayed him: it was the voice in which they all spoke, a
hundred times a day, a voice of hope.

Brunet shrugged. "I suppose the Russians have landed
at Bremen or the British have asked for an armistice; it's
always the same kind of thing." He looked at the printer
without a trace of sympathy. The boy was just longing to
join the others, but did not dare. Brunet gave him no
credit for his timidity. I've only to turn away, and he'll
be off like a shot to stand like a deaf-mute in front of
Chaboche, with goggling eyes, dilated nostrils, and his
ears wide open, just waiting to be filled. "Turn the hose on
me," he said. He took off his pants; his flesh rejoiced at
the feel of the astringent shower; pellets of hail, millions
of little pellets of flesh, vigor. He rubbed his body down
with his hands, his eyes fixed on the gaping listeners.
Marbot had slipped into the crowd and was standing with
his snub-nose upturned toward the speaker. God in
heaven, if only they could get rid of all this ridiculous hoping, if only they could be put to *doing something!*

Before the war, work had been their touchstone, their
test of truth, work had decided their relations with the
world. Now that they cared about nothing, they had come
to believe that anything was possible: they lived in a
dream state, no longer capable of distinguishing the truth
when they saw it. Look at those three dopes walking over
there, loping along with easy strides and a sort of vegetable
smile on their faces! Are *they* really awake? From time to
time a word would ooze from their lips as though they
were half-asleep; they seemed scarcely to notice that they
were speaking. What were they dreaming about? From
morning till night they just drifted around, manufacturing,

like an auto-toxin, that life of sensation which had been taken from them; day after day they told one another about all the things they had once done but could no longer do. Thus they built up a fantasy life full of blood and drama.

"That's enough!" The jet of water fell, the hose lay on the ground, setting up a boil of foam between the cobbles. Brunet dried himself. Marbot came back; on his face was a look of blind triumph. For a moment or two, he swaggered round before making up his mind to speak. With assumed detachment he said: "Well, we're going to have visitors."

The printer's face went a fiery red. "What? *What* visitors?"

"Relations."

"Is that so?" said Brunet ironically. "And when is that to be?"

Marbot straightened himself with alacrity and looked him in the face with the air of one imparting a thrilling piece of news. "Today!"

"Oh, yeah?" said Brunet, "and I suppose they've ordered in twenty thousand beds just so the prisoners can slip it to their wives!"

Dewrouckère laughed. The printer was too nervous not to laugh too, but there was still a hungry look in his eyes. Marbot smiled with self-assurance. "No, no," he said, "this is official! Chaboche has just told us."

"Oh, if Chaboche said so—" said Brunet with a glint of amusement.

"He says it's going to be posted up officially this morning."

"Posted up officially in a pig's arse!" said Dewrouckère. Brunet smiled at him; Marbot looked surprised.

"But this is the real thing; Gartiser heard about it too, he got it from a German truck-driver—it seems they're coming from Épinal and Nancy."

"They? Who's they?"

"Whole families—on foot, on bicycles, in carts and freight trains. They slept on mattresses in the *mairie* and they'll be here this morning with a petition for the German commandant. *Look!* There's the notice going up."

A man was busy sticking a sheet of paper to the door. There was a wild rush; a crowd was soon milling round the steps. Marbot swung his arm in a wide gesture. "What did I tell you?" he asked triumphantly. "How about your pig's arse? Is it yours or the pig's?"

Dewrouckère shrugged. Brunet slowly put on his shirt and trousers, annoyed at having been proved wrong. He said: "So long, boys. Don't forget to turn off the faucet." He sauntered across to the crowd round the door; there was just a chance that this might be another false alarm. Brunet hated the little scraps of undeserved good luck that now and then came to fill the void in the lives of these lily-livered swine: an extra dollop of soup, say, or visitors from outside. Things like that made his work all the harder. From some distance away, over the assembled heads, he could read the notice: .

"The Camp Commandant hereby authorizes the prisoners to see the members of their familes (close relatives only). A room on the ground floor will be set aside for this purpose. Until further orders, such visits will take place on Sundays, between the hours of 2 p.m. and 5 p.m. In no case will interviews be allowed to exceed twenty minutes. Should the behavior of prisoners be found not to justify this exceptional act of clemency, all visits will be forthwith suspended."

Godchaux looked up with a happy chuckle. "You must give credit where credit's due. They're not such a bunch of bastards after all."

On Brunet's left, little Gallois began to laugh; it was an odd sort of sound, rather as though he were laughing in his sleep.

"What are you laughing at?" asked Brunet.

"It's coming," said Gallois. "Slow but sure, it's coming."

"What's coming?"

Gallois looked put out, made a vague gesture, stopped laughing, and said again: "It's coming."

Brunet forced his way through the crowd and got on to the staircase; all around him the dark ground floor was a struggling mob of men; the place resembled an ant heap. Raising his eyes, he could see bluish hands on the banister rail and a long, moving spiral of bluish faces. He pushed his way up, pushed in turn by others; clinging to the rail, he hoisted himself forward. He was crushed against the banisters, which shook under the weight. All day long, men were going up or going down without the slightest reason. He thought: "Nothing to be done; they're not wretched enough yet." They had become gentlemen of leisure, property-owners; the barrack belonged to them; they organized expeditions to the roof and into the basement; they had discovered some books in one of the cellars. There weren't, to be sure, any drugs in the hospital or food in the kitchens; still, there was a kitchen, there was a hospital, there was a secretariat, and there were even some barbers available. They had a feeling that they were part of an organized society. They had written to their families and for the last two days the life that is lived in cities had resumed its humdrum.

When the *Kommandantur* had issued instructions that all watches must be set by German time, they had hastened to obey, even those among them who, from June onwards, had carried on their wrists, in sign of mourning, watches that they had allowed to run down. The vague sequence of the hours, born and nourished among wild grasses, had become militarized, and these Frenchmen had been given German time, true conquerors' time, the same time as ticked away in Danzig and Berlin: sacred time. No, they were not yet wretched enough, for here they were organized, administered, fed, lodged, and governed; they were, in fact, without responsibility. There had been the train in the night, and now their relations were coming to see them, loaded with canned food and consolation. What a squealing, what tears, what a kissing there would be! "It needed only that. So far, they've not, at least, been showing off, but now they're going to feel that they are objects of interest." Wives and mothers, who had had plenty of time in which to build up the myth of the heroic Prisoner, were now coming to infect them with its virus.

He reached the attic floor, went along the corridor, entered his cage, and looked round with anger at his companions. There they were, lying about as usual, with nothing to do, dreaming away their lives, comfortable, and well and truly hoaxed. Lambert, with raised eyebrows and an expression of sullen surprise, was reading *Les Petites Filles modèles*. It was pretty obvious that the news had not yet reached the attic. Brunet hesitated: should he tell them? He could imagine how their eyes would shine, how excitedly they would prattle. "They'll hear it soon enough." He sat down in silence.

Schneider had gone to get a wash; the man from the north had not yet come in; the rest of them looked at Brunet in consternation. "What's cooking?" he asked.

At first there was no reply; then Moulu, lowering his voice, said: "Lice in No. 6."

Brunet gave a start, made a face. He felt nervous and the feeling increased; he said angrily: "I won't have lice in here." Then he broke off sharply, bit his lower lip, and looked at his neighbors uncertainly. No one had reacted to his words. The faces turned to him were as blank and as vaguely sheepish as ever.

"What are we going to do about it, Brunet?" Gassou asked. "I know you don't like me, but when there's anything to be done, it's me you come to for advice."

Very quietly he replied: "You wouldn't move when I told you to."

"Where to?"

"There were plenty of empty rooms. Lambert, I asked you to see whether there was anyone in the kitchen on the ground floor."

"The kitchen!" said Moulu. "No, thanks! Lying on stone gives diarrhea, and it's a gloomy hole anyway."

"Better gloom than lice. Lambert, I'm talking to you. Did you go look?"

"Yes."

"Well?"

"The place was full."

"There you are! You ought to have had a look a week ago." He felt the blood rushing to his head, his voice rose, he shouted: "I'm not going to have any lice in here!"

"Keep your hair on," said Goldilocks; "it's not our fault."

But the sergeant leaped to his defense: "He's right to bawl you out. I was all through World War I and I never had a louse on my body. I'll be damned if I begin now just because a lot of bums like you can't even keep clean!"

Brunet had recovered his temper; in a reasonable tone he said: "We've got to take immediate steps."

Goldilocks laughed. "Sure, but what steps?"

"First," said Brunet, "*all* of you must take a shower every day. Second, each man's got to delouse himself *every evening*."

"How do we do that?"

"You strip, and you go over your blouses, your pants, and your shirts to see whether there are any nits in the seams. If any of you wear body belts, it's their favorite breeding-ground."

Gassou sighed. "What fun we're going to have!"

"When you turn in," Brunet continued, "you must hang

everything, shirts included, on a nail, and sleep naked in your blankets."

"Hell!" said Moulu. "I'll die of bronchitis."

Brunet turned on him sharply. "I was just coming to you, Moulu. You're a regular nest of the things, and that's got to stop!"

"It's a lie!" said Moulu, almost speechless from indignation. "You won't find a thing on me!"

"Not at the moment, perhaps, but if there are any lice within a radius of ten miles, they'll make a bee-line for you as sure as we've lost the war."

"Why should they?" asked Moulu primly. "Why me and not you? You've no call to talk like that."

"Oh yes I have," Brunet thundered, "it's because you're as filthy as a pig!" Moulu threw him a venomous look; he opened his mouth to reply, but the others were laughing and shouting:

"He's right there! You stink! You're humming, you are! You smell like a young girl who neglects herself, you're a tub of shit, it takes my appetite away just to look at you!"

Moulu sat up and glared at them. "I wash myself regular," he said with surprise, "probably more regularly than you. But I'm not like some who strip stark naked just to show off."

Brunet fixed him with a pointed finger. "Did you wash yesterday?"

"Of course."

"Let's see your feet, then."

Moulu jumped up. "What right have you got?" He twisted his feet under him and squatted on his heels like a Turk. "I'll be frigged if I show my feet to anyone."

"Take his boots off," Brunet ordered. Lambert and Goldilocks flung themselves on Moulu and pinned him to the floor on his back. Gassou tickled his legs. Moulu twitched, gurgled, dribbled, giggled, and heaved deep sighs.

"Oh! stop it, boys! Don't be a lot of bastards! I'm ticklish."

"Keep still, then," the sergeant warned. Moulu relapsed into immobility though little shudders still ran over his flesh. Lambert was sitting on his chest; the sergeant un-laced Moulu's right boot and pulled it off. His foot came into view. The sergeant went pale, let go of the boot, and got up suddenly. "Christ!" he said.

"You may well say Christ!" Brunet observed. Lambert and Goldilocks got up too, in silence. They gazed at Moulu in admiring wonder. Moulu resumed his seat, calm and dignified.

A furious voice came from a neighboring cage: "Hi! what the hell are you boys in No. 4 doing? There's a God-awful stink coming from somewhere. It's like rancid butter."

"Moulu's taking his boots off," Lambert explained with simple directness. They looked at Moulu's foot: his big toe, quite black, was poking through a hole in his sock.

"Seen the soles?" asked Lambert. "They're more like lace than socks."

Gassou had buried his nose in his handkerchief. Goldi-locks was nodding his head with an expression almost of respect and saying over and over again: "You dirty old beast! You filthy old beast!"

"We've seen all we want to see," said Brunet. "Hide it away, for God's sake!" Moulu hurriedly put on his boot. "Moulu," Brunet solemnly went on, "you're a public dan-ger. You'll oblige me by going down and having a wash right now. If you're not scrubbed and clean in half an hour, you'll have no supper and you won't sleep in here tonight."

Moulu turned on him with a look of hatred, but got up unprotestingly, merely saying: "Throwing your weight around a bit, aren't you?"

Brunet was careful to say nothing. Moulu went out;

the others laughed. But Brunet did not laugh; his mind was busy with the idea of lice. He thought: "Anyhow, *I* won't get any."

"What's the time?" asked Goldilocks, "my belly's sagging to my toes."

"Noon," said the sergeant. "Noon, time for ration issue. Whose turn for K.P. fatigue?"

"Gassou."

"Come on, then, Gassou, get going."

"Plenty of time," said Gassou.

"I said get going. We always get our grub last when you're on the job."

"Oh, shut up!" Gassou slammed on his cap in a temper and went out.

Lambert returned to his book. Brunet was aware of a nervous itch between his shoulders. Lambert was scratching his thigh while he read; Goldilocks was looking at him.

"Say, have you got 'em?"

"No," Lambert said, "but I've been itching ever since the talk started."

"Same here," said Goldilocks; he began to scratch his neck. "Don't you feel crawly, Brunet?"

"No," said Brunet. None of them said any more. Goldilocks smiled nervously while he scratched; Lambert scratched and went on reading. Brunet dug his hands into his pockets and did not scratch. Gassou reappeared in the doorway; his face threatened trouble.

"Have you boys been kidding me?"

"Hey, where's the bread?"

"The bread, you big chump! Why, there's no one downstairs, the kitchens aren't even open."

Lambert raised scared eyes. "You mean to say it's going to be the way it was in June all over again?" Their lazy and prophetic souls were always ready to believe the worst or the best.

Brunet turned to the sergeant. "What time d'you make it?"

"Ten past twelve."

"Sure your watch hasn't stopped?"

The sergeant smiled and contemplated his watch with self-satisfaction. "It's a Swiss watch," he said, and left the words to speak for themselves.

Brunet called to the men in the next cage: "What time have you guys got?"

"Ten past eleven," came a voice.

The sergeant was triumphant. "What did I tell you?"

"You told us it was ten past twelve, you turd!" Gassou said resentfully.

"Of course I did: ten past twelve by French time, ten past eleven by Boche."

"That was a dirty trick to play, you bastard!" Gassou cried in a fury. He stepped over Lambert and flung himself down on his blanket.

The sergeant, quite unruffled, continued: "Nice thing, just when France has taken the count, to abandon French time!"

"You're nuts; there's no such thing as French time now, there's only Heinie time for everywhere from Marseille to Strasbourg."

"Maybe," said the sergeant, obstinately refusing to let himself be rattled, "but I'd like to see the man who could make me muck around with any newfangled time!" He turned to Brunet. "You'll be glad enough to go back to it," he said, "when Heinie's had a kick in the pants."

"Hey!" Lambert shouted. "Look at Moulu dressed like a man about town!" Moulu had just come into the room looking pink, fresh, and Sundayish. The others began to laugh.

"Pretty good, eh, Moulu?"

"What is?"

"Water!"

"Oh, sure, it wasn't bad," said Moulu carelessly.

"That's all right, then," said Brunet. "From now on, you'll report every morning for foot-washing."

Moulu showed no sign that he had heard; he was flaunting an important and mysterious smile. "News, boys, get on your toes!" he said.

"News? What news?" Faces shone, flushed, brightened up.

Moulu said: "We're going to have visitors!"

Brunet got up noiselessly and went out. Behind him he could hear the sound of voices raised. He hurried on, forced his way through the dense jungle of the staircase, and went down. The yard was swarming with men, all walking slowly round in single file under the thin drizzle. Their eyes were turned inwards to the center of the circle they were describing; every window was festooned with staring faces; something had happened. Brunet joined the procession and followed it round, though without curiosity. Each day in this place there was something happening, men standing stock-still, seemingly in expectation of some imminent event, others circling them, all eyes. Brunet turned; Sergeant André smiled at him.

"Why, if it isn't Brunet! I bet he's looking for Schneider."

"Have you seen him?" Brunet asked quickly.

"Sure, hell yes!" André answered with a grin. "As a matter of fact, he's looking for you." He addressed himself to the others and laughed. "Those two guys, they're as thick as thieves, always together or running after each other!"

Brunet smiled: thick as thieves, why not? He regarded his friendship for Schneider with a tolerant eye because it made no inroads on his time; it was like a steamer acquaintance, it committed him to nothing. If ever they got home from prison camp they'd never set eyes on each other again. It was an unexacting friendship, without claims or responsibilities, just a feeling of warmth in the pit of the stomach. André was walking round beside him, saying nothing. At the center of this slow maelstrom was a zone of absolute calm where a few men in overcoats were sitting on the ground or on their knapsacks. André stopped Clapot, who was just passing him.

"Who are those guys?"

"Punishment squad," said Clapot.

"What?"

Clapot threw off his hand impatiently, "I just told you, punishment." They resumed their circular progress, but without shifting their gaze from the motionless and silent group.

"Punishment!" grunted André. "First time I've seen anyone doing punishment here. Punishment for what? What have they done?"

Brunet's face cleared. He had just caught sight of Schneider grounded on the bank of the maelstrom. Schneider was looking at the little group of men undergoing punishment, and rubbing his nose. Brunet liked Schneider's trick of holding his head sideways; he thought with pleasure: "We'll have a chat." Schneider was very intelligent, more intelligent than Brunet—not that intelligence is so very important, but it does make for pleasant personal contact. He laid his hand on Schneider's shoulder and smiled at him. Schneider smiled back, but without gaiety. Brunet sometimes found himself wondering whether Schneider really enjoyed his company; they were hardly ever apart, but if Schneider had any real liking for him, he did not often show it. At heart Brunet was grateful for this: he had a horror of all forms of demonstrativeness.

"Found your pal Schneider, huh?" said André. Brunet smiled; Schneider did not smile. "Say," said André to Schneider, "what are those guys doing punishment for?"

"What guys?"

"Those bastards over there."

"They're not doing punishment," said Schneider, "they're the Alsatians. Can't you see Gartiser in the front row?"

"Oh, so that's it!" said André. "So that's it!" There was a look of satisfaction on his face. He stood beside them for a moment, his hands in his pockets, informed, assuaged; then suddenly he grew worried. "What are they there for?"

Schneider gave a shrug. "Go ask 'em."

André hesitated, then strolled slowly over to the men with assumed indifference. The Alsatians looked stiff and uneasy; in their insecurity, they sat very upright, their overcoats billowing round them like skirts; they looked like emigrants on the deck of a ship. Gartiser was squatting, tailor-fashion, his hands flat on his thighs, his great farmyard eyes goggling in his big face.

"Hullo, fellows," André said. "So there's nine of you, is there?" They said nothing. André's questioning face seemed to swim above their lowered heads. "Nine?" Still no reply. "I thought there were nine when I saw you sitting here in a circle. Hey, Gartiser!"

Gartiser had made up his mind to raise his head; with a certain arrogance he faced André.

"How come all you Alsatians got together?"

"They ordered us to."

"What about the overcoats and the kit? Did they tell you to take them?"

"Yes."

"Why?"

"Don't know."

André's face was scarlet with excitement. "Haven't you got any idea?"

Gartiser said nothing; behind him there was an impatient gabbling in Alsatian dialect.

André, offended, stiffened. "I see," he said. "You weren't so proud of yourselves last winter, so anxious to chatter in your lingo; but now we're beaten, you seem to have

forgotten how to talk French." The heads remained lowered; the sound of the voices talking Alsatian was like the
natural and ceaseless rustling of leaves in the wind. André
laughed and stared at his audience of bent heads. "Not
much percentage in being French now, eh, boys?"

"Don't you worry about us," said Gartiser sharply, "we
won't be French for long."

André hesitated, frowned, tried to find a stinging reply, and, failing to do so, made a half-turn toward Brunet.
"So that's that!"

From behind Brunet's back came a sound of angry
voices. "What d'you want to talk to 'em for? Leave 'em
alone, can't you? They're just Boches."

Brunet looked at the speakers, at the pale, embittered
faces, all of them the color of sour milk: envy, the envy
of little middle-class minds, of petty tradesmen jealous of
men with an official position, of men with privileges,
jealous now of Alsatians. He grinned and looked at the
rancorous eyes. This little bunch of men were vexed at
being Frenchmen. Well, that was better than passive resig-
nation; even envy was better than that, it was at least
something to work on.

"Did you ever hear of one of these guys lending you a
penny or giving you a helping hand?"

"Hell, no, the bastards! Why, some of 'em actually had
chow when we were first took. What did they do? They
gobbled it up with us looking on; they didn't care if we
starved."

The Alsatians were listening; they turned their fair pink
faces and looked up at the Frenchmen. Perhaps there
would be a fight. A harsh shout sounded: the Frenchmen
jumped back; the Alsatians sprang to their feet and stood
at attention. A German officer, a major, had just appeared
at the top of the steps. He was tall and fragile-looking,
with hollow eyes and a worried face. He began to speak.
The Alsatians listened. Gartiser, red as a beet, was lean-

ing forward. The French were listening, too, not understanding a word, but with faces that expressed tolerant
attention. Their anger had gone cold; they had a feeling
that they were taking part in some sort of official ceremony. There is always something rather gratifying about
a ceremony. The officer spoke on; time passed. The stiff,
strange language had a sacrosanct quality like the Latin
of the Mass. No one dared to envy the Alsatians now; they
were robed in dignity, like a choir.

André nodded and said: "Theirs isn't such an ugly lingo,
after all."

Brunet said nothing: just a lot of monkeys, that's what
they were; they couldn't even nurse their anger for more
than five minutes. "What's he saying?" he asked Schneider.

"He says they've been liberated." The voice of the major
emerged in a series of enthusiastic jerks from his dark
face; he was shouting, but there was no gleam in his eyes.

"What's he saying now?"

Schneider translated in a low voice: "Thanks to the
Führer, Alsace will return to the bosom of the mother-
land."

Brunet glanced at the Alsatians, but their faces were
slow to express their feelings, incapable of keeping pace
with their passions. Two or three of them, nevertheless,
flushed red. Brunet felt amused. The German voice soared
and darted, rising from level to level; the officer had raised
his fists above his head and, with his elbows, was beating
time to his pæan. Everyone felt moved, as when the na-
tional flag goes by, as when the music of a military band
is heard. The two fists opened; the fingers sprang into the
air; the men trembled; the officer yelled: *"Heil Hitler!"*
The Alsatians looked as though they had been turned to
stone.

Gartiser swung round on them, struck them to the earth
with the lightning of his glance; then, facing the major, he
flung his arm forward and shouted: *"Heil!"* There was a

scarcely noticeable silence, then other arms rose in the air. In spite of himself Brunet seized Schneider's wrist and gripped it hard. There was a sound of shouting. Somebody cried: *"Heil!"* enthusiastically; others merely opened their mouths without uttering a sound, like people in church pretending to sing. One big fellow, standing in the back row, his head bent and his hands in his pockets, seemed to be suffering. The arms fell. Brunet let go of Schneider's wrist. The French said nothing; the Alsatians resumed their attitude of attention; their faces were white marble, blind and deaf beneath the golden flame of their hair.

The major barked an order, the column began to move, the French backed away, the Alsatians marched by between two hedges of curious eyes. Brunet turned round; he looked at the excited faces of his companions. He would have liked to see in them fury and hatred; all he saw was a sort of flabby, blinking avidity. Far off, the gate swung open. Upright, on the steps, the German major looked at the receding column with a benevolent smile.

"All the same—" said André, "all the same—"

"Hell!" said a bearded fellow, "and to think I was born in Limoges!"

André nodded his head; he repeated: "All the same—"

"What's wrong?" asked Charpin, the cook.

"All the same—" said André.

The cook had a gay and lively look. "See here, pal," he said, "if you'd only to shout *'Heil Hitler!'* to be sent home, wouldn't you shout? It doesn't commit you. You just shout but you don't say what you're really thinking."

"Oh, *I'd* shout anything," said André, "but it's different for them: they're Alsatians; they owe France a duty."

Brunet made a sign to Schneider. They made their escape and took refuge in the farther yard, which was deserted. Brunet leaned with his back against the wall of the recreation hut, facing the stables. Not far from them, seated on the ground, his arms round his knees, was a tall

soldier with a pointed skull and thin hair. He did not
bother them. He looked like a village idiot.

Brunet kept his eyes on his feet. He said: "See those
two Alsatian Socialists?"

"What Socialists?"

"Among the Alsatian crowd. I saw 'em; Dewrouckère
got in touch with 'em just last week. They told him they
were as keen as mustard."

"What of it?"

"They raised their arms with the rest of 'em."

Schneider said nothing. Brunet stared at the village
idiot; he was a young fellow with a well-modeled, aquiline
nose, the nose of a rich man. His distinguished face,
molded by thirty years of middle-class living, with its fine-
etched lines, its sensitive intelligence, had assumed the
look of tranquil bewilderment that one sees in certain animals. Brunet shrugged his shoulders. "They're all the
same. One day you meet a guy and he seems all right;
twenty-four hours later he's a changed person and pre-
tends not to recognize you." He jerked his thumb toward
the idiot. "I've been used to working with men, not with
objects like that."

Schneider smiled. "*That* was once an engineer in the
Thompson Engineering Works, the kind of young fellow
said to have a future before him."

"Well," Brunet said, "he's got his future behind him
now."

"How many of us are there?" asked Schneider.

"Can't say for certain, the number varies. Let's assume
it's about a hundred."

"A hundred out of twenty thousand?"

"Yes, a hundred out of twenty thousand." Schneider's
question had been put in a colorless voice; he made no
comment on Brunet's reply, but Brunet dared not look at
him. "There's something not quite right," Brunet went on.

"Reckoning on the basis of 1936, we ought to be able to count on one third of the prisoners."

"It's not '36 now," said Schneider.

"I know that," said Brunet.

Schneider touched his nostril with the tip of his fore-finger. "The fact is," he said, "we're recruiting the sore-heads and bellyachers. That explains the instability of our group. A bellyacher isn't necessarily a man with a genuine grievance; on the contrary, he's content to go on belly-aching. If you try to take his words at their face value, he'll pretend to agree, so as not to look like a pricked bubble; but you just turn your back and he evaporates into thin air. That's happened to me more than once."

"And to me," said Brunet.

"What we want to do is to enlist the real malcontents," said Schneider, "the sound Leftists who used to read *Marianne* and *Vendredi*, the guys who honestly believe in democracy and progress."

"I'm with you there," said Brunet. He looked at the wooden crosses on the mound and the grass gleaming under the drizzle. He went on: "Every now and then I meet a guy limping along like a sick man and I say to myself: that's one of 'em. But what can you do? As soon as you try to talk to him he gets scared. It's as though they were suspicious of everything."

"It's not exactly that," said Schneider, "The trouble with most of them, I think, is that they're ashamed. They know that they've been the losers in this war, that they're down and that they'll never get up again."

"They don't really want to go on fighting," said Brunet; "they'd much rather think that they're down and out for good; it's more flattering to their self-importance."

With a strange look Schneider said between teeth: "What can you expect? It's a form of consolation."

"How d'you mean?"

"It's always consoling to think you're not alone in your defeat, that defeat is the common fate."

"The suicide mentality!" said Brunet with disgust.

"Put it that way if you want to," said Schneider. He added quietly: "Still, you know, they are France. If you can't establish communication with them, all you do goes for nothing."

Brunet turned and looked at the idiot; the vacant face seemed to fascinate him. The idiot yawned voluptuously and his eyes watered; a dog yawned, France yawned, Brunet yawned. He stopped yawning. Without raising his eyes, and in a low, hurried voice, he asked: "Is there any point in going on?"

"Going on with what?"

"Our work."

Schneider laughed. The sound was dry and unpleasing. "You ask that of me?" Brunet looked up suddenly; on Schneider's thick lips he caught the vanishing tail of a sad, sadistic smile. "What'll you do if you don't go on?" asked Schneider. The smile had vanished. The man's face was once again smooth, heavy, calm, a dead sea.

I shall never really get at the meaning of that face. "What'll I do? I'll make a get-away somehow and join the comrades in Paris."

"In Paris?" Schneider scratched his head.

"You think things are the same there as here?" Brunet asked sharply.

Schneider thought for a moment. "If the Germans are behaving well—"

"You bet they're behaving well!" said Brunet. "They're helping blind people across the street, I shouldn't wonder."

"In that case," said Schneider, "yes, I expect things are about the same as here." He sat up suddenly and looked at Brunet with an air of curiosity unmixed with distress. "What are you hoping?"

Brunet had gone stiff. "I'm not hoping anything; I never have hoped anything, I don't give a damn for hope. I *know.*"

"What is it you know?"

"I know that sooner or later Russia will join in the dance, I know that she's biding her time and I want our crowd to be ready."

"Her hour's gone by," said Schneider. "England'll be down and out before autumn. If Russia didn't intervene while there was still an opportunity to build two fronts, why should she intervene now when there'll be nobody to help her?"

"The U.S.S.R. is the land of the workers," said Brunet, "and the Russian workers won't let the proletariat of Europe be ground into dust under the Nazi jackboot."

"Then why was Molotov allowed to sign the German-Soviet Pact?"

"At that precise moment it was the only thing to be done. The U.S.S.R. wasn't ready."

"What proof have you that she's any readier now?"

Brunet smacked the wall irritably with the palm of his hand. "We're not at the Café du Commerce," he said, "and I'm not going to argue that with you. I'm a militant and I've never wasted my time in speculating about high politics; I had a job to do, and I did it. So far as everything else was concerned, I put my trust in the Central Committee of the U.S.S.R. and I'm not going to change my attitude now."

"When I asked what you were hoping, I was perfectly right," said Schneider gloomily, "you live on hope." The mournfulness of his tone drove Brunet to exasperation, he felt that this misery of Schneider's was assumed.

"Schneider," he said without raising his voice, "it is conceivable that the Politburo might founder in the depths of stupidity. By the same token, it is conceivable that the roof of this hut might fall on your head, but that doesn't mean you spend your time keeping a wary eye on the ceiling. Of course, if you feel like it, you may say that you hope in God or that you have confidence in the architect, but those are mere words. You know perfectly well that there are certain natural laws and that it is the way of buildings to stay standing when they have been built in conformity with those laws. Why, then, should I spend my time wondering about the policy of the U.S.S.R. and why should you raise the question of my confidence in Stalin? I have complete confidence in him, yes, and in Molotov and in Zhdanov—as much confidence as you have in the solidity of these walls. In other words, I know that history has its laws and that, in virtue of those laws, an identity of interest binds the country of the workers and the European proletariat. I give no more thought to these things than you do to the foundations of your house; my knowledge is the floor under my feet and the roof over my head. In that certainty I live and behind that certainty I shelter. That is what makes it possible for me to carry on with the concrete duties the party assigns to me. When you stretch out your hand to grasp your mass cup, the mere fact of that gesture postulates a universal determinism. Similarly with me, my every act, no matter how trivial, affirms implicitly that the U.S.S.R. is the vanguard of World Revolution." He looked ironically at Schneider and concluded: "That's me. I'm nothing but a militant."

Schneider's expression was still one of discouragement; his arms hung loosely, his eyes were lusterless; it was as though he were deliberately concealing the nimbleness of his mind under a mask of heaviness. It was something that Brunet had noticed in him before now; Schneider was always trying to slow down his own intelligence, as though he wanted to bring it into step with that patient, dogged mentality which doubtless he believed to be the distinguishing mark of peasants and soldiers. Why? So as to assert in the very depths of his being a complete solidarity with them? So as to utter a protest against intellectuals and leaders? So as to express his hatred of pedantry?

"All right, old man," said Schneider, "go on being a militant to your heart's content. Only don't get wild when I say your behavior bears a marked resemblance to the blah-blah-blah at the Café du Commerce. With infinite trouble we have got together a handful of unhappy idealists, and all we give them to bite on is a lot of talk about the future of Europe."

"That's inevitable," Brunet objected. "So long as there's no work for them to do, I can't give them a definite job; the only thing open to us is to talk and to make contacts. But just you wait till they've been deported to Germany. There'll be something for them to do then, all right!"

"Oh, I'll wait," said Schneider in a sleepy voice. "I'll wait. It doesn't seem as though I'd much choice in the matter. But the priests and the Nazis won't wait, and, oddly enough, their propaganda is a good deal more effective than ours."

Brunet looked him straight in the eyes. "What are you getting at?"

"Me?" Schneider looked surprised. "Nothing at all. We were saying how difficult it is to find recruits—"

"Am I to blame?" Brunet demanded with sudden violence, "am I to blame if the French are a lot of bastards without either courage or initiative? Am I to blame if—"

Schneider sat up and broke in sharply on his words. His face had gone hard and now he spoke so quickly and so disjointedly that it seemed as though *someone else* had stolen his voice in order to heap insults on Brunet. "You're —you're always—it's *you* who are the bastard," he shouted. "*You!* It's easy to be superior when you've got a party behind you, when you've been trained in a political dogma and are used to taking hard knocks; it's easy to despise a lot of poor devils who don't know whether they're coming or going." The only effect this outburst had on Brunet was to make him feel guilty because he had been impatient.

"I don't despise anyone," he said. "As for the guys here, naturally I allow for extenuating circumstances."

Schneider was not listening. His great eyes were dilated, he seemed to be waiting for something to happen inside himself. All of a sudden he resumed his shouting: "Yes, you are to blame! Of course you're to blame!"

Brunet looked at him without understanding. An unhealthy color had flooded Schneider's face; it was something more than anger, it was something closer to a long-standing hatred, it was like one of those suppressed enmities which exist among families for years and at last burst out with a kind of wild joy. Brunet gazed at the massive incarnation of fury before him, at this man who looked more like a revival preacher than anything else, and he thought: "Something's going to happen."

Schneider seized him by the arm and pointed to the engineer from the Thompson works, who was innocently twiddling his thumbs. There was a moment's silence because Schneider was seething too violently for speech. Brunet felt cold and calm. When other people lost their tempers, it always made him feel calm. He waited; he wanted to find out the truth about Schneider.

Schneider made a violent effort to control himself. "That's one of the bastards who have neither courage nor initiative, just another guy like me, like Moulu, like all of us except you of course. It's *true* that he's become a bastard, it's *true*, it's so true that he's convinced of it himself. It happens that I saw him at Toul in September. He had a horror of war, but he accepted this war because he thought there were good reasons why he should fight, and I swear he wasn't a bastard then. No, this is what you've made of him! You're all in cahoots, Pétain with Hitler, Hitler with Stalin, the whole lot of you are busy explain-

ing that these poor devils are doubly guilty—guilty of
having made war, guilty of having lost it. You're running
around, taking from them all the reasons they thought
made it necessary for them to fight. That poor guy thought
he was embarked upon a crusade for Justice and the
Rights of Man; now you want to persuade him that he was
just cheated into taking part in an imperialist war. He
doesn't know what he wants, he's not even sure what he's
done. It's not only the army of his enemies that has
triumphed, but their ideology as well. He's bogged down,
he's fallen slap out of the world of men, out of history, and
he's trying to build up some kind of defense mechanism, to
think out the whole situation, to get it straight from the
beginning. But what with? Even his tools for thinking
straight are outdated, thanks to you. He's suffering from
the iron that has entered into his soul and it's you who
are to blame."

Brunet could not keep himself from laughing. "Who do
you think you're talking to?" he asked. "Me or Hitler?"

"I'm talking to the editorial writer of *L'Humanité*,"
said Schneider, "to a member of the C.P., to the fellow
who, on August 29, 1939, filled two pages with pæans of
praise on the occasion of the signing of the German-Soviet
Pact."

"So that's the trouble," said Brunet.

"Yes, that's the trouble."

"The C.P. was opposed to the war, as you perfectly well
know," Brunet explained without any show of anger.

"Certainly, it was opposed to the war, we all know that;
it made no bones about that. But at the same time it ap-
proved the very pact that made war inevitable."

"No," Brunet insisted, "the pact was our one chance of
preventing war."

Schneider burst into a laugh. Brunet smiled, but said
nothing. Suddenly Schneider stopped laughing. "Take a
good look at me, go ahead! I always have a feeling you're

conducting some sort of post-mortem. A hundred times
I've caught you studying us all with cold concentration;
it's as though you were drawing conclusions from what
you saw. Well, what are those conclusions? That I'm just
a waste product of the historical process, all right, that's
O.K. by me; I'm a waste product sure enough, but I'm
not dead, Brunet, oh, no, I'm *not dead*, unfortunately.
I've got to go on living my degradation, with the taste of
it in my mouth, though that's something you could never
understand. You deal in the abstract, and it's you and
others like you who have made of us the scraps and waste
products we are."

Brunet remained silent, looking at Schneider. Schneider
seemed to be hesitating, but there was a sort of terror in
his hard eyes, he gave the impression of a man who on
the tip of his tongue was framing words that, once said,
could never again be unsaid. Suddenly the color drained
from his face, a film of sheer panic seemed to form on his
eyes, he shut his mouth in a grim, hard line. After a moment, in calm, monotonous tones, he continued: "Well,
we're all of us washed up, and that goes for you too, it's
your excuse. Oh, I know you still think of yourself as a
manifestation of the historical process, but your heart's
no longer in it. The C.P. will be re-established without
you and on principles you will know nothing of. You could
escape, but you don't dare to because you're afraid of
what you'll find outside. The iron has entered into your
soul, too!"

Brunet smiled. No, that wasn't the way, they wouldn't
get a rise out of him like that. This sort of talk was just
words which didn't in the least concern him. Schneider
was silent now and quivering faintly. Actually, nothing
had happened, nothing at all. Schneider had not confessed
anything or revealed anything, he was just a man whose
nerves had let him down, that was all. As for that refrain

of his about the German-Soviet Pact, Brunet had heard it all a hundred times since September.

The soldier must have realized that they had been talking about him; slowly he unfolded his full length and moved off on his long, spindly legs, sidling like a frightened animal.

What was Schneider? A bourgeois intellectual? An anarchist of the Right? An unconscious fascist? The fascists, too, had been opposed to the war. Brunet turned and looked at him. What he saw was a down-at-heels, perplexed soldier who had nothing left to defend, nothing more to lose, a man who just stood there rubbing his nose with an absent-minded stare in his eyes. "He wanted to hurt me," Brunet thought. But he could not feel any resentment. Very softly he asked a question: "If that's the way you think, why did you come in with us?"

Schneider looked old, used up. In tones that expressed nothing but wretchedness he said: "So as not to be alone." There was a silence; then Schneider raised his head and with a wavering smile: "A fellow has to do something, eh? It doesn't much matter what. We may not agree about some things—" He broke off. Brunet said nothing. After a moment Schneider looked at his watch. "Time for our visitors. You coming?"

"I'm not sure," said Brunet. "You go along; I may join you later."

Schneider threw him a brief glance, as though he had a mind to say something, then he turned away, moved off, and disappeared. The incident was closed. Brunet put his hands behind his back and started to walk up and down the yard under the thin rain; he was thinking of nothing, he felt within himself a hollow, echoing void. On his cheeks and hands he could feel the impact of tiny wet particles. The iron in the soul—all right, but what then? "Just a lot of psychological balderdash," he said to himself scornfully. He came to a stop, thinking of the party. The yard was empty, a gray, disembodied place, smelling of Sunday, a land of exile. Suddenly he started to run and dashed into the other yard.

The men were crowding round the barrier, silent, all heads turned toward the gate. *They* were there, on the other side of the walls, exposed to the same thin drizzle. Brunet noticed Schneider's muscular back in the front row. He forced his way to him and laid a hand on his shoulder. Schneider turned; his smile was warm and friendly.

"So you did come after all!" he said.

"Yes, I came."

"It's five past two," said Schneider; "they're going to open the gate."

Close beside them a cadet officer leaned toward his friend and murmured: "Perhaps there'll be some girls."

"It'll be fun to see civilians again," said Schneider excitedly. "This reminds me of Sundays at school."

"Were you at boarding-school?"

"Yes. We used to line up outside the parlor door to watch the parents arrive."

Brunet smiled, but said nothing. He didn't give two hoots for civilians, but he felt happy because the presence of all these fellows around him gave him a sensation of warmth. The gate swung back creaking, a murmur of disappointment was audible in the ranks. "Aren't there any more than that?" They numbered about thirty. Above the heads Brunet caught sight of the tiny black, packed group, doggedly waiting under their umbrellas. Two Germans went forward to meet them, all smiles and affability, checked their papers, and then stood back to let them pass. There were women and old men, nearly all dressed in black, looking like members of a funeral procession in the rain; they were carrying suitcases, bags, and baskets covered with napkins. The women's faces were gray; their eyes were hard and they looked tired. They advanced slowly, brushing against one another, embarrassed by the staring eyes that devoured them.

"Hell! What a bunch of apes!" the cadet officer sighed.

"Oh, they've got possibilities," said the other; "look at that kid over there with the dark-haired woman."

Brunet scanned the visitors with a sympathetic eye. Dowdy they certainly were; the women's faces were harsh and set; they looked as though they had come to say to their husbands: "That was a fool's trick of yours to get nabbed! How d'you think I'm going to manage, left on my own with a kid to look after?" Still, there they were. They had come on foot or in carts, carrying heavy baskets of food, the kind of women who are always to be seen waiting motionless, expressionless, outside hospitals, barracks, and prisons; the pretty, young shy-eyed dolls, on the contrary, wear mourning only at home. With emotion Brunet noticed on their faces the traces of wretchedness and poverty which was all that peace had brought them; with just such looks of feverish disapproval, mingled with loyalty, must they have taken meals to their husbands when they were engaged in a sit-down strike.

The men, for the most part, were old and sturdy, with quiet, tranquil eyes. They walked slowly, heavily, they were free; they had won their own war when they were young, and their consciences were clear. This defeat was not *their* defeat, yet they accepted it as their responsibility, carrying the burden of it on their broad shoulders because, when a man has produced a child, he has to pay for any damage it may do. They were neither angry nor ashamed, they had come to see what mischief the young hopefuls had been up to now. On these rustic faces Brunet suddenly discovered what he himself had lost: the meaning of life. These are the kind of men I used to talk with. They made no attempt to understand, but they listened with just such an expression of calm thoughtfulness; they grumbled a bit, but once they had grasped what he was after, they never forgot it.

He felt the recrudescence of an old desire: to work, to feel upon him the eyes of those who were adult and responsible. He shrugged his shoulders, turned from his contemplation of the past, and looked at *the others,* at the crowd of tense, expectant prisoners with their twitching, inexpressive faces. That's where I belong. They were standing on tiptoe, stretching their necks for a glimpse, looking at the visitors with monkey eyes of fear and insolence. They had counted on this war to make men of them, to give them their rights as heads of families and as war veterans; it was to have been for them a solemn initiation, a means of freeing them from the shackles of the other, the *Great* War, the *World* War, which had stifled their youth with memories of splendor. This war of theirs was to have been greater and still more world-wide. By firing on the Heinies they were to have accomplished that ritual massacre of fathers which marks the entry of each new generation into life. But as things turned out, they fired on nobody, they indulged in no massacre, the whole thing had gone wrong. They had remained minors and their fathers were still leading the procession, very much alive, hated, envied, adored, and feared, while the sons, twenty thousand warriors, remained bogged down in a rancorous childhood. All of a sudden one of the old men turned to face the prisoners. All the heads drew back. He had heavy black brows and red cheeks, he was carrying a bundle at the end of a stick. He approached the barbed wire, gripped it with his hand and stared across out of large, bloodshot eyes. The gaze was almost that of an animal, slow, fierce, inexpressive; beneath it the men waited, withdrawn, holding their breath, ready to kick back if they were goaded. They stood there in expectation of a blow.

The old man spoke. "So there you are!" he said.

There was a silence and then someone muttered: "Yes, pops, it's us all right!"

The old man said: "It's a pitiful sight."

The cadet officer cleared his throat and blushed. Brunet read on his face the expression of a furious, frustrated defiance. Yes, daddy, this is us, twenty thousand guys who wanted to be heroes and threw down their arms without striking a blow. The old man nodded his head; heavily, in deep tones, he said: "Poor lads!"

Tension relaxed, faces smiled, heads were stretched forward. The German sentry came up; politely he touched the old man on the arm and signed to him to move on. The old man barely turned his head. "Can't you allow a fellow a minute?" he protested; "I've only just come!" He winked conspiratorially at the prisoners, who smiled in response. They felt happy because of an old man whose glance was warm and friendly, because of a tough old fellow from down their way; they felt as though freedom had been conferred on them by proxy. The old man asked: "Things not too bad?"

Now they'll all start whining, Brunet thought. But twenty voices replied cheerfully: "Not too bad, pops, we'll get along O.K."

"That's fine, then," said the old man, "that's fine." He had no more to say to them, but still stood where he was, a clumsy stocky, rugged figure. The sentry took him gently by the sleeve. He hesitated, scanning the assembled faces. It was as though he were trying to pick out his son's. A deep-buried thought slowly rose to his eyes; he showed signs of embarrassment. At last, in his gnarled old voice he said: "You know, lads, it wasn't your fault." No one answered. The men stood stiffly before him, almost at attention. He tried to express himself more plainly. "No one at home thinks it was your fault." Still there was no answer. He said: "Well, so long, lads," and turned away.

Then, all of a sudden, the crowd was swept as by a

wind; voices rose passionately: "So long, pops! So long! See you soon! See you soon!" The volume of their voices swelled as he moved away, but not once did he turn his head.

Schneider said to Brunet: "You see!"

Brunet started. "See what?" he asked, but he knew perfectly well what Schneider meant.

Schneider said: "It only needs someone to show a little confidence in us."

Brunet smiled and said: "Do I still look like a surgeon at a post-mortem?"

"No," said Schneider, "not now." They looked at each other with the eyes of friends.

Suddenly Brunet turned away and said: "Look at that old girl!"

A small gray figure was limping along, and, as they stared, the woman came to a halt, dropped her bundle in the mud, shifted into her right hand the bunch of flowers she was carrying in her left, and raised her right arm above her head. There was a moment's pause. It was as though that arm had risen of its own accord, in triumph, dragging at her neck and shoulder. Then she threw the flowers from her, but the movement was awkward and they dropped to the ground at her feet. They lay there scattered, wild flowers of every description, cornflowers, dandelions, poppies; she must have gathered them from the roadside. The men fought for them, scrabbling on the ground, gripping the stalks in muddy fists. Laughing, they got to their feet, displaying the flowers as though they were taking part in an act of homage.

Brunet felt a lump in his throat. He turned to Schneider and said angrily: "Flowers! What would it have been like if we'd won the war!"

There was no trace of a smile on the woman's face. She took up her bundle and moved on, only her back was visible as she waddled along in a raincoat.

Brunet opened his mouth to say something, but he saw Schneider's face and thought better of it. Schneider elbowed his way out of the crowd. He looked thoroughly upset. Brunet followed and touched him on the shoulder. "Anything wrong?"

Schneider raised his head and Brunet looked away. The thought of what his own face must look like, what the face of a surgeon at a post-mortem must look like, embarrassed him. "Anything wrong?" he said again, and stared down at his feet. They were standing alone in the middle of the yard, in the rain.

Schneider said: "It's just that I'm a God-damned fool." There was a short silence, then he went on: "Seeing those civilians again, that's the trouble."

Brunet, still looking down, said: "I'm quite so much of a God-damned fool as you are."

"It's different in your case," said Schneider, "you've nobody belonging to you." He paused a moment, then, unbuttoning his blouse and fumbling in the inside pocket, he brought out a wallet that looked curiously flat. Brunet thought: "He's destroyed everything." Schneider opened the wallet; there was nothing in it but one photograph, about the size of a postcard. Schneider held it out to Brunet without looking at it. Brunet saw the face of a young woman with brooding eyes. Beneath the eyes there was a smile. He had never seen anything quite like it. This girl looked as though she knew all about concentration camps, wars, and prisoners herded into barracks; yet, though she knew all about those things, nevertheless she could still smile. It was to the conquered, the deported, the waste products of history that she offered the gift of her smile. In vain Brunet tried to discover in her eyes the base sadistic light of charity. Her smile told of confidence; it was a calm smile, a tribute to the strength in others. It was as though she were asking them to show mercy to their conquerors. Brunet had seen many photographs of late and many smiles, but they, too, had suffered the devastation of war so that he had found it impossible to look at them. But at this one he could look. It was a newborn smile and it seemed to be addressed to him, to him alone, to Brunet the prisoner, to Brunet the waste product, to Brunet the victorious.

Schneider was leaning over his shoulder. "It's getting dog-eared," he said.

"Yes," said Brunet, "you ought to trim the edges." He handed back the photograph, glittering with raindrops. Schneider wiped it carefully with his sleeve and returned it to his wallet. To himself Brunet said: "Is she pretty?" He did not know; he had not had time to notice. He raised his head and looked at Schneider; he thought: "Her smile is for him." It was as though he saw him now with other eyes.

Two men passed, both young, both of them chasseurs. They had put poppies in their buttonholes. They were silent and their lowered eyes gave them an odd look as though they had just taken Communion. Schneider gazed after them. Brunet hesitated. An almost forgotten word rose to his lips. "I find them touching," he said.

"Seriously?" Schneider asked.

Behind them the hedge of curious faces had disintegrated; the visitors had gone into the barracks. Dewrouckère loped up, followed by Perrin and the printer. "Of course," thought Brunet, "it's three o'clock." There was a secretive look on the three faces. It occurred to Brunet, with irritation, that they had been talking among themselves; that was one of the things that were bound to happen. From some distance away he called out: "Hullo, boys!" They came up to him, stopped, and exchanged nervous glances. "Come on, out with it," said Brunet bluntly, "what's the trouble?"

The printer fixed him with his fine, uneasy eyes; he

looked sullen. He said: "We've done what you told us, haven't we?"

"Yes," Brunet answered impatiently, "yes, yes. What about it?"

The printer could say no more; it was Dewrouckère who spoke for him, keeping his eyes down. "We'd like to go on and we will go on for as long as you want us to, but it's a waste of time."

Brunet remained silent. Perrin said: "The boys won't listen." Still Brunet said nothing.

The printer went on in a colorless voice: "Only yesterday I got into a scrap with a fellow because I said the Heinies were going to deport us to Germany. He was plain crazy. He said I was a member of the Fifth Column." All three looked up and stared at Brunet stolidly. "Things have reached such a point that you can't say a word against the Germans."

Dewrouckère took his courage in both hands and looked Brunet full in the face. "See here, Brunet," he said, "it's not that we're refusing to do the job, and if we've started off on the wrong foot we'll try again. But you've got to understand the position. We move about all over this camp. Hardly a day passes but we talk to a couple of hundred, we know what the feeling in this place is like. You, naturally, know less about it, you can't realize what it's like."

"Well?"

"With the guys feeling as they do, if twenty thousand prisoners here were liberated tomorrow, it'd mean twenty thousand additional Nazis."

Brunet felt his face going red. He looked at each of them in turn. "Is that your honest opinion?" he asked.

"Yes," said all three.

"You're all agreed on that?"

They all said "Yes" again, at which he suddenly burst

out: "There are workers and peasants in this lot; you ought to be ashamed even to think they'd become Nazis. If they do, it'll be your fault. A man's not a block of wood, he's a living, breathing, thinking human being. If you have failed to win these guys over, it's because you don't know your job." He turned his back on them, took three paces and then swung round, his finger pointing. "The truth is you think yourselves superior. You despise your comrades. Just you remember this: a member of the party despises nobody." He saw the bewilderment in their eyes, and the sight made him still angrier. "Twenty thousand Nazis! You're crazy as hell. You'll do nothing with them if you despise them. Try, for a beginning, to understand them. These boys have got the iron in their soul; they don't know which way to turn; they'll follow the first man who shows confidence in them." Schneider's presence rasped his nerves. "Oh, come on!" he said to him. Just as he was moving away, he turned to the others, who were standing silent and discomfited. "I consider that you have failed. It's already forgotten. But don't let me have any more of your nonsense. Report again tomorrow."

He ran up the stairs, Schneider panting behind him. He went into the cage, flung himself down on his blanket, stretched out his hand, and picked up a book, Henri Lavedan's *Leurs Sœurs.* He read with concentrated attention, line by line, word by word, until he calmed down. When the light began to fail, he laid the book aside and remembered that he had eaten nothing. "Did you keep my bread for me?" Moulu held it out. Brunet cut off the piece he would give next day to the printer, stowed it in his knapsack, and began to eat.

Cantrelle and Livard appeared in the doorway. It was that time when visits were paid. "Hullo!" said the inmates without looking up.

"Anything nice to tell us?" asked Moulu.

"They say some guys have a hell of a nerve," Livard said. "And who pays for that? Us, as usual."

"What's the news?" asked Moulu.

"One of the noncoms made a get-away."

"Made a get-away? Why?" asked Goldilocks, surprised into plain-speaking. The men took a little time to digest the information; they looked vaguely startled, slightly horrified, as they might have done before the war if, in the bored crowd filling the subway, a madman had unexpectedly started raising hell.

"Made a get-away," Gassou repeated slowly.

The man from the north laid down the stick he was carving. He seemed worried. Lambert munched in silence, his eyes fixed in a hard stare. After a moment he said with an unpleasant laugh: "There's always some who're in a bigger hurry than the rest."

"Perhaps he likes walking," said Moulu.

With the point of his knife Brunet dug out the moldy fragments of bread and let them fall on his blanket; he felt uncomfortable. The murky outer air had drifted into the room; out there, in the dead town, a hunted man was in hiding. Here are we, eating, and tonight we'll have a roof over our heads. Rather reluctantly he asked: "How did he manage it?"

Livard looked at him with a consequential air. "Guess."

"How should I know? Over the back wall?"

Livard shook his head with a grin, he took his time; then, triumphantly: "By the front gate," he said, "at four o'clock this afternoon, under the Heinies' noses!"

The others seemed struck all of a heap by this news. For a moment Livard and Cantrelle reveled in the general amazement; then Cantrelle explained in precise, rapid words: "His old woman came to see him with a suit of civvies in her bag. He changed in a closet and then just walked out with his arm in hers!"

"Didn't anyone stop him?" Gassou asked indignantly.

Livard shrugged his shoulders. "Stop him? Why should anyone do that?"

"If I'd seen him going out," Gassou said, "I'd have called a Heinie and had him locked up!"

Brunet looked at him in amazement. "Have you gone stark mad?"

"Mad?" said Gassou with a spurt of ill-temper. "What's this poor country of ours coming to? A guy tries to do his duty and the only thanks he gets is to be called mad!" He glanced around the circle to see whether the men were with him, and then went on with even greater vehemence: "You'll soon see whether I'm mad when they put a stop to visiting. After all, they let them in of their own free will; they didn't have to. Don't you agree, boys?" Moulu and Lambert nodded, and Gassou added severely: "For once the Heinies behave decently and what happens? We do them dirt. They'll be wild when they find out what's happened, and who's to blame 'em?"

Brunet opened his mouth to say just what he thought of this argument, but Schneider, with a quick glance at him, cried: "Gassou, what a disgusting piece of work you are!"

Brunet held his tongue, but his thoughts were bitter. "He put in that bit of abuse to prevent me from passing *judgment* on him. He doesn't judge Gassou, he never judges anybody. He's ashamed for all of them because I'm here; whatever happens, whatever they do, he'll always be with them against me."

Gassou glared at Schneider, Schneider glared back, and Gassou looked away. "All right," he said, "all right, just you wait till they put a stop to visits and then see whether I'm nuts or not. I don't give a damn, my folks are at Orange."

"I'm an orphan, if it comes to that," Moulu remarked, "but, after all, a guy should think of his pals."

"You're a fine one to talk, Moulu, I must say," Brunet

said, "you who wash yourself so carefully every day just so your pals won't get lousy."

"That's different," said Goldilocks sharply. "We all know Moulu is filthy, but it's only the guys in this room who suffer. We're talking about a bastard who don't care whether he screws up twenty thousand provided he can do as he likes."

"If the Heinies get him and throw him in the hoose-gow," said Lambert, "*I* won't do any crying."

"Only six weeks before we're all demobilized," said Moulu, "and off our fine gentleman goes! He couldn't do like the rest of us, could he, and just wait?"

For once the sergeant was in agreement. "Typical of the French character," he said with a sigh, "that's why we lost the war."

Brunet gave a nasty laugh. "All the same," he said, "you'd be damned pleased to be in his shoes. The trouble with you is you're ashamed you didn't make a bolt for it yourselves."

"That's where you're wrong," Cantrelle said sharply; "if he'd taken a risk, any sort of a risk, say if he'd risked a bullet in the backside, you would have said: 'He's a bas-tard and a hothead, but at least he's got guts.' Instead of that he slips away on the q.t., hiding behind his wife like a God-damned coward. I don't call that an escape; I call it an abuse of confidence."

Brunet felt as though cold water was running down his spine. He sat up and looked each of them in turn straight in the eyes. "All right, if that's how you feel, I give you fair warning: tomorrow evening I'm going to hop over the wall and make a bolt for it. We'll see whether anyone gives me away."

There was general embarrassment, but Gassou wasn't going to let himself be put out of countenance. "No one will give you away," he said, "you know that perfectly well, but when I get out of here, I'll damned well give you something to remember me by; because if you escape, you can be sure that we're the ones that'll have to pay for it."

"Something to remember you by?" said Brunet with an insulting laugh. "I'd like to see you try!"

"Well, if necessary, we'll get up a gang to do the job."

"Time to talk about that ten years from now, when you get back from Germany."

Gassou was about to say something, but Livard got in first. "No point arguing with him. They're letting us out on the 14th, that's official."

"Oh, that's official, is it?" asked Brunet, still laughing. "I suppose you've seen it in writing!"

Livard pretended not to answer him. Instead he turned to the others and said: "Not in writing, I haven't, but it's as good as official." Faces lit up in the darkness like radio dials, with a dark, muffled glow. Livard looked at them with a good-natured smile and proceeded to expatiate: "Hitler said so."

"Hitler!" repeated Brunet, dumbfounded.

Livard ignored the interruption and went on: "Not that the bastard's a friend of mine; he's our enemy all right, and as for Nazism, well, I'm neither for it nor against it. It may work with the Heinies, but it don't suit the French temperament. All the same, I will say this for Hitler, he sticks to his word. He said he'd be in Paris on June 15, and on June 15 there he was, even ahead of schedule."

"And he's said something about letting us go?" Lambert inquired.

"Well, didn't he say: 'On June 15 I shall be in Paris and on the 14th of July you'll be dancing with your wives'?"

A timid voice piped up; it belonged to the man from the north. "I thought what he said was *we* will be dancing with your wives, we, the Heinies."

Livard gave him a withering look. "Were you there?"

"No," said the man from the north, "but that's what they told me."

Livard broke into contemptuous mirth.

"If it comes to that," Brunet asked him, "were *you* there?"

"Of course I was there! It was at Haguenau; we were holding an advance post. I'd been out, and when I got back he'd just finished speaking." He nodded his head and repeated with self-satisfaction: "On June 15 we shall be in Paris and on July 14 you'll be dancing with your wives."

"Ha!" the others, now in a cheerful mood, cried gaily, quoting his words: "June 15 Paris, and on the 14th of July we'll be dancing." Women, dancing! Hunching their shoulders, throwing back their heads, grasping their ground-sheets like partners, they began to dance. The floor creaked as they waltzed and twirled under the stars between the clifflike buildings of the carrefour Châteaudun.

Gassou, in softened mood, leaned across to Brunet and embarked on a logical explanation. "Hitler's not crazy, you know. Why should he want to plump down a million prisoners in Germany? A million more mouths to feed?"

"To make 'em work," said Brunet.

"Work? Alongside the German workers? What'd the Heinies' morale be like after they'd talked with us a little?"

"In what language?"

"Any language, pidgin German, Esperanto, anything you like. The French workman is born cunning; he's a natural grumbler and stubborn as you make 'em; in less than no time he'd have knocked the stuffing out of the Heinies; you can be sure that old Hitler knows all about that. You can bet your life he's pretty shrewd! I agree with Livard: I don't like him, but I respect him, and that's more'n I'd say about a lot of people."

The others nodded their heads solemnly in agreement. "He loves his country, it's only fair to grant him that."

"He's a man with an ideal. It's not the same as ours, but it's worthy of respect, just the same."

"All opinions are worthy of respect provided they're sincere."

"Does that go for ours too? What about our deputies, what sort of ideals have they got, beyond filling their pockets, keeping themselves well supplied with dames, and having a good time generally—on our money? Things are different in Germany: you pay your taxes, but at least you know where the money goes. Each year you get a letter from the collector: 'Dear Sir, you have paid so much. It represents this or that amount of medical supplies for the sick or so many miles of motor roads.' I know what I'm talking about."

"He never wanted to make war on us," said Moulu; "it was us who declared war on him."

"Wait a minute: it wasn't even us; it was Daladier, and he did it without even consulting the Chamber."

"Just what I said. Well, Hitler couldn't take that lying down, could he? 'You've asked for me,' he said, 'and here I am.' And in less than two years he'd got us where he wanted us. So what's he going to do now? D'you think it's any fun for him to have a million prisoners on his hands? You wait and see. In a few days he'll say: 'You're a damned nuisance, boys,' he'll say, 'just get the hell home and stay there.' Then he'll turn round on the Commies and they'll hammer each other flat. Why should France bother? He'll take back Alsace—that's a matter of prestige—and good riddance! I never could stand the Alsatians!" Livard went off into a fit of silent laughter as though at some private joke; he looked thoroughly self-satisfied. "If only we'd had a Hitler!" he said.

"Hitler with the French Army behind him," said Gassou, "Why, there'd have been no holding him. He'd have been in Constantinople by this time, because," he went on with a broad wink, "the French soldier's the best in the world when he's properly led."

How ashamed Schneider must be feeling, Brunet thought, not daring to look at him. He got up and turned his back on the best soldiers in the world; no point in staying there, he thought as he went out. On the landing he paused and looked at the staircase spiraling downwards into the darkness. At this time of night the door would certainly be locked. For the first time he felt himself a prisoner. Sooner or later he would have to return to his jail, lie down on the floor next to the others, and listen to them dreaming. Below him the whole barrack building was alive with sound; a noise of shouting and singing filled the well of the staircase. The floor creaked. He swung round: Schneider was walking toward him down the twilit corridor, crossing, one by one, the last beams of daylight filtering through the windows. "I'll say: 'Don't tell me you've got the nerve to stand up for 'em now!'" Schneider was close to him. Brunet looked at him, but said nothing. He leaned his hands on the banister rail, and Schneider leaned beside him.

Brunet said: "Dewrouckère was right." Schneider made no reply: what was there for him to say? A smile, a few red flowers in the rain, that's all they need to give them a little confidence, and a little's all they need. Confidence! In a fury he broke out: "There's nothing to be done with them! Nothing! Nothing! Nothing!" Confidence was not enough! Confidence in whom? Confidence in what? What they needed was suffering, fear, and hatred; what they needed was the spirit of revolt, massacre, an iron discipline. When they'd got nothing more to lose, when life would seem even worse than death. . . . They both leaned there together above the blackness, which smelled of dust.

Schneider lowered his voice. "Are you really planning

to escape?" he asked. Brunet looked at him without answering. Schneider said: "I shall miss you."

Brunet said bitterly: "You'll be the only one who will."

On the ground floor some men were striking up a chorus: *"Drink up! drink up! let's drain a cup. Here's to wine and women!"* Escape? To pull a fast one on twenty thousand men and leave them to stew in their own filthy dung? Has anyone ever the right to say there's nothing more to be done? Suppose they are waiting for me in Paris? The thought of Paris filled him with a sense of disgust so violent that he was amazed. He said: "No, I'm not going to escape; I only said that because I'd lost my temper."

"But if you really believe there's nothing more to be done—"

"There's always something to be done. You have to do the work that lies to hand with whatever tools you can find. We must wait and see." Schneider heaved a sigh. Brunet said sharply: "It's you who ought to escape." Schneider shook his head. Brunet said shyly: "You've got a wife waiting for you." Again Schneider shook his head. "Why don't you?" Brunet asked. "There's nothing to keep you here."

Schneider said, "It would be worse everywhere else."

"Drink up! drink up! let's drain a cup. Here's to wine and women!"

Brunet said: "And now for Germany!"

For the first time, and rather shamefacedly, Schneider echoed him: "And now for Germany, that's the next step!" And, as in the popular ballad, to hell with the King of England, who has declared war on us!

Twenty-seven men; the freight car creaked; the canal slid by. Moulu said: "Things don't look so smashed around as you might have expected." The Germans had left the sliding doors open and daylight filtered into the car with

a swarm of flies. Schneider, Brunet, and the printer were
seated on the floor in the opening of the door, dangling
their legs outside. It was a fine summer day. "No," said
Moulu with satisfaction, "it isn't too bad."

Brunet looked up. Moulu was standing, obviously
pleased by the spectacle of the fields and meadows slipping by. It was warm; the men gave off a strong smell;
someone at the far end of the freight car was snoring.
Brunet leaned out. He caught the glitter of German helmets in the caboose above rifle barrels. A fine summer day
in a peaceful world. The train rumbled on; the canal
glided by. Here and there a bomb had torn a hole in a
road or scarred a field; at the bottom of the craters water
reflected the sky.

The printer said, as though speaking to himself: "Easy
enough to make a jump for it."

Schneider jerked his shoulder in the direction of the
rifles. "They'd knock you over like a rabbit." The printer
said nothing. He leaned out as though about to take a
dive. Brunet held him back by the shoulder. "It'd be easy
enough," said the printer again like a man in a trance.

Moulu patted him on the back of the neck. "What's the
point, aren't we off to Châlons?"

"But are we? Is that really where we're going?"

"You read the notice, same as I did."

"But it didn't say anything about Châlons."

"No, but it did say we were staying in France. Didn't
it, Brunet?"

For a moment Brunet said nothing. *It was true* that the
evening before a notice stuck on the wall and signed by
the commanding officer read: "The prisoners in the camp
at Baccarat will remain in France." But that didn't alter
the fact that here they all were in a train, borne off to
some unknown destination.

Moulu pressed his question: "Is it true or isn't it?"

From behind them came impatient voices: "Of course

it's true! Why are you trying to scare the hell out of us? You know damn well it's true."

Brunet glanced at the printer and said quietly: "Yes, it's true."

The printer sighed. He was smiling now and looked reassured. "It's funny, traveling always gets me like this." He laughed gaily; still turned toward Brunet, he said: "I've only been in a train about twenty times in my life, and it always gets me like this." He laughed, and Brunet thought: "He's in bad shape."

Lucien was seated slightly behind them, his hands clasped round his ankles. He said: "My people were to have come on Sunday." He was young and gentle-looking and wore spectacles.

"Wouldn't you rather find them waiting for you at home?" Moulu asked.

"Well, yes," said the boy, "but as they were coming Sunday, I'd rather we hadn't started till Monday."

Protests rose from all sides. "Here's a dope who would have liked to stay there another three days! Some guys don't know when they're well off! If we'd waited any longer, we might as well have stayed there till Christmas."

Lucien smiled sweetly. "You see," he explained, "they're not young any more, and I don't like to see them put to all that trouble for nothing."

"Bah!" said Moulu, "when they get home, it'll be you who let's them in at the front door."

"That's what I'd like," said Lucien, "but no such luck! It'll take 'em at least a week to demobilize us."

"Who knows?" said Moulu, "who knows. Heinie's a quick worker."

"All I'm bothering about," said Jurassien, "is being home in time for the lavender-picking."

Brunet turned his head. The car was full of white dust and white smoke. Some of the men were standing, others sitting. Across the bent trunks of this forest of legs he could see placid faces, each vaguely smiling. Jurassien was a great lout of a fellow who looked tough, had had his head completely shaved, and wore a black bandage across one eye. He was squatting tailor-fashion in order to take up less space.

"Where're you from?" asked Brunet.

"Manosque; I was in the merchant marine. Now I live ashore with my wife, and I don't like the idea of her having to do all the cutting without me."

The printer was still staring at the rails. "It was high time," he said.

"What's the trouble, my boy?" asked Brunet.

"High time they let us go, high time."

"Why so?"

"It was getting me down," said the printer. Brunet thought: him too! But seeing the feverish eyes in their dark sockets, he said nothing. "He'll find out soon enough," he thought.

Schneider said: "That's right, it was no laughing matter. How're you feeling now?"

"Oh," said the printer, "I'm fine now." There was something he wanted to explain, but he could find no words for it. He made a gesture as though to excuse his silence and merely said: "I'm from Lyon."

Brunet felt embarrassed. He thought: "I'd forgotten he was from Lyon. I've been making him work for the last two months and I don't really know a thing about him. Now he has a grudge against me, and he's homesick."

The printer had turned his head and Brunet could see behind his eyes a sort of anguished gentleness. "Is it certain we're going to Châlons?" the printer asked suddenly.

"Still on that song?" said Moulu impatiently.

"What's it matter?" Brunet asked. "Even if it's not Châlons, we'll get home sooner or later."

"It must be Châlons!" said the printer. "It must be Châlons!" The words sounded almost like a prayer. "If it hadn't been for you, you know," he said to Brunet, "I would have taken a chance ages ago."

"If it hadn't been for me?"

"Yes. As soon as I felt there was somebody ready to take responsibility, I had to stay."

Brunet said nothing. He thought: "It was I who made all that difference." But the knowledge gave him no pleasure.

The printer went on: "I would have been back in Lyon by this time. I've been in the army since October '37 and that means I've forgotten my trade."

"It'll come back pretty quick," said Lucien.

The printer shook his head with a look of wisdom. "Not so quick as all that," he said. "It'll be hard starting in again, as you'll soon find out." He sat motionless, his eyes staring at nothing. Then he said: "When I was at home evenings with my old parents, I used to give everything a good polishing; I hated doing nothing, and I wanted the whole place to look spick and span."

Brunet glanced at him out of the corner of his eye. He has lost his neat, sprightly appearance; his words came lolloping out of his mouth; there were scattered tufts of black hair on his thin cheeks. A tunnel swallowed the cars ahead of them. Brunet looked at the black hole into which the train was plunging. He turned sharply to the printer. "If you really want to take a chance, now's the moment."

"What?" said the printer.

"You've only got to make a jump for it as soon as we're inside the tunnel."

The printer stared at him, then all went black. Brunet got smoke in his mouth and eyes; he coughed. The train slowed down. "Jump!" said Brunet, coughing. "Go on, jump!" There was no reply. Daylight began to show gray through the smoke. Brunet wiped his eyes. Suddenly the car was filled with sunlight; the printer was still where he had been. "Well?" Brunet asked.

The printer blinked his eyes and said: "What's the point, if we're really on our way to Châlons?"

Brunet shrugged and looked at the canal. There was a tavern standing on the bank, with a man drinking; they could see his cap, his glass, and his long nose over the top of the hedge. Two other men were walking along the towpath. They wore straw hats and were talking quietly together; they did not even turn their heads to look at the train.

"Hey!" shouted Moulu. "Hey, pals!" But already they were out of sight. Another café, brand-new, came into sight: *A la Bonne Peche*, "Headquarters for Fishermen." The metallic neighing of a mechanical piano struck Brunet's ears, then died away: by now the Heinies in the caboose must be hearing it. Brunet saw a château that was not yet within their range of vision, a château in a park, white, and flanked by two pointed towers. A small girl in the park, holding a hoop, stared at them with solemn eyes; it was as though all France, an innocent and outmoded France, through those young eyes was watching them pass. Brunet looked at the little girl and thought of Pétain; the train swept across her gaze, across her own future of quiet games and healthy thoughts and trivial worries, on toward fields of potatoes and factories and armament works, on to the dark, real future of a world of men. The prisoners behind Brunet waved their hands; in all the cars Brunet saw hands waving handkerchiefs; but the child made no response, she only stood there clasping her hoop.

"They might at least say hello," said André. "They were glad enough to see us in September when we were off to get our faces bashed in to defend 'em."

"Yes," said Lambert, "but the trouble is there wasn't any bashing."

"Well, is that our fault? French prisoners deserve a salute."

An old man seated on a camp stool was fishing; he never so much as looked up. Jurassien laughed. "They've just sunk back into their old, easygoing ways."

"Looks like it," said Brunet.

The train rolled on through a land at peace: fishermen, taverns, straw hats, and the quiet summer sky. Brunet glanced over his shoulder; the faces he saw were discontented but fascinated.

"Between ourselves," said Martial, "I don't blame the old boy. Within a week *I'll* be going fishing."

"What sort of fishing? Just hook and line?"

"Not on your life! Fly fishing."

Their liberation had become something they could almost touch, a picture with, for background, this familiar countryside, these calm waters. Peace, work, the old man coming home at night with his bag of carp—within a week they would be free: the proof of it was there before them, gentle and insinuating. Brunet felt ill at ease: it is a bad thing to be the only one in a crowd who has a true vision of the future. He turned his head away and watched another set of rails branching off from the track they were on. He thought: "What can I say? They won't believe me." By rights he ought to be rejoicing; at long last they were about to have understanding forced upon them; at long last he would be able to get to work. But against his shoulder and along his arm he could feel the feverish heat of the printer's body, and his heart was heavy with something very like remorse. The train began to slow down.

"What gives?"

"Switches," Moulu replied with complacent knowingness. "Not much of this line I'm not familiar with. I used to go on it regular ten years ago, every week. We'll turn off left here, you see if we don't. That right-hand track goes to Lunéville and Strasbourg."

"Lunéville?" asked Goldilocks. "But I thought we had to go through Lunéville?"

"No, no, I tell you I know this line. Probably the track is up over Lunéville way, and we've gone round by Saint-Dié to avoid it; now we're working back."

"Is Germany over there to the right?" Ramelle asked in an anxious voice.

"Yes, we'll swing to the left. To the left is Nancy, Bar-le-Duc, Châlons."

The train came to a halt. Brunet turned and looked at them. Their faces were calm and peaceful, a few were smiling. Only Ramelle, the piano teacher, kept biting his lower lip and fingering his spectacles in a worried and unhappy manner. All the same, no one spoke.

Suddenly Moulu shouted: "Hey, babes, blow us a kiss!"

Brunet swung round sharply. There were six girls in light summer dresses; they had fat red arms and healthy complexions. Six pairs of eyes watched from behind the gate of a grade crossing. Moulu was busy throwing kisses. None of the girls smiled. One of them, large, dark, and far from plain, began to sigh; her sighs distended her ample bosom. The other five stared out from wide and mournful eyes; six mouths in six rustic and inexpressive faces puckered up like those of children on the verge of tears.

"Come on!" said Moulu. "Give us some sign of life, girls!" Then, moved by sudden inspiration, he added: "Spare a kiss for a lot of poor devils on their way to Germany?"

Protesting voices rose behind him: "Hey there! Don't say things like that, it's unlucky!"

Moulu turned, completely at his ease. "To hell with it! I only said that to get a smile out of 'em!"

The men now were laughing, and shouting: "Come on, girls, come on!"

The dark-haired one was still staring hard with frightened eyes. Hesitatingly she raised one hand, put it to her flacid lips, and threw it forward with the movement of a mechanical doll.

"Better than that!" said Moulu. "That's not good enough for us, you know!"

A furious voice shouted at him in German, and he hurriedly withdrew his head.

"You God-damned fool!" said Jurassien, "they'll be shutting the door on us if you're not careful!"

Moulu made no reply; he was grumbling away to himself: "God, what dumb bitches they raise in this dump!"

There was a sound of creaking; the train began to move forward slowly; the men stopped talking; Moulu, his mouth hanging half open, stood waiting. They were gathering speed. Brunet thought: "Now's the moment." There was a noise of banging and a sudden shock. Moulu lost his balance and caught at Schneider's shoulder.

He gave a cry of triumph: "What did I tell you, boys! We're off to Nancy!" Everyone started laughing and shouting. Ramelle could be heard saying nervously: "Then it's sure we're going to Nancy?"

"Look for yourself," Moulu said, pointing to the track. Sure enough, the train had diverged to the left. It was strung out now in the arc of a circle; without leaning forward it was possible to see the small locomotive.

"Is this the direct route?"

Brunet turned his head. Ramelle's face was ashen, his bloodless lips were still trembling.

"Direct route?" Moulu asked with a laugh. "Do you think they're going to make us change trains?"

"All I meant was, are there any other switches?"

"There are two others," Moulu replied. "There's one just before we get to Frouard, another at Pagny-sur-Meuse. But we needn't worry; we've turned left, and left we ride to Bar-le-Duc and Châlons."

"When can we be sure of that?"

"What more do you want? We *are* sure."

"But what about the switches?"

"Oh," said Moulu, "if that's what's bothering you, the second. If we went to the right there, it'd mean Metz and Luxembourg. The third don't count; to the right would take us to Verdun and Sedan, and why in the world would they be sending us there?"

"So it's the second," said Ramelle, "the one that's coming next. . . ." He relapsed into silence, and lay curled up with his knees drawn to his chin, looking lost and cold.

"Oh, give it a rest!" said André. "You'll see soon enough."

Ramelle did not answer. Silence lay heavy on the car; the men's faces were without expression, but rather tense. Brunet heard to his left the sound of a harmonica.

André gave a start, "Hey! Cut it out, we don't want no music!"

"I've got a perfect right to play the harmonica," said a voice from the shadows.

"No music!" said André. The man stopped his playing. The train had gradually been gaining speed; it ran across a bridge.

"That's the last of the canal," remarked the printer with a sigh.

Schneider was sleeping where he sat, his head jerking to the movement of the train. Brunet felt bored; he looked out at the fields, thinking of nothing. A moment later the train began to slow down and Ramelle straightened up, his face haggard.

"What's happening?"

"Don't get scared, it's only Nancy," Moulu told him.

The sides of a railroad cut rose above the level of their heads, topped by a street wall with a cornice of white stone, and atop the cornice there was an iron paling.

"Must be a road up there," said Moulu. Brunet felt suddenly as though he were crushed under an enormous weight. The men all around him leaned out, supporting themselves on his shoulder; they were staring upwards. Great puffs of smoke drifted into the car. Brunet started to cough.

"Look at that guy up there," said Martial.

Brunet tilted his head back; it struck something hard; hands were pushing him. A man stood leaning against the paling. Through the iron latticework, they could see his black jacket and striped trousers. He was carrying a leather briefcase, and seemed to be about forty.

"Hello!" called Martial.

"Good morning," said the man. His face was thin and hard. He had a neat mustache and very light blue eyes.

"Hello! Hello!" cried the prisoners.

"How are things going in Nancy?" asked Moulu. "Has the town been blitzed?"

"No," said the man.

"Good," said Moulu, "good." The man said nothing; he was staring hard at them with an air of curiosity.

"Business starting up again?" asked Jurassien. The engine whistled; the man curved his hand round his ear and called: "What's that?"

Jurassien gestured over Brunet's head, in an attempt to convey the fact that he couldn't shout any louder.

Lucien said: "Ask him about the prisoners from Nancy."

"What about them?"

"Ask him if he knows what's happened to them."

"Pipe down," said Moulu, "a guy can't hear himself speak."

"Hurry up and ask him, we'll be off again in a minute."

The whistling had stopped. Moulu shouted: "Business as usual?"

"Plenty doing with all these Germans in the place!"

"Movies open again?" Martial asked.

"What's that?" the civilian shouted.

"Hell!" said Lucien, "I'm sick of movies! For God's sake,

let's give 'em a rest! Here, let me do the talking." Without pausing for breath, he added: "How about the prisoners?".

"What prisoners?" asked the civilian.

"Weren't there any prisoners from here?"

"Yes, but they're not here any more."

"Where have they gone?" Moulu shouted.

The civilian looked at them with an air of mild astonishment. "Germany, of course!"

"Stop pushing!" said Brunet. He braced himself with his two hands against the wall of the car. The men were crowding on top of him, they were all speaking at once.

"Germany? Are you crazy? You mean Châlons! Germany! Who says they've gone to Germany?" The civilian made no reply; he fixed them with his untroubled gaze.

"Shut up, boys!" Jurassien ordered. "Don't all talk at once." There was silence and Jurassien shouted: "How d'you know?"

The sound of a voice raised in anger reached them; one of the German guards, with fixed bayonet, jumped from the caboose and ran up along the train. He was very young, his face scarlet from anger. He began to yell in very rapid German; his voice was hoarse. Brunet felt himself suddenly freed from the enormous weight that had been pressing on him; the men must have sat down suddenly. The guard stopped talking; he stood in front of them, his rifle resting on the ground. The civilian was still there, leaning over the paling and looking down at them. Brunet could feel behind him all the fevered faces raised in a mute questioning.

"A hell of a God-damned note!" Lucien muttered at his back. "A hell of a note!"

The man up on the road was motionless and dumb, useless from their point of view, yet filled with some secret knowledge. The engine whistled, a great eddy of smoke poured into the car, the train gave a shudder and began to move. Brunet coughed; the guard waited until the caboose came alongside and threw his rifle into it. Brunet could see two pairs of hands, projecting from greenish sleeves, catch him by the shoulders and hoist him up.

"What does that bastard know about it, anyhow?"

"Yes, what does he know? They went off somewhere and he saw 'em go, that's all there is to it." There was an outburst of angry voices at Brunet's back; he smiled, but said nothing.

"He was only guessing, that's all," said Ramelle; "he *guessed* they were going to Germany."

The train began to move faster, past long, empty platforms. Brunet saw a sign with the words: "Exit. Subway." The train drove onwards. The station was dead. Brunet could feel the printer's shoulder trembling against his own.

The printer gave vent to a fit of temper. "Dirty swine, to say a thing like that if he didn't know for sure!"

"That's right," said Martial, "the bastard!"

"Nothing to worry about," said Moulu. "The guy is probably nuts."

"Nuts?" said Jurassien, "Did you take a look at him? Nothing nuts about that pissant, he knew what he was doing all right!" Brunet turned his head. Jurassien showed a nasty smile. "One of the Fifth Column," he commented.

"Say, guys, suppose he was right?" asked Lambert.

"For God's sake, if you want to go join the Boches, get going, but don't frighten the shit out of us!"

"Well, anyhow," said Moulu, "we'll know when we get to the next set of switches."

"When'll that be?" Ramelle asked. His face looked green: he was drumming with his fingers on his overcoat.

"Quarter of an hour, maybe twenty minutes."

The others sat waiting. Since catastrophe had overtaken them Brunet had never seen their faces so tense, their eyes so fixed. Silence fell, heavy and complete; there was no sound save the creaking of the train. It was hot. Brunet would have liked to take off his blouse, but he was wedged between the printer and the wall of the car. Sweat was trickling down his neck.

The printer, without looking at him, said: "Say, Brunet."

"What?"

"Were you joking just now when you told me to jump?"

"Why?" asked Brunet.

The printer turned up his face; wrinkles, dirt, and stubble could not age its air of childlike charm. He said: "I just couldn't stand being packed off to Germany." Brunet said nothing. "I just couldn't stand it, it'd kill me. I'm sure it would kill me."

Brunet, shrugging, said: "We'll all be in the same boat."

"But we'll all die, it'll kill the lot of us," said the printer.

Brunet freed one hand and laid it on his shoulder. "Get hold of yourself, boy," he said affectionately. The printer was trembling. Brunet went on: "If you start talking like that you'll end by scaring the hell out of everybody."

The printer swallowed; all the fight seemed to have gone out of him. He said: "You're right, Brunet." He made a little movement, expressive of despair and helplessness; Sadly he added: "You're always right." Brunet smiled at him. A moment or two passed, then the printer began again in a dull voice: "Then you were kidding me?"

"What d'you mean?"

"When you told me to jump, you were kidding me?"

"Oh, forget it," said Brunet.

"If I jumped now," said the printer, "would you hold it against me?"

Brunet looked at the glitter of the rifle barrels projecting from the caboose. "Don't be a fool," he said, "you'd only get yourself bumped off."

"Let me take a chance," said the printer, "let me take a chance."

"This is the wrong moment," said Brunet.

"I don't care," the printer argued, "if they take me to Germany, I'll die anyway. One way's as good as another." Brunet remained silent. The printer said: "All I want to know is, would you hold it against me?"

Brunet's eyes were still on the rifle barrels. Slowly, coldly, he said: "Yes, I would. I forbid you to do anything of the sort." The printer hung his head; Brunet could see his jaw moving.

"What a brute you are!" said Schneider. Brunet turned his head; Schneider was looking at him with a hard expression in his eyes. Brunet did not answer him, he pressed against the door; he would have liked to say: "Can't you see that if I don't forbid him to jump, he'll get himself killed?" But he could not do so because the printer would have heard him. He had an uncomfortable feeling that Schneider was passing judgment on him. He thought: "What nonsense!" He looked at the skinny back of the printer's neck; he thought: "Suppose he really did die in Germany? Hell! What's the matter with me?"

The train slowed down, they had reached the switches. All of them knew perfectly well that it was because of the switches they were stopping, but not a word was uttered. The train came to a standstill, there was silence. Brunet raised his eyes. Moulu was leaning across him, looking at the track, his mouth open; his face was livid. The chirp of crickets could be heard coming from the grass that grew on the embankment. Three Germans jumped down onto the siding to stretch their legs. They sauntered past the car, laughing. The train began to move; they made a half turn and ran to get into the caboose.

"It's left all right, boys!" Moulu yelled. "We're going left!"

The car creaked and vibrated; it felt almost as though the rails would be torn from the ties. Once again, Brunet was conscious of ten heavy bodies leaning forward on his shoulders. The men shouted: "We're going left! We're going left! We're off to Châlons!" Laughing faces, blackened by smoke, appeared in the doorways of the other cars. André shouted: "Hey, Chabot! We're off to Châlons!" Chabot, who was leaning out of the fourth car from them, laughed and shouted back: "About time too!" Everyone was laughing. Brunet heard Gassou's voice; "They were just as scared as us." "What did I say, boys?" Jurassien asked. "That guy was a Fifth Columnist all right!"

Brunet looked at the printer. The printer said nothing; he was still trembling and a tear ran down his left cheek, making a furrow in the grime and coal dust. Somebody started to play a harmonica; somebody else struck up a song: "Kaki, my sweet, I'm ever thine." Brunet felt horribly depressed; he watched the track slipping by, he wanted to jump. Theirs was the front car; behind them the whole train was singing. It was like a prewar excursion. He thought: "There's a hell of a shock waiting for them."

The printer heaved a sigh of relief. "Ah-h-h!" he sighed. He eyed Brunet shrewdly. "*You* thought it was going to be Germany." Brunet stiffened slightly; he felt that his prestige had suffered, but he said nothing. The printer, by now in a friendly mood, hastened to add: "Any guy can make a mistake sometimes. As a matter of fact, I thought so, too." Brunet still said nothing. The printer started to whistle. A moment passed, and then he said: "I'll send her word before I show up."

"Who's her?" asked Brunet.

"My girl," said the printer. "If I don't do that, she might throw a faint."

"You got a girl, at your age?" asked Brunet.

"You bet your life!" said the printer. "We would have been married by this time if it hadn't been for the war."

"How old is she?"

"Eighteen."

"Did you meet her through the party?"

"N-no, not exactly," said the printer; "it was at a dance."

"Does she think the same as you?"

"What about?"

"Everything."

"Damned if I know what she thinks," said the printer, "Actually, I don't believe she thinks at all; she's just a kid. But she's a decent kid and a good worker and—steady." He brooded for awhile, then said: "I think it was that got me down. I was feeling bored with her. You got a doll, Brunet?"

"No time for that," said Brunet.

"How d'you manage, then?"

Brunet smiled. "Oh, just a pick-up now and then."

"I couldn't live like that," said the printer. "Don't you ever feel you'd like a place of your own with a wife and all?"

"I wouldn't ever be there."

"Yes, of course, I see that." The printer seemed slightly abashed; as though to excuse himself, he went on: "I don't need much, nor does she. Three chairs and a bed." He was smiling at nothing in particular; he added: "If it hadn't been for this war, we would have been happy."

Brunet felt irritated; he looked at the printer without sympathy. The thinness of the man's face made it easy to read, and Brunet deduced a strong desire for simple happiness. He said quietly: "This war wasn't a matter of chance. You know well enough it's impossible to live under an oppressive system."

"Oh," said the printer, "I'd have dug a little hole for myself somewhere."

Brunet raised his voice and said sharply: "Then why are you a Communist? Communists aren't made to dig holes for themselves."

"Because of the others," said the printer; "there was so much poverty where I lived, I wanted to see that changed."

"When a man joins the party, nothing but the party matters," said Brunet. "You must have known what you were letting yourself in for."

"Oh, I knew all right," said the printer quickly. "Have I ever refused to do anything you asked? Only, don't you see, when I'm with my girl, the party's not looking on. There are moments when—" He looked at Brunet and broke off short. Brunet said nothing; he thought: "He's acting like this because he thinks I've made a mistake. One ought to be infallible."

It was getting hotter and hotter. His shirt was soaked with sweat, the sun was beating straight on his face. It was important to know why all these young men had joined the C.P. When the reason's been based on generous impulses, there always comes a moment when the enthusiasm begins to flag. *And what about you, why did you join?* "Oh, well, all that's so long ago it doesn't matter any more. I'm a Communist because I'm a Communist, that's all there is to it." He freed his right hand, wiped the sweat from his eyebrows, and looked at his watch. Half past four. What with all these detours, we're nowhere near getting there. Tonight the Heinies will bolt the doors and we'll sleep on a siding. He yawned and said: "Schneider, you're not doing much talking."

"What d'you want me to talk about?" Schneider asked.

Brunet yawned again; he looked at the track streaming by. A white face was grinning up at him from between the rails—ha, ha, ha!—his head was falling. He awoke with a start; his eyes were hurting him. He pushed his way backwards in order to avoid the sun: someone had said: "Sentenced to death." His head fell; he awoke again and raised his hand to his face, his chin was wet. "I've been dribbling, I must have gone to sleep with my mouth open." It was something he had a horror of doing.

"Want to piss?" A hand pushed an empty can at him; it felt warm.

"What's that for?" he said. "Oh, thanks." He emptied it

out of the door; the yellow liquid rained down on the track.

"Hey! Pass it up, quick!" He handed it back without turning his head; it was taken from him. He wanted to go to sleep again, someone tapped him on the shoulder, he took the can and emptied it.

"Let me have it," said the printer. Brunet held out the can to him and he struggled, with difficulty, to his feet. Brunet dried his damp fingers on his blouse. A moment later an arm was extended above his head and the tin can was again tilted. The yellow water fell, blown into white bubbles in their wake. The printer resumed his seat, wiping his fingers. Brunet let his head droop on the printer's shoulder; he could hear the music of the harmonica, he could see a lovely garden full of flowers, he fell asleep. He was awakened by a violent jerk.

"What the hell!" he exclaimed. The train had come to a halt in open country. "What's up?"

"Nothing," said Moulu, "you can go to sleep again; it's only Pagny-sur-Meuse."

Brunet turned his head; peace lay over the scene. The men had grown accustomed to their new happiness; some were playing cards, some were singing; still others, silent as though under a spell of magic, seemed to be telling stories to themselves; their eyes were full of memories that now, at last, they could let come to the surface from the depth of their hearts. No one was taking any notice of the fact that the train was standing still. Brunet was fast asleep; he dreamed of an unfamiliar plain where men, naked and thin as skeletons, with gray beards, were seated about a great fire. When he awoke, the sun was low on the horizon, the sky was mauve, two cows were grazing in a meadow, and the train was still motionless. The men were singing. German soldiers were picking flowers on the grassy embankment. One of them, a fattish little man with a great spread of shoulder and pink cheeks, approached the prisoners. He had a daisy between his teeth and was smiling broadly. Moulu, André, and Martial smiled back at him. For a moment the German and the Frenchmen remained looking at one another and smiling; then Moulu said quickly: "*Cigaretten. Bitte schön, Cigaretten.*"

The soldier hesitated and turned toward the embankment; his three companions, bending over, showed only their rumps. He hurriedly felt in his pocket and threw a pack of cigarettes into the car.

Brunet heard behind him a noise of scrambling. Ramelle, who did not smoke, stood up and shouted: "*Danke schön!*" to an accompaniment of smiles. The squat little German made a sign to him to hold his tongue.

Moulu said to Schneider: "Ask him where we're going."

Schneider said something to the soldier in German, the soldier answered with a grin. By this time the others had finished picking flowers and approached the train, holding bunches in their left hands, upside down. The group consisted of a sergeant and two privates; they seemed to be in a hilarious mood and were laughing a good deal as they talked.

"What are they saying?" Moulu asked, smiling likewise.

"Wait a moment," said Schneider impatiently. "Let me see if I can understand."

The soldiers flung a final pleasantry, then started unhurriedly back to the caboose. The sergeant stopped to piss against one of the wheels; he stood with his legs apart, buttoning his fly. He took a quick look at his men, and, while their backs were turned, threw a pack of cigarettes into the car.

"Ha!" said Martial with a chuckle, "they're not such evil bastards!"

"It's because we're being released," said Jurassien, "they want to make a good impression on us."

"Maybe," said Martial, musing. "Actually it's all propaganda."

"What were they saying?" Moulu asked Schneider. Schneider made no answer; there was an odd expression on his face.

"Yes," said André, "what were they saying?"

Schneider swallowed with difficulty; he said: "They're from Hanover. They've been in action in Belgium."

"Where did they say we're going?"

Schneider spread his arms, smiled apologetically, and said: "Trèves."

"Trèves?" Moulu commented. "Where's Trèves when it's at home?"

"It's in the Palatinate," replied Schneider.

There was a scarcely noticeable silence, then Moulu said: "Trèves in Bocheland? Then they must have been kidding the hell out of you." Schneider said no more. Moulu went on with calm assurance: "You don't go to Bocheland by way of Bar-le-Duc." Schneider still remained silent.

André asked nonchalantly: "Were they kidding you or what?"

"Must have been," said Lucien; "they were kidding the pants off you."

Reluctantly Schneider said: "They weren't joking when they told me that."

"Didn't you hear what Moulu said?" Martial asked angrily. "Bar-le-Duc's not on the way to Bocheland. It doesn't make sense."

"We don't go by Bar-le-Duc," Schneider explained; "we branch to the right."

Moulu began to laugh. "Poppycock! I suppose you'll admit I know this route better than any of you? Well, to the right it goes to Verdun and Sedan. If you kept on to the right, you might find yourself in Belgium, but not in Germany!" He turned to the others with the reassuring air of one who knows. "I used to travel this territory every week.

Twice a week sometimes," he added, his face expressing a desperate conviction.

There was a chorus of voices: "He knows! He can't be wrong."

"We go via Luxembourg," said Schneider, speaking with an effort. Brunet had the impression that, now he had started, he meant to drive the truth into their heads; he was pale, and avoided their eyes as he spoke.

André thrust his face close up to Schneider's and shouted: "But why should we have come this roundabout way?" The men behind chimed in: "Yes, why? They wouldn't be such fools. Why? They could take us round by Lunéville."

Schneider was scarlet. Suddenly he swung round toward the back of the car and confronted the men who were making all the noise. "I know nothing about it," he shouted angrily, "*nothing!* Maybe it was because the track was destroyed or because there are German troop movements on the other lines. It's no use your trying to make me say more than I know. You can believe what you damned well please."

A shrill voice sounded above the hubbub: "No need to lose your tempers, pals, we'll soon know for certain."

The others repeated the words: "That's right, we'll soon know. What's the use of squabbling?"

Schneider sat down without saying any more. From the next car but one emerged a curly head, and a boy's voice shouted: "Hey, guys! Where do they say we're going?"

"What's he want to know?"

"He's asking where we're going." There was a roar of laughter in the car.

"Couldn't have chosen a better moment to ask!"

Moulu leaned out, put his hands to his mouth and yelled: "Up my backside!" The head disappeared. Everyone laughed, then the laughter stopped.

Jurassien said: "What about a game, boys? Takes our minds off it."

"All right, come on."

The men squatted tailor-fashion around an overcoat folded into four. Jurassien took up the cards and dealt. Ramelle sat biting his nails in silence; the mouth organ was playing a waltz. A man standing against the end wall was smoking a German cigarette; he looked thoughtful. As though speaking to himself, he said: "It's good to have a smoke."

Schneider turned to Brunet. "I couldn't lie to them," he said with something almost defensive in the tone of his voice. Brunet merely shrugged. Schneider went on: "I just couldn't."

"It wouldn't have done any good if you had," said Brunet; "they'll have to learn sooner or later." He noticed that he had spoken gently and he felt annoyed at Schneider, because of the others.

Schneider gave him a queer look and said: "Too bad you don't know German."

"Why?" Brunet asked surprised.

"Because breaking the news might have been more up *your* alley."

"You're wrong," said Brunet wearily.

"But you always wanted it to be Germany."

"Yes, I suppose I did," said Brunet.

The printer was trembling again. Brunet put his arm round his shoulder and pressed it with a clumsy show of affection. Silently, he drew Schneider's attention to him and said: "Shut up."

The astonished smile with which Schneider looked at Brunet seemed to say: "Since when have you bothered about sparing other people's feelings?" Brunet turned away his head only to see before him the printer's hungry, supplicating gaze. The printer returned his look; his lips

moved, his great soft eyes turned in his shadowed face.
Brunet was on the point of saying: "I wasn't so wrong,
was I?" but he said nothing; he looked at his legs dangling
over the motionless wheels and began to whistle.

The sun went down; the heat grew less. A small boy was
chasing cows with a stick; they galloped across a field,
then quieted down and ambled majestically onto the road.
A boy going home, cows making for the cowshed: it was
a sight fit to break your heart. Very far off, high above a
meadow, dark birds circled: not all the dead had been
buried.

Brunet was beyond knowing whether this heart's anguish was his own or that of others. He turned to look at
his companions, trying to see them objectively. Their faces
were gray and preoccupied, almost peaceful. He recognized their expression; it was the curious mental emptiness
of crowds just before they are shaken by a gust of anger.
He thought: "That's fine. That's as it should be." But he
experienced no sense of pleasure.

The train shuddered throughout its length, continued
on its way for another few minutes, then stopped. Moulu
leaned out and stared at the horizon. "The next switch
is a hundred yards ahead."

"Don't you realize they're going to leave us here till
morning?" Gassou inquired.

"A swell case of jitters we'll have by that time," André
said.

Brunet could feel in his very bones the dead weight of
the train's immobility. Someone said: "It's the cold war all
over again." A dry cackle ran through the car, then the
laughter died out. Brunet heard Jurassien say imperturb-
ably: "Trump you once, trump you twice!" He felt another
jerk and turned. Jurassien's hand, holding an ace of hearts,
hung motionless in the air. The train moved slowly forward. Moulu was watching. A moment later it gathered

speed; two rails leaped into view from under the wheels, two parallel flashes of light that showed for a moment and then vanished over to their left among the fields.

"Shit!" said Moulu. "Shit! Shit! Shit!" There was complete silence: the men had understood. Jurassien let his ace fall on the coat and took the trick. The train was running smoothly with a regular puffing sound; the setting sun turned Schneider's face red; the air felt suddenly much cooler.

Brunet looked at the printer and gripped him sharply by the shoulders. "No funny business, eh? No funny business, my boy!" The thin body went taut under his fingers; Brunet tightened his grip, and the body grew slack. Brunet thought: "I'll keep a hold of him till nightfall." When darkness came, the Heinies would shut the door; by morning he would have calmed down. The train ran on under the mauve sky in absolute silence; they knew now, in each separate car they knew. The printer had dropped his head on Brunet's shoulder, like a woman. Brunet thought: "Have I any right to keep him from jumping?" But he kept a tight grip on him.

He heard a laugh at his back and a voice: "My old woman wanted a kid! I'll have to write and tell her to get the neighbor to do the job." They all laughed. Brunet thought: "The laughter of despair." Laughter filled the car, and a rising anger; somebody spluttered through his mirth: "What shits we were! What God-damned shits!" A field of potatoes, steel factories, mines, hard labor—what right have I to hold him back?

"Were *we* cunts! Were *we* cunts!" the voice continued. Anger rumbled and rose. Brunet could feel beneath his fingers the twitching of the thin shoulders, the movement of the slack muscles; he thought: "He'll never be able to stick it out." He tightened his hold—by what right?—he tightened it still more.

The printer said: "You're hurting me." Brunet maintained his grip. This is a life vowed to Communism; so long as he lives, he belongs to us. He looked at the small, squirrel face: so long as he lives, yes, but is he still alive? He's finished, the springs are broken, he'll never work again.

"Let me alone!" shouted the printer, "for Christ's sake, let me alone!"

Brunet was conscious of the queerness of his position; there he sat keeping tight hold on this rag of a man, this member of the party, who would never again be of the slightest use. He wanted to speak to him, to cheer him, to help him, but he could not: his words belonged to the party, the party alone gave to them any meaning they might possess; only within the party could Brunet love, persuade, console. Now that the printer had got himself into a position where he was outside the range of that immense and wheeling light, Brunet could find nothing more to say to him. Nevertheless, the kid was still a suffering human being; it was death either way. Oh, let him decide for himself! If he could make a get-away, so much the better for him; if he stayed, his death might be of some use to the cause.

The laughter grew louder. The train was running slowly; it seemed to be on the point of stopping. Inspired by a sudden cunning, the printer said: "Pass me the can, I want to piss." Brunet said nothing, but looked at him, and what he saw was death, the vast freedom of death. "Hell," said the printer, "why can't you pass me the can? Do you want me to piss in my pants?"

Brunet turned his head. "Pass the can!" he shouted. Out of darkness aglow with anger came a hand holding the can. The train slowed down; Brunet hesitated; he dug his fingers into the printer's shoulder, then suddenly relaxed his grip and took the can. How God-damned silly it all was! How silly!

The men had stopped laughing. Brunet felt his elbow

jarred; the printer had dived under his arm. Brunet stretched out his hand; it closed on emptiness: the dark mass, bent double, was falling, had fallen, ponderously through the air. Moulu uttered a cry, a shadow struck the embankment, legs apart, arms flung wide. Brunet waited for the rifle-shots, the sound of them *already* in his ears. The printer rebounded from the embankment; they could see him standing upright, now, a figure of blackness, free. Brunet *saw* the flash of the rifles: five frightful jets of flame. The printer began to run along the train; seized with panic, he was trying to climb back again into the car.

Brunet shouted to him: "Get up the bank! For God's sake, get up the bank!"

All the men were shouting: "Jump! Jump!"

The printer did not hear. He was running as hard as he could, he was drawing level with them, he extended his arms. "Brunet!" he called out. "Brunet!" Brunet could see his terrified eyes. He yelled at him the two words: "The bank!" but the man seemed deaf; he was nothing now but a pair of enormous eyes. Brunet thought: "If he can climb back quickly, he may have a chance." He leaned out. In a flash Schneider realized what he was after and flung his left arm round him to keep him from falling. Brunet stretched out his arms. The printer's hand touched his. The Heinies fired three times; the printer slumped backward and fell. The train drew away from him. The printer's legs leaped once into the air and fell; the tie and the clinkers beneath his head were black with blood. The train jerked to a standstill.

Brunet collapsed on top of Schneider; between his clenched teeth he said: "They must have seen he was trying to climb back. They shot him down just for fun."

The body lay some twenty yards away, already a mere object, already free. *I'd have dug a little hole for myself.* Brunet noticed that he was still holding the can; he had reached out his hand to the printer without letting go of

it. It was warm. He let it fall on the stones by the side of
the track. Four Heinies jumped out of the caboose and
ran toward the body. Brunet could hear the men behind
him growling; their anger was no longer under control.

From one of the cars ahead ten Germans emerged.
They clambered up the embankment and faced the train,
their tommy guns leveled. None of the prisoners showed
any sign of fear. Someone behind Brunet shouted: "Bastards!"

The tall German sergeant, with a look of fury on his
face, bent over the corpse, lifted it, let it fall back, and gave
it a kick. Brunet struggled round. "Hey! You'll push me
over!" Twenty of the men were leaning out. Brunet saw
twenty pairs of eyes with murder in them: there was going
to be trouble.

He shouted: "Don't jump, boys! You'll only get yourselves slaughtered!" He got to his feet with difficulty,
struggling with them. "Schneider!" he shouted. Schneider
had got up too. Each had his arm round the other's waist;
with their free hands they clung to the jambs of the door.
"No one's leaving this car!"

The men pushed. Brunet could see their hatred, *his*
hatred, the tool ready to *his* hand, and he felt afraid.
• Three Germans approached the car, their rifles pointed at
the men inside. The men growled, the Germans kept their
eyes on them. Brunet recognized the big fellow with the
curly hair who had tossed the cigarettes to them; his eyes
were the eyes of a murderer. The Frenchmen and the
Germans glared at one another. *This was war.* For the
first time since September '39, this was war. Gradually
the pressure relaxed, the men drew back, he could breathe
again.

The sergeant walked up to the car. *"Hinein!"* he shouted.
"Hinein!"

Brunet and Schneider were pressed against a wall of
chests; behind them the Heinies were closing the sliding

doors. The car was plunged in darkness; it smelled of sweat and coal dust; it echoed with a low growl of anger. Feet were stamping on the floor; the sound was that of a crowd on the march. Brunet thought: "They won't forget this; the game's won." He felt ill, he was finding it hard to breathe. His eyes were wide open in the darkness; at times he felt them swell up until they seemed to be two great oranges about to start from their sockets. In a low voice he called: "Schneider! Schneider!"

"Here I am," said Schneider. Brunet groped around him, he felt a need to touch Schneider. A hand found his and pressed it.

"That you, Schneider?"

"Yes." They stood side by side, hand in hand, both silent. There was a jerk; the train creaked into motion. What had they done with the body? He could feel Schneider's breathing close beside his ear. Suddenly Schneider withdrew his hand. Brunet tried to retain it, but Schneider shook him off and melted into the darkness. Brunet was alone, rigid and uncomfortable; the place was hot as an oven. He stood there on one foot, the other jammed in a confusion of legs and boots. He made no attempt to free himself; he was obsessed by the need to feel that everything about him was provisional, that he was passing through something, that his thoughts were passing through his head, that the train was passing through France. Ideas leaped from his brain, vague, indistinct, and fell on the railroad track behind, even before he had had time to identify them. He was moving farther and farther and farther away; only when life was moving at this speed was it endurable. Complete immobility: speed slid by and dropped at his feet. He knew that the train was moving, grinding, bumping, shuddering its way onward, but he was no longer conscious of movement. He was in a great ash can; somebody was kicking about inside it. Behind him, on the embankment, lay a body, limp and boneless; Brunet knew that they were moving farther from it with each passing second, he longed to feel it, but he could not: complete stagnation reigned. Above the dead body, above the inert freight car, the darkness wheeled; it alone was living. Tomorrow's dawn would cover all of them with the same dew. Dead flesh and rusted steel would run with the same sweat. Tomorrow the black birds would come.

VINTAGE BELLES—LETTRES

VINTAGE FICTION, POETRY, AND PLAYS

VINTAGE CRITICISM: LITERATURE, MUSIC, AND ART

VINTAGE WORKS OF SCIENCE AND PSYCHOLOGY